JANNAWAY'S MUTINY

By the same author:

Novels:
The River Running By
The Raging of the Sea
The Believer
Armada
The Fighting Spirit
The Crying of the Wind

Philosophy:
Basic Flying Instruction

JANNAWAY'S MUTINY

Charles Gidley Wheeler

iUniverse, Inc.
New York Lincoln Shanghai

Jannaway's Mutiny

iUniverse books may be ordered through booksellers or by contacting:

iUniverse
2021 Pine Lake Road, Suite 100
Lincoln, NE 68512
www.iuniverse.com
1-800-Authors (1-800-288-4677)

ISBN: 0-595-33956-5 (pbk)
ISBN: 0-595-79136-0 (cloth)

Printed in the United States of America

PART I

▼

1895–1914

1

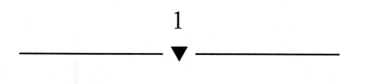

Far back in the early morning mists of memory there was a time when it was always raining and nothing ever changed. That dimly remembered time was real and yet not real. The person who remembered it was the same person and yet not the same person who had experienced it.

When Frank Jannaway thought very hard about it, which he often did, it seemed to him that in those half-forgotten dreadnought days when they lived in Devonport, where the streets were full of sailors and the harbor full of ships, he was not really a person so much as a seething whirl of sights, sounds, smells, tastes, and tactile impressions of everything and anything: bread and dripping, bacon and mushrooms, boiled potatoes, hoar frost, horse manure, hot milk, tram bells, church bells, fried onions, margarine, dirt, drains, damp laundry, and rain, rain, rain. It was only very slowly that real thoughts and facts began to emerge from the fog. He chased after them, but they were as difficult to catch as falling leaves.

Ma took in washing for Warrant Officers. She had black boots and red elbows. When he went to bed it was empty, but when he woke up it was full, because Ma was there, warm, big, soft, and heavy.

He came to believe that he had two fathers. One was a sailor called Jack, who was at the bottom of the deep blue sea my darling; and the other was somebody mysterious called Witchart in Heaven.

He sat under the table and looked at Ma's boots. They made the world safe even when the Warrant Officers' washing wouldn't dry. He found a ball of string and wound it round all the table legs and the chair legs, and threaded it through the handles of the dresser drawers; and when Ma saw what he had done she said, 'Frank, Frank, Frank, what am I to do with you?'

The sun came out, the rain stopped, and the front door onto the street was opened. He ran out in front of a tram and would have been killed—but he wasn't. Ma hugged him so hard he couldn't breathe. He could hear her heart churning and bumping about like milk turning to butter.

The next day the postman brought a letter, and when Ma read it she made him kneel down with her and say thank you to Our Lady because she (Ma, not Our Lady) had found a position and they would be going away to a place where there would be no more Warrant Officers' washing, no more trams, no more ships, no more sailors and no more rain. Indeed, from what he could make out, it seemed likely that they were going to see Our Father Witchart, in Heaven.

Ma woke him before it was light, and told him it was time to get ready, because they were going in a train. He had new second hand shoes that fitted perfectly. She put paper in the toes and told him to be careful not to trip. She put all their things in a small suitcase and sat down at the table and cried. Then she took his hand and they went out into the morning mist and closed the door behind them.

He was five years old. Everything changed after that. Nothing was ever the same again.

They came to Meonford. The new century had just begun. On their first day, Ma taught him to make the sign of the Cross. She said he had to be good *all the time*, because otherwise she might lose her position. He had to be good, and respectful, and always do what he was told. He must always tell the truth, sit up straight, wash his hands, comb his hair, and only speak when he was spoken to. It was no longer Ma or Ma's boots that made the world safe and reliable, but Sir Jervis and Lady Yarrow. 'Is Sir Jervis Witchart in Heaven?' he asked one night when he was tucked up in bed; and Ma said 'No, Frank, you don't understand. God is our father in heaven. God made you to love him and serve him in this world, and to be happy with him for ever in the next. That's who we pray to when we say the Our Father.'

She kissed him goodnight and took the candle out with her and closed the door; and he lay listening to the soft sounds of hooves on straw that came up from the stables below; and the wind sighed in the eave—and suddenly it was morning again. Cocks were crowing and dogs barking and milk churns clattering, and Ma was already up and dressed because it was after five and time to start another day.

He began to remember things and understand things. His head was full of questions. Why did porridge swell? Why did milk turn to butter? How far away was the moon? What was earth made of? Where was the next world? Why did a horse-shoe turn red when it got hot? How big was God? Who was Hail Mary? If everything was always changing, how could anything be the same?

He started school in Droxford village. Ma took him the first day, but after that he walked to school with Alan Roughsedge, who had a bad leg and a funny eye. He sat beside Alan on the bench in the schoolroom, and dawdled with him on the way home. Alan was the best friend he ever had. He lived in a cottage with a thatched roof, and had four elder brothers: George, who worked at Nailer's sawmill, Harry and Sidney, who labored on Tonks's farm, and Walter, who was apprenticed to a carpenter in Bishop's Waltham.

Alan's Ma had floury hands and cracked thumbs. She gave Frank bread and dripping and a glass of milk fresh from the cow for his tea. Mr. Roughsedge was gamekeeper to Sir Jervis. He had a red face and black hair and blue eyes and big fists with black hairs on the backs of his fingers. He smelled of earth and blood and sweat. He came in by the back door and threw four rabbits on the kitchen table and put his shotgun in the corner and lit his pipe, and unlaced his boots and sat down in the chair with a patchwork cover and closed his eyes; and his arm dangled down beside his chair, and a black cat came purring and pushing his whiskers against his hand.

It seemed like a miracle that they should have been plucked from that damp place on the main road out of Devonport with the trams clanking by every minute of the day, and had come to this fine, grey-stone mansion, with its tall grey chimneys, its magnificent conservatory, its stables and dovecot and dairy and boiler house, its sloping lawns and rose beds, the summer house, the tennis court, the walled vegetable garden, the orchard, and the high boundary wall overlooking the River Meon. Ma said she felt as if she'd died and gone to heaven.

Frank's world was one of gardeners, valets, chauffeurs, laundry maids, kitchen maids, and ladies' maids. When he was seven, Ma said he had to start pulling his weight. Bob Ramage, who was valet to Sir Jervis, and whose face was cratered with pox scars, taught him to clean boots. He had to clean Master Roddy's boots when he was on leave from the naval college at Osborne on the Isle of Wight. Bob Ramage said Master Roddy was Trouble with a capital T. Alan hated him, but would never say why. Ma told Frank that he should always show extra special respect to him because he was Sir Jervis's son and heir.

'What's an heir?' Frank asked, and when she told him he wanted to know if he was an heir, and she laughed bitterly and said, 'No, my darling, you're no heir and you never will be.' He asked why he didn't have brothers like Alan. She said it was because his father had gone down with his ship. He was a hero, and he had gone to be with Jesus.

'At the bottom of the deep blue sea, my darling?' he asked, and Ma looked cross and said, 'Frank. It's not funny.'

The school mistress was called Miss Pinkham. She was the tallest woman in the world. Her hair was piled on top of her head like a stork's nest. It was impossible to get away with anything she didn't want you to get away with, because she had eyes in the back of her head. When she caught you putting a barley husk down the back of Doris Bloodworth's pinafore she took you by the ear and pulled you to your feet and said, 'You bother me and I'll bother you, Frank Jannaway,' and you had to stand in the corner until the end of class. She said that love of money was the root of all evil. They sang *All Things Bright and Beautiful*:

> The rich man in his castle,
> The poor man at his gate;
> God made them high and lowly,
> And ordered their estate.

> All things bright and beautiful,
> All creatures great and small;
> All things wise and wonderful,
> The Lord God made them all.

'Now close your eyes,' said Miss Pinkham, 'and put your hands together. Oh Heavenly Father we ask thee to watch over and bless His Majesty King Edward and the royal family, and give succor to the starving millions in India, and bless the work of the missionaries in darkest Africa.'

She taught them how to make their letters and join them up, and she made them read out loud from the Bible and say their times tables and learn the rhyme about the Kings of England, which went 'Willie, Willie, Harry, Stee; Harry, Dick, John, Harry Three.' They colored a map of the British Isles that showed where the coal and the sheep and the herrings were; and the Cotswolds and Chilterns and Cheviots as well. They drew pictures of a Viking ship, a Brixham trawler, and a Lowestoft drifter. They learnt that Paris was on the Seine and London was on the Thames and Lisbon was on the Tagus, and that Christopher Columbus had found America and George the Third had lost it, which was a pity.

It was a twenty minute walk to school and back every day, but Frank and Alan, who became close friends and partners in crime, seldom made it in less than forty. Alan liked dares, challenges and competitions, and he had a repertory of songs that he had learnt from his elder brothers, one of which went:

Be I Bristol?
Be I buggery!
I comes up from Sareham;
Where all the girls wear calico drawers,
And I knows how to tear 'em!

They were singing this one afternoon as they came marching round the corner and down the hill into the village, when they ran into Mr. Middleton the village blacksmith, who collared them, took off his wide leather belt, and gave them each three of the best and one for luck. After that, they were more careful.

They had spitting competitions, pissing competitions and competitions to see who could endure the most pain; and it was Alan who showed Frank a special secret place where they weren't supposed to go. A high stone wall ran along at the bottom of the orchard, and if you crawled in under the laurel bushes you came to a sort of tunnel that led along beside the wall; and further along, almost as far as the walnut tree by the summer house, there was a stone which stuck out. They managed to climb up, and there was a sort of seat up there, a smooth stone that was shaped like a saddle, and they used to sit astride it with their heads among the branches of an old ash tree and their feet among the ivy leaves, and watch the gentry having their scones and China tea in the summer house.

Sometimes Frank went and sat on the boundary wall on his own and thought about his father. He wished it could be possible to get him to come back alive again so that he could talk to him and ask him all the questions that Ma couldn't answer. She kept a little sepia photograph of him inside the front cover of her missal. He was standing on Plymouth Hoe with his cap on the back of his head, a pipe between his teeth and a big grin on his face. He was called Jack Jannaway and he looked like the sailor on the front of a packet of Players cigarettes. He had been the boatswain's mate on board the battleship HMS *Victoria*, and was helping to steer the ship when she collided with the *Camperdown* in 1893. Ma said it was a tragedy that should never have happened. She said the cause of it was a disagreement between two admirals who hated each other. She said it was a terrible thing that a petty squabble like that could cause the loss of so many fine men.

'Your father was a hero,' she said. 'He stayed at his post and went down with his ship. You can be very proud of him.'

'What *is* a hero?' Frank asked.

'Someone who gives his life in the service of others,' said his mother.

He wanted to know so much about his father. He wanted Ma to tell him every single thing about him. But she said that it was impossible. 'Though there is one thing I haven't told you before,' she said. 'He used to play the fiddle.'

'What's the fiddle?' he asked, and she laughed quite a lot, then stopped and said, 'Ask your teacher.' So he did, and the next day Miss Pinkham brought her own violin for them to see.

In the winter time he got out of bed at six every morning, cleaned out the grate in the library, and helped Ramage with the boots. He had porridge for breakfast and walked to school with Alan Roughsedge and Doris Bloodworth and Lucy Ashton. There were mornings when the trees were hung with frozen fog, and the ring of the hammer in Middleton's forge sounded muted because it was so cold. When spring came, he delighted in the blooming of snowdrops and aconites under the walnut tree on the upper lawn, and the crocuses and daffodils poking up through the grass when the snow had gone. The early mornings echoed with birdsong, and wild flowers grew along the hedgerows. The forest was carpeted with blue-bells: the whole world seemed to shout for joy.

In the summer, he and Alan climbed trees, stole apples, teased Doris Bloodworth, spied on the gentry, and sometimes bought a penny-worth of fruit gums from Mrs. Ashton's village shop; and when the weather was really hot, they swam in the River Meon with other boys from the village, making dams and having water fights among the watercress and kingcups, splashing and shouting and laughing.

These were the years of Frank's innocence. They came to an abrupt end one July afternoon two months after his tenth birthday, when he was sitting up in his secret place on the orchard wall thinking about his father and wondering what it would be like to be a hero. He was disturbed by someone coming along the tunnel under the laurel bushes by the boundary wall. A few moments later, he saw Master Roddy enter his private den. He was wearing his naval cadet's uniform and was back for the summer leave from Osborne naval college.

Roddy entered the clearing below where Frank was sitting, set down his suitcase on the leaf mold, opened it, and took out a parcel. Hardly daring to breathe, Frank watched as he removed the wrapping paper to reveal a wooden box, and used the blade of a knife to prize the box open; but as he did so, an ivy root under Frank's foot came loose, and a trickle of dry dust and earth fell down onto the white cover of Roddy's uniform cap.

Immediately, Roddy twisted round and looked up, and Frank found himself staring back into his pale blue eyes. Then Roddy grabbed him by the ankle and pulled him down off the wall, and within the space of a few minutes took away the happiness and innocence of Frank's life.

2

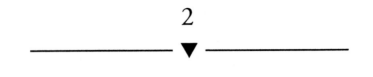

At seven o'clock in the morning on Tuesday, September 16th 1903, Roddy Yarrow woke up, and immediately remembered what was going to happen that day.

He was thirteen years and two months old, the sole surviving son of Commodore Sir Jervis Yarrow Bt., Royal Navy; younger brother to the late Lieutenant Clive Yarrow (Fifth Irish Lancers, killed in action, 1899); half-brother to three-year-old Anita, and stepson to his father's fancy woman, the Russian opera singer Irina Yuryevskaya. He feared his father, couldn't really remember his mother, hero-worshipped his dead brother, disliked his stepmother, and had as little to do with Anita as possible.

This was the first day of his naval career.

He took his new uniform jacket out of the wardrobe and admired its yellow cotton lining in the sleeves, its neat white twist and brass button on each lapel, and the two rows of four brass buttons. He took a new white cotton shirt, collar studs, and a stiff white collar from his chest of drawers, and put them on. He struggled for a while with the business of knotting the black uniform tie; and having done so, sat on the side of the bed to pull on his uniform trousers. Having donned and buttoned his uniform reefer and put on his uniform cap, he looked in the mirror and, like God on the seventh day of creation, was pleased with what he saw.

'Naval Cadet Roderick Yarrow,' he said to his reflection. And then: 'Midshipman Roderick Yarrow…Commander Yarrow…Captain Sir Roderick Yarrow. Vice Admiral Sir Roderick Yarrow.' He snapped to attention and saluted. 'Admiral of the Fleet Lord Yarrow of Meonford.'

There were about seventy cadets in the new term, which was the first to go to Osborne Naval College. They gathered on The Hard at Portsmouth and watched as a paddle tug maneuvered alongside.

Going on board, smelling the tar and the funnel smoke, and seeing the crew manhandle the ropes, Roddy became aware of a feeling of distaste. While he liked the idea of being a naval officer, he now realized, with something of a shock, that he didn't actually like ships or sailors, and he had absolutely no wish to go to sea.

The paddlewheels churned up the muddy waters of the harbor. The last line was cast off, hauled in, and coiled down. The cadets, some of whom had been chattering excitedly, fell silent. One was standing apart from the others and staring astern. Tears were streaking down his cheeks.

Roddy felt suddenly more cheerful. He turned to the boy beside him. 'What's your name?'

'Coolser. What's yours?'

'Yarrow. Is your father in the Navy?'

'No.'

'Mine is. At least, he was. He's a Commodore. Is your father titled?'

'No.'

'Mine is. When he pops it, I'll be a baronet.'

The tug went down the harbor, out past Fort Blockhouse and into the Solent. It was a windy day with the sun coming out and going in behind the clouds.

Coolser blew his nose.

'Do you sail?' Roddy asked.

'Sail what?' said Coolser.

'Yachts, of course.'

'No.'

'My father does. His yacht's the *Clover*. She did awfully well in the Solent regattas last year.'

The paddlewheels beat a steady rhythm and left a broad wake. Skinny Radcliffe, who had been the head chorister at Stubbington House Preparatory School, burst suddenly into tears. The effect was catching: within seconds, half a dozen of the new naval cadets were sniffing and blowing their noses. Fortunately, the voyage across the Solent was long enough to give them time to regain their control before the tug came alongside at East

Cowes, so that there was a full roll call of British stiff upper lips by the time they disembarked.

Standing on Trinity Pier, Captain Rosslyn Wemyss looked on as the cadets disembarked. A naval pensioner fell them in on the quay and ordered 'Quick march!' and off they went, up the hill to the grounds of Queen Victoria's old summer residence, to be drilled in the Nelson Room before sitting down to tea in the Mess Hall.

After tea they were addressed by Commander Yelland, a ginger-haired officer who looked fierce and held a telescope under his arm and paced up and down with his hands behind his back as he addressed the new term.

'You young gentlemen are entering the Service at a most important time in the Royal Navy's long and glorious history,' he told them, and went on to extol officer qualities like loyalty, honesty, good manners and a sense of humor.

When Yelland had done with them they were handed over to Mr. Sweeney the Cadet Gunner, a warrant officer of the old school who had a very thin gold stripe on his sleeve, a whistle on a chain round his neck and legs encased in shiny black gaiters. He shouted at them unintelligibly in a strong Belfast accent for several minutes before handing them on to a slow-speaking naval pensioner in a plain serge suit with brass buttons and an anchor for a cap badge, who told them to call him 'Chief.'

The Chief led the way to a dormitory in an outbuilding. This was the chest flat. There was a sea chest at the foot of each bed and each boy's trunk had been placed beside it. The Chief showed them how to stow their kit in their chests and how to lay it out for rounds.

Then there was supper, and after supper a belly muster, in which Surgeon Lieutenant Bolam, who had soft, sweaty hands, soulful eyes and a melancholy air, inspected each boy's belly and checked that his balls had dropped. After that the cadets undressed and put on pajamas and prepared for rounds; and after rounds Lieutenant Merrion, a dapper little man who had dressed for dinner and was wearing a bum-freezer jacket, a brass-buttoned waistcoat and a wing collar and black bow tie, introduced himself as their term officer.

Pacing up and down between the lines of chests, Lieutenant Merrion talked about famous admirals like Drake, Hawke, Hood and Nelson; and the traditions of the service which they upheld, like fighting spirit, loyalty, honor, and duty.

'I hope and expect,' he concluded, 'that some of you will rise to the very highest ranks in the Service. Perhaps one of you will, one day, proudly wear the five rings of gold lace on your arm that denote the rank of Admiral of the Fleet. But whatever rank you achieve, never forget that the Royal Navy's history imposes upon you the privilege of carrying on the tradition which Drake began: for we are all servants; servants of His Majesty the King, servants of the British Empire, servants of Almighty God. Now goodnight to you and God bless you.'

'Goodnight, sir!' shrilled the cadets; and a moment later a boatswain's call trilled high-low-high, and the lights went out.

They lived life at the rush: doubling from class to class, drilling, exercising, reporting, and mustering. Their day started with cold baths and continued with an extraordinary mixture of professional and academic study: squad drill, English literature, anchor work, naval history, boat pulling, spherical trigonometry, divinity, engineering, French, and physical training.

Many of them had known each other at prep school, but by unspoken agreement, arrival at Osborne allowed each boy to make a new start. Old nicknames were discarded and new nicknames were invented. Fishy Pike became The Squeaker because his voice was breaking. Sniffer Yates turned into Liver Lips. Hugh Barrow, who had passed in top with an unimaginable score of ninety-six percent and who had a voice that sounded as if he were perpetually on the brink of tears, became known as The Blubber. Toss Yarrow, Squitters Bruford-Jones and Smelly Greenlow earned their nicknames for more obvious reasons. The Honorable Ernle Fairfax-Notley became known initially as Four-Fucks-Nightly, but that was later abbreviated to Fortnightly.

Camaraderie teetered permanently on the brink of homosexual flirtation. Initiation ceremonies, de-bagging, 'cock-fighting' and the unending innuendos and repartee broke down what barriers of natural modesty still remained. Roddy, whose bed squeaked rhythmically every night after pipe down, was set upon, stripped of his pajamas, tied up in his mattress cover, and given a cold bath. Liver Lips was tied to his bed and tickled with a feather until, to cheers that were unanimous with the exception only of The Blubber, his member stood to attention.

The Blubber was the only cadet who came out of his first term entirely untouched by any sort of physical or sexual assault. On the first evening he astonished the whole chest flat by kneeling by his bed, making the sign of the Cross, and saying a decade of the rosary in an audible whisper. But he got away with it, because there was something untouchable about The Blubber that rendered him proof against any attempt at bullying or taunting.

When Roddy came home at the end of his first term, he seemed at first to be a changed person. He was bigger and tougher, and he had a wary look in his eye and a curl to his lip that had not been there before. Having been subjected to a strict routine for three months, he was at first unable to throw it off. He marched about the house giving himself orders to 'move to the left in threes' or 'into line, right turn' in order to get from the breakfast room to the conservatory.

He spoke in a new, clipped jargon, referring to the holidays as leave, his room as his cabin, and the floor as the deck. But three days after his homecoming, his term report arrived and the truth emerged that he was under official Admiralty warning for withdrawal from the college.

His position in the term was second from bottom; his term officer said that he was untidy and lazy, and his tutor reported that his carelessness in Mathematics stemmed from a lack of self-discipline.

'He must pay particular attention to the above criticisms if he is to stay the course here,' added Captain Wemyss as a footnote.

His father sent for him. Sir Jervis had bristly black eyebrows that were matched by the black, wiry hairs growing out of his nose and ears. He had fallen foul of Admiral Fisher back in '93, and had lost his career. His first wife, Laura, had committed suicide as a result of nervous depression brought on by his womanizing, and he had met his second wife Irina, who was a cousin of the Grand Duchess Vittoria of Russia, while standing in as naval attaché in St Petersburg during the Peace Conference at The Hague. Irina presented him with a daughter, Anita, three weeks into the new century. Anita was the apple of her father's eye, and Roddy knew it.

'This is not good enough,' said Sir Jervis, tapping Roddy's report with his forefinger. 'Not good enough at all.'

'No, Father.'

'So what are you going to do about it?'

'I don't know, Father.'

'In that case I shall tell you.' Sir Jervis' eyes swiveled like the twin barrels of a naval gun turret. 'Yes,' he said. 'I shall tell you. His voice sank to a whisper. 'You are going to sharpen up.'

There was a long pause. Jervis squared off the blotter and pen on his desk, and then glanced up at his son.

'Did you hear me?'

'No, Father. I beg you pardon—'

'I said you are going to SHARPEN UP!' roared Sir Jervis.

'Yes, Father.'

'You are going to work harder, do you understand? A great deal harder or I shall know the reason why. I shall be seeing Captain Wemyss next week and I shall have a word with him about you. I shall ask him to have a very strict eye kept on you. I've moved heaven and earth to get you into Osborne, and I'm damned if I'm going to see you fall by the wayside for lack of self-discipline. That's what it is, isn't it? I think your tutor has hit the nail on the head. Too much self-indulgence, I fancy. Do you hear what I'm saying?'

'Yes, Father.'

'Very well: the only way to stop the rot is to get your books out and work like a coolie. Let us have no further comments about laziness or lack of self-discipline, do you hear me? That's the beginning of the slippery slope. You're not Mummy's boy any longer, you're a naval cadet. You've got to start playing the man.'

'Yes, Father.'

'Very well. Go to it. And Roddy—'

'Yes Father?'

Yarrow glanced down at a private letter from the captain of the college. 'I understand there's been some sort of unmanly behavior among a few of the cadets. I'll say just this. Never have anything to do with that sort of thing, do you understand? Just keep well clear of it, my boy. Right. You can go now.'

Roddy went down to his den at the bottom of the orchard, hid himself among the rhododendron bushes, and set about ignoring his father's advice.

As the terms went by, Roddy wore the loop of his white lanyard lower and lower, until in his final term it plunged down to the top buttons of his reefer jacket. He was fifteen years old now and in his sixth and final term. It was the summer of 1905, the centenary of the Battle of Trafalgar. Admiral Fisher had achieved his ambition of becoming First Sea Lord, and a new naval college at Dartmouth was to be opened.

The day after his birthday in July, and about three weeks before the end of term, Roddy received a parcel chit with his mail at breakfast. Parcels had to be collected from the college post office, which was a quarter of a mile or so from the college, and you were supposed to get permission from the duty petty officer to go there.

As it was a Wednesday, which was a make-and-mend, he decided to risk it and walked over to the post office without obtaining permission. He handed the chit over the counter to Miss Tucker, who examined it, went to the parcel rack, took out a parcel, and handed it over. But as he took it from her hands he saw that it was not addressed to himself, Naval Cadet R. Yarrow, but to The Blubber, Naval Cadet H. Barrow.

He never knew why he didn't hand it straight back and say that there had been a mistake. It was somehow easier not to: after all, it was the day after his birthday and the parcel chit had his name on it. The fact that the parcel did not actually belong to him was somehow blocked out of his mind, so that although it had the wrong name on it, he felt that he had a right to it.

He thanked Miss Tucker, took the parcel and walked out of the post office and up the steps; but instead of following the path that went straight back to the college, he took another path that went up between bushes where he would not be seen.

When he was out of sight he stopped and had another look at the parcel. It was a square, heavy package with a London post mark. Perhaps it was a tin of marmalade. That was one of the things parents were allowed to send through the post to cadets. He weighed it in his hand, wondering what to do.

Nobody had ever played any sort of practical joke on the Blubber. He had sailed through Osborne taking top marks at everything, stuttering and sobbing out the right answers in class, never being picked up on divisions or rounds, never rising to taunts about being a Holy Roller or a Left Footer, never joining in the cock-fighting or de-bagging sessions, excelling at everything, whether it was navigation, sailing, engineering or French. He even played the oboe.

Nobody would know. He could say he'd opened it by mistake, couldn't he?

He pulled the string off it, tore the brown paper with his finger—and revealed a stout wooden box whose lid was firmly nailed down with tin tacks. He tried to prize the top off with his fingers but failed. He needed a screwdriver or a knife or the end of a pair of scissors.

He was still wondering what to do when he heard footsteps coming along the path. He dived into the bushes and crouched out of sight. It was one of the gardeners. He waited for him to go past, then, wishing that he hadn't accepted the parcel in the first place, put it roughly back in its wrapping and hid it in the bushes under some leaves. That done, he walked quickly back to the college, went in by the side door, changed into sports rig (white rugby shirt, blue shorts, tennis shoes), waited to see that the coast was clear, and set off on a cross-country run that took him on a five mile circuit inland, back to the coast and up via the boat sheds to the college, where he arrived, hot and sweaty, forty-five minutes later.

Two days later, when they had just come off the parade ground from morning divisions and were mustering outside a classroom, Barrow came up to him and stuttered, 'I s-say, Yarrow—did you get a parcel chit addressed to me the other day?'

'No.'

'It's awful rot. Mater s-says she ordered a parcel to be s-sent from London a week ago, and it hasn't arrived. Fortnightly s-says he thought you had a parcel chit.'

'Well I didn't.'

'What a dashed nuisance. I'm going to the post office to ask.'

The next morning he was listed in the Daily Orders as being required to report to the commander in the visitors' waiting room immediately after breakfast.

He went along and waited outside with a few other cadets. When his name was called by Mr. Sweeney, he walked smartly in, took his cap off, and stood to attention.

'Naval Cadet Yarrow, sir,' said Sweeney.

'Did you go to the post office after lunch on Wednesday last?' asked Commander Yelland.

He feigned surprise. 'No, sir.'

'Are you sure of that?'

'Yes, sir.'

'Did you receive a parcel chit that morning?'

'No, sir.'

Yelland looked at Sweeney and pursed his lips and stared for a long time into Roddy's eyes. Yelland had ginger hair and red eyes. He looked as if he were about to burst into flames. Roddy met his stare as well as he could, though he couldn't help blinking in the way he did when he was nervous.

'Very well,' Yelland said suddenly. 'Carry on.'

He went out into the corridor and doubled along to rejoin the first class of the morning. 'Isn't it rot,' he remarked to Fairfax-Notley in Stand Easy when they were eating ships biscuits and drinking cocoa. 'The Blubber hasn't had a parcel and he's accusing me of pinching it.'

He was called to the commander's office again after tea. There were three others: Barrow, Fairfax-Notley, and Coolser. They were called in one by one. Yelland and Sweeney were there, and Miss Tucker was sitting on a chair to one side. He was called in third and was told to look at Miss Tucker. He met her gaze as steadily as he could, sure that they must be able to hear his heart beating.

'Carry on!' barked Mr. Sweeney.

He changed for Evening Quarters and went to the locker room to polish his boots. While he was doing so, Barrow came in. 'I say, Yarrow,' he said, 'if you did collect my parcel by mistake, I won't s-say anything more about it if you just give it back. I'd just like to have it, that's all.'

Roddy spun round to face him. 'Are you calling me a thief?'

'No!'

'It sounded like it. It sounded like deuced rot. Actually.'

'I'm s-sorry. I just thought—'

'Well you thought wrong. I haven't got your wretched box.'

Barrow looked at him for a moment and said, 'How do you know it's a box?' But before Roddy could answer, he had left the locker room.

He was sure they must suspect him now. He wondered what to do. If he was had for stealing he'd be chucked out. It was a prospect that terrified him. What would his father say? What would happen to him?

But he hadn't stolen—not really. The parcel chit had had his name on it, not Barrow's. Was that his fault? Was it his fault that he'd been given the wretched parcel? In any case, he didn't have the parcel any more, did he? It wasn't in his possession, so he hadn't stolen it and he hadn't lied. All he had to do was sit tight and wait for the whole thing to blow over. They couldn't prove that he had collected the parcel. They couldn't even prove that the parcel had been delivered to Osborne, because it wasn't registered.

So it had been lost in the post, hadn't it?

He went along to the quarterdeck for evening quarters. Normally the parade was run by the cadet captains, but that evening Mr. Sweeney was there, and just as the chief cadet was about to give the order to dismiss, he bawled, 'Steady the parade!' His fists pumped downwards at his sides as he shouted. 'At the order dismiss, all cadets will double away and stand by for locker inspection. Evening quarters, dismiss!'

Lieutenant Merrion carried out the locker search. Each cadet had to open his private till, take out the contents, and place them on the top of his chest. When Merrion came to Coolser's chest, Coolser broke down and wept, because two weeks before he had found a wristwatch with a bro-ken strap on the cricket pitch and had failed to hand it in. Coolser was already under Admiralty Warning for lack of officer-like qualities, so this was the end of his naval career. He cried all night, and when the cadets came back into the chest flat the following day for the compulsory fifteen minutes' rest after lunch, Coolser's bed and chest had been removed and the word went round that he had been sent home in disgrace.

Roddy began to hope that he was off the hook. It was the last week-end before the end of term, and Sunday Divisions was a dress rehearsal for the passing-out parade the following week.

The cadet captain took charge of the squad and reported them for inspection to the term officer, after which Fairfax-Notley, the chief cadet captain, called the parade to attention and reported to Commander Yel-land, who reported to Captain Wemyss, who inspected the entire parade of three hundred and ninety-two cadets, walking slowly up and down the ranks, trailing his sword behind him. When his inspection was complete, the whole parade marched off to the strains of 'Hearts of Oak' played by the College Band.

After Divisions came Church. The service finished with 'Eternal Father Strong to Save,' after which the congregation recited the naval prayer:

> O eternal Lord God, who alone spreadest out the heavens and rulest the raging of the sea; who hast compassed the waters with bounds until day and night come to an end; be pleased to receive into thy Almighty and most gracious protection, the persons of us Thy servants and the Fleet in which we serve….

When the final blessing had been given, the music master played a toccata on the organ, and the cadets streamed out of church to enjoy their Sunday afternoon.

Outside the chapel door, Mr. Sweeney, lurking like an angel of doom in black gaiters, was waiting.

'Cadet Yarrow!'

'Sir!'

'Report to the visitors' room immediately!'

He doubled along the corridor, a voice inside his head saying, 'Oh God, oh God, oh God…!'

On reaching the visitors' room, he paused. There could be no going back now. He must keep his nerve. He must say as little as possible. Above all, he must admit nothing. He would have to deny this charge, even if it meant doing so for the rest of his life.

He knocked on the door.

'Enter!' said a voice; and he entered.

Sir Jervis turned back from the window. 'Come in, Roddy. Sit down.'

He sat on the upright chair and looked at the Regency wallpaper opposite him. His father remained standing. Roddy could hear his breath whistling among the black hairs in his nose. 'Right,' he said eventually. 'I'm sure you know why I'm here.'

Roddy said nothing. He kept his lips tightly compressed and gazed straight ahead.

'I've spoken with Captain Wemyss. He's given me all the relevant facts. The duty mail cadet believes that you had a parcel chit that day, but he can't be sure of it. The post mistress says that she handed over a parcel to a cadet on the afternoon in question, but she can't identify him. I understand that you went on a cross-country run that afternoon, but as far as can be established it was the first and only cross-country run you have done voluntarily in your entire time at Osborne.'

His father fell silent.

'I wonder…I wonder if you realize the seriousness of this charge, Roddy. You see, it isn't just your good name at stake here. It's my name as well. It's the family name. That's what's at stake. Do you understand that? Well? Do you?'

'Yes, Father.'

'I wonder.'

There was another long silence.

After a heavy sigh, his father started again.

'It was extremely kind and courteous of Captain Wemyss to contact me personally. He felt it only right that I should be given an opportunity to speak to you before the matter was reported to Their Lordships at the Admiralty.'

Roddy was aware of a sense of unreality. All the time, the same thought ran through his head: *They can't prove it was me. They can't prove it was me.*

'The next step is that Captain Wemyss will write an official report to Admiralty. I have asked him, as an old shipmate, to grant me the favor of having one last word with you before he takes that step, because I believe that, as your father, I can persuade you to tell me the truth.' Sir Jervis took out a handkerchief and mopped his face. 'I know that you have already denied that you collected Cadet Barrow's parcel. But I am now going to ask you once more whether or not you collected that parcel from the post office last Wednesday. You are my son, Roddy, my only son, the son who, when I die, will inherit the family title. As a father to his son, I ask you now to tell me the truth, however painful that may be. If you did take the parcel, tell me, and I shall do everything in my power to see to it that the family name is protected and your life is not ruined by this most unfortunate incident. If you are innocent, I undertake to move heaven and earth to see that you are completely exonerated and cleared of all suspicion. Now look at me. I put you on your honor to tell me the truth. Look at me, boy. Did you steal that parcel?'

He looked his father directly in the eye and said, 'No, Father. On my honor, I did not.'

Sir Jervis went to the window and stared out over the parade ground for so long that Roddy began to wonder if he might have forgotten that he was still sitting there behind him.

'Very well,' Sir Jervis said, turning back. I put you on your honor, so I have to take you at your word. I shall speak with Captain Wemyss this afternoon, and I shall do my utmost to ensure that this charge against you is dropped. You may go.'

For a moment, Roddy stared in disbelief. Then he turned and bolted from the room.

He was called to Commander Yelland's office the following day and told that the whole thing had been dropped. When he came out he felt quite light-headed. It seemed that he'd got away with it. He'd held his nerve, stuck to his story and it had paid off. Father had come up trumps. He'd pulled strings with Wemyss and it had done the trick. Walking back along the corridor he could hardly stop himself laughing aloud, the relief was so great.

But then it occurred to him that this might be a trick. They might have told him he was off the hook in the hopes that he would give himself away. He had nearly done that with the Blubber. So he had to be careful. Having got so far, he mustn't lose it all by making any more silly mistakes.

There was another problem: the parcel. It was still hidden under the bushes near the college post office. He wondered about leaving it there. But if he left it the chances were that one of the grounds men would find it sooner or later and the enquiry would be re-opened. So there was only one thing to do. He had to recover it straight away.

He kept himself awake that night until after one o'clock, climbed out of a bathroom window, ran barefoot in his pajamas through the college grounds to the spot where he had hidden the parcel, collected it, and put it in the locker room before returning to his bed; and three days later when he boarded the Admiralty tug at East Cowes, having left Osborne for the last time, the parcel was safe inside his suitcase.

He took a trap from Wickham station and stopped in Meonford village in order to arrive home the back way. He went along the path beside the church which lead into the water meadow by the Meon, and crossed over by the wooden foot bridge which led directly to the high stone boundary wall of Meonford Hall.

There was a heavy wooden door set into the wall which he pushed open; but instead of going on up through the orchard and the vegetable garden to the house, he ducked down under the laurel bushes to his right and made his way along the tunnel by the wall to his secret den. He put the suitcase down on the leaf mould, sprang the catches, and took out the Blubber's parcel. He prized it open with the blade of his sailor's knife; and after removing some newspaper and sawdust, took out a model steam engine, painted dark green.

There was a sheet of instructions with it that told you how to fill the boiler with distilled water and bring it to the boil using a spirit burner, and he was reading these instructions when he felt a little shower of earth fall onto his uniform cap. He looked up quickly, and found himself face to face with the housekeeper's ten year old son, who was staring down at him from a vantage point on top of the wall.

When it was all over and he had let the boy run off, Roddy hid the model steam engine in the wall behind a loose stone. He brushed himself down and straightened his tie and smoothed his hair and straightened his cap and buttoned his fly. Then he picked up the suitcase and sauntered up the garden to the house.

He could hear his stepmother playing the piano in the drawing room, so he went in via the conservatory, through the hall and straight upstairs to his room. He changed out of his uniform and put on a clean white shirt, flannel trousers, and a blazer. He wet his hair, went to the mirror, and used a pair of bristle hairbrushes with monogrammed silver backs to restore his parting to pristine condition.

He crossed to the window and stood looking out over the valley, where the river Meon was reflecting the afternoon light between the water meadows and the church.

What had happened ten minutes before was already like a confused dream. Images jostled with each other in his mind: the model steam engine; the housekeeper's boy looking down at him; that overpowering feeling of intimacy when he was beating him. And then…

He felt confused, and frightened. It was as if some demon were inside him that kept taking decisions and doing things that he knew were wrong, but over which he had no control.

He turned away from the window and shut the door on the whole thing. It didn't happen. He didn't give the housekeeper's boy a beating, and he didn't do anything else to him, either. There was nothing hidden in the wall. He told the truth to Commander Yelland, and Mr. Sweeney, and his father; because the parcel chit was addressed to him, so it was his parcel, and he didn't steal it.

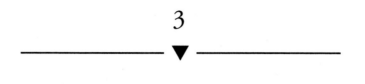

3

Head down and blinded by tears, Frank ran out of the orchard, over the footbridge and past the cattle that were cooling their legs in the river. He ran, stumbling and weeping, up the hill to the copse by the railway line; and there, like Adam after the fall, he hid himself, taking refuge under the heavy branches and thick foliage of an ancient beech that he called the Elephant Tree.

He squatted down and watched the activities of a beetle that was attempting to climb up one of the gnarled tree roots. Its back was like two shiny black shields. It climbed laboriously upward, patiently turning aside and trying a different route when it found its way blocked.

What had happened was too horrible to think about at first, and it was mercifully blocked from his mind. But it soon dawned on him that his encounter with Roddy under the rhododendrons by the boundary wall must surely mark a change more radical than his departure from Devonport five years before.

He saw that his life could never be as straightforward as it had been in the past. It would no longer be possible to qualify for the title 'good boy' by being respectful to his elders and betters, by telling the truth, by working hard, and by going to Confession once a month. Within the space of a few minutes, Roddy had changed all that.

The memory of what had happened was by no means the worst part, however, because although he had fought with Roddy and had tried to struggle free, he now felt guilty that he had not fought harder.

'How on earth did you get into such a state?' his mother asked when he walked in through the kitchen door. 'Have you been in a fight?'

He was prepared for that question. Roddy had made him swear that he would never breathe a word of what he had seen or what had happened, warning that if he ever told anyone, or if any sort of rumor went around, he would see to it that he and his mother would be thrown out into the street.

'I fell off the wall,' he said.

'What wall?'

'The wall at the bottom of the orchard.'

She gave him a look. 'Are you lying to me, Frank?'

'No,' he said. 'I'm not lying.'

'Are you sure?'

'Quite sure.'

'Well I hope you're not,' she said, 'because if you're lying you'll be in mortal sin, won't you? And if you're in mortal sin and you don't confess it you won't be in a state of grace; and if you get run over by a tram you won't go to heaven to be with Our Lady.'

He didn't confess it. There weren't any trams at Meonford, and he decided that he would rather forego the company of Our Lady than be thrown out on the street and have to go back to Devonport and start taking in Warrant Officers' dirty laundry all over again.

But although he never confessed it, he thought about little else for weeks and months afterwards. He wished he could forget it, or at least stop thinking about it, but he couldn't. He had a recurring nightmare in which Roddy's face came very close, his eye getting bigger and bigger and bigger until he seemed to be right inside it and was trapped and unable to escape.

He never dared breathe a word about what had happened, because he was terrified that if a rumor got out, Roddy would come to hear of it and would carry out his threat. He found himself trapped in a paradox of truth and lies; obedience and disobedience.

His mother had always insisted that he should tell the truth and do as he was told, but Roddy had made him promise never to breathe a word about what he had seen. So whether he told the truth or lied, he would have to disobey either Roddy or his mother. If he told the truth about what Roddy had done, he would be disobeying Roddy; and in disobeying Roddy he would be disobeying his mother. On the other hand, if he didn't tell the truth about what had happened, he would be disobeying his mother by telling lies. Whatever he did involved disobedience or telling lies or both. So, because the lesser of two evils was to obey Roddy and deceive his mother, that was what he decided to do.

No one can appreciate or value the meaning of innocence until it has been lost. Frank appreciated it all too well now, and would have given anything to have it back; but because he had been sworn to secrecy, he had to feign what he had lost.

He worked hard at home and at school. He was cheerful, and respectful to his betters. He served Mass for Father Purbright, who looked deeply into his eyes and patted his head and squeezed his knee and said he was a good Catholic boy and a great credit to his mother.

He felt himself sinking ever deeper into deceit and hypocrisy. He went to Confession once a month and made up fictional sins to whisper into Father Purbright's hairy ear; and when he came out afterwards he told his Ma what penance he had been given, and assured her that he had said his *Ave Maria*'s slowly and thoughtfully, and had made a good act of contrition.

'That's a good boy, Frank,' she would say. 'So you're in a state of grace. Just mind you keep it that way.'

His life became founded on deceit. All that his mother had taught him about God, Jesus, Mary, and Joseph—not to mention telling the truth and being respectful and obedient—turned into a not very good joke that he could share with no one. None of his mother's pious exhortations applied or could ever apply to his situation. He didn't doubt for a moment that they applied to everyone else in the world, but his case was different.

The only way to get along through life, he decided, was to laugh at it and make others laugh with him. He set about courting popularity. He entertained the maids with impersonations of Sir Jervis on the throne or Master Roddy eating muffins or Lady Yarrow practicing her scales. He taught himself to whistle through his fingers, and sang songs to small audiences on the way home from school.

It was his talent for singing that set him on a new and upward path, because one day when he was lighting the fire under the boiler in the laundry, Lady Yarrow overheard him doing a passable imitation of an aria from *Tosca*, with the result that a week later Miss Pinkham took him back to her cottage in Droxford after school and gave him his first piano lesson, which he enjoyed very much because there were pancakes and butter for tea. So when she asked if he would like to learn to play the piano and have regular lessons he said, 'Yes please.'

Lady Yarrow had an upright piano moved down to the billiard room so that he could practice for an hour every day after he got home from school. Ma could hardly contain her excitement. Sir Jervis was paying for his lessons and had become his patron.

He fell in love with Miss Pinkham. She used to play Chopin to him after each lesson. When he heard her play the Prelude No.7 in A Major for the first time, he made up his mind to learn it and play it for her as a surprise. He didn't say anything to her but worked on it every evening for several weeks. He came to know it so well that he could see the score and hear the melody in his mind when he was lying in his bed in the room above the stables.

On the last day of school before the Christmas holiday, a cold blustery day with showers of sleet and snow, he played the piece to Miss Pinkham in her cluttered sitting room with its tiger's head on one wall, its elephant's foot coal scuttle by the fire and its antimacassars of Goan lace over the backs of the two armchairs.

When the last chord had died away, he turned on the piano stool and was amazed to see tears in Miss Pinkham's eyes. She took his hands in hers and told him Plato's story of prisoners that are chained up in a cave, who believe that the shadows they see on the wall are the only reality. 'They are prisoners of illusion,' she told him, 'and it is my task in life to lead people like you out of the cave of falsehood and into the daylight of knowledge and truth. You have a good brain, Frank Jannaway, and it is my duty to see that good brains don't go to waste. So I'm going to ask Sir Jervis if I may start coaching you for the scholarship examination for entrance to Wykeham School.'

The pace of his life accelerated. The possibility of going to a proper school and improving himself drove him on. His mother and all the staff below stairs encouraged him. Everybody in the village was on his side: all hopes were pinned on him. He was the Meonford boy who everybody hoped would make good.

He rose at five each morning in order to study for an hour before lighting the boiler and laying the grates and cleaning Master Roddy's boots. In the afternoons he was allowed off classes to go home and study on his own in his room over the stables. He wrestled with Euclid's theorems and quadratic equations; and in the evenings he sometimes spent as much as two hours at piano practice in the billiard room.

He sat the scholarship examination a month after his thirteenth birthday. Three weeks later a letter addressed to his mother was delivered to Meonford Hall. She opened it with a table knife and read it in the kitchen in front of Mrs. Spooner the cook and Mr. Apps the butler.

'Glory be to the Holy Ghost!' she whispered. 'They've given him a scholarship.'

He was sent for by Sir Jervis, who rewarded him by employing him as a deck hand aboard his racing yacht. He spent six weeks putting sails into bags and taking them out again, polishing brass, scrubbing decks and running errands in Cowes where the yacht was berthed; and at the end of that time he used the six shillings he had been paid to buy a bicycle.

His mother took him into Fareham to buy a second-hand school uniform with money donated by Lady Yarrow; and a week later she watched from the kitchen door as he swung his leg over the cross-bar and cycled at break-neck speed out of the stable yard to start his first day at the Wykeham Grammar School for Boys.

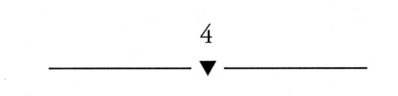

4

Roddy's ship, HMS *Terrific*, had been appointed guard ship to the Royal Yacht for Cowes Week, and Captain Tapprell had granted permission to Midshipman Yarrow and a friend to accept Commodore Yarrow's invitation to race aboard his yacht.

Being aware of Sir Jervis's reputation for writing angry letters to the *Times*, Captain Taprell invited Yarrow to lunch on board after the Church service on Sunday. Jervis came up the accommodation ladder dressed in yachting reefer, cap and white flannels, and was welcomed aboard by the officer-of-the watch, the midshipman-of-the-watch and the captain.

Taprell was an urbane man, unusually softly spoken for a naval officer, with a rather ingenuous manner. By contrast, Sir Jervis was very much the Old Salt, with a nose like a parrot's beak and a way of dragging his lower lip backwards and downwards when waiting for a reply.

'I thought you might find a tour of the ship instructive,' Taprell said when he had shaken hands with his lunch guest, and, without turning he beckoned to a midshipman, who doubled across the quarterdeck, snapped to a halt and saluted.

'Bring our guest to my stateroom on completion of your tour, Mr. Yarrow.'

'Ay ay, sir,' said Roddy.

He was not much taller but a lot chunkier. He was also afflicted by some sort of nervous rash which, if the eruptions on his face were anything to go by, must have made shaving extremely uncomfortable.

He led his father up to the bridge, and proceeded to point out and explain all the latest devices with which the ship was fitted. He showed his father the new experimental gyro compass and explained that a disc, floating in mercury, and driven by an electric motor, rotated at over twenty thousand revolutions per minute, keeping the compass card exactly aligned with true north.

'Is it reliable?' Jervis asked.

'Well, the Germans are fitting it in their ships.'

'That doesn't answer the question, does it Roddy? What happens if the motor fails?'

'Well, if the revolutions drop below a certain point, we change back to the magnetic compass.'

'And how do you know when to change?'

'A warning bell rings.'

'Oh yes? Where?'

Roddy blushed. 'I don't know, father. Actually.'

'Well you ought to. If you're giving a visitor a tour of the ship, you must know all the answers.'

'Yes sir.'

'Never mind. Show me the gun direction platform.'

'It's just behind the bridge.'

'*Abaft* the bridge, Roddy! Whoever taught you to say "behind" on board a ship?'

'Sorry, Father.'

They walked round to look at the gun direction tower. Yarrow looked it up and down with some suspicion. 'I understand all the turrets can be controlled from a single point these days, is that right?'

'Yes sir.'

'How does it work?'

'Well, it's all done electrically, Father. You have an aimer up there on that platform, and a range finder as well, and as they wind their handles to get the bearing and range, other pointers move in the turrets, so that all the gun layers and trainers have to do is keep their pointers lined up to make sure the gun is aimed. It's frightfully cunning, don't you think?'

'What about aim-off for enemy movement? What about wind allowance?'

'The gunnery officer does that, sir.'

'How? Where?'

'I don't know an awful lot about that yet.'

'I thought you wanted to be a gunnery officer.'

'We'll be doing all that on sub lieutenants' courses, Father.'

'That's not good enough. You should keep ahead of the hunt. All right. Let's have a look at the flag deck. I doubt much has changed in that department.'

After visiting the flag deck, they went down to the forecastle and stood looking aft at the main armament, which Roddy described in some detail.

'Do you realize Father,' he concluded, 'that this ship could take on the whole of Lord Nelson's line of battle and win with her secondary armament alone?'

'Hmm,' went Jervis. 'That's what we used to say thirty years ago aboard the old Colossus.' He saw Roddy's face fall. 'Never mind. What about torpedoes?'

'Three submerged tubes, sir—but I believe that's secret.'

'In that case you shouldn't have told me.'

They strolled forward, picking their way over the anchor cables, and stood looking out over the sail-dotted Solent.

Roddy wondered if he ought to talk about the centre-line capstan and the breaking strain of cables, but just as he was about to start, his father turned to him and said rather gruffly, 'How's it been, then? Your time as a midshipman?'

'Oh,' said Roddy. 'Jolly fine, sir.'

'Good. Good.'

There was a silence.

'And you'd like to race in *Clover* would you?'

'Yes please, sir!'

'You're bringing a chum?'

'Yes, sir. Ernle Fairfax-Notley. He's an awfully decent fellow. His father's a Viscount.'

'I'm aware of that, Roddy.'

'Sorry, Father.'

'We'll be berthed in the Medina River. I'll send the dory ashore for you at eight-thirty. Don't be late.'

They strolled aft. 'Would you like to see the engine room, Father?' Roddy asked.

'Is there much to see?'

'Well—you can't see the turbines themselves because they're encased in steel. And…it's awfully hot and unpleasant down there.'

'In that case, I'll settle for lunch.'

Taprell appeared as anxious to make a good impression as Roddy. 'Just my luck to pick the year the Court's in mourning to do guard ship during Cowes week!' he remarked as they sat down to green pea soup. 'No Squadron dinner, no firework display, no balls. It's a damned shame.'

'I should imagine it's rather pleasant,' Jervis said. 'In my day there were too many balls, not too few.'

'I think you would see a great change in the Navy now, Sir Jervis. We're very much more conscious of the need for readiness these days, as you probably noted during your walk round the ship. I hope you saw everything you wanted to see?'

'Yes, I think so. I wasn't expecting a conducted tour in the first place.'

Taprell looked deflated. 'Did you visit the engine room?'

'No, there wasn't time for that.'

'So how would you describe your general impression of the ship, sir?'

'Oh, very favorable. Very favorable indeed.'

A uniformed servant collected the soup plates and served roast beef and Yorkshire pudding, roast potatoes, carrots, and peas.

'You have no criticisms at all?' Taprell smiled. 'I'm sure you appreciate that I'd prefer to hear criticism from your lips now than to read it in correspondence columns of the *Times* next week.'

Yarrow said he didn't think there was much likelihood of that.

'I expect you were pleased to see your son after his year away? Did you see a big change in him?'

'He seems to have matured somewhat. How's he doing?'

Captain Taprell decided that tact was called for. 'Well,' he started, 'he has bags of enthusiasm, there's no doubt of that.'

'Does he have the makings of a useful officer?'

Taprell made a play of looking thoughtful. 'He's been my doggy for the past three weeks. I would say...I would say that he is somewhat lacking in self-assertion, Sir Jervis. Mind you, he's come on tremendously during his time on board—no doubt of that.'

Jervis had consumed two pink gins before lunch and was beginning to feel their effect. 'Do you think he's suited to the naval service?'

Taprell removed a bone from the gap between his front teeth and set it on the side of his plate. 'Yes, I think I can dispel your doubts on that account. Your son obviously enjoys his chosen occupation and, given time, I think he may do well. His seamanship examination result was a little disappointing admittedly, but then we cram a great deal of knowledge into young heads these days. What he needs is to gain self-confidence. That was an excellent idea of yours to invite him to sail with you. I think you can help him even further by letting him know that you have confidence in him, wouldn't you agree?'

After lunch, Captain Taprell accompanied Yarrow aft to the quarter-deck to see him off. 'I wonder if you realize, Sir Jervis,' he said, with the air of one about to make a devastating revelation, 'that I could take on and sink Nelson's entire battle fleet with my secondary armament alone?'

Yarrow was still chuckling about it ten minutes later when he landed at the Royal Yacht Squadron steps.

'What's the rig?' Fortnightly asked the following morning when the midshipmen were lashing hammocks.

'Yachting rig,' replied Roddy. 'Uniform reefers, white trousers, white shoes, and caps. And watch out. Pater's awfully particular. If you have a grubby collar or a broken shoelace he'll have a fit.'

'What about oilies?'

'Better take them. It's blowing a hooligan out there.'

'I say,' said Vanning when they were eating toast and marmalade in the gunroom. 'I believe the German Emperor's racing today. You're frightfully lucky, Toss. I'd give anything to race at Cowes.'

Yarrow and Fairfax-Notley went aft for Colors at eight o'clock, and five minutes later the duty picket boat came alongside and embarked the captain's steward, the stores petty officer and the two midshipmen, Fairfax-Notley embarking last as he was the senior officer present.

After landing at the public hard, the midshipmen walked through the town and got lost in the wrong boatyard; with the result that when they finally found the right landing stage they were ten minutes late and *Clover*'s dory had just departed. Roddy hailed it. On seeing the two midshipmen, the oarsman brought the boat back alongside.

'What the hell do you think you're doing?' Roddy said as he came down the steps to the boat.

'I beg your pardon, sir,' said Jannaway. Sir Jervis hoisted my recall, and I didn't see you until I'd cast off.'

The two midshipmen stepped into the boat and sat in the stern sheets. Jannaway pushed off with the loom of his oar and started rowing out into the river. Fairfax-Notley gave him a kindly grin, but it did nothing to dispel the feelings of repulsion that he always experienced in Roddy's presence. For the merest flicker of a second, his eyes met Roddy's, and there flashed through his mind the thought; 'Yes, Master Roddy, sir, I remember what you did to me, and I can see that you can remember it too.'

'Oars!' ordered Roddy as they were approaching *Clover*. Jannaway glanced over his shoulder and continued to row. 'Ship your starboard oar,' ordered Roddy. 'Hold water port!'

'It's all right, sir,' Jannaway said. 'I've done this before.' He glanced again over his shoulder, stopped rowing, shipped one oar, and at the last moment, when Roddy was convinced the bow was going to savage *Clover's* pristine black hull, held water with the outboard oar so that the dory came snugly and gently alongside.

'Better late than never, better never late!' Jervis said as the two midshipmen came aboard. 'Right—we're going to put you young gentlemen to work straight away. You can start bending on the number two jib. It's going to be quite choppy today. Just the sort of weather I like.'

There was a hard south-westerly gale blowing by the time *Clover*, under reefed main, staysail, and number two jib, came out of the Medina River and into Cowes Roads.

As they cleared the lee of the shore, the full force of the gale made itself felt, and within minutes the yacht was sailing close-hauled past the Prince Consort buoy, with the wind howling in the stays and the sea foaming up over the lee gunwale.

'What are those marks on my jib?' Sir Jervis asked. 'They look like footprints to me. Has either of you young gentlemen been walking on my sails, by any chance? Come on, Roddy. Let's have a look at your shoes. Yes you have, you miserable fellow!'

'Sorry, Father.'

'Right, Mr. Healey, we'll scrub those marks off, if you please. I'm not racing against Kaiser Bill with my best jib covered in horse shit.'

It wasn't the best of starts to the day, but Jervis had the magnanimity to put it behind him, and when the jib had been scrubbed clean and re-hoisted, he invited his son to take the helm.

'Here you are, Roddy! You can take her while I have a look at the chart. You should be able to make the East Lepe on this tack. No need to pinch her. Just keep her full and by.'

He turned away and studied the chart for a minute or two, but then, when the luff of the mainsail flapped, he looked up. 'No—look, you're pinching her, Roddy. Watch your luff, and when it begins to tremble ease her away. That's better. But don't go off the wind! Use smaller movements of the helm!'

Sir Jervis returned to the chart, but not for long.

'You're right off the wind, Roddy. Are you steering on a landmark? You are, aren't you, you wretched fellow! That doesn't work when you're close hauled, see? It's no good steering on a landmark, because you've got the flood tide and lee-way taking you down. Look! Look at the luff! You're pinching again. That's because the wind veers with the gust. Keep your weather eye lifting. Watch out for the cats' paws, and ease her as they hit us. All right, I'll take her now. Ready about! Sheet's in hand! Stand by the lee runners! Helm's a-lee!'

There was a brief clapping of canvas, the main boom swung over from starboard to port, and immediately *Clover* heeled over again and shot forward on the new tack.

'What do you think, Mr. Healey? Shall we have a topsail? I think so, don't you?'

The boatswain, an ex-petty officer with a well-trimmed white beard, grinned and ordered a couple of hands to prepare the topsail for hoisting.

As soon as they were ready, Yarrow brought Clover into wind and all hands tailed on the halyards to hoist it as quickly as possible. Then the fun started. Close-hauled, the yacht sailed right over on her ear, and every time the bow hit a wave an explosion of spray flew back over the boat.

After a sailing back and forth between Needs Oar Point and the approaches to Newtown River, Jervis put the helm up and eased the sheets, so that they ran before the wind. 'Going like a blessed train!' he shouted.

A gun fired from the Royal Yacht Squadron and a moment later a flag hoist fluttered to the masthead to indicate fifteen minutes to the start of the race.

Lord Dunraven's ketch *Cariad II* was out in Cowes Roads now, as were the German Emperor's *Meteor*, Lord Wandsworth's *Zaneta*, and the Earl

Fitzwilliam's *Kathleen*. At the ten minute gun, Jervis started his stopwatch and ordered the crew to lie down on the deck to decrease the windage. 'Here you are, Mr. Fairfax-Notley,' he shouted. 'Take the stopwatch and sing out the time every minute down to one minute, and every five seconds thereafter.'

Jervis turned to Roddy. 'I'm going to make a long leg on the starboard tack, then go about just before the start, so that we cross the line on the port tack, high up to windward and well inshore.'

'Seven minutes to go, sir!' Fairfax-Notley sang out.

'Ready about! Helm's a-lee!'

When the five-minute gun went, they were fairly well off-shore, heading back towards Cowes on the starboard tack inside the start line. There were now six large cutters and ketches maneuvering under full sail in a high wind.

'Oh—oh! Look at that! *Zaneta's* mainsail's gone! Ha! That'll teach him to penny pinch on his outfit of canvas!'

'Two minutes, sir!' shouted Fairfax-Notley.

'Thank you! We shall put about half a minute before the start!'

'One minute! Forty seconds! Thirty-five! Thirty!'

Suddenly, under *Clover's* lee bow, the German Emperor's yacht *Meteor* appeared at close quarters on the port tack. 'Give way, sir!' Jervis shouted, and everyone aboard *Clover* held their breath as the two yachts converged—and let it out again as the *Meteor* bore away at the last moment, to pass so close to Clover's stern that Frank Jannaway, who was sitting right aft, could have stepped onto her bow as she passed.

'Twenty seconds!'

'Ready about! Helm's a-lee!'

'Ten…nine…eight…' And *Clover* was round on the other tack with all sheets hardened right in, surging forward over the start line no more than three seconds after the gun.

'Best start ever!' Sir Jervis chortled. 'Where are the others, Mr. Healey?'

The boatswain raised his telescope and reported, 'The Kaiser hasn't crossed the start line yet, sir. *Zaneta's* retiring on account of her mainsail. *Kathleen's* under headsails only. I think she's retired from the race as well.'

'Thought this weather would sort the men from the boys,' said Sir Jervis, and he took a nip of brandy from his hip flask.

Clover sailed fast down-tide. She made a short tack inshore when off the Gurnard Ledge, and then a long one up to Lymington Spit, round which they made a carefully controlled gybe. This left *Clover* with a clear lead of fifty yards over *Cariad II*, her nearest rival.

They were running on a broad reach now and making a fine pace. Jervis ordered the crew to come as far aft as possible to balance the boat. The masthead staysail was hoisted, and with the topsail set as well, it seemed that *Clover* was drawing still further ahead of the other three boats in the race.

'Here you are, Roddy!' Jervis said. 'You can sail her down to the next mark. You've got a soldier's wind. Just keep her as she goes, straight as a dye down towards the Bullock Buoy.' He handed over the helm to his son and looked about him. 'Hello, who's this coming out of Southampton Water?' He lifted his binoculars, and focused them on the liner that was making her way out of Southampton Water past the Calshot Spit.

Roddy had no desire to take the helm. He hadn't genuinely wanted to come sailing with his father in the first place. Sailing in *Clover* held unhappy memories for him. The last time he had done so was on the day his mother died.

On that day, his father, who was the Queen's Harbor Master at Devonport Dockyard, had taken him and his elder brother Clive out for a sail round the Eddystone lighthouse, off Plymouth. Roddy was four years old at the time, and could just remember it. His nanny, Miss Cook, had been very seasick.

On their arrival back at the house, he remembered the crunch of his father's footsteps as they went up the gravel drive, and Miss Cook telling him that he could run ahead to see Mama and tell her how he had been allowed to steer his Father's yacht.

He ran into the hall and went up the wide staircase. 'Mama! Mama!' he called, running along the landing to her room. But on entering, he stopped dead.

She was in bed, lying with her head right back and her mouth full of vomit. Her eyes were open and not blinking. There was a smell, and a terrifying silence. He backed away, and was still staring when Nanny Cook came and swept him up in her arms; and always after that day his life had been hateful. He hated yachts and he hated the sea. He hated his father and he hated the woman his father brought back from Russia as his wife, who said she was going to be his mother. He hated this woman's shining blond hair and her dark blue eyes. He hated her big bust and narrow back, her fine clothes, the smell of her soap, the sight of the back of her head, the sound of her voice, the arias she sang, and the pieces she played on the Bechstein grand piano in the drawing room. He hated the way she doted on Anita and called her 'Anuchka.' He hated Anita herself, that romantic little fair-haired fairy who was always dressing up and dashing about and giggling and falling in love with her ponies and making eyes at her cousins and pretending she was famous like her mother. Above all, he hated this Jannaway brat, the housekeeper's son, who his father and stepmother had taken under their wing—this paragon of virtue and excellence who could do no wrong in his father's eyes.

Frank was sitting right aft, directly behind Roddy, his arm looped round the back stay. With the wind right aft, he was in the best position in the boat to detect changes in the relative wind direction, and he was becoming concerned that Roddy seemed unaware that *Clover* was dangerously close to a gybe.

Frank's training as a deck hand at the hands of Mr. Healey had not been for nothing. It had been drummed into him that the safety of the boat must always come first, even when that meant speaking out of turn or interrupting his superiors. Now, as he felt the wind move from being on his right cheek to his left, he knew that it was his duty to sound a warning, whatever the consequences.

'Sir,' he said quietly. 'You're by the lee.'

Roddy turned quickly and glared at him. 'When I want advice from you,' he said, 'I'll ask for it.'

'White star Line,' commented Sir Jervis, who was still looking at the liner through his binoculars. 'Looks like the *Lusitania*.'

As Roddy turned back to look ahead, a strong gust of wind sent cats' paws scattering across the choppy water. Roddy saw that *Clover* had lost her heading, because the Bullock buoy was now under the port bow rather than dead ahead. At the same moment, Sir Jervis lowered his binoculars and glanced up at the sails. Fearful of a rebuke for being off course, Roddy pulled the helm sharply up to alter course to port.

'Helm the other, way, sir!' shouted Healey.

But it was too late. The wind, catching the big mainsail on the wrong side, lifted the boom higher and higher until it slammed across to starboard.

There was a cracking sound like the noise a tree makes when it is felled. The topmast snapped off at the throat halyards and came down in a tangle of canvas and cordage that fell over the side and stopped the boat dead in the water.

His father turned on him. 'You bloody fool! You've lost me the race! You've humiliated me in front of the Kaiser!'

Roddy rose immediately in his own defense. 'Father—it wasn't my fault! You said that on the port tack—'

'To hell with what I said! You were at the helm! It was your responsibility! Even the wretched deckhand saw that you were by the lee!'

Two white spots appeared on Roddy's temples. His mouth became misshapen and he had difficulty forming his words. 'Every bloody thing I do is wrong, isn't it?' he shouted, his voicing breaking into a falsetto. 'I don't know why the hell I agreed to sail with you in the first place. I don't give a fish's tit for your bloody yacht. You can stuff it up your backside as far as I'm concerned. I never want to set foot on it again.'

'And you shall not, Roddy,' said his father. 'I can promise you that. After your performance today, you certainly shall not.'

They were still clearing the wreckage when the liner slipped majestically past. Sir Jervis was right: it was indeed the *Lusitania*. Some of the passengers waved to crew of the yacht with the broken mast, but no one on board *Clover* waved back.

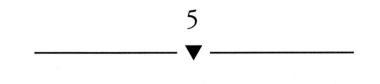

5

By the time she celebrated her seventh birthday, Anita Yarrow had come to the conclusion that all grown-ups were silly. She saw it in everything they said and did, and because she saw it so clearly and so distinctly, she was absolutely confident that it was so. But while ladies were understandably and predictably silly, gentlemen were silly in a quite incomprehensible and unpredictable way. This, she began to suspect, was because gentlemen had Persons like Madrigal, whose Person was, on occasion, clearly displayed to view when the poor darling was standing in the paddock feeling lonely.

Searle the head groom ('Searle by name, surly by nature,' her mother used to say), explained to Anita that the reason for this was that Madrigal was probably thinking about his lady friends, a piece of information that Annie accurately reported to her governess, the love-lorn, pock-marked Mademoiselle Chateauneuf; who in turn passed it on, inaccurately, to Lady Yarrow.

Anita's mother was not amused. 'That is not a subject of conversation that is of concern to young ladies, Anuchka,' she said. 'Nor should you make it your practice to engage the servants in conversation. If you have questions, ask them of Mademoiselle Chateauneuf or myself.'

Mademoiselle Chateauneuf was always saying that this or that was '*très très romantique*,' an expression that applied particularly to Mama, who had fallen in love with Father when she was an opera singer and he was a captain in the Navy. It was a story of rides round London in closed carriages, of late night suppers on oysters and *crèpes suzettes*, of performances of *La Traviata* at the Royal Opera House, and—a few years later—of a cab chase across St Petersburg, at the end of which Father finally caught up with

Mama in the Café Literaturnoy, presented her with a large bunch of white irises and went down on one knee to propose marriage. '*Bien sûr*,' Mademoiselle would say, '*c'était très, très romantique*, Miss Anita.'

When summer came, there were garden parties and house parties and tennis parties and croquet parties and dinner parties; and the world filled up with young men in white flannel trousers and striped blazers and straw boaters whose entire lives seemed to be given over to playing the fool. They were always playing practical jokes on each other and roaring with laughter. Anita could never understand why they all laughed so much.

Every year at the end of July, her parents rented the same villa at Bembridge on the Isle of Wight. She had a straw hat with a black ribbon to go with the black silk bow on her sailor suit. There were blisters in the varnish on the deck seats of the paddle steamer which took them across to the Isle of Wight, and she liked to burst them with her thumb nail when Mademoiselle wasn't looking. The villa's garden ran down to the sandy beach of St Helen's Bay. Hordes of friends and relations descended: the Collard cousins and the Talbot cousins and the Braddle cousins, and one or two maiden aunts who looked acutely uncomfortable and totally disapproving most of the time.

Anita's favorite cousin was Tom, who was in the Navy and Doing Very Well. She was going to marry him, though he didn't know it yet. He was the only grown-up she knew who wasn't silly. He sent her a picture postcard from Gibraltar and showed her how to do mirror writing; and he taught her how to make up codes so that you could send secret messages to people or keep things secret in your diary. He carried her on his shoulders and pretended to be a camel. He ran along the sandy beach, his enormous toes splashing up the sea. She asked if he would marry her. He said he would have to think over that proposal very carefully indeed.

All the things she most wanted to do on those Bembridge holidays were the things that her mother said she was not allowed to do. She wanted to go for a ride in a goat cart, watch the Punch-and-Judy show, listen to the minstrel play his banjo, and go in a bathing machine. But whenever she asked if she could do any of these things, Mama always came back at her with a 'Certainly not, Anuchka.'

Uncle Vernon hired a horse-drawn *charabanc*, and they went on an excursion up to White Cliff. Her cousins played cricket on the turf and they had bacon and eggs for lunch in a café that was used by the lower classes. Uncle Vernon, who had a wooden leg and side whiskers and a voice that Father said was like a foghorn, sang a sea shanty about shaving under the chin and drinking whisky and gin, and the way he sang it made everyone laugh. He had been the captain of a gunboat on the Nile when General Gordon was besieged at Khartoum.

Mama called Uncle Vernon an Old Salt, but he was a very nice Old Salt and Anita's favorite uncle. He and Aunt Constance lived in a little cottage with only four bedrooms in Hambledon and Aunt Constance sometimes made butterfly cakes for tea, which was amazing. Uncle Vernon had a brother who was dead. He had been a friend of Winston Churchill, and was killed at the battle of Omdurman. Roddy's elder brother, Clive, had been named after him, and he had been killed at the beginning of the Boer war. His body had been brought back to England and was buried under the yew trees in the churchyard of St Bartholomew's Church, with the family motto, *suaviter in modo, fortiter in re,* on the tombstone.

One evening at Bembridge, Mama gave one of her soirées. They put chairs in rows in the drawing room, and Mama wore her glorious cream taffeta. She accompanied herself on the piano and sang her best arias, after each of which the guests clapped and clapped and clapped, and some of the gentlemen stood up and shouted 'Encore!'

The following day they had a picnic on the beach, but she had Eaten Something and had to go back to the house to be sick. Mademoiselle took her back, and they went up the long back garden that had banks of hydrangeas and lupines and hollyhocks on either side. Mademoiselle said she was to spend the rest of the day in bed, but quite soon she felt very much better, so she put her clothes back on and went down to talk to the servants in the kitchen, where Mrs. Jannaway and her son were podding broad beans. She said she would like to help them, and sat down at the scrubbed table beside Mrs. Jannaway, who had thick dark eyebrows and sallow skin and a severe manner. Her boy, who did the boots and cleaned the grates, was sitting on the other side of the table opposite her. He was called Frank. He had a shock of hair the color of dark sand, and seaweed eyes, and a saucy smile that made her heart go pit-a-pat.

She was beginning to get the hang of pressing the end of each bean pod with her thumb to push the pale green beans out, when Mama appeared in the kitchen doorway. One moment she wasn't there, the next moment she was: tall, magnificent, her shining hair packed up underneath her hat, her pale blue reticule hanging from her wrist, the ivory handle of her parasol gripped tight in her delicate hand.

'Anita,' she said, beckoning with a gloved finger. 'Come.'

Later, Anita tried to explain about being bored, but Mama would not listen. She said she was very, very cross. 'How many times have I told you,' she said, 'that it is quite, quite improper to mix with the servants?'

'Why is it improper?' Anita asked, but was given no satisfactory answer.

She began to suspect that her mother and Mademoiselle Chateauneuf were conducting a campaign to prevent her from finding out certain things about the world—things that everyone else seemed to know about, talk about and laugh about, but that were for some reason forbidden to be known about by yours truly, Anita Yarrow.

The activities of boys and young men with girls and young women seemed to be a particularly sensitive subject, and she realized that the only way to find out about such matters was to keep her ears and eyes open, while pretending to be not in the slightest bit interested.

She became adept at standing in places that were out of sight but within earshot of interesting conversations. She discovered that the world that was forbidden to her had its own jargon. It was a world in which things and people went from bad to worse, or down the drain; a world whose inhabitants looked up furtively at her approach, or laughed behind their hands for no good reason. The servants were part of that world. They seemed to know far more about it than Mama or Father, or, for that matter, Mademoiselle Chateauneuf, who seemed to think she knew just about everything.

One of the best vantage points from which to observe the goings on in the underworld of lower-class life was the servants' lavatory at the top of the back stairs, from where, if she stood on the mahogany seat, she could see through a small window, straight across the stable yard into Frank's room where he studied in the evenings. Also, when Frank was practicing on the piano in the billiard room, she sometimes watched him through the crack in the door; and in the afternoons, she always tried to be in the yard when he came home from school on his bicycle.

But Frank always seemed to be looking the other way. She became increasingly angry about it, and ever more determined to make him notice her. Every evening, as soon as he had stopped his piano practice, she went up to the servants' lavatory, stood on the seat and looked out of the little window to catch a glimpse of him studying in his room. And one evening, he *did* look up. Anita smiled and waved to him, but instead of smiling back, he waved his finger at her as if to warn her about something. As he did so, the lavatory door opened behind her, and Mrs. Jannaway walked in.

Mrs. Jannaway reported the matter to Mademoiselle Chateauneuf, and Mademoiselle Chateauneuf reported it to Mama. Anita was duly sent for.

She had never seen Mama so angry. She said that her behavior had been grossly, *grossly* improper. She was sent to her room and had to stay there with only bread and water to eat for two whole days; but the punishment did not lessen her curiosity. Rather, it convinced her that she would have to be much more careful in future.

Two weeks before Christmas, the gardeners were sent out into the forest to chop down a Christmas tree, which was set up in the refectory. The servants decorated the house with ivy and holly, and on Christmas Eve the Mummers came in to perform their play, and were given mince pies and hot drinks. The servants and their children crowded into the refectory, the smallest children sitting in a semi-circle on the floor.

'Here comes I, soldier of the King!' said the Soldier; and the Doctor brought him back to life after he was killed by giving him some medicine from a bottle.

Anita, who had seen the whole performance before, concentrated her attention upon Frank. She stared at him and went on staring at him until he glanced back, giving her the barest hint of a smile.

She decided there and then that she would marry Frank instead of Cousin Tom, who she couldn't marry because he was her cousin, and marrying one's cousin was not, according to Father, an Awfully Good Idea.

Her birthday was on January 17th, and her age went with the year, so she was ten in 1910. That was the year that her parents took her to Russia. They went by steamer across the Baltic Sea, and when they arrived at St

Petersburg they were rowed ashore in a barge and taken by coach-and-four to her grandfather's summer palace.

It was midsummer. One night Mama woke her at midnight to see the sun on the northern horizon. They went on a picnic by the sea at Peterhof, and Father played with a boat which was driven along by pedals, like a bicycle. The ladies were all in cream and white and the gentlemen, who were all Life Guards or Hussars or Sappers, wore splendid uniforms. She was taken to a military parade on the Field of Mars and was presented to the Grand Duchess Vittoria, who was a distant cousin and who painted a beautiful little miniature of her, which later hung by the hearth in the drawing room at Meonford Hall.

She went riding side-saddle with her mother through birch forests to a dacha for an *al fresco* lunch with more of her cousins, and one of them, Cousin Georgi, showed her his tree house and tried to make her play doctors and nurses, but she wouldn't, and went off in a huff to find Mama, who showed her how to make strawberry jam the way they used to when she was a little girl, by holding wild strawberries in a kitchen spoon over a candle flame.

At the end of their stay, Mama took her to the opera at the Conservatoire on Mariensky Square; and on her last evening she dined at table with her grandparents. The following morning, dressed in her new Russian sailor suit, with black stockings and a floppy Russian sailor hat, she sat between her parents in the landau as they drove back to the landing stage to embark for England.

The ship sounded a deep, long blast on its siren as it began moving away down the River Neva. The palace roofs and shining domes of St Petersburg slipped away out of sight. The sound of shots came from the city. The proletariat were having one of their riots.

Anita stood on the passenger deck with a lump in her throat. It was like a dream.

She was given a diary for her eleventh birthday, and began to record the every-day events at Meonford Hall. But while her parents and relations did only boring things, like going to London and coming back again, or giving dinner parties, or going to hunt balls, or getting promoted, the lives of the servants seemed altogether more colorful.

Servants died, fell in love, broke things, stole things, and went from bad to worse. They misbehaved, were dismissed and (whisper it soft) drank. In the world of servants there were tears, laughter, courage, and adversity; while in the world her parents inhabited there were only problems about the Empire, the price of diamonds, Germany, the Duma, suffragettes, and the Navy. Upstairs all was dry propriety and the stiff upper lip; below stairs there was passion and drama.

One of her earliest diary entries recorded the death of Aggie Roughsedge, who died of a fever at the end of January. Later that year there was talk below stairs of Tom Roughsedge marrying Mrs. Jannaway, but nothing ever came of it because if they had married, Mrs. Jannaway would have had to give up her position as housekeeper, and Frank would have had to leave his grammar school, which was out of the question because he was doing so well.

That summer there was a vacancy for a new table maid, and Becky Summers from the village was engaged; but she only lasted three weeks because she and Frank had been to school together and she was always giggling and making eyes at him. She was caught trying on one of Mama's hats, and this gave Mrs. Jannaway the excuse she needed to get rid of her, so Becky was exchanged for one of Lord Romsey's maids: a gorgeous, soulful individual with russet hair, dark blue eyes, and freckles all over her face and arms.

While Becky Summers was only sixteen—the same age as Frank—her replacement, Gert, was a fully mature woman of twenty-two. Wherever she went, she turned men's heads. The valet fancied his chances with her but was sharply rebuffed. The driver suffered the same fate. The head groom called her a 'man-eating tigress.' She seemed to exert a magical influence over men. Father went out of his way to be charming to her. Even Roddy, who was usually very off-hand with the servants, treated Gert with a certain deference.

'That girl has the manner of a *femme fatale*,' Mama remarked one afternoon, and when Annie asked what that meant she was told to ask her governess, which she did, with the result that she decided that it would be very interesting to become a *femme fatale* herself one day.

It was about that time that the King died, which Annie was supposed to be very sad about but wasn't; and the year after that her parents went to London for the Coronation.

She was left behind in the charge of Mademoiselle. There was a village party to mark the occasion. Because Mademoiselle liked looking at young men with long legs, she decided that it would be good for Anita's education to attend.

She would have liked to wear her Russian sailor suit and have her hair loose down her back, but Mademoiselle insisted on plaiting it very tightly, and made her wear a green velvet dress, which had horrible lace cuffs that tickled her wrists.

Trestle tables were set up under the willow trees in Stapleton's meadow by the river, and the villagers sat jammed up together on benches dressed in their Sunday best, the men looking hot and polished, the military men wearing their campaign medals pinned to their lapels; the women chattering nineteen to the dozen, and kicking their husbands under the table if their eyes wandered in the direction of Doris Bloodworth's burgeoning cleavage.

The vicar said a very long Grace, in which he asked God's blessing on the new King; and Sergeant Thompson, who was eighty and had lost his balls in the Crimea, made a speech about the new era that had dawned. But Anita was not as interested in talk of past battles or new eras as in the fact that Gert was making advances to Frank.

Her parents came home on Wednesday. On Thursday, her father went down to Gosport to finalize the arrangements for chartering a yacht. Anita asked her mother why her father wanted another yacht, and was told that this was a steam yacht that he was going to hire for the day because they were going to attend the Royal Fleet Review.

'Shall we take the servants?' Anita asked.

'Of course,' said her mother.

'Shall Mrs. Jannaway be coming?'

'Yes.'

'And Frank?'

Mama gave her a severe look. 'I have told you before, Anuchka, that it is extremely bad form to take an interest in the servants. Whether or not Frank will be present should be a matter of supreme indifference to you. Do you understand?'

They had a Bentley with a long bonnet and a walnut dashboard. It was driven by Purviss, who had a reputation with the ladies, though which ladies and what sort of reputation Annie had no idea. He wore a black jacket with black buttons, leggings, gauntlets, and a peaked cap with a black badge. Father complained that he drove too fast, and Mama that he drove too slowly. Mama was like that. She was full of suppressed vivacity. She pined for the bright lights and the *crèpes Suzettes*.

Along with Aunt Constance and Uncle Vernon, they all drove down to Portsmouth harbor, where they embarked in a freshly painted black and cream yacht, with bright red insides to the ventilators that poked up through the decks. It was like a floating tennis party without the tennis. Her father and several of his gentlemen guests wore naval uniforms with white trousers, and the ladies tied their hats on with chiffon scarves. Before they cast off, four huge hampers were delivered, and carried aboard by the servants, one of whom, Annie was pleased to see, was Frank.

She went up on deck and sat with Mama and the ladies as the yacht gave a bleat on its siren and the ropes splashed into the water; and as they came out past Fort Blockhouse and into the Solent it dawned on her for the first time what a fleet review was, because there now appeared line upon line upon line of warships, all painted dark grey, their guns huge and menacing, their funnels tall, and their flags fluttering on strings that went up to their masts from both ends. She had never seen so many ships. She had never even dreamt that there could be so many ships in the whole world.

Father began pointing them out with such evident pride that you would have thought he had built every single one of them with his own hands. They sailed down the line between the *Good Hope* and the *Warrior*, the *Black Prince* and the *Achilles*. Some of the battle cruisers had modern names like *Indefatigable* and *Invincible* and *Indomitable*; others, like the *Euryalus*, *Juno*, and *Isis* had a classical ring about them.

Anita had been told often enough that the Royal Navy had made Britain great, but there seemed to be something dark and foreboding about so many floating weapons of war. There was no doubt what Father expected her to feel about them, however. He held forth at great length about the complexity and speed and power and invincible nature of each one they passed.

The battle cruisers were the most terrifying. They were like awful iron monsters, decked out with flags today maybe, but just waiting, like alligators, to snap their steel jaws. Then there were the submarines: nasty, black iron cigars floating so low in the water their decks were awash. The destroyers were no better—they looked sleek and fast and merciless, like ferrets.

As the yacht steamed up and down the lines, Sir Jervis explained to his guests which ship was which and what sort it was and how far its guns could fire and what the white or red stripes on their funnels meant.

'Here you are, now this one is the *Dreadnought* herself. See the St. George's Cross at the masthead? That's Admiral Sir John Fisher's personal flag. Twenty thousand tons! Over eight hundred men! Twenty-one knots! Twelve inch guns! What do you think of that? Isn't she a fine sight?'

When they had steamed once up and down the lines, the yacht dropped anchor, and luncheon was served in the main saloon. Soon after two o'clock, word came down from the bridge that the Royal Yacht *Victoria & Albert*, with the King embarked, was on her way out of Portsmouth harbor, so the whole company of guests proceeded on deck again; and after a slight delay, the reviewing ships—the *Victoria & Albert*, the *Alexandra* and the *Enchantress*—came into view.

'Now, ladies and gentlemen,' said Sir Jervis, 'the Royal Yacht has just hoisted a signal giving the preliminary order for the massed gun salute, and at two-thirty when the order is executed, every ship in the fleet will fire a colossal combined salute, the like of which has never before been heard by human ears.' He took out a pocket watch, flipped it open and announced, 'One minute to go.'

But then something awful happened, because as the *Victoria & Albert* neared the head of the lines, and everyone held their breath for the signal to be made for a massed gun salute, one of the ships let off a gun by mistake, and the result was a sporadic popping that was not at all in keeping with the original concept of a mighty roar of synchronized gunfire.

Anita got the giggles. It seemed that not only were all grown-ups silly, but the entire Royal Navy was silly as well. The silliest one of all was her father. He became almost apoplectic with fury. He strode up and down muttering to himself and going red in the face, until Mama told him to come and sit down, because there was nothing at all he could do about it.

The *Victoria & Albert* steamed slowly down between the lines of ships, and as she passed each one, the sailors cheered three times, waving their caps in a circle with each cheer. While this was going on and all attention was focused on the Royal Yacht, Annie turned to look behind her at the gathering of servants who were looking out through the saloon windows. Frank was among them. He was standing beside the new maid, and must have been unaware that he was being watched, because Annie saw Gert link fingers with him.

When the review of the fleet was over, the Royal Yacht anchored in the line and there was an immediate flurry of activity as captains and admirals went in their barges to call upon the newly crowned King and, as Father explained, offer him their Humble Duty. While that was going on, tea was served in the saloon, but before Annie had managed to get anywhere near a cheese straw, Father called for silence to make another announcement.

'Ladies and gentlemen, as you know, it was our intention to return to harbor on completion of the review after his Majesty departed, and I can confirm that he has indeed now done so. However, because of the state of the tide, I am afraid to say that we are at present unable to proceed into harbor.'

There was a buzz of conversation among the guests.

'Are we aground?' asked a retired admiral.

'I regret to say we are, sir.'

'So how long are we stuck here for?'

'We shall have to await the flood tide.'

'How long will that be?'

'At least seven hours, I'm afraid.'

'But my dear Jervis,' said Aunt Constance. 'That won't be until after midnight!'

'I'm afraid so. And, unfortunately, as we are not permitted to go along-side between the hours of midnight and six a.m., I regret to inform you that we shall be obliged to spend the night on board. However, there is one consolation in that we shall have a front row seat for the fleet illuminations scheduled for nine-thirty.'

Anita was allowed to stay up to see the illuminations, which were much prettier than she had expected them to be, because every single ship had a string of electric lights running up to the mast from bow and stern.

The servants brought hot beef tea up on the deck, and there was something of a party atmosphere. Mademoiselle Chateauneuf flirted with the yacht master, and Mama flirted with the old admiral. While this was going on, Annie noticed Frank walking off by himself; so when no one was looking, she slipped away after him.

She couldn't find him at first. She went up and down ladders, looked in through brass portholes and climbed up to a small deck just below the bridge, which afforded a rather better view of the illuminated ships. She paused to look out across the fleet and at the lights on the foreshore beyond, and it was while she was up there that she saw, on the deck below, a door open, and Frank emerge. He stood for a moment in the doorway looking up and down the boat deck in a rather furtive way before going back inside and closing the door after him.

Anita descended the accommodation ladder and went along to the door. It was smaller than the normal doors in the ship and had a brass plate with UPPER DECK CLEANING STORE on it. With her heart pounding, she put her ear to the keyhole and listened. Yes. He was in there. She wondered if she dare open the door, and was about to do so when she heard footsteps behind her.

She spun round and came face to face with her father.

'What the hell is going on here?' he muttered, and, pushing her to one side, he pulled open the door to the upper deck cleaning store. Inside, jammed up together among the mops and buckets, clasped in a close embrace, were Frank and Gert.

Her father was as furious as only her father could be. He took her by the arm and marched her back to the other side of the yacht, where he handed her over to Mademoiselle Chateauneuf, who was instructed not to let her out of her sight; and she spent an uncomfortable night in a cabin which she shared with her mother, Aunt Constance and another lady, who snored.

Gert was put ashore the following morning when the yacht berthed at Portsmouth. She was never seen again, though a rumor went round below stairs that she had gone from bad to worse. On Sir Jervis's orders, Frank was given a thrashing by Tom Roughsedge. Mademoiselle Chateauneuf informed Anita that he had been warned that this was his last chance: any further misbehavior on his part would put an end to his education at Wykeham Grammar School.

Outraged on Frank's behalf, Anita decided that he was a 'darling,' and confided the fact in code to the pages of her diary, which she kept completely safe from prying eyes in the secret drawer of her Davenport.

6

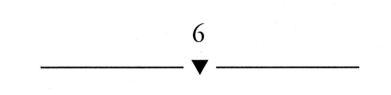

Towards the end of August, Roddy decided to spend a night at Meonford Hall with the aim of talking his father into buying him a motor car. He caught a train from Portsmouth, and traveled in the station trap from Wickham to Meonford.

He had passed his sub-lieutenant's courses, done the London Season, and now, as sub-lieutenant of a gunroom, was terrorizing midshipmen aboard one of the new battle cruisers in the Grand Fleet. He had filled out considerably in the past year, and had a rather bloated look, with a small plantation of mutton-chop whiskers on his cheeks, which he referred to as his 'bugger's grips.'

The front door of Meonford Hall was left open during the summer, so Roddy arrived unannounced. Inside the hall he stopped and listened. All was quiet. He went into the library and had a look at the papers on his father's desk, among which he found a letter from the headmaster of Wykeham Grammar School confirming that, in view of his good showing in the recent examinations, Francis Jannaway would remain at the school a further two years until the age of eighteen.

Roddy found this irritating. He had no idea why his father was taking so much interest in the housekeeper's son, and suspected that Jannaway's gain was his loss. In this rather negative frame of mind, he went up the wide staircase past portraits of his ancestors, most of whom had been generals, admirals, lord lieutenants, or justices of the peace.

Fifteen minutes later, having changed into a blazer and flannels and had a bit of fun at the expense of the new housemaid, who he caught posing in front of the mirror in Lady Yarrow's boudoir, he came out of the conservatory and down to the lower lawn, where he found a tennis party in progress.

His step-mother, father, Uncle Vernon and Aunt Constance were sitting outside the summer house taking tea. On the tennis court, Cousin Tom was playing pat-ball with Anita and Maisie, the youngest of the Collard cousins.

Uncle Vernon was sitting in an old wicker chair with his wooden leg supported on a stool. 'Roddy!' he bellowed. 'Home is the sailor, home from the sea!'

'Hello old man,' said Sir Jervis rather stiffly, and Lady Yarrow said, 'Roddy, dear boy! What a lovely surprise!'

Cousin Tom broke off his game and came over to shake him by the hand, and Cousin Maisie went on tiptoe to kiss him on the cheek.

'Aren't you going to come and kiss your brother, Anuchka?' her mother asked, so Anita came over and gave him a perfunctory kiss before returning to the court, where she stood bouncing a ball with studied impatience.

'Haven't seen you since you were at Osborne, old boy,' Tom remarked. 'How goes the battle? I gather they've given you a gunroom and some midshipmen to play with?'

Roddy was in awe of his cousin who, at the early age of thirty-two, had just been selected to be promoted to the rank of commander. 'Yes-that's-right,' he said, adopting the staccato delivery which is associated with 'tautness' in the Royal Navy. 'I'm sub of the gunroom.' He turned. 'I say, Mater—is there any tea going?'

Irina turned to her sister-in-law. 'You see? He hasn't changed a scrap. He still thinks only about his stomach, don't you dear boy?'

He had never liked being made fun of, and was particularly sensitive to his step-mother's brand of condescension. 'Well who knows, Mater?' he said briskly. 'Perhaps this dull little brain of mine is *occasionally* occupied by thoughts of other things.'

Irina ignored his sarcasm and rang a hand bell for the maid. Roddy helped himself to the last of the scrambled egg sandwiches, poured himself a cup of tea from a fluted silver tea pot, and sat down in a wicker chair.

'Why don't you join us, old boy?' Tom asked. 'We could have a game of mixed doubles.'

'It's much more fun with just we three,' Anita said.

'With *us* three,' her father corrected. 'You wouldn't say "with we" would you?'

The maid arrived, in some distress.

'What on earth is the matter, Doris?' Irina asked.

Doris glanced at Roddy and said quickly, 'Nothing ma'am—nothing at all, ma'am.'

'Another pot of tea, please,' said Lady Yarrow.

'And more scones, strawberry preserve and clotted cream,' added Roddy.

Doris collected the teapot and departed back across the lawn.

'Crossed in love, I expect,' Irina said. 'That one seems to spend her entire life in a dream.'

From the house came the sound of a piano. 'That surely can't be your housekeeper's boy playing?' Constance asked.

'Yes—that's our resident pianist,' said Jervis.

'And the cause of the maid's distress, no doubt,' added Roddy.

Irina laughed lightly. 'Yes, I think you may be right there.'

Roddy bit into a scone. 'What happened to the redhead? The one with freckles.'

'The less said about her, the better,' said his mother. 'She was dismissed.' Irina nodded in the direction of the house. 'And *he* was extremely fortunate not to be given his marching orders at the same time.'

'It was his last chance, wasn't it, Mama?' Anita called from the tennis court.

Constance said: 'I must say he does play remarkably well, don't you think? Who is his teacher?'

'A chap called Strong,' Jervis said. 'Though he hardly lives up to his name. One of these effete long-haired types.'

'You know Eleanor Pinkham?' Irina said. 'Sir Basil Pinkham's spinster daughter? It was she who started him off. He has perfect pitch, you know.'

Roddy snorted. 'Perfect pitch? What's that when it's at home? Some sort of tar?'

'It means he can tell which note is which without having to use a tuning fork,' Anita said from the tennis court. 'Even I know that!'

'We decided to encourage him,' said Irina. 'He's gone from strength to strength.'

'He may even go to university,' said Anita, who had abandoned the tennis court to join the grown-ups, and was standing by her father's chair patting the top of her head with her tennis racquet.

'That is by no means certain,' said her father. 'And it is no concern of yours, Annie.'

'The housekeeper's brat going to university?' said Roddy. 'Pull the other one!'

Jervis shook his head. 'He's going to have a damn good try, and provided he behaves himself I think he'll succeed. His headmaster is very enthusiastic.'

'And who'll pay for it?'

'Your father is acting as his patron,' Irina said.

Constance clapped her hands. 'What a splendid thing to do, Jervis! Do you think he will be a concert pianist?'

'An engineer, more likely. His headmaster tells me that he has a mathematical brain.'

'He could do anything he liked,' Anita said, her eyes shining.

Irina turned to her and put a finger to her lips. 'That is quite enough from you on the subject, Anuchka.'

'I say, do you know,' said Roddy, 'I do believe my little sister is blushing.'

Jervis put his arm round his daughter. 'Don't take any notice of him, sweetheart. He's just jealous.'

Roddy said, 'Well that didn't take long, did it?'

Jervis looked up quickly. 'I beg you pardon? What didn't take long?'

'Nothing important.'

Anita leant against her father and stared at Roddy, her fair curls over one eye, the collar of her sailor suit crumpled up on her shoulder. She raised one eyebrow and put her head on one side. 'If it's not important, why did you say it in the first place?'

Roddy waved a finger at her. 'Don't be cheeky, you.'

'Fair's fair, Roddy,' said his father. 'After all, you started it, didn't you?'

Annie put her tongue out at Roddy when no one else was looking.

'Just had a thought,' Roddy said abruptly. 'Excuse I, one and all.'

'Oh dear,' he heard Anita remark as he went up the lawn towards the house. 'Roddy's up the miff tree.'

He went through the conservatory and upstairs to Anita's bedroom. He didn't know what he was going to do, but he was determined to teach her a lesson she would not quickly forget.

Anita had never played with dolls, but had a greatly favored teddy bear called Disraeli that had patched paws and wore an old red jersey. Seeing it on her bed did nothing to improve Roddy's mood. He felt like wrenching its head off, but decided against that. There were more subtle ways. He went to her Davenport, opened the secret drawer, found her diary, and scanned the pages.

Most of the entries contained the usual sort of rubbish about ponies and parties and cousins and her governess; but every so often he discovered the same group of capital letters: GTBOL, and, on one page, the letters UBTNKOH GTBOL. So she was using a code. He flicked through the unused pages, and on the last but one found the key to it. It was a simple Playfair cipher using the word MEDUSA as the keyword: the same code and the same keyword that Cousin Tom had taught him years before.

Taking the letter to the left, GTBOL came out as 'Frank.' This was an interesting discovery, but when he decoded UBTNKOH and it came out as 'darling,' he knew that he was on to something that might prove useful. He looked back through the diary and found the entries, 'Saw GTBOL,' 'Waved to GTBOL' and, on one of the latest pages, 'UBTNKOH GTBOL passed exams!' But the most interesting entry of all was on the last page but one: 'Wrote to GTBOL.'

He could still hear the piano being played in the billiard room, and it occurred to him that as long as he could hear it he could be sure of the pianist's whereabouts. He put the diary back into the drawer and closed the desk. Then he went down the back stairs, out through the tradesmen's entrance, across the yard and up the stairway to Frank's room over the stables.

It was as much a study as a bedroom now, with a plain pine table under the dormer window, complete with inkwell and blotter, and a single well-stocked bookshelf. He looked in the small chest of drawers, but it contained clothes. He searched in the table drawer but found only odds and ends: a penknife, a spare packet of nibs, a ball of string, shoe laces, and a photograph of the housekeeper in her best hat at Wickham fair.

He looked round the room, shaking his fists in frustration. He took a copy of Euclid down from the shelf and held it upside down so that all the markers and penciled notes fell out on the floor. Nothing there. He took another book down: *Introduction to Trigonometry*. What was this? A card. A picture of the Virgin Mary and a note on the back: 'To Frank on your confirmation day, with fondest love, Mother.'

He snorted in disgust and took more books down. He went systematically through them, leafing quickly through each and putting it back on the shelf when nothing had been found.

He realized, with a slight shock, that the piano had been silent for some time. Quickly, he put all the books back on the shelf, and stooped to pick up the markers and notes. As he did so, his eyes came down to the level of the table top, and he noticed the edge of an envelope which had been slipped in underneath the single drawer in the table. He pulled it out, and knew immediately that the letter it contained was just the sort of thing he needed to sort both Anita and the housekeeper's son out once and for all:

Dear Frank,

I would like to talk to you but I am FORBIDDEN to. I think you are VERY clever doing so well in your examinations. Well done! Please can we be secret friends? I am ~~groin~~ growing very fond of you.

With lots of love from
Anita.
xxx

He met Frank as he was crossing the stable yard. 'The maestro himself!' he said. 'That was a fine performance you put on for us, young Jannaway. We were all singularly impressed, I must say. And I hear we have hopes of sending you off to university one of these fine days, is that right?'

Frank was lighting the boiler in the laundry when his mother came to tell him that Sir Jervis wanted to see him. She was flushed and excited. 'Go and wash your hands and brush your hair,' she said. 'You can't go looking like that.'

He entered the library believing that Sir Jervis had good news for him. But when Sir Jervis held up Anita's note, he knew instantly that Roddy must have taken it from his room.

'Have you seen this before?'

'Yes, sir.'

'How many other letters has my daughter written to you?'

'None sir. That was the only one.'

'Have you written back?'

'No, sir.'

'Have you had any other contact with my daughter?'

'No sir.'

Sir Jervis put Anita's note carefully down before him, adjusting it so that it lay exactly square and central on the desk. Then he looked up and fixed him with a piercing stare from beneath his bushy eyebrows and asked, 'Do you realize what this means?'

'No, sir.'

'Then I shall tell you. It means the end of our plans for your education. It means an end to your hopes of staying on at school. It also means the end of your mother's employment with us here.'

Frank felt tears start to his eyes. 'Sir,' he said. 'My mother hasn't done anything wrong. If I have to go, I have to go, but if you dismiss her, I doubt she'd ever find another position. She hasn't any money. She'd be destitute. It'll mean the workhouse. Please, sir. I beg you.'

But Sir Jervis was shaking his head. 'You were warned, weren't you? You were told that you had been given your last chance. We gave you the benefit of the doubt. We trusted you. You have abused our trust. If your mother stays here, you will inevitably return to see her, and if you return, my daughter will be in moral danger.'

'But I never wrote to her, sir! She wrote to me!'

'You kept her letter did you not? You failed to destroy it. Why was that I wonder? No need to reply, Jannaway, no need to reply. You kept it because you were flattered by it and unwilling to discourage a clandestine correspondence. Can you deny that? No you can not. And that is why I am unwilling to have you at Meonford Hall a day longer than is absolutely necessary.'

Sir Jervis leant back in his chair and stared at Frank for several seconds. Then he started again. 'A couple of years ago, your mother came to us for advice. She had received a proposal of marriage from my gamekeeper, and was at her wit's end about whether or not to accept it. Did you know that?'

'Yes, sir.'

'What you may not know, however, is that had she married Mr. Roughsedge, she would have had to relinquish her position with us here, and our financial support of your school education would have come to an end. Do you know what she did?'

'She didn't marry, sir.'

'Quite right, Jannaway. And you know why? It was for *your* sake. That was why. To keep you at school, she gave up the chance of having a husband to support and comfort her in her declining years. That was a selfless act of hers, don't you agree?'

'Yes sir.'

'I think, therefore, that you owe her a debt of gratitude.'

'Sir,' Frank said. 'I would do anything to prevent her having to lose her position—anything at all.'

Sir Jervis's expression relaxed immediately. 'I'm glad to hear you say that, Jannaway, very glad indeed. Because if you will now give me your solemn undertaking that you will follow the course of action which we propose, then it will be possible for your mother to retain her present position. So. Here is what we have decided. First, you will be sent into the Royal Navy. Second, you are never to return here to Meonford. And finally, you are not to reveal to your mother—or indeed to anyone else—the circumstances attending our decision. If you do so, your mother will be summarily dismissed. Is that understood?'

7

A chief petty officer was waiting on the platform at Harwich when the London train pulled in. It was a wet and windy September evening, and it was getting dark. 'Follow me!' bellowed the chief, and the new entrants trooped along behind him.

He led the way through the town to the harbor, where an Admiralty trawler lay alongside. They were ordered below into the hold, and moments later the vessel maneuvered away from the quay.

The boat smelt strongly of tarred rope, a smell that embedded itself in Frank's memory, so that he could never smell it again without remembering that journey across the nautical Styx they crossed that night—the stretch of water that separates the civilized world from Shotley Boys' Training Establishment.

The engine slowed its beat, paused and raced as it was put astern. Feet clumped on the deck overhead and fenders squeaked as the boat came alongside.

'Up top, the lot of you! Chop-chop! This way! Follow me!'

They went up flights of stone steps and along a road towards buildings with saw-tooth roofs. They came to a long, low building and were hustled in through a door. Inside, three petty officers sat behind three tables, and a warrant officer in a stiff wing collar and tie stood behind them. They were split into three groups, each of which lined up at a separate table behind which sat a petty officer.

'Answer your names! Adams! Ackroyd! Bell! Biggs! Bradley…!'

'Name?'

'Jannaway, sir.'

'Full name!'

'Francis John Jannaway, sir.'

'Date of birth?'

'Thirty-first of May, 1895, sir.'

'Next of kin?'

'Mother, sir. Ethel Jannaway.'

'Religion?'

'Er—'

'C of E. Next boy. Name?'

'You have joined the Royal Navy,' said the warrant officer, pacing up and down with his hands behind his back. 'You are Boys Second Class. You will address all petty officers and chief petty officers as "sir," and when an officer passes you will stand to attention and salute. From tomorrow, you will proceed at the double at all times. There are two sorts of boys at this establishment: the quick and the dead. Make sure you are numbered among the quick. Any boy found smoking or in possession of smoking materials of any kind, including matches, will be given official cuts. Any boy who deserts or attempts to desert will be given official cuts. Any boy who willfully disobeys the order of his superior officer or shows disrespect to those in authority will likewise receive official cuts. Carry on, chief petty officer!'

Frank was placed in a group of twenty under the charge of one of the gunnery instructors, Petty Officer Litton. They followed him outside onto a wide road, where he stopped and addressed them in a voice that sounded like boots on gravel.

'This is the quarterdeck,' he said reverently, as if it were the Taj Mahal. 'This is the first and last time you will walk across it. In future you will always salute as you step onto it and cross it at the double.'

They came to low buildings between which led a narrow street that had been roofed over with corrugated iron. 'This is the Long Covered Way,' said Litton; and after leading the way up it for some distance, turned in through a door to the wash places.

'Strip off, the lot of you,' he ordered. 'It's bath time for babies.'

It was a disinfectant bath. Frank had not expected to be molly-coddled, but this was humiliating and inwardly hurtful in a way that shook him. It was the first thing about the Navy that really hurt.

White duck uniforms, one for each boy, had been laid out on the benches. Most of them were too big or too small, and there was some sub-dued laughter. Frank's outfit was too small, and he was approached by a scrawny Irish boy called Lewtas, who was holding up his trousers to keep them from falling round his ankles.

'Want to swap?'

'Sure.'

'What's your Monica?'

'Frank. Yours?'

'Steve.'

With sailors' caps on their heads for the first time, they followed the petty officer along to the galley, where tripe and onions awaited them. They loaded up their plates and took them to the mess tables and sat down, jammed side-by-side on wooden benches. There was dry ship's bis-cuit to go with it and mugs of watery cocoa to wash it down.

When they had eaten, they were led further along the Long Covered Way to Grenville mess. It was more of a shed than a dormitory. The roof was supported by iron girders and the only furniture was the beds and the kit lockers. 'Get turned in, nozzers,' Litton said. 'Lights out in fifteen min-utes.'

They slept in their shirts under rough blankets. Some had come from orphanages and were used to sleeping in a dormitory. Others looked sud-denly frightened and vulnerable. Undressed, they seemed to revert into children: children with anxious faces, pinched faces, spotty faces, cruel faces, kind faces, old faces.

'First time I slept in a bed on me own in me life!' Steve Lewtas remarked.

'Pipe down!' shouted Litton. 'Silence on the mess deck! No skylarking! Stay in your beds until Charlie. Unless you want the heads.'

Then the lights were out and the wind was moaning through the open windows; and Frank lay on his back thinking about the day and trying to fight back the bleak feeling of hopelessness that had been dogging him from the moment he stepped off the train.

When dawn came up, the wind was battering in off the sea and bringing spatters of rain in through the half open windows. That day, and every day, started with Charlie, the bugle call that blasted every last thought and memory from the mind and jerked you into a grim recollection that, whether you liked it or not, you were in the Navy. 'Wake up Charlie,' it went, 'lash up your hammock. Wake up Charlie, lash up and stow…'

So now they were nozzers, the lowest of the low, Boys Second Class who messed and slept in an annex building for the first five weeks in order to be instructed in the necessary skills of marching, saluting, eating and sleeping in what the training petty officers termed the 'proper service manner.'

From Charlie to Pipe Down there was hardly a minute of free time. If they weren't scrubbing the mess they were scrubbing the heads or the bathrooms or their white duck uniforms. When they weren't scrubbing they were marching and counter marching, wheeling left and right, moving into line, forming fours, forming two-deep, saluting to the front, to the left, to the right. When they weren't on the parade ground they were in the gym, where they spent two hours of every day. There were also school lessons and seamanship classes and gunnery drills; and when those were over any spare time was spent on the playing fields.

Autumn turned to a bitter winter. Clad only in flannel shirts and duck suits, with biting east winds blowing in off the North Sea, they were sent barefoot up and over the rigging and the upper cross-trees of the mainmast. It was a test of courage to touch the very top, which could only be reached by shinning the last ten feet up the bare pole to a two-foot wide circular platform that was known as the button, to which was attached a short steadying pole called the gallows. Whenever a course passed out, the mast would be manned, and one boy, picked for the length of his arms and lack of imagination, would stand on the button with only the tip of the gallows to steady him and a one hundred foot drop to probable death if he lost his nerve and fell.

In the spring, they went for a cruise in HMS *Tring*, the training sloop. They did seamanship drills, fire drills, gun drills, anti-torpedo drills, and boat drills. They slept in hammocks, stood night watches, vomited into buckets, kept look-out, and learned to handle anchor cables and berthing hawsers.

Gradually, as the months passed, they were turned from boys into the sort of men the Royal Navy demanded they should be: men who obeyed with knee-jerk immediacy, men who were tough and fearless, and whose humor seldom failed them. Friendships formed that would never completely fade. Surnames were dropped. They knew each other now as Smudge, Ginge, Scouse, Shiner, Mick, and Jan. And quite suddenly it was July again, and they were counting Charlie's to the last Charlie of their time at Shotley.

The day before the passing out parade, Ginge Waller, the button boy, broke his arm in the gym. That evening Lewtas was sent for by Chief Grier. When he came back to the mess deck, he looked decidedly pale.

'What's up, Mick?' asked Smudge. 'Seen the bleedin' 'oly ghost, 'ave yer?'

Lewtas had not seen the Holy Ghost. He had been told that he was to take over from Waller as button boy.

'I'll go into a boxing ring with anyone,' he confided to Frank at supper, 'but the thought of goin' up on that bleedin' button frightens me fuckin' fartless!'

'You've been on it before, haven't you?' Frank said.

'Ay, but I swore I'd never go on it again. It's not the gettin' on I mind. It's the getting off the bugger that puts the fear in me. Jesus! Just the thought of it brings me out in a sweat! And if I'm feelin' like this now, me hands'll be so sweaty tomorrow I'll be bound to slip.'

Frank told him that he would be up and down all in five minutes, and then he'd be shaking hands with the First Lord of Admiralty.

'Stuff that for a bleedin' game of darts!' he said. 'I don't want to shake hands with that bleedin' toff!'

They were up before Charlie the next morning. They put on their best uniforms, adjusted the bows of their cap tallies and the knots of their black silks, brushed the last specks from their bell-bottomed trousers, and emerged into the sunlight to wait out of sight behind the buildings for the bugle call to fall in for divisions.

The notes brayed out over the morning. A thousand boys rushed out and fell in by divisions. When the First Lord appeared, the flag of Admiralty was hoisted, a musical salute was played by the bluejacket band, and the guard presented arms. Accompanied by the captain, the commander, the divisional officers, the medical officer and three chaplains, the First Lord of Admiralty walked up and down the lines of boys.

Then the moment came and the Warrant Officer Gunner ordered, 'Grenville mess, man the mast!'

The only way to do it was to forget everything else, sprint to the rat-lines, hurl yourself at them and climb, climb, climb: up the square-meshed foot-holds of the shrouds, swaying and bouncing as dozens of other boys climbed with you; up, swinging up, over the Devil's Elbow; suspended momentarily over thin air as you heaved yourself over it; and up again to the half-moon and the foot of the Jacob's ladder that led up to the button. It was here that Frank caught up with Steve Lewtas, who was clinging to the Jacob's ladder, frozen with fear, unable to go higher, unable to descend.

'I can't do it, Jan! I can't do it!'

There was no time to think. He didn't think. He climbed on, past Steve, up the Jacob's ladder, up the rungs to where they stopped. He put his hands up and gripped the bare pole, wrapped his legs round it and hoisted himself up, up, up…up…up…up again, and up once more. Got one hand up over the button. Didn't think. Just reached out and got his fingers over the far edge. And heaved; and lay over the button; and gripped the gallows with one hand. Pulled himself up, slowly, carefully, into the kneeling position. Didn't look down. One foot on. Crouching now. Holding the gallows with his left hand.

Standing…up…straight. And—salute.

But Lewtas was right. It was the getting down that was the worst bit, because there was a moment when you had to get your legs back round the pole, and then let go with your hands and trust your legs to grip and keep you from falling.

He was the last to reach the ground. He doubled across the parade ground to where the captain of the college stood with the First Lord. 'Boy Jannaway down from aloft, sir!' he reported, and heard Mr. Churchill's gruff, 'Well done.'

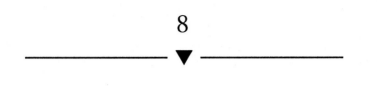

8

From his first days at Stubbington Preparatory School to his time as a trainee gunnery lieutenant at HMS *Excellent* in Portsmouth, Roddy Yarrow had played rugby football, with the result that, over the years, he had developed an extensive repertoire of the sort of songs that are sung after rugger matches by naked young men relaxing in communal baths of hot, muddy water.

Roddy's favorite, with variations corresponding to each of the positions in a rugby team, went:

> If I was the marrying kind,
> Which thank the Lord I'm not, sir!
> Oh what fun in the middle of the night,
> To play at Rugby full back!
> I'll make touch, you'll make touch
> We'll make touch together!
> Oh what fun in the middle of the night,
> Making touch together!

As every moral and religious leader knows, the more often a belief is repeated, the more surely does that belief take hold; so by the age of twenty-four there was no doubt in Roddy's mind that he was *not* the marrying kind. But fate is an unpredictable thing and coincidence has a long arm; and when they work together—which they always do—unlikely consequences can result.

This was the case in the peculiar circumstances of Roddy's meeting and mating with Geraldine Malone.

Geraldine was one of those unfortunate people who, from her earliest childhood, had been led to believe that whatever she wanted, she could have. Her father, Tip, was a bullet-headed self-made tycoon who, with the help of cheap immigrant labor, had amassed a fortune to rival that of J.P. Morgan. Geraldine, who was known as Toots to her family and close friends, said she should have been a boy. Her father agreed with her. He would certainly have preferred her as his heir to either of her two elder brothers. Scott was a bully and Henry was a sap. Between them, they had tormented, teased, and taunted their younger sister, so that by the time she was sixteen the three Malone siblings were locked together by dark secrets and a perpetual fear that Toots might carry out her threat to go tell Mommy.

With the onset of middle-age, Mommy slipped into the role of an ill-used neurotic. While Tip built palaces, collected art treasures, competed in yacht races, and launched transatlantic liners, Winnie Malone stayed in her bed, humming the Baptist hymns of her childhood, feeling her own pulse, and wondering if she was strong enough to ring for the maid.

Toots was so named because of an early tendency to bawl the house down if there appeared the remotest possibility that she might not have her own way. The nickname stuck with her when she grew up, because the necessity to out-shout her father developed in her a voice that could penetrate all the four floors of the Malone family residence.

By the time she was sixteen, her uncomfortable relationship with Scott and Henry had given her a rather warped attitude towards the opposite sex. She regarded herself as a prize that would be awarded to the suitor with the most to offer by way of status, real estate, and hard cash, being confident that, with her daddy's influence and connections, she would be able to find the perfect young man.

And she did. His name was Benjamin J. Porterman. He was four years younger than she, and first in line to inherit a cotton mill in North Carolina which, thanks to the employment of ten-year-old children with empty bellies and quick fingers, had turned honest John Porterman into a millionaire.

Geraldine first put her hooks into Benjamin when she was seventeen and he was thirteen. Tip took them sailing off Long Island and they spent the following four summer holidays riding and swimming and canoodling on the Porterman estate in the mid-west.

Toots teased out the romance with an expertise of one who has been a victim of teasing. If ever a girl knew how to keep a boy teetering on the edge of satisfaction, it was Toots. Over and over again, the romance lurched in the direction of the ultimate intimacy; over and over again there would be a crisis, tears, recriminations—and then a kiss-and-make-up resolution.

Ben came of age on December 29th 1913. Three evenings later, at the Long Island Sailing Club New Year's Eve Ball, Toots took him outside, compromised them both, and having done so made him an offer he would have been unwise to refuse. That done, she led him back to the ball to announce their engagement.

Enter a dark, gentle, svelte young lady called Rachel Joseph. How she and Ben Porterman met, nobody knew. All that was certain was that it was one of those amazing love-matches that no one believes is possible unless it happens to them. Well, it happened to Rachel and Benjamin, and within a matter of hours of their meeting, Benjamin knew that he could never marry Geraldine Malone.

He struggled with the dilemma for several weeks. Sensing that the relationship was cooling, and suspecting competition lurking in the wings, Geraldine responded by intensifying what might be called the koochy-koo aspects of the relationship, which only sickened Ben the more.

One grey-skied afternoon in Central Park, Henry saw Ben out with Rachel and reported the fact back to Geraldine. She went immediately to work. She interrogated Ben and wheedled Rachel's name out of him. That done, she called round on the lady in question and told her, 'Hands off, he's mine.'

Throughout this encounter, Rachel behaved with admirable restraint, which infuriated Geraldine to such a degree that she started tooting. Rachel showed her the door, and Geraldine went down the steps into the street shouting that this would not be the last Rachel heard of it. Nor was it.

Geraldine was a great one for her daily routine, in which Benjamin was included. After she had taken a leisurely breakfast and spent what remained of the morning with chocolates and fashion magazines on the settee, Benjamin was expected to arrive at midday on the dot to take her out to lunch. But on the day after the rumpus with Rachel, he arrived an hour early.

He had put on a brown suit and a brown bowler hat, which he brought into the lavishly furnished sitting room instead of leaving with the servant at the door. Toots bit into a marsh mallow and asked why he had arrived early. He replied that he had come to tell her that he couldn't take her out to lunch.

Her upper lip, which protruded slightly over her lower, twitched petulantly. 'What do you mean, "can't"? There's not such word as "can't."'

He tried again. 'All right—I'm *not going* to take you out to lunch.'

'Why?'

'Because I heard what you said to Rachel yesterday, that's why.'

'That bitch!'

'Now listen here, Geraldine—'

'What are you calling me Geraldine for? You never called me that, long as I can remember!'

'Look, let's both try to keep calm, shall we? I've come early because I've something to say to you—something important and serious.'

'Like what?'

'The fact of the matter is,' he started, and, after a deep sigh, came out with it: 'I've come to ask you to release me from my promise.'

'What promise?'

'To marry you. I can't do it. I like you, but, well, I guess I don't love you.' He shrugged and opened his hands. There was nothing more he could say.

'Wait a minute,' growled Geraldine. 'Are you saying what I think you're saying?'

His Adam's apple jerked up and down. 'I'm not going to marry you, Geraldine. That's the beginning and end of it.'

Geraldine threw the marshmallows on the parquet, and hollered for her daddy.

Daddy galloped to the rescue. No son of a bitch, not even the heir to the Porterman fortune, could hurt his little girl and get away with it. He was going to sue. He was going to sue Ben Porterman and his father for breach of promise, and if there was any justice in the United States of America, he was going to win.

The battle lines were drawn, the attorneys were engaged, and dates for a hearing were set aside. The gentlemen of the press sharpened their pencils. The broken engagement between the heir and heiress to the Porterman and Malone fortunes became a talking point in the society columns. The Number One subject of conversation at smart dinner parties became that of Malone versus Porterman.

The day came. The court was full. The press was there. Malone's counsel opened with a speech that made all the salient points. At the end of the day, the gentlemen of the press scurried off to write their pieces; and the next morning the nation read all about how Miss Malone had fallen in love and waited for her childhood sweetheart to grow up and come of age. How tragic it was that this fine girl, this lovely young lady, this burgeoning flower of American womanhood, should, for four long years, keep herself so exclusively for the boy she loved and then, only a matter of weeks after accepting his proposal of marriage, made of his own free will and under no sort of duress, have that precious thing called love flung back like a torn and soiled rag in her face!

There was no doubt about it. Miss Malone was going to walk away with this, and when it was over, there would surely be no shortage of suitors queuing up to prove that love and honor still counted among the young men of America.

Even while the New York cabbies were assuring their fares that the Malone heiress was bound to win her case, the Porterman family attorney was on his feet, quietly asserting that his client's defense was one of justification.

Before a hushed court, Rachel took the stand. Quietly but confidently, she told the court what Geraldine had said about Ben Porterman behind his back. She had said a lot, it appeared. Geraldine had gained Ben's confidence, and he had confessed to some pretty intimate feelings and habits which had long troubled his conscience. Now, the court heard that Miss Malone had abused his trust in her.

Before Rachel finished giving evidence, Geraldine broke down in court and was helped out, shouting that it was all lies. The case was adjourned, which gave the press another field day and another cliff-hanger. By morning, Geraldine had become the 'Kiss-and-tell Heiress,' and the cabbies in New York had revised their opinions of her chances.

The outcome was a nice exercise in justice. The plaintiff was awarded damages in the sum of fifty cents, and ordered to pay costs, which were considerable.

Though it was a devastating loss of face for Tip, he at least had his steel mills, his presidency of the United States Line, his art treasures, his yachts and his fortune to console him. His daughter was left with nothing. Toots had tooted once too often. She was twenty-five going on twenty-six. She was the Kiss-and-tell Heiress. She was the young lady any bachelor with any sense of self-preservation would run a mile to escape.

She had a nervous collapse.

Tip called in a gentleman who had awarded himself a doctorate in psychology and who, for a fee of a hundred dollars, told Tip what he knew already, namely that Geraldine needed rest and a complete change.

Geraldine hated change above all things. She liked what she knew and was used to. She liked punctuality, reliability, and routine. For weeks she resisted all suggestions of a trip to Europe; but then Tip started talking about how J.P. Morgan's daughter had married the son of Lord Fisher, the famous British admiral. So why shouldn't she do the same sort of thing? Everyone knew that titles were ten a penny over in England, and if she played her cards right she might end up a Duchess. He offered her the use of his house in Hyde Park Square if she would give it a try.

Gradually, she became attracted to the idea of mingling with the English aristocracy; so that when Tip hinted that if she were to go to England she might get to meet the Prince of Wales, who was undoubtedly the most eligible bachelor in the whole world, Geraldine showed a perceptible flicker of interest.

Tip engaged the services of Miss Slocombe, a tortured lady, who agreed to act as his daughter's companion and minder; and three weeks later, when Tip's flagship moved slowly down harbor past the Statue of Liberty, Geraldine was sitting in the first class saloon, smoking a Balkan Sobranie cigarette in a jade holder and wondering what the future might hold.

Geraldine was not one to do things by halves. Her father had opened a bank account for her in London, and her credit was good. She had come to England to do the season and find herself a titled husband, and she set about the task with characteristic directness. On arrival in the capital she fitted herself out in the latest fashions and signed the visitor's book of every hostess with a handle to her name.

Within two weeks of docking at Southampton, the entries in her appointment book included balls to be thrown by Lady Inchcape, Lady Aird, Lady Lucas-Tooth, Lady Henry, the Marchioness of Salisbury, and Lady Melksham.

She said 'yes' to a picnic in a naptha launch at Henley, 'yes' to the Derby, 'yes' to Ascot and 'yes' to the Wimbledon Championships; and at every occasion, she took care to wear a different outfit, so that she very quickly succeeded in getting herself noticed. But while a large number of chinless young men danced with her, dined with her and dallied on balconies, terraces and lawns with her, the elusive Duke of Right or Marquis of Desirability continued to elude her.

One evening she met Lieutenant the Honorable Ernle Prescott Bertram Fairfax-Notley, Royal Navy, and he happened to let drop that he had been sub of the Duke of York's gunroom. Exactly what that meant, Toots had no idea; what she did know was that this honorable lieutenant might provide her with an entrée into the coveted naval circle—and he did.

For Royal Ascot, she wore white satin. The dress was made with a bodice fastened with round, fat pearl buttons down the front from throat to well below the waist. The sleeves were long, and tight, and ruffled over the hands. A faint tulle frill lay round her neck, and the skirt was made with a long tunic which formed a point at the front. White satin shoes and paste buckles, white gloves, a parasol, and a magnificent black hat completed the picture. It was a modern edition of a courtier's dress in the time of Watteau, and it was Parisian to the last degree.

Lieutenant the Honorable Fairfax-Notley escorted her to the naval tent, where she was given caviar and a glass of well chilled Moet & Chandon, and was quickly surrounded by jovial young naval officers. After quite a lot of banter and repartee among them, none of which Geraldine understood, a plump lieutenant with blue eyes, a pink face and blond side-whiskers, elbowed his way towards her. 'Did I hear correctly that your father is the President of the United States?' he asked.

'Where the heck did you get that idea from?' Geraldine returned. The lieutenant looked confused. He blinked rapidly and made little grunting noises. She was aware of ill-suppressed mirth on all sides. 'I guess some-one's been pulling your leg,' she said. 'My Daddy's President of the United States Steam Shipping Line, not the United States of America.'

His fellow lieutenants roared brutishly.

'I say you chaps!' complained the object of their mirth, 'That was a rotten trick to play on a fellow. Actually.'

He looked so demolished that Geraldine took pity on him. 'What did you say your name was?'

Fairfax-Notley stepped forward. 'Allow me to introduce you. Miss Malone, this is Lieutenant Roderick Yarrow. Lieutenant Yarrow, may I present Miss Geraldine Malone.'

'Roddy,' said Roddy, and bowed.

'So what sort of lieutenant are you?'

'Oh. I'm on the 'G' course at the moment.' He blinked nervously. 'Gunnery, actually.'

'You like that?'

'Absolutely. Are you over here on holiday, Miss Malone?'

'You mean a vacation? I guess so.' She glanced at his beaming comrades-in-arms. 'I'm doing the season.'

'Have you been presented?'

'Have I what?'

'Been presented.'

'Who to?'

'His Majesty. The King.'

'Oh! Oh, I guess so, yes. I went to the garden party at the royal palace last week. What about you?'

He laughed a snorting sort of laugh. 'Chaps aren't presented. My younger sister will be though. When she's seventeen.'

'So where do you live, Roddy—may I call you Roddy?'

'Of course! Ah—in Hampshire. Actually.'

'He's rich as Croesus and his father's a baronet!' said one of his friends.

'Is that true? Have you got one of these fancy titles?'

'Not yet, unfortunately!' Roddy laughed his porcine laugh, which was more of a 'snort-snort-snort' than a 'ha-ha-ha.'

'So you will one day?'

'Yes. When Pater pops it, I'll inherit.'

'What?'

'I beg your pardon?'

'What will you inherit?'

'The title.'

'What title?'

'The baronetcy.'

'So your father really is a baron?'

He stroked his side-whiskers with his knuckle. 'In a manner of speaking. Yes.'

'And when he goes you take over?'

'Yes.'

'That's neat.'

He smiled and tapped his foot. 'I say,' he said, 'would you care to stroll over to the paddock? I've a tip for the next race. Or—or perhaps you'd care for another glass of fizz?'

'A stroll would be just fine,' she said; and as they walked out of the tent and she accepted his arm, she had a feeling that this might be her man.

9

▼

HMS *Dominant*, Frank's first ship, was an elderly coal-burning cruiser. He joined at Portsmouth on a Wednesday, the ship commissioned on Thursday, and they sailed for the China Station the following Monday. She was not a happy ship. The captain, Henry Barker-Parsons, had an obsession about cleanliness and smartness. He used to wear a pair of white gloves when he did his weekly rounds, and would stage a petulant loss of temper if he picked up dust or oil or any sort of dirt when he ran his fingers along the tops of pipe runs or lockers. 'Help, help!' he would cry. 'Dig me out! Dig me out! I'm up to my neck in shit!'

Because of her limited coal capacity, the ship visited practically every naval coaling depot between Portsmouth and Shanghai; and Frank, along with the whole of the ship's company, found himself engaged in an endless struggle to keep the coal bunkers replenished and the ship up to the impossibly high standards of smartness and cleanliness that Barker-Parsons demanded.

Coaling started with the boatswain's mates going through the mess decks and flats piping, 'Heave out! All hands heave out, coal ship!'

Every man had his station, whether on the inhauls or the outhauls, the whips, the winches or down in the coal lighter filling the bags from the trap-doors to the coaling chutes. The seamen filled the bags in the hold of the collier. They were then winched up, swung across and dumped on the deck. Marines with dump trucks rushed to wheel them away to the manholes spaced out on the upper deck, seamen tipped them, and the signalmen piled the empty bags on barrows, take them to the ship's side, and throw them back into the hold to be filled again.

At the beginning of the commission when everyone was new to the ship coaling was a nightmare, with the officers shouting at the petty officers, and bags taking charge and splitting open against the ship's freshly painted side, and Captain Barker-Parsons, who became known as 'Flaming Henry' on the lower deck, fuming up and down his quarterdeck and sending for the first lieutenant to tell him that there was 'something wrong with your bloody organization, Number One.'

After that, the first lieutenant, who was frightened that he wouldn't get his promotion to commander if he didn't cut the time taken to coal ship, began cracking the whip, insisting that the Royal Marines wheeled the barrows of coal at the double. Crushed hands, dislocated shoulders, and bruised heads became a commonplace; but the pace was never slackened.

The best way to get through coaling was to switch off and turn yourself into a machine—a machine for filling and lifting and heaving and shoveling, on and on and on, with the dust choking in your throat and getting in your eyes and up your nose; the clanking and chuffing of the steam winch; the scream of the block as the derrick swung across; the heavy crunch as another bag landed on the deck, and your own sweaty grunt as you up-ended it into the open mouth of the coaling chute.

As soon as the lighters were clear, the task of washing down the ship started, and as soon as that was done, you washed yourself and your kit. There were no basins, just buckets. You stood in your bucket and scrubbed yourself down from top to toe in salt water. The dust got into everything: the seams of your clothes, your skin, and the teak decks.

Sometimes the officers had one of their parties on the evening after coaling, which meant all hands had to scrub down the decks, and men had to go over the ship's side on stages to wash off the coal streaks.

But the washing and scrubbing didn't stop when you sailed out of harbor: the funnel smoke made the masts and upper decks filthy. Almost every night the stokers blew soot out of the funnels, and in the morning after both watches of the hands had mustered, the chief boatswain's mate would stare at the fresh soot on his decks and boat covers and carry on about the fucking stokers pumping shit all over the fucking upper scupper.

'Fuckin' bastard stokers!' he would shout. 'Look at my fuckin' screens! Black as a fuckin' cow's cunt!'

But no one ever gave him 10A punishment for swearing, because 10A punishment was reserved for junior ratings only.

There were four classes of punishment: minor punishments, summary punishments, warrant punishments and court martial punishments. The minor punishments were things like extra work and drill and could be dished out by the officer-of-the-watch if you broke any of the hundreds of Ship's Standing Orders. The summary punishments meant coming up in front of the commander, and were usually for breaking your leave, returning on board drunk, being slack in obeying an order or being absent from your place of duty. You could be sent to pick oakum in the cells, or have your leave, pay, and grog stopped. The warrant punishments, which were usually things like disrating or detention quarters or second class for conduct, could only be given by the captain.

The older men on the mess deck said things weren't as bad now that the old prison sentences with hard labor had been replaced by the new naval detention quarters, but they were bad enough. They had to have a warrant from the senior officer present to send you over the wall; but as often as not Flaming Henry was the senior officer present, so you could be committed for ninety days in detention quarters if you broke ship or argued the toss or got into a fight ashore.

If you were in the rattle too often, you would be labeled a troublemaker. Once that happened, it was virtually impossible to get back into the Navy's good books, and the chances were high that they would find some way to get rid of you. But before they got rid of you they usually stuck you in the second class for conduct, so it wasn't made easy for a man to work his ticket out of the Navy.

Second class for conduct was the most hated punishment of all. It cut your pay, stopped your leave, stopped your privileges, and forced you to work extra hours when your messmates were ashore. Second class for conduct made you wonder why you ever joined up in the first place. It made you detest the Navy with a deep, smoldering hatred, and when you remembered how everyone had said how wonderful it was that you were going off to join the Senior Service, you were filled with impotent rage and burning resentment. There weren't many who went into the second class for conduct who came out smiling, and still fewer who had a good word to say for the Royal Navy. It was a punishment that made you want to get even with the system. If you didn't think in terms of 'us and them' before you were put in the second class for conduct, you certainly did afterwards.

When the ship was in harbor, shore leave was granted to the boy seamen until sunset. You always had to wear uniform ashore and, because leave was so short, there wasn't much time to get into trouble.

On a make-and-mend with leave, if you could be bothered and you had a shilling to spare, you put on your best ducks and fell in with liberty men; and after being inspected by the duty petty officer you gave in your leave card and went down the ladder into the steam cutter, to be ferried ashore and stroll up and down the streets of Gibraltar or Valletta or Trincomalee or Singapore City, spending your money on a postcard or a souvenir for your Mother.

On your eighteenth birthday, your Man's Time started. You were allowed all-night leave and you had to choose whether to draw your spirit ration and be marked 'G' for grog in the spirit issue book or 'T' for temperance, and get a penny a day in lieu.

Before your eighteenth birthday the chaplain, who enjoyed his whisky as much as all the other officers in the wardroom, did everything he could to discourage you from taking your tot, but on the mess deck they virtually forced you to be 'G' because that meant that the mess would get a larger issue of rum every day.

Rum was what the lower deck ran on. You offered your messmates sippers or gulpers, or sometimes your whole tot in exchange for favors. If you helped someone out of a hole or prevented him from getting punishment, you would say, 'I'll see you at tot time.' If ever you got in the rattle and the commander stopped your tot, your messmates made sure you still got your share from the rum fanny at dinner time.

You had to get drunk on your eighteenth birthday, and everyone on the mess deck made sure that you did. They gave you sippers all round, and after dinner when you mustered with both watches of the hands, and you could barely stand up, the petty officer looked the other way.

The ship was in Singapore dockyard and the petty officer made sure you didn't have to go over the side on a stage, but sent you down into the bottom of the dry dock with a long handled scraper. You tried to focus your eyes on the barnacles, and felt a lot better after vomiting up a mixture of rum, minced meat with carrots, and yellow rice pudding.

In the dog watches, when you'd sobered up, they helped you get into your best ducks and took you on your birthday run ashore. You went in a rickshaw up Bugis Street. You rolled up your cuffs to stop the sweat itching and put your cap flat aback and undid the top flap of your duck trousers. You went into a bar and drank beer.

A Chinese Malay came and sat on your knee. She slipped her hand into yours and asked if you were a clean boy. She said her name was Dahlia. You went out of the bar and up the stairs with her. She led you into a room where an oil lamp with a red shade was burning, and joss sticks were smoldering before a shrine to a god called Ama.

She took off her sarong and lay on the bed and opened her legs, and you did it; and when you went downstairs with her, your mess mates were singing:

> Rule Britannia!
> Marmalade and jam!
> Five Chinese crackers up your asshole,
> Bang-bang-bang-bang-bang!

The ship went back to Hong Kong and into dry dock. They painted out the mess decks, dismounted the eight-inch gun barrels, and landed the anchor cables for their half-yearly inspection.

The officers went ashore every afternoon to go shooting or play golf, and came back on board in the evenings to hold parties under the striped awning on the quarterdeck, to which were invited school mistresses from the British School, nursing sisters from the British Hospital, and all those who had taken the trouble to sign the High Commissioner's visitors' book.

At the weekends there was special leave from 1.30 in the afternoon to 6.30 in the morning, but Frank didn't go with any more whores because he was terrified of getting the clap. On Christmas Day the ship spliced the main brace, and the captain and the officers visited the mess decks at dinner time before going to the wardroom and getting drunk.

After Shanghai the ship steamed up the River Yangtse to Chinkiang, and stopped for a couple of days before proceeding to Nanking, where they secured to head and stern buoys.

As soon as the buoys had been secured, awnings were spread and the seamen went over the side on stages to paint the ship and make her look tiddly for the officers' reception to be held on the quarterdeck that evening.

Frank was detailed off to paint the forward mooring bridle. He collected a two-inch brush, a pot of white paint, and a butcher's hook from the paint shop; climbed out over the bows, and set to work, sitting astride the mooring bridle and shifting further down with each link completed. This was a job he always volunteered for, because it was the one time that he could be completely on his own and think his own thoughts.

He was almost half way down the bridle when he heard shouting coming from upstream. A junk under sail was crabbing across the river. The wind had died and the Chinese crew was frantically getting out oars in an attempt to row the junk clear and avoid colliding with the mooring buoy.

Everything happened quickly. The coolies aboard the junk were shouting, a dog was barking, and women were screaming. The stern of the junk crashed into the mooring buoy. As it did so, a little Chinese girl with short black pigtails fell overboard right underneath him, so he jumped in to fish her out.

10

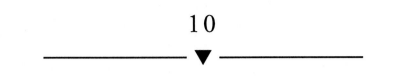

Captain Barker-Parsons had been ashore paying formal calls on the local dignitaries. He wore full tropical dress: white tunic, brass buttons, sword, medals, epaulettes and high-hat. When he arrived back at the landing stage, a blue haze was rising from the polished brass funnel of his steam barge, and the bow and stern men were standing barefoot in their best white ducks, ready to cast off.

The bow and stern lines were slipped and hauled quickly inboard, and a moment later the steam engine chuffed, a wisp of brown smoke emerged from the funnel, and the barge proceeded from the berth, crabbing across the strong river current towards HMS *Dominant*.

Barker-Parsons cast a practiced eye over his ship to see that everything was just so. The awnings had been spread, the booms had been lowered, and the sides had been touched up with grey paint to conceal the rust streaks. He inspected the canvas screens and saw that they were immaculate. He noted that all the brass scuttles had been polished and were glinting in the sun. He checked that the signal halyards were taut, and that a clean White Ensign flew from the ensign staff. He saw with satisfaction that the boot-topping had been scrubbed clean of weed and that the draught marks on bow and stern had been picked out in white paint.

He also saw the junk drifting downstream towards the ship's bow, and the panic on board as the wind died and collision became inevitable. He heard the shouts, and witnessed the collision with HMS *Dominant's* mooring buoy, and the splash as the man painting the forward bridle leapt into the water. Then the junk went down-stream on the far side of the ship, and was lost to view.

The coxswain took the captain's barge in a gentle, curving sweep in order to make the approach to the gangway where the commander and side-party were fallen in to pipe him aboard. The bugler sounded the Alert. Every man working on the upper deck stopped what he was doing, faced to starboard, and stood to attention. As the barge made its final approach to the gangway, the bow and stern men performed the ceremonial boathook drill in strictly synchronized time, raising the boathooks horizontally above their heads, down to shoulder level and finally at the ready.

The barge slid alongside. The boatswain's calls trilled low-high-low as the captain mounted the accommodation ladder, and the commander, the officer of the watch and the midshipman saluted.

'All well?' Barker-Parsons enquired of the commander as he came aboard.

Commander Vavasour was a lean man with a worried look. 'Yes, sir, all well.'

'Sure?'

'Yes, sir.'

'Quite sure?'

'Yes, sir. Absolutely sure.'

'In that case,' said the captain, 'I shall be in my cabin.'

'Thank you sir.'

Barker-Parsons walked across the quarterdeck to the hatch down to his stateroom. When he was a few steps down the accommodation ladder, he paused with his head just visible above the hatch coaming.

'I observed,' he remarked, in a voice loud enough for all on the quarterdeck to hear, 'that half of the forward bridle is unpainted, and that one of the hands has jumped overboard.' Then he went on down the ladder, pausing in his cabin flat until he heard the cry of 'Man overboard!' and the thudding of bare feet on deck as sailors ran to man the cutter.

Later that afternoon, Commander Vavasour came to the captain's cabin and reported the circumstances of the incident. 'To his credit, the rating concerned jumped in to rescue a child who had fallen overboard from a junk, sir.'

'Well he's a bloody fool,' said Barker-Parsons. 'You can tell him that when you see him with his cap off.'

'You mean as a defaulter, sir?'

'What the hell do you think I mean?'

'I felt in the circumstances, as he acted without regard for his own safety—'

'Any man who jumps off my ship without permission is to be seen as a defaulter, Commander.'

Ordinary Seaman Jannaway was brought before the commander the following day on a charge of desertion, which the commander reduced to one of 'improperly leaving His Majesty's Ship *Dominant*.' This lesser charge was found proved; but, while Commander Vavasour would have preferred to let the young sailor off with an admonition, he knew that Captain Barker-Parsons would examine the ship's quarterly punishment return and ask questions if he had not been punished. So Jannaway was awarded a punishment of fourteen days' stoppage of pay, fourteen days' stoppage of leave and fourteen days' Number 10A, for failing to complete painting the forward bridle, improperly leaving his ship, and losing one two-inch paint brush, the property of the Crown.

The punishment was not completed. That evening in the dog watches, while doubling up and down the upper deck with a Lee-Enfield rifle above his head, Jannaway collapsed, and had to be carried down to the sickbay in a Neil-Robinson stretcher.

Surgeon Lieutenant O'Malley made a quick examination of the patient before going aft to report to the captain, who he found stripped to the waist in front of his bathroom mirror, trimming his nose hair with a pair of nail scissors.

'Sir,' reported the Surgeon Lieutenant, 'We have a suspected case of cholera.'

Barker-Parsons looked sideways at his own reflection. 'What action do you propose?'

'I think we should land him, sir. At once.'

'Very good,' said Barker-Parsons. 'Make it snow.'

That was one of his jokes.

11

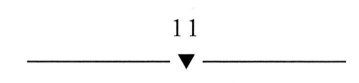

Roddy's motor car was a six cylinder monster with wire wheels, drop-hood, long bonnet and a deafening exhaust. It was painted British racing green, and the two hinged sides of its bonnet were secured by a leather strap and brass buckle. His personal servant cleaned and polished it every morning. It was his pride and joy.

After meeting Miss Malone at Ascot, he drove her back into town; and by the time they drew up outside her father's house in Hyde Park Square she had dropped several hints that if he cared to invite her to dine that evening, she would cancel going to Lady Melksham's ball and accept. Roddy got the message and asked her what she would say to a quiet night out.

She put her gloved hand on his arm. 'I'd be delighted, Lieutenant. Just delighted.'

'So…where would you like to go?'

'What about the Ritz?' She saw his face. 'Anything the matter?'

'Well, the fact of the matter is, I'm a bit strapped for cash at the present moment—'

'That's no big deal. I'll fund you.'

He puffed out his cheeks and blinked rapidly. 'I don't know if I could accept that sort of generosity—'

She gave him a sidelong glance. 'Give it a try, Lieutenant. You'll get the hang of it.'

They danced. He was not a great dancer, but she didn't mind because they looked well together, and people were watching. He was perhaps half an inch shorter than Geraldine, and a year or two younger, but she didn't mind about that either, because he was presentable, wealthy and heir to a title.

'You know something?' she said over the Stilton, 'I think you and I are going to get on real well, Roddy.'

He looked pleased.

'So tell me about yourself. Why did you join the Navy?'

He blinked and tapped his foot. 'I...I was half-hitched by Pater. Actually.'

'You mean you didn't want to join?'

'Not at first. I was only ten when the decision was taken.'

'You joined the Navy when you were ten?'

'No, I was thirteen. But Pater decided I was to join when my brother was killed. He was with General Symons in the Boer War. We received the news on New Year's Day of the new century. I was dragged in and told I was to join the Navy.'

'Do you regret it?'

'Heavens no! Best decision I ever took!'

'It sounds as though you're doing quite well.'

'Yes, I am, as a matter of fact. I'm one of the youngest on the gunnery course, and I got an awfully good flimsy from the captain of *Vindictive*.'

'So...do you plan to be an admiral one day?'

'Absolutely!'

'And your family? Your father and mother live down in Hampshire, right?'

'Father and step-mother, yes. Mother died when I was small.'

'Do you remember her?'

'Not really. That is—'

'Yes?'

'Well, I found her, you see. After she...took her life.'

'That must have been quite ghastly!'

'Yes. It was. Actually.'

'Why did she do it?'

He lowered his eyes. 'Because of my father's womanizing.'

She reached her hand under the table and placed it on his knee, put her head on one side, and gazed into his eyes.

They danced again, and talked some more, and danced again. She paid the bill and they went out into a clear, warm night. He asked her if she would care to take a walk. She said she would just love that.

They strolled through the park to Buckingham Palace, up the Mall, under the Admiralty Arch to Trafalgar Square, and back along Piccadilly; and by the time they arrived at his car she had heard all about how he had never got on with his father; how his half-sister was the spoilt favorite of the family, and how he was determined to outshine his father, whose naval career had gone into the doldrums as the result of some sort of political skullduggery back in the nineties when he was at the Admiralty on the staff of Admiral Fisher.

It was late when they drew up at her house. He left the engine running and turned to face her.

'May I call you tomorrow?'

'Please do.'

'And on Saturday evening it's Lady Inchcape's ball isn't it? Will you be there?'

'I don't have an escort as yet.'

'In that case, may I have the honor?'

'You certainly may.'

'I feel I've known you all my life, Geraldine.'

'I guess that's how I feel about you.'

He swallowed. 'Until tomorrow then.'

'Until tomorrow,' she replied, and lifted a gloved hand for him to kiss before going up the steps and into the house.

They went from party to party and from strength to strength. She had money, dress sense and a striking presence. He had rank, an automobile, and a title in the offing. They felt good together. Roddy's standing in society was heightened and his self esteem enhanced: he was particularly gratified one morning to find his name and Geraldine's in the society column of *The Times*.

Geraldine was similarly gratified, but also determined. This time there must be no mistakes. Frightened that her reputation might follow her across the Atlantic and kybosh her chances of landing a husband, she was in something of a quandary over delaying too long and losing her quarry, or being too forward and frightening him off.

Within the space of three weeks, she was confident that she could extract a proposal of marriage out of him at the drop of a monogrammed handkerchief, so that hers was no longer a dilemma of when to shoe-horn Roddy into a proposal, so much as whether to do so at all.

It was quite a dilemma. Lingering at the back of her mind was the uncomfortable awareness that of all the young men she had met in England Roddy was the only one who had shown any positive interest in her. And, while his class and status made him suitable husband material, he was also a bit of a dope. He was always opening his mouth and putting his foot in it. He was also inclined to drink rather a lot and become unpleasantly loud.

On the other hand, weren't most men like that? Besides, she felt quite sympathetic towards him, as he seemed to have had a raw deal in life, what with his mother committing suicide and his father being such a tyrant.

She hadn't breathed a word about the Porterman business. She had left all that behind her on the other side of the Atlantic. No, her only problem now was that if she extracted a proposal of marriage out of Roddy Yarrow and accepted it, wouldn't it be just her rotten luck if the real Duke of Dreams came along the next day when it was too late?

After appearing on Roddy's arm at three society balls, two garden par-ties, one tennis match and a picnic on the Thames, at which she tore an expensive dress while watching an electric canoe going over the mechanical conveyor at Boulter's Lock, Geraldine decided that she had waited long enough.

On the last Saturday in June, Lady Fairfax-Notley was throwing a ball at her house just round the corner in Gloucester Square, to which Roddy and several of his contemporaries on the gunnery course had been invited. This seemed to be a suitable occasion upon which to make her move, and the day before the event she dragged Miss Slocombe round the West End in search of a suitable ball dress.

This time, she was dressing to kill.

It was a sultry, thunderous evening. Miss Slocombe fussed her unneces-sarily; Geraldine's period was imminent, and the tulle and taffeta dress she had bought at Harrods was too tight round the bust, too low at the neck and, in this light, too livid a green.

To make matters worse, the moment Roddy was shown in by the maid, she detected a change in him. The rapport they had shared the day before had vanished.

'Is anything wrong?' she asked as they walked across Hyde Park Square.

'Nothing at all,' he replied.

'You didn't bring me any flowers.'

'Sorry about that.'

She tapped his wrist. 'You're a very naughty boy!'

He said nothing.

They went up the steps to the front door, but before ringing the bell she said: 'Something is wrong, isn't it? Is it me? Have I said something? Or done something?'

'There is nothing wrong,' he said.

'Pardon me,' she said. 'Sorry I spoke.'

His mood didn't improve when they arrived at the ball. All his previous enthusiasm for her had evaporated. But there was worse to come. Within minutes of their arrival, she became aware that he was not the only one whose attitude had changed, because his naval friends seemed to be regarding her in a different light, as well. She was used to being the centre of attention, and always knew when she was being pointed out. That evening she had the distinct impression that people were deliberately shunning her. Roddy certainly was. He was drinking heavily, and within half an hour of their arrival he was flushed and becoming incoherent.

'Are you trying to get yourself pie-eyed or something?' she asked.

'What I drink is my business,' he retorted.

She tried a different tactic. 'Please,' she whispered. 'Please tell me what I've done. Tell me what's happened, what's gone wrong.'

He looked at her briefly, smiled, shook his head, and looked away. She excused herself and went to the bathroom. Five minutes later, when she came back, he had gone. She was about to panic when he reappeared. They met in the hall. 'I have to leave,' he said. 'My father is dangerously ill. I'm going to drive straight down to Hampshire.'

'Tonight?'

'Yes. He has pneumonia. He may not last.'

'I'll come with you.'

He shook his head. 'I'd rather you didn't. I'll escort you home straight away.'

'I said I'm coming with you.'

'It's not a good idea. It's a long drive. Nearly seventy miles.'

'That's nothing where I come from!'

'All the same—'

'You won't change my mind. If your father's dying, you'll need me with you. I'm coming. That's final.'

'No,' he said. 'I won't have it. I don't need you with me and I would prefer to go on my own.'

She turned on him. 'Why? Why? Because you don't care for me any more? Is that it? It is, isn't it? You've been acting strangely all evening.'

'You'll just have to accept it,' he muttered. 'I'm going down to Hampshire, and I'm going alone.'

'You'll need someone with you, Roddy. I know you will.'

He shook his head. 'I'm perfectly capable. I don't need a nursemaid.'

It was happening all over again. He had the same look in his eye that she had seen in Ben's the day he had told her it was all off. 'You know, don't you?' she said. 'You know about me.' She looked back into the ballroom where the quartet was striking up a military two-step. 'Do you think I'm dumb and blind? Do you think I didn't see the way you've been treating me all evening?'

'Don't be ridiculous!'

'You think you can fob me off with some sort of damned lie?'

'I beg your pardon?'

'I don't believe your father's ill. It's an excuse, isn't it? It's an excuse to get rid of me.'

'It is nothing of the kind. If you're accusing me of lying, you're making a big mistake.'

'Let me come with you then. If you don't want to get rid of me you must want me with you.'

'You're twisting what I said. I said I'd prefer to go on my own.'

'Well I'd prefer to come with you, thank you very much, and if you don't like that just—just try to stop me.'

He went white about the temples and his lips began to quiver. 'I will not have this. I will not tolerate it.'

'Don't talk to me like that. I'm not one of your midshipmen, you know.'

'I shall talk to you any way I like.'

Fairfax-Notley came into the hall. 'I say,' he said. 'Have you heard the news? Pater's just had a telegraph saying that the Archduke Ferdinand has been assassinated.'

Geraldine rounded on him. 'Stay out of this, Ernle. It's none of your business.'

Fairfax-Notley bowed, apologized, and went back into the ballroom.

Roddy turned to Geraldine. 'I have to go. Excuse me.'

She grabbed a passing flunkey. 'Here, you. I want my things. Now.'

'And mine,' Roddy added.

They waited.

'If you think you're coming with me you're mistaken, Geraldine.'

'We'll see about that.'

The footman returned with her things. She threw them on and left immediately. She crossed the road and walked fast round the corner into Hyde Park Square; and when Roddy arrived she was sitting in the passenger seat knotting a chiffon scarf under her chin.

He came round to her side. 'Geraldine, please get out.'

'Uh-uh,' she went. 'If you want me out of this car, honey-pie, you're going to have to drag me. And if you lay a finger on me I'll scream until that cop on the corner comes running. So what do you say? Shall we take a ride?'

A thunderstorm was threatening, so he put up the hood before they set out. They drove to Marble Arch, down Park Lane and turned right at Hyde Park Corner to go through Knightsbridge and head west out of town. For a long time, neither spoke. The brilliant headlights stabbed ahead into darkness as they left Esher, Cobham, and Ripley behind. When they reached Guildford, Roddy slowed and drew up alongside a petrol pump.

'What's the matter?' asked Geraldine. 'Are we out of gas?'

'Not quite.'

'It's after nine. They'll be shut.'

'I know that. I'm not a complete fool.'

He knocked on the door and went on knocking until a head appeared at the window on the first floor. There was a delay before the owner came down and filled up the tank from a hand-pump.

'That'll be seven and nine,' said the man.

Roddy gave him a half-sovereign and told him to keep the change. He got in behind the wheel and switched on the ignition. The man swung the engine; it roared into life, and moments later they were off again, and the speedometer needle was creeping up past forty miles an hour.

'Roddy?'

'What?'

'Can we be friends?'

He said nothing.

She tried again. 'You know, don't you? Someone's said something to you about what happened to me in the United States. Am I right?'

She looked to him for an answer. He gave it with a brief nod of the head.

'What have you heard?'

He delayed before answering; then he sighed and said, 'That you're the kiss-and-tell heiress.'

'Who told you?'

'I'm not saying.'

'Were you told anything else?'

'I don't want to talk about it.'

She laughed without humor. 'Ha! That's great! You don't want to talk about it. It's my reputation. Don't I have a right to know what people are saying behind my back?'

He shook his head. They went up a hill and turned right. The road was perfectly straight ahead, and the land fell away on either side. He put his foot down on the accelerator, and she saw the speedometer needle creep on past fifty. A rabbit ran into the road. There was a soft thump as they went over it. She was gripping her seat with both hands and bracing her feet against the foot rest.

He slowed, and as the speed came back below fifty she relaxed again. Then, extraordinarily, Roddy was his old self. 'That was the Hog's Back,' he remarked. 'I've touched sixty on that stretch before now.'

She reached out and placed her hand on his knee, and was gratified to feel his hand close over it.

They went through Farnham and on towards Alton.

'So, are we friends again?'

He nodded: a single, sharp nod.

'You're a proud man, aren't you, Roddy?'

'Is that a bad thing?'

'Not a bit. I love you when you're all stiff and British.'

He smiled and blinked and puffed his cheeks out; and when he put his hand back on the steering wheel, she moved her hand higher up his thigh.

Going through West Meon, there was a crash of thunder and the heavens opened. Roddy hunched over the wheel, peering through the small fan-shaped space made by the windscreen wiper. The rain was so heavy that they had to shout over the din.

'Nearly there!' Roddy shouted. 'Only a few miles to go!'

They went through Droxford, up a slight hill, over a crest and then down through the last S bend before Meonford village.

Going into the second bend, a fallen branch came into sight on the road ahead, and Roddy swung the car onto the other side of the road to avoid it. As he did so, the headlights picked out a man pushing a bicycle up the hill towards them.

They were going too fast for there to be any possibility of avoiding him. One moment he was there, lit up by the glare of the headlights, the next there was a sickening thump and a dark shadow flew up over the windscreen.

They drew up a hundred yards further on. Geraldine glanced across at Roddy. He was gripping the wheel, staring ahead, shaking visibly.

'We'd better go look at him, I guess.'

He made no move.

'Come on, Roddy. Get a grip.'

He turned to her. His mouth opened and shut but no sound came out.

'We've got to go back to him,' she repeated.

He shook his head.

Then, she lost her temper. 'What's the matter with you? Turn around and drive back, will you? Or do you want me to walk it and get a drenching?'

He drove twenty yards on and did a three-point turn, backing into the entrance of a field before driving slowly back up the hill.

The bicycle was lying in the road but there was no sign of the man. The rain was still pelting down. A torrent of water was going down the hill. The lightning flickered again. 'Oh sweet Jesus!' whispered Geraldine. 'He's over there. For God's sake will you look where I'm pointing? Up on the bank. There.'

He was lying huddled up like a baby under the cut-and-laid hedgerow. Roddy put his head out of the window and shouted, 'Are you all right?'

'You imbecile!' said Geraldine. 'Of course he's not all right!'

He pulled his head back in, then a moment later opened his door, leaned out and vomited.

'For God's sake!' Geraldine whispered. 'What kind of a man are you?'

Thunder cracked and rolled round them. Roddy closed his door. 'I think I know who it is,' he said.

'Where can we get a doctor?'

'There's no point.'

'What do you mean, there's no point? Of course there's a point!'

'He's dead.'

'How do you know?'

'The back of his head…it's…missing.'

He bowed over the steering wheel.

'We've got to figure what to do,' Geraldine said. 'First off—it was an accident, wasn't it? You weren't to blame.'

'I'll be blamed all the same. I'm always blamed. I'll have to resign my commission. Pater will cut me off. I'm finished. Oh, Christ! Oh, Christ, Christ, Christ!'

'Come on Roddy. We can get out of this.'

'How?'

'What's the time?'

He looked at the dashboard. 'Half-past ten.'

'There you are then. We could be back in London by a half after midnight if we start right away. We can go back to the ball.'

'You mean—'

'Did you tell anyone where you were going?'

'No.'

'So there you are. We were never here, were we? We can go back. We can walk right back into that ballroom and no one will be any the wiser.'

'What about the man at the garage?'

'You mean the gas station? That's a million to one chance.'

'What about the tire marks in the mud back there?'

'There won't be any tire marks after this rain.'

'What if I'm asked?'

'You won't be.'

'But what if I am?'

'We went for a spin around town, didn't we? Maybe we had a stroll by the river. Heck—we got carried away, didn't we? But we never came down to Hampshire, right?'

'Jesus Christ!' he whispered. 'Jesus Christ!'

'It's our only chance. The sooner you get us back into that party, the better for both of us. So what do you say? Shall we get going?'

'There's something I have to say to you,' Geraldine said when they were clearing Guildford on their way back to London.

'What?'

'Well, I've been figuring what we're going to say when we get back into that party.'

'Ball. It's a ball.'

'Okay, it's a ball. But what I was thinking was, when we walk in there, it's got to seem like we know what we're talking about, right? I mean, it's got to seem natural. Otherwise people are going to smell one big rat.'

He nodded. 'I was thinking the same.'

'A girl can't walk out of a party at nine in the evening and come back four hours later without people asking questions, right?'

'I suppose not.'

'There's no suppose about it. I've got my reputation to consider.'

'So what are you suggesting?'

'What I'm thinking is, there's got to be something in this for me. Sure, I can lie for you and we can make out we never went south. We can act coy and say we went for a drive around town. But is that story going to hold up?'

'That's what I said back there! But you made me drive off!'

'I made you do nothing of the kind, Roddy. And I wasn't the one who smashed the brains out of that poor boy we left lying by the roadside.'

'You were the one who suggested we cut and run.'

'Try saying that to a judge and see where it gets you.'

'What are you trying to do? Blackmail me?'

'No, I'm trying to make some kind of plan. So we know what we're talking about when we get back into that ballroom. That's all I'm trying to do.'

He drove for a mile or two in silence.

Geraldine tried again. 'The way I see it is, you want an alibi, right? Well, I'm your alibi. But to be your alibi, I'll have to admit I was alone with you for the best part of five hours, right? Now that doesn't do a lady's reputation much good, does it? I had a bit of trouble in the past as you know, and I can't afford to have any more. So what I want to know is this: if I speak up and give you the alibi you need, what'll you do for me in return?'

The tires swished through a large puddle. A fountain of water shot up on either side.

'Have you any suggestions?' he asked.

'Well as a matter of fact, I have. What's more, it'll make your alibi rock solid. And—and it's not such a bad idea when you think about it. My daddy's a wealthy man like yours. We're well matched, wouldn't you say?'

'Go on.'

'Well, when we walk back into that party—'

'How many times do I have to tell you? It's a ball.'

'Ball then. Ball! Ball! Now you've made me lose my thread, damn it!'

'We were walking back in.'

'Right. We have to say *something* don't we? Otherwise it'll be a fine piece of scandal for the press to get their teeth into. As far as I can see, there's only one thing we can say.'

'What's that?'

'For God's sake, you dope! We've got to go in there and tell them we've gotten ourselves engaged to be married! That's the only way I can walk back in there with my reputation intact. So are you going to pop the question or am I?'

He sighed, but said nothing.

'I'm serious, Roddy. We have to do this. I don't see any other way.'

'Do you really want to marry me after this?'

'Of course I want to marry you! I've wanted to marry you from the moment I set eyes on you!'

He was silent again. When she looked at him she saw tears going down his cheeks.

'Stop the car. Come on, Honey. Pull in. You can't drive like this.'

He stopped, put on the handbrake and burst into tears. She held him in her arms. He told her about his memories of his father and his elder brother. He told her about hearing his father shouting at his mother, how his father had taken him sailing, and when they got home how he ran up to see his mother and found her dead in bed. And he told her how the whole of his life had been one endless and futile attempt to please his father and live up to his expectations.

Geraldine soothed him, patting his back, and kissing him. He wept and hiccupped and said that everything he touched turned to rats.

'You touched me,' she said. 'I'm not going to turn into a rat.' She kissed his forehead, undid a couple of buttons, and put his hand to her breast. 'We'll be good together, you and me. We'll have ourselves some fun, just see if we don't. We'll get married straight off—as soon as we can, agree? We can live in my daddy's house in town and you can play with ships, and we'll give parties—balls—and you'll end up an admiral of the fleet, right? You'll be a baron and we'll have lots of little baronets. Okay?'

'Okay.'

'So we're engaged, right?'

'Right.'

She reached for her evening purse and took the ring Ben had given back to her a few months before. 'Here you are. You can put it on my finger right away.'

He did so, started to speak, and then stopped himself.

'Now what is it?'

'Well, you won't ever breathe a word, will you, Geraldine? About what happened this evening?'

She looked at him sideways. 'And you won't ever leave me or two-time me, right? You'll be a good husband? No messing with other women? If you start messing around, or treat me badly or leave me—'

'What?'

'If you ever leave me, I'll tell the world what happened this evening.'

'If you ever tell,' Roddy said quietly, 'I'll leave you.'

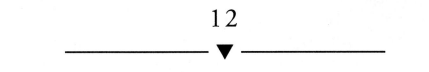
Frank was carried on a stretcher up the hill to the British Hospital in Nanking, and within hours of his arrival was reduced to a wasted invalid whose only hope was that he should die, and die quickly.

He floated in and out of consciousness. From time to time he was aware of the attentions of a dark-haired nurse in a high, starched collar. She held a cup to his lips. 'Drink!' she ordered. 'For God's sake drink, will you?'

He heard his own voice asking if he was dying.

'Not if you drink, you aren't,' said the nurse. 'Now come on. Take it down.'

He drank, vomited, purged, and drank again.

'I want to die,' he whispered.

'Oh no you don't!' said the nurse. 'We won't allow that.'

He heard himself babbling, asking questions. The room whirled and swayed. He seemed to be flying up out of himself. It was a quite a pleasant feeling because it was a total surrender. Nothing mattered. The whole of life—it was nothing in comparison to this. Life passed, but death had no end. Death was infinitely bigger than life. It was an all-encompassing otherness and it was beckoning him to itself.

He was being drawn towards a door out of a room, on the other side of which was something huge and incomprehensible. But it was not at all frightening. The life that he was leaving behind, was it so very important? What did it matter if he slipped out of the room? No one would notice. And there was no pain any more: that was the good thing. No pain, no tears, no worry, no anxiety. The door was open and it seemed to be coming towards him of its own accord. Not long now, and he would be through it.

Yes. Yes, that would be good.

He became aware that someone was in the room with him. He opened his eyes. Miss Pinkham was standing at the foot of his bed looking at him very intensely. Immediately, he sank into a deep sleep.

When he woke up and saw the blades of the fan going round overhead he knew that he was not dead. Was he pleased about that? No, not pleased: quietly content.

He watched the blades of the fan going round and round, and his thoughts meandered round with them. It was odd to think that he might have died. But he hadn't, and he wasn't going to, either. From now on, all of life was a bonus. There was no need to fear death, or life, for that matter. His time was limited. It was ticking away even now. He must make the most of every second of it.

Nurse McGowan, the one with dark hair, came in. She was large and forthright, with her sleek hair put up in a bun. She looked at him and he looked back at her and they smiled at the same moment. She put a thermometer under his tongue and held his wrist to take his pulse.

'That's a bit more like it,' she said, when she took it out. She flicked the thermometer and put it back in her top pocket. 'You're a lucky boy,' she said. 'We nearly lost you.'

The senior medical officer examined him the next day, and gave orders that he must make a complete recovery before being allowed to rejoin his ship.

When he was fit enough to get out of bed, he discovered an upright piano on the verandah, and asked Nurse McGowan if he might play it. She gave him an odd look and said, 'Well, I suppose you can try.'

He sat down in his hospital night shirt and played an arpeggio. It was hopelessly out of tune. Nurse McGowan watched him from the door. 'It hasn't been played in over a year. The last person who played it was a young midshipman, but he wasn't as fortunate as you.'

'Why was that?'

'He died of blood poisoning. Timothy Whettingsteel was his name. A nice boy. He's in the British cemetery.'

He opened the top lid of the piano. A tuning lever and a tuning fork were inside. He asked if he might try to tune it.

McGowan shrugged. 'Certainly you may. I don't suppose you can make it any worse than it is.'

He took the front off the piano and surveyed the strings. Before his illness he would never have considered attempting to tune a piano. But now, having been close to death, anything was worth a try. He struck the tuning fork smartly on the floor and held it to the piano frame so the note, 'A' natural, reverberated. Then he located the 'A' string and inserted the tuning lever.

It was a much bigger task than he had expected, because most of the notes had three strings, and they had to be tuned in perfect unison. But once started he became totally absorbed, and he made up his mind to tune it as perfectly as he was able.

He spent several hours each day at it. As the work progressed he began to feel that he was tuning more than a piano. It was as if he were tuning himself as well. Before coming to Nanking, he had been out of tune: railing against every injustice, still at war with himself over whether he should be a Catholic or a Protestant, angry with his mother, resentful at the Yarrows, vindictive towards Roddy.

His response to each one of these jarring situations had to be adjusted and modified, tuned up or down so that while the situations remained the same, his reaction to them changed.

He spent a week working on the piano, and continued making fine adjustments until he could play arpeggios up and down the keyboard in every key without a single jarring note.

When he had finished, he sat down and played Chopin's Prelude No.7 in A Major, and the playing of it awoke in him a sense of optimism that three years of naval service had all but destroyed.

As the last chord died away, he sat with his head bowed over the piano. He was still weak, and the music had moved him. He felt a touch on his shoulder. He turned. Staff Nurse McGowan was standing at his side, staring down at him.

'Come here,' she said quietly. 'I think you could do with some loving kindness, couldn't you, my dear?' She drew him to her and held him. 'Just let go,' she whispered. 'Just let go.'

When he had been convalescing at the British Hospital for nearly a month he received orders to proceed by rail to Shanghai, where he joined HMS *Campion*, a destroyer that was on her way home to England to pay off.

He had hoped that he would be due some back pay, but on the first pay day received nothing. When he went down to the ship's office to enquire about it, the paymaster clerk gave him short shrift. 'You had fourteen days pay stopped in *Dominant* and there are thirty-one days hospital stoppages on top of that,' he said.

'Hospital stoppages, sir?

'You don't get paid while you're in hospital, Jannaway. What do you think this is, a holiday home?'

Frank realized that if he was to stay sane he had to stop raging inwardly at the injustices of the Navy and start working actively to improve the pay and conditions of men on the lower deck. So on passage back to England he made contact with one or two like-minded men in the ship's company and started work on an article about lower deck life for submission to the editor of a magazine called *The Fleet*, which was widely read on the lower deck.

He taught himself to touch-type on the ship's office typewriter, and posted the completed article when the ship arrived at Malta. But he never received a reply because on the day the ship arrived at Gibraltar war was declared on Germany, and his literary and political aspirations were abruptly curtailed.

PART II

▼

1914–1922

13

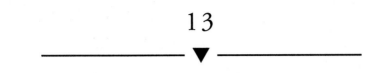

The green seas came over everywhere. The destroyer lurched and tumbled, pitched and rolled and wallowed. You turned in wet and you turned out wet, day after day, for however long the patrol lasted. Most were seldom seasick; a few unfortunates threw up in a flat calm. But when a gale was blowing and the ship was doing twenty knots into sea, the lurching and shuddering, together with the combined smell of vomit, food and gash between decks left only a stalwart few unaffected.

There were smells and tastes, sights and sounds that you could never forget: the hot, horrid smell of tobacco smoke coming up through a voice pipe; the sight, looking aft, of the stern wallowing as the seas smashed over her, the skyline swinging violently, the funnels crazy against the sky, the wake making a zigzag as the man on the wheel struggled to keep her on course; the crash of pots and pans and the shouted curses between decks as the ship rolled past thirty degrees; the taste of salt pork that had been soaked for twenty-four hours to get some—but never all—of the brine out of it; the queer taste of duff made with moldy flour; the smell of tarred cordage down in the tiller flat, and the way the screw thundered as the stern topped a wave; the stores petty officer chipping the dark red wax off the cork of a new rum cask. The queasy smell of rum that made you catch your breath.

HMS *Campion* did the blood run to Flanders for several months, escorting convoys carrying fresh meat and provisions from east coast ports to Ostend for the troops in the trenches. The ship was seldom in port for more than twelve hours, and the ship's company were in two watches. As one of the sea boat's crew and lowerers of the port watch, Frank spent many long hours huddled up for warmth against the funnel. They wore black oilskins and sea boots, and towels round their necks to keep out the spray. Every hour, they brewed up 'ki' (hot chocolate) in the galley, and at the beginning of the watch one of the ordinary seamen was sent down to the boiler room to bake potatoes in the asbestos cladding round the steam pipes.

Now it was two in the morning and the ship, fully darkened, was plunging into a northwesterly gale. It was just one more middle watch. Another night of counting the minutes until you could get back into your hammock and catch an hour's sleep before Charlie. Frank was struggling to keep his eyes open, watching the foam-flecked waves march by in unending procession.

A jarring shock. A mighty explosion. A dark orange flash.

When he recovered consciousness, the emergency steam valves were making a deafening din, and the first lieutenant was giving orders to lower the sea boat. Frank had been detailed as bow man of the sea boat, but the moment he got to his feet he collapsed, so he crawled under the torpedo tubes to keep out of the way.

The alarm bells were ringing for emergency stations. The ship was already down by the head. The first lieutenant was bellowing orders through a megaphone, and the stokers were coming up through the hatch from the boiler room like rabbits coming out of a hole. Life rafts splashed down into the sea. 'Lower to deck level!' bellowed the first lieutenant, and the sea boat juddered down from the davits and rapidly filled up with stokers.

He watched the performance like a spectator at a horror show. 'Lower away!' ordered the first lieutenant—but he made no allowance for the fact that the ship was down by the head, and a wave swamped the boat and overturned it, tipping all the men in it into the sea.

Shadowy figures emerged from the superstructure and jumped into the sea. Frank made no attempt to follow them. It wasn't that he had decided to die, more a case of not making any undue effort to survive.

The ship's bow tipped further down, and he found himself alone; and it was at that moment, as he prepared to go down with the ship, that the captain, who was known on board as Gentleman Jim, came along the iron deck and found him huddled up under the torpedo tubes in his personal pool of blood.

'Are you hurt old man?' he asked. 'Give me your arm. That's the way. Easy does it. Here we go. Ready? Jump!'

Arm in arm with Gentleman Jim, he went down into the North Sea. The captain towed him to a life raft float, and when he had been pulled aboard, swam off into the darkness to help someone else. But moments later the ship upended and went down in a cauldron of bubbles and steam, her screw still turning, and lengths of timber shooting vertically out of the water. Gentleman Jim was never seen again.

As dawn broke, they were picked up by a herring drifter, which took them to Lowestoft.

Wilma was a probationary nurse at the cottage hospital. She changed his dressings and brought his Bovril and lit his cigarettes and rubbed his bottom and tucked him up at night; and the day before he was due to go to Chatham to join his new ship, when his ribs had mended and he could get his jumper on over his head without too much pain, they went for a walk together. They stood under a tree and kissed. She was a slow, soft spoken, Norfolk lass, and he loved her. On the way back to the hospital he asked her to marry him when the war was over. He told her that they could save up and rent a little seaside cottage with roses round the door and hydrangeas by the wicket. They would be Mr. and Mrs. Jannaway, Frank and Wilma. He would mend watches, tune pianos, teach at the village school, fish from the beach, grow potatoes, keep a pig, and work for the Labor Movement. They would have five rosy-cheeked mites with flaxen hair and dark blue eyes like their mother. And they would be happy. Yes, he was sure of that. There would be no more war, no more middle watches, no more destroyers or submarines or mines or torpedoes or zeppelins or trenches or whiz-bangs or mustard gas. The sun would come out over England. People would live in peace and prosperity. The Labor Party would be voted in and there would be fair shares for all.

He warmed to his theme. The first Labor government would do what should have been done a hundred years before. It would introduce socialism to England. They would have a Workers' Charter. They would nationalize the major industries—water, gas, coal, steel, electricity, public transport—and provide free medical care and education for all.

'That's the meaning of socialism,' he explained, aware that he was pontificating, but unable to stop himself. 'It's the only way we'll ever be able to create a fair society. Any other is doomed to fail. If you want a happy society you must have a fair society, and if you want a fair one, it has to be a socialist one, because capitalism is just another word for inequality. There's no alternative. It's as simple as that.'

She looked at him as if he was barmy.

'So what do you say?' he asked. 'Why don't we get married? Not such a bad idea, is it?'

Wilma dissolved into silent tears.

'What's matter?' he asked.

She shook her head, unable to tell him that, because she had already accepted two proposals of marriage and both her fiancés had been killed, she was terrified of acquiring a reputation for bringing bad luck. So her answer was no; and after she had given it they walked back in silence.

Before they parted, he held her hands for a few moments. 'I think I understand,' he said.

She nodded, unable to speak.

'Shall I write to you?'

'Better not,' she replied, the tears standing in her eyes. 'No, Frank, better not.'

His next ship was HMS *Essex*, a light cruiser. After a few months of North Sea patrols, they put into Rosyth for essential maintenance, and five days' leave was given to each watch. He had not been home since joining the Navy, and although he knew he wasn't supposed to go back to Meonford without prior permission, he couldn't believe that Sir Jervis would object now that there was a war on, so he decided to use his travel warrant to go and see his mother.

It took him eighteen hours to get to London, and another three down to Wickham. He arrived at seven in the morning and set out on foot to walk from the station; but on the way he was given a lift in the trap that was delivering the London newspapers to the outlying villages.

Mrs. Ashton, the Meonford postmistress, came out of the village shop to collect the bundle and pin up the latest casualty lists on the village notice board. She stared at him. 'It's Hetty Jannaway's boy, isn't it? Look at you, you're a grown man!'

He followed her into the shop and bought a quarter of a pound of tea as a present for his mother. While he was doing so, Tom Roughsedge arrived, had a look at the casualty list, and walked off without uttering a word.

Mrs. Ashton took down the big square tin of Lipton's from the shelf and glanced back. 'Poor old Tom,' she said. 'He lost George last autumn and Sidney in the spring. So now he's left with Walter, and he's at the front too, by all accounts.'

'What about Alan?' Frank asked. 'Hasn't he joined up?'

She weighed the tea and poured it from the tray into a brown paper bag. 'Didn't you hear about Alan?'

'No?'

'He's in his grave, my dear. He was knocked off his bicycle by a motor car on his way to fetch the doctor to Sir Jervis when he had the pneumonia.' She folded the paper bag into a V and tucked the flap back in on itself. 'That was a bad business. Never stopped, whoever it was. Who would do a thing like that, I ask you? Knock a young lad down and leave him to die?'

'Did they find out who did it?'

'No they did not. Though there was one name that was on a lot of people's lips round these parts. But they never proved anything so we can only trust that whoever it was will get his just deserts one day, whether in this world or the next.'

He paid for the tea and went across the village green and into St. Bartholomew's church yard, where he found a new tomb stone with Alan's name on it. He stared at the name. It was all very well to lose messmates when your ship went down, because that was war and you became hardened to it. But this was different. This awoke in him all the old anger he thought he had managed to put away.

He crossed the river and went up through the orchard and the walled garden to the back of Meonford Hall. Mrs. Spooner was frying Sir Jervis's breakfast; and the kitchen maid, who he didn't recognize, was laying a tray. Then his mother bustled in, saw him, and immediately wanted to know what he was doing arriving back at the house without prior permission. He hadn't seen her in four years, and yet the first thing she did was to give him a ticking off.

They were awkward together. She seemed more concerned that Sir Jervis or Lady Yarrow might find out that he was there than pleased to see him. She made no pretence of the fact that she found his unexpected arrival an embarrassment. He could hardly believe that she was the same person.

They went out into the stable yard to talk. She looked him up and down and began firing questions at him. 'Are you still going to Mass, Frank? What about the rosary I gave you? Have you still got it?'

He said he had lost it. She gave him a long, hard look, and asked him when he last went to Confession. He said he couldn't remember.

'So you're in mortal sin. Do you realize that? If you're not taking the sacraments and you're not going to Mass, you're in mortal sin. If you get yourself killed, you'll go to hell.'

He said he didn't believe in any of that.

'What do you mean? Of course you believe it. You're a Catholic. You have to believe it.'

'I've changed,' he said. 'I've given up religion. I'm an atheist.'

She told him not to talk nonsense. He said it was a fact and she would have to like it or lump it.

'Why, Frank? Why?'

He shrugged. 'Does it matter?'

She said she felt as if her whole life had been a waste of time. What had she done wrong? Hadn't she brought him up in the Catholic Faith? Hadn't she worked and worked to provide for him?

'Atheist?' she repeated. 'Atheist? How could you, Frank? How could you?' She burst into tears, but quickly regained her composure. 'Can't you see that you've made a terrible mistake? Why not come to Confession with me tomorrow and put it all right? I could never forgive myself if you were to die in mortal sin. Please. For me, Frank. Do it for me. Come and put it right with Father.'

'It's no good,' he said. 'I don't believe in any of that.'

'What do you believe in?'

'That's my business, isn't it?'

'No it is not, Frank. It's mine as well. You're not yet twenty-one.'

'You won't change my mind,' he said.

At that, the light of her motherly love was suddenly extinguished. 'I'm not at all sure that you can stay here,' she said. 'Your room's been taken by the new driver. Besides, what am I to say to Lady Yarrow? You gave your word you'd not come back without permission.'

'In that case I'd better say goodbye.'

'What do you mean? You're not going are you? You've only just arrived!'

'I can't stay, can I? You said so yourself.'

'I said no such thing, Frank!'

'I'm not supposed to be here, am I?'

She sniffed and looked up at him. 'Perhaps if you could take rooms somewhere. Just for the time being. Until I can sort it out with her ladyship.'

'I've only got four more days, and one of those will be taken up traveling back.'

Inside the kitchen, a bell rang. 'There now,' she said. 'That'll be her ladyship ringing for me.'

'Look,' he said, 'Maybe I'll come back later.' He moved to kiss her, but she avoided him.

'Yes,' she said. 'Maybe that's for the best.'

She went back into the kitchen, and he remained in the stable yard, wondering what to do. It seemed that whatever he did would be wrong. He had been wrong to come home in the first place, and now he would be wrong to leave. There seemed no point in trying to please her. He was still shocked by the news of Alan's death, and his arrival back at Meonford Hall had brought back a flood of unwelcome memories.

There didn't seem much point in anything. He had never known his father, and now he was estranged from his mother. He didn't have a place that he could call home—indeed, he didn't really know what he was doing walking this earth. It would have been a lot more convenient if he had gone down with his ship.

Fuck it, he thought. Fuck it. Fuck it. Fuck it.

He picked up his kitbag, slung it on his shoulder, and walked back to Wickham. He took the train to Portsmouth, got drunk that evening, and spent the night on a bench on Southsea Common. The following night he went to Aggie Weston's rest home for sailors, and the day after that he took the train north and returned to his ship.

HMS *Essex* was up in the Orkneys with the battle fleet for most of the following winter and spring. The war dragged on and on. There was ample time to talk, and most of the men on the seamen's mess deck agreed that keeping so many ships swinging round anchors the whole time was a funny way to fight a war.

They reflected that if the Navy was as wonderful as the recruiting posters always said it was, they should have been able to up-anchor, steam into German waters and blow Fritz out of the water by now, which was surely what Drake or Nelson would have done. But Admiral Fisher hadn't taken mines and torpedoes into account when he built his Dreadnoughts, and was terrified that he would lose the war in an afternoon. So there they were, bottled up at Scapa Flow for month after month, while the German fleet was bottled up in the Baltic for exactly the same reason.

The officers had a grand time at Scapa. The junior officers had mess dinners and inter-ship sports events, and the signalmen were for ever passing the letters 'RPC' by semaphore or light, which stood for Request the Pleasure of your Company. The captains and commanders gave dinner parties for each other and took their retrievers ashore to shoot grouse on the moors, sometimes coming back later than they said they would and keeping the boats' crews waiting in the drizzle.

Commander de Salis, the second in command of HMS *Essex*, was worried that the men might become bored and cease to be on a split yarn for action, so he organized events to keep the lads amused. He had a fund of bright ideas, nearly all of which turned out to be paper-chases or treasure hunts. All the midshipmen and fifty seamen would be landed and sent off along bleak little Orkney lanes, pounding along in the rain to find the answers to clues. Usually the treasure hunts ended with the promise of ten shillings hidden in the bosom of the fairest maiden in the village, and the place would be terrorized by whooping sailors chasing the local girls round the crofts.

There were no boom defenses at Scapa, so apart from the cruiser and destroyer patrols, there was nothing to stop a German submarine coming straight in and blowing a few battle cruisers to the bottom. One quiet afternoon the alarm went up that a periscope had been sighted in the anchorage, and all hell was let loose. The duty destroyer started dropping depth charges, and thick black smoke rose from the funnels of the battle cruisers as they got up steam and prepared to weigh anchor. Frank was sent away as bow man of the picket boat on anti-submarine patrol, and spent three hours searching without seeing a thing.

Apart from these and a few similar incidents, life at Scapa was monotonous and frustrating. There was a limit to the entertainment you could achieve from jousting with deck mops, or the quizzes organized by the surgeon, or the commander's treasure hunts, or the first lieutenant's kite flying competitions; so when, on the afternoon of Frank's twenty-first birthday, the sparkers spread the buzz that the battle fleet was to put to sea, it was as if the whole ship had been electrified.

The cruisers sailed first and steamed at full speed, heading south-east. The ship went to action stations. Every gun was loaded with shell. Large quantities of ready-use ammunition were brought up from the magazines and stacked round the ammunition hoists. All the torpedoes were prepared for firing. The torpedo crews checked and double checked the compressed air pressures. They inserted the primers and detonators. They hoisted each torpedo in turn, and inserted it carefully into its tube.

How the admirals knew that the Germans were coming out of the Baltic at that particular place and time was a mystery, but the sudden sight of those dark grey ships appearing through the drizzle caused a drop in the pit of the stomach, a feeling of being winded.

There was little time for fear. The six-inch turrets swung round. The gun barrels elevated. Hooters sounded and bells rang as the layers and trainers indicated that they were on target—and then the whole ship jolted as the first broadside fired. Almost immediately, shells were falling around them, sending up great fountains of water.

For a while, it seemed that the light cruiser squadron was taking on the full might of the German fleet. The cruisers fought for three hours before the main battle fleet arrived, and when they did the Germans immediately altered course to the south. Both fleets chased about, wheeling and trying to cut each other off in poor visibility. One moment you could see nothing except the splashes from shells that rained down all around; the next, Admiral Jellicoe's battle fleet was in clear view, steaming at full speed in line ahead, twelve-inch guns roaring, thick black funnel smoke spreading out in a great cloud overhead, and the arriving German shells sending up fountains of white water.

Frank stared in wonder at this spectacle of Armageddon. As he watched, one of the German shells scored a hit on the battleship *Queen Mary*. One moment she was steaming at full speed in the battle line, and the next there was a monumental explosion. She went down in minutes, and a thousand sons, brothers and fathers went with her.

In the early hours of the morning, the ship blundered into two German cruisers. They trained searchlights on HMS *Essex* and opened fire at close range. *Essex* turned away, and the order came down from the bridge to fire torpedoes. They were charging along at thirty knots, the spray hurtling in sheets up over the bridge, and whipping back over the torpedo deck. Frank was manning the torpedo rangefinder and singing out ranges of the enemy for the torpedo gunner; but seconds before they were to fire they took a shell inboard and the gunner went down, so he closed the circuits to fire the torpedoes without further orders.

Dawn came up. The battle was over. The German fleet was on its way back to Kiel. The ship was full of the acrid stink of burnt Lyddite. No one had had any sleep for thirty-six hours and you knew that you looked as red-eyed and grey-faced as everyone else. There was no sense at all of victory. Rather, there was a feeling of disillusionment and guilt. Two of the petty officers had been killed during the action, and as he had been recently advanced to Leading Seaman, Frank was made coxswain of a steam cutter for the first time in his life and sent away to pick up survivors and corpses.

There were more corpses than survivors. They pulled them in over the side of the cutter, their bodies blackened and bloody, their faces smashed in, some naked, some legless, some headless, a few still alive, staring up with pitifully grateful eyes as they were helped inboard and comforted.

The burial at sea started at noon. All hands off watch were mustered on the quarterdeck. The ship had no chaplain on board, so Commander de Salis conducted the service. 'Man that is born of a woman' was how it started, and while he continued, canvas body bags splashed one by one into the sea.

HMS *Essex* buried one hundred and thirty-two German and British sailors that morning.

The next day, they put in to Newcastle-on-Tyne to land the wounded and repair the battle damage. Within minutes of the first brow going across, dockyard workers in brown overalls were swarming on board, and riveters were starting up their pneumatic hammers to patch the shell-hole in the ship's side. The seamen were set to work scrubbing off the stains of burnt Lyddite, and the stokers started the work of unraveling the fractured pipes and twisted metal in number three boiler room.

There were other ships in harbor, and that night the pubs were full. The Chiefs and Petty Officers drank in the saloon bars; the junior rates went to the public. They stood on the sawdust-littered floor, jam-packed together, smoking and drinking and talking. It was more of a wake than a celebration. Everyone had messmates who were dead or injured or shell-shocked, and the price they had paid seemed too high for the result that they had achieved.

Since the first days of the war, the expectation of taking part in a major battle had buoyed up spirits. Everyone had been confident that when the German fleet came out, there would be another Trafalgar, and a glorious victory that would bring the war to an end. But it had not turned out that way. Something had gone wrong. Too many ships had been sunk, and too many men had seen the *Queen Mary* blow up and the *Invincible*'s bow and stern sticking up out of the water.

There was a buzz going round that Admiral Beatty had muttered, 'Something wrong with our bloody ships' during the battle. Well, he wasn't the only one who felt that way. Everyone on the lower deck knew damn well that quite a lot was wrong. There wasn't enough armor plating to stop twelve-inch shells penetrating, and there weren't enough bulkheads on the passageways to stop fire spreading. Between decks, there were no escape scuttles big enough for a man to climb through, so that hundreds of good men had gone needlessly down with their ships.

Before the battle, the old peacetime grievances about pay and punishments and conditions of service had been put aside. Afterwards the people on the lower deck felt less inclined to give their service and loyalty so unreservedly.

A man could be pushed only so far. Thirty pounds a year for an able seaman wasn't enough. It was a change of attitude that went unnoticed among the officers in the wardroom, but on the mess decks of HMS *Essex* it was impossible to ignore it.

14

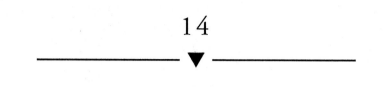

Anita served as a volunteer auxiliary nurse in the last three months of the Great War, and after the armistice went to Turkey, where she worked as an assistant secretary to the Military Attaché in Constantinople. Now she was back in England. The bluebells were out in the Meon Valley, and the people of Meonford village were trying to pick up the pieces of their lives and return to some semblance of normality.

Her parents had been deeply affected by the war. Her mother was in mourning for members of her family who had been murdered by the Bolsheviks, and her father seemed to have lost his former self-confidence, clinging to the life he had known before the lamps went out in 1914.

It was no use telling them that the world could never be the same again, nor was Anita able to explain to them how radically her own attitudes had changed. They had no concept of the horrors she had witnessed, and she could hardly inform them that she had lost her virginity to a Royal Flying Corps observer barely out of his teens in the upstairs bedroom of a French *estaminet*.

On the overland journey home from Constantinople, she had thought hard about what she wanted to do with her life, and her ambitions were so completely different from her mother's hopes for her that she felt it kinder not to mention them. The thing to do, she decided, was to honor her parents' wishes while losing nothing of her independence of thought.

While she had no intention of finding a husband, she would at least go through the motions of looking for one. She would do the Season, have a bit of fun, dance the summer nights away, and then, with her independence still intact, apply for a place at the new Academy of Dramatic Art in Gower Street.

But of course it didn't turn out that way—how could it? Yes, she was presented at Court; yes she danced with plenty of young men just back from the war, and yes, she went to dinner parties, supper parties, garden parties, boathouse parties and picnic parties up and down the Home Counties from Bexley Heath to Bampton, from West Meon to Wickhambreux and from Islip to St. Ippolyts.

She mixed with the Ogilvie-Grants, the Bells, the Actons and the Nicolsons; and as party followed party and ball followed ball, she found herself being sucked, willy-nilly, into a social whirlpool of Bright Young Things. She had never intended to let herself go to quite such a degree, but everyone was doing it, and one quickly fell into the habit of playing the part. She had her hair bobbed, flattened her chest, wore trousers and taught herself to blow cigarette smoke through her nose. She swam across the Thames at Henley at three o'clock in the morning for a bet, and did an Immelmann turn in a bi-plane with Cecil Lewis at the controls.

It was at a house party in Bampton that she met Basil Walmshurst. He was nearly forty, unattached, had pots of money and owned a literary and theatrical agency in Great Russell Street.

On first acquaintance, Basil struck Anita as a perfectly frightful man. He had long fingernails and dirty habits, and seemed incapable of eating a meal without throwing half of it down his shirt front. He wore pebble glasses, had blubbery lips that made the end of his cigars go soggy, took snuff, dropped names, called young men 'darling' and wore obscenely fat neckties, loathsome pointed shoes, and a wildly ostentatious fedora.

But for all that, Basil Walmshurst held a horrible fascination. He was so lewd, so devoid of tact and so amoral that she found herself drawn to him; and, once he had taken a liking to her, he proved to be a determined and entertaining suitor.

He introduced her to a surreal world that was peopled by several imaginary military men. General Good-Times was a great chum and Private Means was a useful chap to have around. Major Catastrophe had to be avoided at all costs, and if one ever came into contact with Private Parts it was important to keep an eye out for General Consternation, who was liable to send for Major Embarrassment and his nasty little side-kick, Corporal Punishment.

In the cold light of early morning such wit seemed puerile, but when you were full of Veuve Clicquot, and half naked in a dress which showed your all (or ninety-nine percent of it) when you sank into a sofa without crossing your legs, it could be hysterically funny.

Perhaps she was more impressionable than she had thought, or perhaps she was just rebelling. Whatever the cause, within the space of three weeks she felt herself becoming dangerously but excitingly entangled with him.

Roddy was still serving abroad in the Mediterranean, so Anita spent the London season with Geraldine in Mayfair. Basil sent her roses and chocolates every morning and took her out to lunch every day. No door was closed to him. When you went into a room full of strangers with him the crowd would open and there would be shouts of 'Baz, old boy!'

She shut her eyes to his awful behavior. He called her Poppy and he made her laugh. He was ugly, cynical, and totally outrageous. Obscenity and blasphemy tripped off his tongue with an easy nonchalance that had you doubled up with laughter, although you knew you should pretend you hadn't heard what he had just said.

Wherever he could find a tide of opinion, Basil Walmshurst swam against it. He could be a bright pink Socialist one moment and a raving blue Tory the next—and argue both sides against each other so cogently that you were left totally confused.

They went to Deauville. He lost over five hundred pounds at the casino, hired a Lagonda, and roared her up to Paris for the weekend, where he bought her a Degas at the *Salon des Refusés*. They took a hamper of *paté de foie gras*, freshly baked *baguette*, and a bottle of chilled Chablis, and picnicked in the grounds of the Trianon Palace.

Anita sat on the bank of the lake and cooled her bare toes in the water. Basil went down on one knee, swept his hat off his head, and flung his arms wide.

'Poppy!'

'What?'

'Marry me!'

She was watching the giant carp that were milling round the bread crumbs in the water. 'What a ridiculous suggestion,' she said. 'I wouldn't dream of it.'

'Why not?'

'Well, I was hoping to go to ADA and learn how to be an actress, if you remember.'

He put his hat back on and sat down beside her again. 'My dear, sweet, innocent, infuriating, adorable child, will you kindly do me a great favor and *bugger* ADA? How many times do I have to tell you that you have a natural talent? Marry me, and I'll have you treading the boards in the West End within the year. Isn't that what you want?'

A carp was tentatively nibbling at her toes. She was pleasantly squiffy and having difficulty thinking straight. Did she know what she wanted? And wouldn't it be something to go straight to stardom in the West End?'

'Well?' he asked.

She sighed. 'Oh, I don't know, Baz. There's such a sense of futility now, isn't there? I mean, there's nothing to *do* now the war's finished. Nothing to achieve. England isn't a land fit for heroes. It never was and it never will be. Nothing matters any more, does it?'

Basil took out a fresh cigar and ran it under his nose. 'It never did in the first place.'

The carp that was nibbling her toes had protruding lips like Basil's. She shrugged. 'Okay.'

'And what does that abominable colonial expression mean?'

'It means…oh, it means bugger ADA, I suppose. It means I accept.'

Basil put on the best possible act for her parents on his first visit to Meonford Hall. He listened with rapt attention to her father's longest and most boring story about winning a pulling regatta in Wei Hai Wei, talked about Turgenev to her mother, complimented Cook, flirted with the maids and on one memorable occasion managed to coax a smile out of Mrs. Jannaway.

'I wasn't at all sure about him at first,' Anita's mother confided on the third day of his visit, 'but now I really am beginning to like him.'

Her father was delighted that she had found a man of substance and maturity to take her off his hands. Everyone was thrilled—everyone, that is, except herself, because she knew in her heart that this was all wrong, that she had agreed to marry on an impulse, that she didn't love Basil, could never love him and indeed found him physically repulsive.

The wedding was set for early September. She and her mother spent a week in London ordering the dress and the trousseau. Basil had to catch up on work in town and she saw much less of him. By now she was fully aware that she was making an awful mistake; but her father was so pleased that she was marrying money, her mother was so excited at the thought that she might become a grandmother, and such vast quantities of money had already been spent on the wedding, that she delayed saying anything to anyone until it was too late.

As the day approached, she fell into a depression that she had difficulty disguising. Her mother reassured her. 'We all go through it, Anuchka,' she said. 'There's never been a bride who hasn't had qualms before the day.'

The wedding was perfect. The marquee stayed up. The sun shone. Everything went according to plan. But although Major Catastrophe stayed away, General Good-Times was not among the guests either, and as Basil's new Bentley scrunched away down the drive, a voice inside her head asked repeatedly, 'What have you done, what *have* you done?'

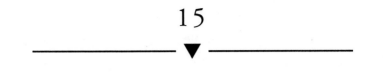

15

Roddy arrived at his front door in Hyde Park Square on a damp November evening, a year almost to the day after the armistice had been signed. His ship, the light cruiser HMS *Andromache*, had paid off in Devonport only three days before, and he was now on leave pending his next appointment. He had been at sea on war service in the Mediterranean and the Black Sea almost continually for five years, and had nothing but a row of campaign medals to show for it.

It takes a strong character to resist the assault that naval life makes on a man's individuality, and Roddy had not been able to resist it. What gentleness, what enquiring doubt, what love, or peace of mind or humility he had once possessed, was gone. His years of naval routine, naval standing orders, naval customs, naval values, naval aims, and naval arrogance had, by degrees, superimposed a new personality on him.

And now the job was done. He had become a naval officer through and through. He was in the Royal Navy, and the Royal Navy was in him. His world was the Royal Navy: nothing outside it had any value or reality for him: he saw everything in terms of his naval experience.

He paid off the cabbie, went up the short flight of steps to the newly-painted black front door, and rang the bell. The door was opened to him by a maid, who took his overcoat and bowler hat and asked what name to announce.

Without a word, Roddy pushed past her and walked into the drawing room, where he found an informal party in progress. A drinks trolley was loaded with bottles, glasses, ice bucket, and a cocktail shaker. On an occasional table, a gramophone was grinding out one of the new dances, to which a couple of flappers were jerking and twitching their heels amid shrieks of laughter.

While he reviewed this scene, a girl smoking a cigarette in an ivory holder came and took his arm. 'You look lost, darling. What's the matter?'

'I'm looking for my wife,' he said. 'Actually.'

The girl's eyes opened wide. She let go of his arm, went to the door and called, 'Gerry, darling! There's someone important here to see you!'

There was a short delay; and then Geraldine, who had put on a stone in weight since he last saw her, appeared in a crochet dress with several long strings of pearls, whose milky parabolas swooped to her navel. She looked momentarily stunned when she saw Roddy, but made a quick recovery, feigning initial coyness before opening her arms wide. 'Piggy Poo!' she gushed. 'Come and give Gerry a big kiss!' She drew him to her, fluttered her eye-lids, and kissed the air in his general direction.

'Too, too moving,' murmured a young man on the *chaise longue*, and one of the flappers added in a stage whisper, 'Isn't he simply divine?'

Geraldine kept open house. People dropped in at any time of day or night, wound up the gramophone, and helped themselves to cocktails.

'A chap can't even read his own newspaper at breakfast,' Roddy complained one morning. 'There was a lounge lizard with his nose in my *Morning Post* when I came down this morning. And he'd polished off the kedgeree, what's more. It's damn bad form if you ask me. Actually.'

'Piggy Poo,' said Geraldine, 'don't be so stuffy!'

He didn't like being called Piggy Poo. When he mentioned the fact to Geraldine she told him not to be so touchy. Within a week of his arrival, it seemed that as far as she was concerned whatever he did or said was either stuffy or touchy or boring or stupid.

There was also the delicate matter of sex. He had been sent off to sea within a week of their wedding in August 1914, and apart from a couple of romps with prostitutes had little practice between the sheets since then. As far as he was concerned, sex was the price a wife had to pay for the security and companionship of marriage. It never occurred to him that Geraldine might expect any enjoyment from the act, and he felt resentful when she criticized his prowess.

The trouble was that he had a tendency, to use one of his gunnery expressions, to go off at half-cock, so that more often than not the performance was over for him before it had begun for Geraldine.

'Honey,' she sighed one night after another premature salvo, 'You're a nice guy, but you're not the world's best lover, are you?'

That remark hurt him more than he was prepared to admit. Removed from the structured routine of naval life and submitted constantly during daylight hours to her condescension and sarcasm, he began to feel increasingly defensive and resentful. He concealed his resentment successfully for a while, but one night Geraldine referred to his penis as Wee Willie Winkie, and threatened to put a clothes peg on it to stop him coming before she was good and ready.

Something snapped. He lost his temper, put his hands to her throat, and started to throttle her. Geraldine had not had two elder brothers for nothing, and knew how to look after herself in a fight. She led off with a knee to the groin, which made his eyes water, and followed it with a karate chop to the nose, which made his nose bleed. He tried to whack her across the face but she ducked and repaid the compliment by hurling the bedside carafe, which missed his right ear by a hair's breadth, smashed through the sash window and shattered on the courtyard below.

He spent the night at the Naval Club.

The following day he lunched alone at the club and sat reading the papers into the late afternoon. He regretted marrying Geraldine now. He felt no love for her whatsoever, and never had. He detested the crowd of vacuous young people she had gathered about her, and already longed to get back to sea, to be a man amongst men once more and escape the eternal chatter of the Mayfair set.

The gas lamps were being lit by the time he left the club. He began walking home, but had barely gone fifty yards when he was accosted by a young woman in a fox fur who fell into step alongside him and said he looked as if he could do with a bit of company. 'I'll give you a nice time for half a crown, sir,' she said.

She took him to her room in a cheap hotel. He was appalled at the tawdry décor and the smell of cheap scent and stale cigarette smoke. She dropped her fox fur over the back of a chair, kicked off her shoes, slipped out of her dress, and asked him if he had any particular likes or dislikes.

He coughed, and blinked rapidly. 'Not really.'

'Come off it! You naval types—there's no knowing what you don't get up to!'

'How do you know I'm naval?'

'Because I saw you come out of your club, that's why. In any case, I'd know your sort a mile off. So what's it to be, then? Naughty boys and naughty girls? Or would you like a spanking?'

He arrived home an hour later feeling dirty and ashamed. He had the maid run a bath and washed himself with obsessive thoroughness. But when he was in his dressing room, Geraldine came in, wrapped her arms round him, gave him a wet kiss, and asked if they could be friends.

He shed a few tears and blamed everything on the war. He said he was worried about the future. His commanding officer had told him, at his farewell interview before he left his ship, that his chances of promotion were minimal.

Geraldine surprised him. She was warm, sympathetic, loving, and understanding. She said that she realized that it must be difficult for him, coming straight back from sea into a completely different way of life, that she too was bored with having so many people in the house, and intended to put a stop to it. She asked if they could start again, on a completely new basis.

The following evening he took her out to dinner at the Curzon, and they had a long talk. He opened up to her and told her what his captain had said about his low chances of promotion. He said he had been advised to consider leaving the Navy straight away in order to start a new career in civilian life.

Geraldine was horrified. 'You can't possibly leave the Navy,' she said, wiping traces of chocolate profiterole from her lips with a table napkin. 'It's your life!'

He explained that there were too many lieutenant commanders chasing too few promotion jobs, that they couldn't find plum jobs for everyone, and that if Geddes had his way, the strength of the Navy would be halved within five years.

'Who is this Geddes man?' asked Geraldine. 'Couldn't we have a talk with him?'

'Hardly. He's the First Lord of Admiralty.'

'What about your old man, then? Couldn't he put a good word in for you?'

He laughed bitterly. 'There's not much chance of that.'

'Don't be such a wet blanket!'

'Listen. To have any chance of promotion, I need to get on an admiral's staff as a flag lieutenant or staff gunnery officer. Something like that.'

'So what's the job you'd really like?'

He smiled. 'Ideally, flag lieutenant to C-in-C the Nore.'

'Then why don't you apply for it?'

'You don't understand, Gerry. Things don't work that way in the Service.'

'Of course they do! The Navy's no different from any other organization. It's not *what* you know it's *who* you know. Get off your backside! Take a few admirals out to dinner! Butter them up! Make a few telephone calls, for God's sake! Start dialing numbers!'

She made sure he did as he was told. The next day he rang the Directorate of Naval Officer Appointments and asked for an interview.

The appointing officer was a genial officer called Barham, who had just been promoted to captain and was about to leave his job in the Admiralty to take over command of an aircraft carrier. He confirmed all Roddy's worst fears, telling him to abandon any hope of an appointment to an admiral's staff because although his confidential reports from HMS *Andromache* hadn't been adverse, they hadn't been superlatively favorable either, and there were brighter stars than his in the ascendant.

'So what's on offer?' Roddy asked.

Barham interlocked his fingers and made his knuckles crack, a trick he had learnt at the hands of a Swedish masseuse. 'How about first lieutenant of Chatham barracks? That's a very responsible job.'

'Is there nothing better than that?'

Barham shook his head. 'I'm afraid not, Yarrow. The truth of the matter is that your commanding officer's advice is sound. It'll be the people who leave early who find the best posts outside.'

'Well, that's that,' Roddy told Geraldine when he got home. 'I'm going to resign my commission.'

She wagged a finger at him. 'Oh no you don't! Not before I've talked to your father, you don't!'

She traveled on her own down to Hampshire and arrived at Meonford Hall on a frosty afternoon when the fields were carpeted in white gossamer and the sun was a white disc in the evening mist. Her father-in-law was out on a shoot, so she took tea in the sitting room by a roaring log fire with her mother-in-law.

Geraldine had matured considerably during the war years, and she and Irina were on good terms. They caught up with family news. Little had been heard of Anita since her wedding in September, except that Basil had taken her on a cruise to Venice.

'Lucky girl!' Geraldine remarked. 'I wish Roddy would do the same for me. His trouble is that he needs to be told what to do the whole time. Now he says he wants to leave the Navy and be a farmer. I ask you! The prospect of Roddy playing at farmers horrifies me. I mean—a farmer has to work, isn't that right? He doesn't know the meaning of the word. And do I want him hanging round wondering what to do next for the rest of his life? No, Ma'am I do not. We'd be at each other's throats within a month.'

Irina was sympathetic but held out little hope. Most of her husband's old contacts at the Admiralty had long since died or retired to the country.

'Well at least he could try,' Geraldine said. 'At least he could take an interest.'

Irina agreed with that. She had thought for some time that Jervis took far too little interest in his son's career. But when she raised the subject over dinner that evening he was immediately dismissive. 'I've pulled enough strings for that young man to last him a lifetime,' he said. 'Besides, I don't know anyone with any influence these days.'

'What about Vernon?' Irina asked. 'Isn't he the editor of a naval magazine?'

'The *Naval Review*, yes.'

'Well then. He's sure to be in touch with all sorts of people.'

'That doesn't mean to say he has any influence on the appointment of officers.'

'Surely the family can do *something* to help!'

They were both looking at him.

'Blood's thicker than water, isn't that right?' Geraldine said.

'And he is your son,' added Irina.

'Yes, he is your son,' echoed Geraldine; and when Jervis looked up from his plate they were looking at him in a way that made him feel guilty, frustrated, and angry.

'God damn it all to hell!' he exclaimed, and stamped out of the dining room.

'Splendid!' said Irina after he had gone. 'That means he'll do something.'

16

▼

Jervis hated asking favors of anyone, and had severe misgivings about asking one of his brother-in-law. But at the same time he did feel that this was one occasion when it was his duty to try to help Roddy out, so when Vernon and Constance came to dinner the following Friday he waited until the ladies had withdrawn and he was alone with Vernon before approaching the subject in the most oblique way possible. When the port had been poured and the cigars were alight, he enquired first of Tom's career.

Tom had just been promoted to captain after serving as flag commander to an admiral, and Vernon proudly informed Sir Jervis that he had heard only that day that his son had received his new appointment, which was on the staff of the Director of Officer Appointments at Admiralty. It was, Vernon said, a plum job; witness the fact that his predecessor, Bobby Barham, had been given command of an aircraft carrier.

'Tom's only trouble is that he hasn't found himself a wife,' Vernon said. 'Of course, Connie and I are delighted that he's doing so well, but we would dearly like to see him settle down and provide us with some grand children.'

'My sentiments entirely,' Yarrow replied. 'We've been waiting six years for Roddy and Geraldine to provide a grandchild to carry on the family name.'

'Roddy's on leave at the moment isn't he?'

'That's right. He hasn't received his next appointment yet. I think he's finding the peacetime Navy rather frustrating. Geraldine says he's considering asking for early retirement.'

Vernon tipped the ash off the end of his cigar. 'I don't suppose that pleases you very much does it?'

'No it doesn't.' Jervis allowed a silence to develop. 'As a matter of fact, I was going to ask your advice about it.'

Vernon inspected the end of his cigar. 'Not sure that's worth much these days, old boy. Senility's creeping up, you know. I can never find my glasses. Connie says I need a nurse maid.'

'What about this editorship you've taken on? I should imagine that's stimulating the grey matter a bit?'

'Not so much as you might suppose. An awful lot of rubbish is submitted, you know. Chaps who fancy themselves as wordsmiths are unbelievably touchy. You wouldn't believe some of the stuff I have to read. Half of it has more to do with the self-esteem of the authors than the good of the Service. But I'm not complaining. I'm lucky to have any connection at all with the Navy at my advanced age.'

'Yes, you are lucky in that respect.'

Vernon looked up. 'That was said with feeling, old boy.'

Jervis smiled. 'I was thinking about Roddy.'

'Is he set on leaving the Service?'

'Far from it. The problem is that he's been told that his reports aren't good enough to get him into the mainstream for post list promotion. In the current climate he thinks it might be better to cut his losses and start a new career.'

'Difficult,' said Vernon. 'Very.'

'I...wondered if there might be any possibility of your putting a word in the right ear.'

Vernon looked up quickly. 'Are you asking me to pull strings, Jervis?'

'Not exactly.'

'It sounded like that to me.'

'Well...you know how it is. Roddy's my son. I have to try. Ever since Laura died I—I've felt a bit guilty, I suppose. You must have contacts all over the place. What about Dewar? Or Richmond? Or Reggie Plunkett?'

Vernon shook his head. 'It doesn't work, old boy. You have to leave them to cut their own careers out for themselves. I made that quite clear to Tom when he joined the old *Britannia*. I told him he had to sink or swim by his own efforts. I hear what you say, and I understand how difficult it must be. But I'm sorry. The answer has to be no.'

Jervis nodded jerkily and gave a short, rasping laugh. 'To be frank, I didn't expect any other reply. Indeed I apologize if I've embarrassed you in any—'

He was interrupted by the sound of raised voices in the hall. Vernon turned in his chair. 'Who on earth—?'

'That sounds like Anita,' Jervis said.

It was Anita. She burst into the dining room in her overcoat and hat. She looked cold, wet, and distraught.

'My dear child!' her father said. 'What on earth is the matter?'

Her mother and aunt came to the door behind her. Irina said, 'She's run away from Walsmhurst.'

Jervis blew out a cloud of cigar smoke. 'In that case I suggest she run straight back.'

Anita turned to her mother. 'You see? I told you he wouldn't listen. I'm going up to my room.'

But her father called her back and demanded to know what it was all about. He said that there was absolutely no question of her running away from Walmshurst, because she was bound by her wedding vows. 'You don't belong here any more,' he said. 'You're Mrs. Walmshurst. You belong to your husband.'

'In that case,' said Anita, 'I want a divorce.'

'Don't talk rubbish,' said her father.

'Why don't you tell us exactly what happened,' Aunt Constance said gently. 'I expect there's been some sort of misunderstanding that can be very quickly sorted out.'

Anita looked as if she might at any moment spring on her father like a wild cat, and tear him with her claws. 'All right,' she said. 'All right, I'll tell you. If you really want to know, I'll tell you. Do you want to know?'

Her mother put her hands on Anita's shoulders, trying to calm her. 'Of course we do, Anuchka.'

'He sodomized me, that's what. Buggery and rape. That's the reason. So if you still think I should go back to him, Father, just think again, because I'm not going to. Not now, not in the future, not ever.'

For Jervis, a divorce in the family was every bit as bad as a suicide, and when all attempts at persuading Anita to go back to Walmshurst had failed, he began to cast about for ways of limiting the damage. He contacted his lawyer, who advised him that while the divorce proceedings were set in motion it would be best for all concerned if Anita moved away to live quietly somewhere where she was not known.

That was easier said than done. It was not for nothing that Anita had been cast as Helen of Troy in her first year at Winchester High School. She had been referred to as 'the Beautiful Miss Yarrow' in the pages of the *Tatler*, and there had been occasions on which she had been photographed in the street by news reporters. She was well known: her marriage to Walmshurst had received publicity on both sides of the Atlantic.

It was Constance and Vernon who came to the rescue. They offered to have Anita to stay on condition that she did some secretarial work for her uncle, who had been asked to judge an essay competition set by the *Naval Review*. Glad to escape her father's disapproval, Anita accepted the offer straight away, and moved to Little Nest Cottage in Hambledon a few days later.

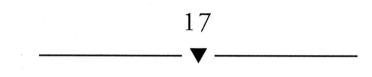

17

Anita was made very welcome by Aunt Constance, who told her that she was going to put the color back in her cheeks. She was given clotted cream with her porridge every morning, brisk winter walks in the afternoons and country roasts and stews for dinner.

Little Nest Cottage was far less grand than Meonford Hall, but much more cozy. Uncle Vernon's study had a long, low lattice window that overlooked a walled garden, with the fields sloping up under oak trees beyond. There was a roaring fire in the inglenook, and the study was littered with piles of books and manuscripts.

On the first morning after her arrival, her uncle threw half a dozen competition essays into her lap, and said, 'Tell me what you think of those.'

She settled down to read, and became quickly immersed in a world of speeds and tonnages, gun ranges and anti-submarine tactics.

'I don't think I'm qualified to give an opinion on this sort of thing,' she said when they paused for lunch, but Uncle Vernon said that you didn't have to be a carpenter to tell if a table was well made. Her private view was that there were quite a lot of rickety tables. She was amazed at the earnestness of the essayists, but also disturbed at the way they seemed to take it for granted that sooner or later there was bound to be another war with Germany.

Although the secretarial work proved rather tedious, she was glad to have something to occupy her mind, and threw herself into it with enthusiasm. Of Basil she tried to think as little as possible, but that was difficult, because his behavior had been so despicable that sometimes she would lose her concentration and find herself staring at the leaping flames, remembering the night she had run from him.

Cousin Tom came home for a week's leave over Christmas, and the moment he walked in through the front door the household came to life. Anita had always adored Tom. He was over six-foot, with a huge, humorous jaw, a deep, rumbling voice, and hands the size of meat cleavers. She hadn't seen him since she was thirteen, but he hadn't changed a bit.

Aunt Constance must have said something to him about what had happened, because he went out of his way to cheer her up, and insisted on taking her and the Springer spaniels for long walks on Soberton Heath every afternoon, returning at dusk in time for hot buttered toast in front of the fire.

On the third of these walks, Tom suggested that it was much nicer on a cold winter's day for cousins to walk arm in arm; and on their walk the following day he discovered that her hand was cold, so he put it into the pocket of his British Warm and held it in his own.

Immediately, she experienced a flood of emotion, and her eyes filled with tears. Their easy conversation dried up. They walked on and on—much further than they had walked before. 'Perhaps we should turn back?' she suggested eventually, and tried to withdraw her hand; but he held it all the tighter and said that when he was with her he never wanted to turn back.

'Tom,' she said quietly. 'Please don't be nice to me. I'm not used to it and it makes me wobbly and tearful.'

He stopped and faced her, and took both her hands in his. 'There's no point in pretending any more,' he said. 'I love you, Annie. I always have. I've loved you for as long as I can remember.'

'Don't,' she said. 'It won't get you anywhere.'

'I don't want to go anywhere. At least, not without you. I've always wanted to marry you. Did you know that?'

'I'm finished. I've made a complete muck of my life.'

'You're not finished. You haven't even begun.'

'I'm not available. I'm married.'

'But you will be divorced.'

'We're cousins, Tom!'

'I don't care. I adore you. We belong together. We were always just right together. Even when you were small. It's true, isn't it?'

She nodded.

'We only have to wait for you to divorce that frightful man,' Tom said. 'Once that's over and done with, we can marry.'

She said it was out of the question, that it would be the most awful scandal and would wreck his career.

'Nonsense,' he said, and kissed her forehead. 'We're in the twentieth century, now. The world's changed. People accept divorce, these days. In any case, my career is of no importance to me. If I don't marry you I'll never marry at all.'

'You can't possibly say that!'

'I can. I'm sure of it.'

They walked back in silence. 'I don't think we should even consider it,' she said as they were crossing the field at the back of the house. 'I'm sorry, Tom. I think it would be madness.'

They stopped under an ancient oak tree. 'Love *is* madness,' he whispered, and took her in his arms.

The telephone rang after dinner when Jervis was sitting in the library smoking a cigar and reflecting on past glories. It was Vernon, sounding uncharacteristically agitated.

'Is that you, old boy? Look here—I need to talk to you. At the earliest possible opportunity.'

'Oh yes?' said Jervis. 'What's this about?'

'I can't tell you on the telephone. I'll come and see you first thing tomorrow, if I may.'

'Not possible. I'm shooting.'

'In that case I shall have to ask you to cancel. We must talk straight away.'

'It's damned inconvenient,' Jervis said. 'And why the secrecy?'

'I'll explain that tomorrow,' Vernon said, and rang off.

He arrived in a shooting brake at eight the following morning when Jervis and Irina were at breakfast. He was not his usual hearty self. He greeted Irina quietly and sat down at the table, declining all but a cup of tea. 'I think you had better both hear what I have to say,' he said gravely.

'It concerns Anita. I'm afraid I must ask you to take her back. She can't remain at Little Nest a day longer.'

'Take her back?' Yarrow said. 'Why?'

Vernon looked down at his teacup, then up at Irina and Jervis in turn. 'I dislike having to tell you this, but you will have to know. The fact of the matter is that she has been making advances to Tom.'

'Advances?' Irina whispered. 'What sort of advances?'

'Do I have to spell it out?'

'Yes,' said Jervis. 'I think you had better.'

'She's set her cap at him.'

'No!' Irina whispered. 'I don't believe she would be so foolish.'

'I'm afraid it is so. I appreciate how painful this must be for you, but Constance became aware that she was making eyes at him from the first moment of his arrival.'

'But my dear chap they're cousins! They've always been devoted! In any case, I'm sure Anita would never intend any sort of improper advance by a mere look.'

'This is not a case of a look,' said Vernon. I saw them together. With my own eyes. They were...embracing.'

'Aren't cousins allowed to embrace?' Irina enquired.

'This was not a cousinly embrace,' Vernon said. 'It was a lovers' kiss.'

'How can you be sure that Anuchka is to blame?' Irina asked. 'Why is it never the man's fault?'

Jervis said, 'I'm afraid that is usually the way of it, my dear.'

Vernon turned to Jervis. 'Could we have a word in your study?'

They excused themselves. A minute later, when Mrs. Jannaway came in to the breakfast room, she found Lady Yarrow in tears.

'It's not merely a question of the family name,' Vernon was saying. 'It's also a question of Tom's career. Fortunately, I think I have acted in time to nip it in the bud. But you know what Hampshire is like. It only takes one person to get hold of the story and it'll be the talk of every saloon and public bar in the county within a week. Tom has a brilliant career ahead of him. I will not stand by and see it wrecked—not even by your daughter. An affair with a married woman is bad enough. An affair with a married woman who is one's first cousin and who, only two weeks before, ran away from her husband—frankly it beggars belief. Your daughter must be sent away, Jervis. Right away. Out of the county. Out of the country.'

'That's for me to decide,' said Yarrow. 'I'm not having anyone dictate to me what's best for my daughter. Not even you, old boy.'

'Then allow me to draw your attention to an aspect of this which may have escaped your notice. Anita hopes to divorce Walmshurst, isn't that so? Have you considered the consequences if the smallest whisper of this leaks out? That Walmshurst fellow will be able to stand up in court and say that his wife ran off with her cousin. How will that look in the *Hampshire Chronicle* law reports, do you suppose?'

'So what you're saying—'

'The only possible solution, as I see it, is for the two of them to be separated immediately. The whole business must be finished now. Straight away, before it can go further. And we have to act quickly. Not the smallest whisper of this must get out.'

Jervis heaved a sigh. 'Go on. What do you suggest?'

'She must go abroad.'

'Easier said than done.'

'Not at all. Send her out to Malta. If she wants to fish, let her join the fishing fleet.'

'What if I say no?'

'You won't, if you have any sense at all.'

'Are you absolutely sure that this whole business isn't a storm in a teacup?'

'Absolutely. You didn't see them kissing. I did. From my study window. They were locked in a lovers' embrace.'

'Of course—it does take two, doesn't it? How can we be sure that it wasn't Tom who made the running? Irina does have a point there. It seems hardly credible that Anita could be so foolish as to make advances at this particular moment in time.'

'For God's sake, man! Of course it was her doing! You must know very well that she has a reputation as a tear-away! She was the talk of the town last year—you admitted as much to me yourself. Not without a certain paternal pride, as I recall. "Nice to see a bit of spirit in a girl," wasn't that what you said when we lunched at the Squadron last August?'

Jervis went to the window and looked out over the wintry garden. He had the impression that he was being maneuvered into a corner.

'I have plenty of contacts,' Vernon said. 'What about the Gosthwaites?'

'What about them?'

'Johnny Gosthwaite has just hoisted his Commodore's broad pennant out in Malta. I heard from him only three weeks ago. He's moving the family out. Sylvia's still living at Exton, but she'll be traveling out with the family within the next few weeks. I understand they're taking a lease on a villa. Anita could go out and be a companion to Sylvia. Wouldn't that make sense?'

Jervis turned quickly back from the window. 'That's the way of it, is it? When I ask you to use what contacts you have to help Roddy find an appointment that will take him forwards rather than sideways in his career, the answer is no. "You have to let them cut their own careers out for themselves." That was how you put it. But now that *your* son's career is in danger of faltering, pulling strings becomes perfectly acceptable.'

'This isn't pulling strings, old boy!'

'Then what is it? Asking favors? Oiling wheels?'

Vernon Braddle spread his hands. 'We live in a wicked world, Jervis. It's dog-eat-dog out there, and the Navy's no exception, however much we would like it to be. Of course this is upsetting for you—both of you. I understand that. But we have to grapple with the situation realistically. Believe me: Tom and Anita are in love. They probably realize already that it's an impossible love. So we'll be doing them both a favor by separating them. If Tom were your son, wouldn't you do exactly the same?'

'Very well,' said Jervis. 'I've listened to your proposal. Now here's one for you. Tom's starting his new appointment at the Admiralty next week, isn't he? If anyone can find Roddy a decent appointment it'll be him. You're obviously quite determined to protect Tom's career, so I don't see why you shouldn't do the same for Roddy. I think that's only fair, isn't it? Wouldn't you agree?'

'I could say so much,' said Aunt Constance when she came up to see Anita in her room, 'but you are an intelligent girl and I'm sure there's no need. All I will say is that you must not blame yourself or feel that we blame you either. What has happened has happened. The thing to do now is to accept our decision with a good will and start a completely new page.'

It was so tactfully and gently done, and the time Anita had spent in Tom's company had been so short, that she felt little more than a sense of having messed things up all over again.

So she arrived home again. In disgrace? Yes, in disgrace, though of course that was never stated in so many words. Nevertheless it quickly became apparent that her parents' attitude towards her had changed. She had the impression that they despaired of her and wanted to wash their hands of her. Her father seemed unable to treat her as a daughter, and had become aloof and unapproachable; while her mother, who was still very distressed by the fate of her family and the reports of Red Army advances, was quite unable to cope with another emotional crisis.

On her second day back, her father called her into the library and informed her that arrangements were being made to pack her off to Malta. She was given no say in the matter. She would travel with Mrs. Gosthwaite and her ten-year-old daughter Clara.

'You must realize that your uncle went to a great deal of trouble to arrange this for you,' her father said. 'It is therefore essential that you do not abuse his kindness or, for that matter, Commodore Gosthwaite's. I believe Commodore Gosthwaite may be able to find some sort of secretarial work for you in Malta. If that is the case, there is to be no question of shirking it. You will find that life goes along much more pleasantly when you think more about others and less about yourself. Do you understand?'

'Yes, Father.'

There was a lot of 'Yes, Father' and 'No, Father' at that time. Indeed, she said little else to him. A great gulf opened up between them; and because her mother seemed reluctant to challenge her father's attitude, she felt estranged from her as well.

It was a quiet Christmas, but not a happy one. On Christmas afternoon she went for a solitary walk by the Meon. On her way back she stopped and gazed across the river at the cozy, picture-book village. It was all so perfect! The Norman tower of St. Bartholomew's church; the frost-white meadows, the cattle standing so still, half lost in the mist that was rising like smoke from the river. Perhaps her father was right. Perhaps she had had it all too easy. Perhaps she was just a poor little rich girl. She wished she could vent her feelings: let fly, shout, scream, or throw a tantrum. But that wasn't done, was it? One had to keep up appearances and set a good example.

A quite inconsequential incident finally lifted the lid off her feelings. She was to sail in early January aboard the SS *Corfe Castle*, which would stop at Malta on passage to Cape Town via the Suez Canal. She was to take two tin trunks of clothes with her, and they had been freshly painted by the gardener in accordance with her parents' instructions. When the paint was dry they were brought up to her room for packing by two of the maids. Painted in white lettering on each trunk was the name Mrs. B. Walmshurst followed by the letters N.W.O.V., which meant Not Wanted on Voyage.

When she saw those letters, she began to laugh and cry. 'You see? You see? I'm not even allowed to have my own name on my trunk! I'm not allowed to be me! Mrs. Walmshurst—not wanted on voyage! I'm not wanted on this voyage or in this house, for that matter! They might just as well have tied a label round my neck and sent me through the post!'

Her mother heard the commotion and came upstairs. Anita turned on her. 'You're just getting rid of me, aren't you? You don't want me. Aunt Constance doesn't want me. Father doesn't want me. I'm an embarrassment to you all, aren't I? Father can hardly be in the same room with me. He looks at me as if I'm something the cat brought in!'

'Don't be so silly, Anuchka!'

'Why shouldn't I be silly? Haven't I a right to be silly? I can't even have my own name back, can I? I can't be Anita Yarrow. I'm Mrs. B. Walmshurst. I'm a chattel, a piece of luggage. That's all I am.'

She took a long time to calm down, and lay awake for most of the night with a blinding headache; but by morning, she had undergone what amounted to an inner revolution, having made up her mind that this was the last time she would take orders from her father—or indeed from any man.

She went up to London to stay for a few days with Geraldine. Roddy was in ebullient form, having recently heard that he was to be appointed to the Britannia Royal Naval College, Dartmouth, where he would be responsible for the welfare and training of thirteen-year-old cadets.

Geraldine proved to be a good listener. Hers was the most encouraging voice Anita had heard for some time. 'Just leave it all behind you,' she said.

'That's what I did. You've got nothing to lose. You can go out to Malta and have a ball.'

'I don't want to have a ball. I had my ball last summer and look where it got me. Besides, I can't stand the company of naval officers. All they ever talk about is sport or ships or guns or promotion. They drive me mad.'

'Honey—all men are the same. The trouble is we can't do without them.'

'I'm beginning to think I could.'

'Well be careful, okay? You don't want to end up, well, kind of—odd. Don't let it get to you. Just let it ride. Let it ride, go somewhere new, make the most of what you've got. That's what I did.' They looked at each other and laughed at the same moment. 'Okay—so I got myself lumbered with your brother. But he's not as bad as all that. He's just a cub scout in long pants like they all are.'

Anita had intended to replenish her wardrobe while in London, but in the event did hardly any shopping at all. What was the point? She wasn't going to compete any more. There would be no obligation to follow the fashion or go to parties. She could be as dowdy and dull as she liked, and to hell with keeping up appearances.

Browsing one afternoon at a book stall in the Charing Cross Road, she came across a second-hand copy of the Communist Manifesto. She bought it for sixpence and read most of it in the taxi on the way back to Geraldine's apartment. It suited her mood of black rebellion perfectly. The abolition of bourgeois property, the overthrow of the privileged class, the pooling of resources for the common good—the whole thing was positively exhilarating.

No wonder there were so many strikes! No wonder the Labor party was poised to take over from the Liberals as the party of opposition! She flipped to the last page and smiled at the closing paragraph.

Marx was right. So was Geraldine. She had nothing to lose but her chains.

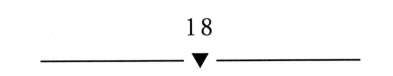

18

The sea calmed down and the sun came out on the last day before the SS *Corfe Castle* was due at Valletta. Having spent most of the voyage in her cabin, Mrs. Gosthwaite left Clara in the care of her nanny and came up to the first class sundeck, where she found Anita reading Rousseau's *Social Contract*.

Sylvia Gosthwaite was in her mid thirties, and very much a naval officer's wife. 'What on earth are you reading?' she asked as she settled herself in a deck chair. 'It looks frightfully serious!'

'Well, it's political philosophy really. But interesting, all the same.'

Sylvia laughed shrilly. 'Philosophy! My dear girl you won't have much time for philosophy in Malta!' She beckoned to a steward and ordered beef tea. 'The chief officer was saying at breakfast that the Mediterranean fleet might be in, and if that's the case, you can expect a pretty hectic time for the next week or two. Mind you, I don't suppose it will be in for long. The last time I was in Malta, just before the war when the commodore was a commander, life was so much more leisurely. But everything's changed, hasn't it? The chief officer was saying that the White Russians seem to be running out of steam. Oh dear! The world is such a complicated place these days, don't you think? I mean, one would have thought that we could all settle down and live peaceably together. But not a bit of it! It's the politicians I blame, don't you agree? Oh—jolly good, here comes the beef tea!'

The ship was to berth at ten o'clock the following morning. Sylvia suggested that they all get up early to watch the entry into harbor. When they came up on deck they found that the fine weather had been short-lived.

The sea was dark green, and the tops of the waves were being blown off by the wind. The ship was steaming along the coast, and the roofs and domes of Valletta were in sight. Sylvia had brought a pair of opera glasses up with her. She lent them to Clara on condition she didn't keep them for too long.

'That must be Sliema Creek, and the next one along is Msida,' Sylvia told anyone who happened to be listening. 'Oh and look! Look Clara, darling! See? The ships are coming out!'

Six destroyers emerged one by one from behind a rocky headland, and formed up in a line. Black smoke poured from their funnels as they increased speed, and they came past with the spray flying up over their bows, flags jumping up and down at the yards, and signal lanterns twinkling messages from the bridges.

Sylvia became girlishly excited. 'I'm so glad we came up on deck! Clara darling you will remember this for the rest of your life!' She turned to Anita with tears in her eyes. 'Isn't the Navy wonderful? So silly—it always makes me emotional when I hear them go "whoop, whoop!" like that.'

The battlements and vedettes of Grand Harbor slid slowly past. Tugs maneuvered the ship between buoys. Sylvia trained the opera glasses on the buildings overlooking the harbor and let out a sudden 'whoop!' of her own. 'I can see the commodore! He's on the admiral's balcony!' She waved and sniffed and laughed and turned Clara's head in the right direction, and they both waved again; and on the balcony a naval officer raised his hat to them and gave a single, heroic wave of acknowledgement.

Commodore Gosthwaite had a large head, a loud voice, and an eye for the ladies. He welcomed Anita a little too warmly. 'Aha!' he said, taking her hand in his and not letting it go 'The fair Mrs. Walmshurst! How good to meet you. I understand you've come out to Malta to help the war effort?'

'I didn't realize—'

'There was a war on? Aha! Nobody does! The war may be over back at home, but out here we're still hard at it.'

The commodore's residence was on the Strada Mezzodi not far from Admiralty House. The entrance was gained by high wrought iron gates to a walled front garden filled with poinsettia and potted geraniums. You went up a flight of steps and into a porch where the visitors' book lay open, with a quill pen and silver inkwell at hand. Into a marbled hall with potted palms, where Maltese stewards in white jackets were standing to attention looking frightened. Heels clicked and footsteps scurried. There was a glimpse of a dining room with a mahogany table laid for dinner; a Maltese steward with long eyelashes and liquid eyes picked up her suitcase and hat box, and led the way up three flights of stairs to a room with painted furniture, louvered shutters, and a four-poster bed with a mosquito net.

Anita sat down on the bed and took off her hat. In any other circumstances she might have been excited, but however hard she tried to put the past behind her, the fact remained that she had been packed off to the colonies in disgrace.

After cocktails that evening there was a dinner party for sixteen to welcome Mrs. Gosthwaite and introduce her to some of the naval shore staff and their ladies. The next morning, Anita accompanied Mrs. Gosthwaite and Clara to the Baracca Gardens overlooking Grand Harbor to watch the fleet come in, which it did amid bugles sounding, flags waving and gun salutes, the noise of which echoed back and forth between the old limestone fortresses on either side of the harbor.

In the two weeks following the fleet's arrival, Anita attended three dances, five dinner parties, one tennis tournament, and a windy picnic at St. Paul's Bay.

When they arrived back at Villa Rosa after the picnic, the commodore's yeoman was in attendance with a clipboard full of signals. There had been a debacle on the Russian front. Preparations were to be put in hand for the Mediterranean Fleet to embark thousands of refugees, as it was expected that if the White Russians were overrun by the Bolsheviks, no mercy would be shown.

Anita was given the task of making dozens of cardboard notices announcing (in Russian) 'MEN,' 'WOMEN,' 'THIS WAY,' 'NO ENTRY,' and 'NO SMOKING'—but a few days later when she went into the office she discovered that the fleet had sailed at dawn and had left all her carefully sign-written notices behind.

Commodore Gosthwaite found a temporary job for Anita as a filing clerk in the dockyard offices which, though hardly inspiring, was better than sitting at home in Villa Rosa playing beggar-my-neighbor with Clara. Whether the job was intended as an apprenticeship she never discovered, but after four weeks she was moved to a cluttered fourth-floor office over-looking Grand Harbor, and installed as a secretarial assistant and Russian translator in the Commander-in-Chief's intelligence office.

This was much more interesting because she began dealing with secret reports and briefings relating to naval operations in the Mediterranean and Black Sea. It was also quite demanding, because much of the material for translation contained naval technicalities and expressions not found in the only English-Russian dictionary in the building.

Her immediate boss was a weary old lieutenant commander called Berty Arborfield. He used to sit in the corner behind his cluttered desk with his chair tipped and his feet on the desk smoking a pipe, pontificating on the way the politicians seemed bent upon emasculating the Navy, the decline of the Empire, and the axe that was expected to fall on the careers of passed-over lieutenant commanders like himself.

One of Berty's heaviest burdens was the drafting and production of the Mediterranean Intelligence Summary. When he discovered that Anita could write clear English, he gave her the bulk of the work. 'Trust you won't mind if I take the credit, my dear,' he used to say, 'but I have a wife and five to support, so my need is greater than yours.'

Spring came, and for a few weeks the chopped-up little fields of Malta were ablaze with wild flowers. She went on a few outings with watercolors, but was continually pestered by peculiar animals known as 'shoats'—a cross between sheep and goats—and came back hot, dirty and discouraged.

Berty Arborfield tried to persuade her to join CADS, the Corradino Amateur Dramatic Society, but she had a private horror of amateur dramatics and declined. And all the time the parties went on: tea parties, garden parties, lunch parties, tennis parties, polo parties, and cricket parties. Her name was on every admiral's list, and as a guest of the Gosthwaites she was obliged by good manners to accept every invitation in which she was included.

Quite quickly, however, a new cloud came up over her horizon, because it became apparent that Commodore Gosthwaite fancied his chances with her. Whatever the occasion, and however hard she tried to avoid him, he always managed to arrange matters so that he was by her side. 'Aha!' he would say when she came into the room, 'If it isn't the fair Mrs. Walmshurst!' Then he would engage her in close conversation, his eyes traveling up and down her as if estimating her price at auction.

At first she told herself that she was being over-sensitive. Later it became so obvious that it seemed only a matter of time before Sylvia noticed and a domestic crisis ensued.

On a Saturday afternoon in May, when the sixth destroyer flotilla was to play cricket against the staff of the Senior Naval Officer in Charge, Malta (SNOIC for short), Sylvia confided to Anita that she had the curse, and asked her to accompany her husband to watch the cricket match.

Gosthwaite lunched her at the Marsa club and was very fruity, nudging her foot under the table and putting his hand on her knee when no one was looking. After lunch, they went to watch the match from deck chairs on the boundary. After sitting in silence for ten or fifteen minutes of extremely slow cricket, Gosthwaite turned to her and said: 'You know what I think? I think we should take the rest of the afternoon off. I have the keys to a flat not far from here. Why don't we bunk off and have a bit of fun between the sheets?'

Unhurriedly, she gathered her things, stood up, and excused herself, saying that she was finding it a little hot, and that she was going to sit in the shade by the pavilion.

She left him looking deflated, and settled down with a book. She put Malta, cricket and the commodore's romantic aspirations out of her mind. But a little while later, two officers in SNOIC's team came out onto the verandah of the pavilion and, with their backs to her, engaged in a conversation which she could not help overhearing.

'The one staying at villa Rosa,' she heard one say.

'The nanny?'

'No, not her! The blonde. Keeps herself to herself. Bit of a bluestocking, but quite a little firecracker all the same.'

'But—that's Mrs. Walmshurst.'

'That's who she is! So who's Mr. Walmshurst when he's at home?'

'Some sort of thespian poof. She ditched him. You know Toss Yarrow? She's his sister.'

'Didn't I see his name in the CW lists the other day?'

'I believe he's gone to BRNC.'

'How on earth did Yarrow get a plum job like that?'

'Well, Daddy's a baronet.'

There was applause for a boundary four. 'That's the stuff! We could do with a few more of those.'

'So is she fair game?'

'You are a randy old sod, Mike Purdy!'

'Well! I'd be doing her a favor! Married women get a taste for it. And if her husband's a homo she's probably longing for a touch of the you-can't-bend-it.'

'You'd better watch your step. You could get yourself into deep trouble with that one.'

'I bet she's a tiger between the sheets.'

'Doubtless. She's a man-eater. She'd have you for breakfast.'

'She can have me for dinner and tea as well, if she likes. I'll play her silly games.'

There was a sudden roar of 'Howzat!' from the pitch.

'Stuff a chocolate pig! Look at that! He's out, LBW! That's me. I'm in.'

As Mike Purdy went down the pavilion steps with his cricket bat under his arm, Anita threw down her book and intercepted him. 'I am Mrs. Walmshurst,' she said quietly, 'and I should like you to know that I heard every word of your despicable conversation.'

She didn't wait to see his reaction. She turned on her heel, collected her hat, her bag, and her book, and walked out of the club grounds and all the way back to Villa Rosa, where she arrived with a blinding headache and a raging thirst nearly two hours later.

She spent two days in bed recovering from sunstroke, and used the time as an interlude in which to think.

She regretted her outburst. It would have been better to keep her mouth shut. But that incident was insignificant in comparison with the problem she now faced of dealing with Gosthwaite's unwelcome attentions. He was the real cause of all this: if she hadn't had to fend him off for the past three months she could have laughed off Purdy's conversation as an interesting example of the average naval officer's adolescent attitude towards the opposite sex.

She did some private weeping during those two days, and the only comfort she received came from Clara. Clara was a dumpy little girl, very phlegmatic, and appallingly well behaved. She came up to Anita's room after tea to play Racing Demon. Anita wished that she could herself have been so unquestioningly obedient, so well-behaved, so docile, and so entirely accepting of parental authority.

She wondered if she was exaggerating the whole thing, but the answer to that was a definite 'no.' She could no longer trust Gosthwaite to behave himself if they were left alone together for two minutes. All the danger signals were there for her to see. If she gave into him, he would undoubtedly use her and then cast her on the rubbish heap along with all his previous conquests. But what if she resisted him? She had known him long enough now to be aware that he was the sort of man who was prepared to trample on anyone who dared to thwart him. He was the sort who might bring immense pressure on her, and if she refused to give him what he wanted, might retaliate by destroying what was left of her good name.

She had to be honest to herself if to no one else. The first step was to acknowledge that she was now deeply unhappy. She felt she was turning into an outsider. There was no one on the island she knew well enough to go to for advice. She was obviously regarded as a woman of doubtful reputation and considered fair game by the Purdys of this world. And now Gosthwaite's attentions had rendered it impossible for her to stay on at Villa Rosa. If she did, something awful would happen, she was certain of that. At best it would be Basil's old enemy Major Embarrassment. At worst she would be compromised, Gosthwaite humiliated, Sylvia's marriage wrecked, and the innocent happiness of Clara's childhood destroyed.

The only thing to do, she decided, was to return to England. The more she thought about it, the more certain she became. In England she could go to her mother and explain. If her mother took her father's side, there was always Geraldine, who would surely understand and support her.

On her first day back at work she composed a telegram which, when finally reduced to the minimum number of words, read: PLEASE MAY I COME HOME. GOOD REASONS. ANITA.

She used the office address, hoping that her parents would have the insight to use it for their reply, but three days later when she arrived back at from work, the Maltese servant brought her a telegram on a silver salver. She took it up to read in the privacy of her room, which was just as well because it would have been difficult to conceal her feelings about it in Sylvia's presence: WALMSHURST REFUSES TO GRANT DIVORCE. LAWYERS

ADVISE YOUR RETURN WOULD ADVERSELY AFFECT OUTCOME OF YOUR DIVORCE PETITION. REMAIN IN MALTA FURTHER SIX MONTHS. FATHER.

She sat on her bed and stared at the words. She felt at the end of her tether. Who said that you can never be injured by another, you can only injure yourself? Did she believe that? If she did, was she co-operating with fate to make her predicament worse? Had she been wrong to run away from Basil? Were there such things as 'just desserts' and was she now getting them? Had she brought all this on herself?

Suddenly, the mists cleared. There was nothing for it but to move into digs. It was such an obvious solution that she couldn't imagine why she hadn't thought of it before. The only difficulty was how to break the news of her decision to Mrs. Gosthwaite. But it had to be done, and there was no time like the present.

'My dear girl, why?' was Sylvia's immediate reaction.

Anita was prepared for that one. 'Because I feel it would be unfair to impose on you any longer, Mrs. Gosthwaite.'

'That's ridiculous! How can you possibly feel that you're an imposition?'

'It isn't exactly that.'

'What is it then? Are you unhappy here?'

'Not at all. It's just that I don't want to become a burden. I never felt that I should stay with you for the whole of my time in Malta.'

'What about Clara? She's absolutely devoted to you! As for being a burden, that is complete nonsense. We have plenty of servants and plenty of room.'

'I'm sorry, Mrs. Gosthwaite. I feel that it would be better if I moved into digs.'

'Better? How could it possibly be better?'

'I would rather not go into my reasons too deeply, Mrs. Gosthwaite. I'm sure you understand.'

'I don't understand at all. What reasons?'

'I can't explain.'

'So there *is* a reason! I think I should be allowed to know what it is, Anita. Don't you?'

'Can't I just be allowed to take this one decision for myself, Mrs. Gosthwaite?'

'I see,' said Sylvia. 'What you are saying is that there is a reason, but you're not prepared to divulge it. Am I right?'

Anita felt as if she were under interrogation. She put her hands up to her face.

'No,' said Sylvia Gosthwaite. 'You can't hide behind tears this time. I won't accept that. The commodore and I agreed to take you on as our guest here. I think we have shown you every possible kindness, don't you?'

'Yes, I acknowledge that and can't thank you enough.'

'So why do you want to leave us all of a sudden?'

She shook her head. 'Can't I be allowed to have private reasons?'

Sylvia smiled. 'Of course. I should have thought. It's to do with a man, isn't it?'

'I'm sorry, Mrs. Gosthwaite, but I'm not prepared to say.'

'Well I'm sorry too, but I consider that I am in a position to insist that you tell me. You're not twenty-one yet, are you? We're acting as your guardians. If you're involved with a man, we have a responsibility to protect you. And in order to do that, I must insist on knowing who that man is.'

'Mrs. Gosthwaite, I really cannot divulge—'

'So it is a man! Are you in love with him? Is that it?'

'Quite the reverse.'

'Then tell me who it is, and I shall put a stop to it.'

'I'm afraid it would do more harm than good, Mrs. Gosthwaite. I'm sorry.'

'Sorry? You're sorry? How *dare* you say you're sorry! I think there are a few things that need to be said, Anita. We were aware of your situation when we agreed to take you on, and we made allowances for it. But what have we had in return from you? Nothing. You have behaved like a spoiled, sulky child.'

'I know I haven't always been the best of company, but I have been through a lot—'

Sylvia shook her finger. 'Don't you *dare* come to me for sympathy! That really would be too much. Your ingratitude takes my breath away. We agreed to take you in after your—your experience, which you seem to have brought on yourself, I may say. We went out of our way to entertain you, to introduce you to our circle and make you feel welcome and happy among us. And now you say you want to live elsewhere for reasons you are not prepared to explain. Do you think that is any way behave? Well do you?'

'I feel that whatever I do will be wrong, Mrs. Gosthwaite. If I leave Villa Rosa I shall upset you and Clara, and if I stay—'

'What?' Sylvia slammed the word out like a gunshot. 'Well? What if you stay? Is this man of yours in this house? Oh my God! Is it one of the Maltese staff?'

'No! No!'

'Who then? Who?'

She tried as hard as she knew how not to give in, but the force of Sylvia's questioning was irresistible. 'It's the commodore,' she said at last, and the moment the words were out she knew that she had made the one mistake she had been determined to avoid.

Sylvia went ice cold. 'How dare you? How dare you say such a thing? You of all people. With your reputation.' She breathed in heavily through her nose and the corners of her mouth turned right down. 'Very well. I agree. You had better leave. As soon as possible. I shall have your dinner sent up to your room, and tomorrow morning you can pack up your bags and go.'

She took a house in the back streets of Sliema. She had a small income from her office work and this, added to the allowance from her father, was enough to make ends meet provided she did her own washing and cooking and cleaning.

The flat was furnished in dreadful Maltese Victoriana. In the front room there was a black sideboard, and pride of place was given to a picture, bolted irremovably to the wall, of Christ wearing a crown of thorns and revealing his sacred heart. The kitchen was minuscule, and the cooker ran off bottled gas. The first time she lit the oven she blew her eyebrows off and frazzled her hair, thereby putting paid to any thoughts of accepting invitations to cocktail parties even if they were to come her way, which was unlikely.

But the place did have one redeeming feature in the form of a magnificent honky-tonk piano; and in the piano stool she found a collection of old music hall songs from the nineties, which she played for her own entertainment.

After a week or so at 33, Don Rua Street, she began to realize that she was happier now than she had ever been in her life. For the first time she was entirely independent of men. She had a place of her own into which she could retire and shut the door on the world. She had this marvelous jangly piano, some books, enough to live on and no appearances to keep up. She could wash the dishes when she felt like it, eat as much or as little as she cared to cook for herself, leave her bed unmade—even pad about the house stark naked when felt like it, which she often did, that summer.

But the best part of all was that she could leave the silly season behind. Sometimes she looked at herself in the mirror and laughed at the thought that she need never go to another cocktail party in her life.

But living alone did have strange effects, and she observed them with a growing sense of unease. 'You really must stop talking to yourself,' she said aloud to the mirror one day. She felt a little like Alice in Wonderland. There seemed to be a voice that was not entirely hers inside her head which scolded, nagged, and praised her.

She found out where the market was and acquired a taste for simple food. She ate a great deal of rice, fish, and fresh vegetables. On Sunday evenings when she was tired of her own company she would go and mingle with the throng promenading on the Sliema waterfront.

She remembered Geraldine's warning about becoming 'odd.' She was certainly becoming so in some respects. The kitchen sink was always stacked with dirty dishes, and she managed to make her bed linen last three weeks before changing it. She knew that she was letting her standards slip but it didn't seem to matter.

In spite of all that had happened she did not feel at all anti-man—quite the reverse. She had a recurring dream of being with a man who she knew loved her above all others, and with whom she felt entirely safe, happy, and secure.

On leaving Villa Rosa, Sylvia had been gracious enough to agree not to report the reasons of her departure back to her parents, and although her mother wrote to say that she could not understand why she would want to live on her own, she did accept the fact. In July, her father wrote to confirm that Walmshurst was still contesting the divorce petition, that it would all take time, and that she would be well advised to stay abroad until the New Year.

June, July and August passed. She lived in a strange limbo. She got to know the Zammitts next door, saw back-street life at first hand, and mingled with the Maltese lower classes. She learnt to cook with pasta, and developed a passion for squashes with butter and white pepper.

One Saturday night in August she put on a yellow cotton dress and sandals and went down to the Sliema waterfront. The destroyer flotilla was in, and the bars were full of sailors. The locals were promenading up and down and the lights of the ships made moving patterns on the water. She passed a group of sailors and felt their eyes on her. When she glanced back, they were looking back at her. She was so tempted to go and get herself picked up that she paid a boatman sixpence to take her round the ships in his *dghaisa*.

She sat in the stern while the boat jerked forward with each stroke of the sweeps. She had never before experienced such a raw feeling of sexual desire. Perhaps it's the heat, she thought; but her Alice-in-Wonderland voice chipped in and said, 'It's nothing of the kind, Anita Yarrow. It's the way you're made.'

On landing she walked straight home, made herself a pot of strong coffee, and, pacing about between the kitchen and the front parlor, smoked three cigarettes in a row. She caught a glimpse of herself in a mirror and stared. 'You're morally unstable,' she told her reflection. 'That's your trouble.'

A few days later when she had arrived back from work and was lying on her bed, there was a knock at the door. She stubbed out her cigarette, threw on a dress, hunted for her sandals, found only one, gave up, and went to the door barefoot, expecting to find Mrs. Zammitt bearing one of her delicious rice puddings. But it was not Mrs. Zammitt. It was Sylvia Gosthwaite in a cream dress, cloche hat, and pearls.

She came into the house and glanced nervously about her.

Anita was about to apologize for the mess, but stopped herself. After all it was her mess and she liked it that way.

Sylvia was obviously undergoing a culture shock. 'Perhaps it would be better if I came back later?' she said a little faintly.

To give me time to clear up? Anita thought. No fear. Aloud, she said, 'I don't mind if you don't mind, Mrs. Gosthwaite. Would you like a cup of tea?'

'Oh!' exclaimed Sylvia, as if Anita had suggested sending out for a gigolo. 'Well—that would be lovely, thank you.'

'I'll put the kettle on.'

'Don't you have a maid?'

'No, I do without.'

'In that case please don't go to the trouble.'

'It's no trouble, Mrs. Gosthwaite. It won't take a moment. Please do sit down—but not on that chair! It's liable to collapse. Sorry! The sofa's probably safest. Half a tick. I'll just move these books.'

While Sylvia perched, Anita went into the kitchen and waited for the kettle to boil. 'You are not to let her intimidate you,' said her Alice voice; and having made the tea and loaded a tin tray, she padded back barefoot into the front parlor.

She sat down and poured the tea. 'I hope you don't mind it strong, Mrs. Gosthwaite. This Sliema water tastes so filthy one has to disguise it.'

Sylvia smiled weakly. Anita felt sorry for her. She made a mental note that she must never on any account allow herself to marry a naval officer.

'I expect you're wondering why I've come,' Sylvia said.

Anita smiled sweetly, and waited.

Sylvia took a little breath, was about to say something, changed her mind and then started again. 'The reason I've come is that we are worried about you.'

'There's no need, Mrs. Gosthwaite. I'm managing perfectly well.'

'That may be so, but it is not just a question of how you are managing. It is a question of what you are becoming.'

'Oh? What am I becoming?'

'Now please don't be hostile, Anita. I'm saying this for your good, not mine.'

'I really don't know how to tell you this any other way but bluntly, my dear. The fact of the matter is that you have been seen alone here in Sliema.'

'Is that so surprising? I live in Sliema.'

'That's not what I meant at all. I don't think you appreciate how vulnerable a woman is if she goes out alone in a naval port on a Saturday night when the fleet's in.'

'Oh. I *see*.'

'Yes.'

'I have never once been approached or pestered.'

'Perhaps not, but you've been seen on your own in an area full of bars and sailors. Surely you must realize how risky that is? How harmful it could be to your good name?'

'I don't think I have any good name left, Mrs. Gosthwaite.'

'Don't be so silly! Of course you do! Nothing at all has been said about the reasons for your departure from Villa Rosa. As far as I am concerned that is water under the bridge. But we do still feel responsible for you. We agreed to have you as our guest. When we heard that you had been seen wandering about alone on the Sliema front, naturally we were concerned.'

Anita shrugged. 'All I can say is that what people think of me is entirely a matter for them.'

'No. That is not so. It is of concern to us, too. Whether you like it or not, we bear a responsibility for you. If we see that you are in moral danger, we have to act to protect you. If you come to any harm, it will reflect directly on us. Do you understand?'

Anita reflected that it would hardly assist Gosthwaite's promotion chances if his charge were to be branded as a loose woman. 'Yes,' she said demurely. 'Yes, I do understand that, Mrs. Gosthwaite.'

'Oh, I am glad, my dear! I was so worried that you might show me the door. Now let's really try to heal the wound, so to speak, shall we? As I said, your reputation on the island is unsullied. You may be regarded in certain quarters as an unusual personality, but of course in some ways that is what you are. But don't you think that it might be an idea to play your part in the social life of the island again? Our friends are constantly asking after you, and we could have accepted any number of invitations on your behalf these past three months. Such a pity. But it can't be helped. What's done is done, isn't it? Have you heard from your parents lately?'

'About three weeks ago. They—'

'And what about the divorce? Has there been any further progress?'

'That's still going through, yes. I shall probably—'

'Well that's good news, isn't it? When that happens you will be able to start again as it were, won't you? My dear—I know you must think me just another brainless naval wife, but I do have eyes in my head. I know how difficult it was for you during your time with us at Vila Rosa, and on reflection I think it was courageous of you to take the decision you did, even though your reasons for it were somewhat misjudged. All right. I have said what I wanted to say on that subject, so let's leave it well alone, shall we? Now. I don't think you've met SNOIC, have you? Rear Admiral Bartelot. He's an awfully nice man. Well, he's invited us to have a picnic on his barge next Saturday and has asked us to bring you along. Now wait a minute! Before you refuse out of hand, can I persuade you to think about this? Brian Bartelot is such a splendid chap. He and the commodore have known each other for the best part of forty years. It won't be at all formal, just a very jolly picnic and probably swimming too, with supper and dancing to gramophone records afterwards at the admiral's residence. Ben Moberly—the flag lieutenant—will be there and his fiancée Lady Margaret Hennessy—do you know her? And we'll invite another young officer to even up the numbers. Please say you'll come. It will be so good for you to get out and meet people of your own sort again. The commodore says I'm not to take no for an answer. He says you are to treat it as a royal command. And please—do remember that even if you may have been embarrassed in the past, men are men, and they do seem to find you extremely attractive. I think we have to make allowances from time to time. Don't you?'

A little before midday on Saturday, Anita walked down to the naval landing stage on Sliema Creek, where she was joined by the Gosthwaites and Lady Margaret Hennessy. The commodore was very courteous, and Sylvia a little nervous. Lady Margaret said hello. They had met briefly during the season the previous year. 'Please do call me Maggie,' she said. 'Everybody does.'

After a short delay, the barge appeared. It made a wide sweep and was brought expertly alongside so that it stopped dead in the water six inches clear of the quay and exactly parallel to it.

'Hello everybody!' said the admiral.

'Hello Brian!' said Sylvia. 'Isn't it a glorious day?'

Gosthwaite, in blazer and white flannels, stiffened to attention. 'Good morning, sir!'

'Morning Fudge!' replied the admiral.

Sylvia convulsed with giggles. 'Oh darling,' she said, 'I haven't heard you called that in years!'

'Morning, sir!' said Flags to Gosthwaite. 'Morning ma'am.'

Sylvia introduced Anita to the admiral.

'Where's Michael?' asked the flag lieutenant.

'Parking the Morris,' said Maggie. 'He won't be a tick.'

Sylvia turned to Anita. 'Mike is such a card. I'm sure you'll get on famously.'

'Shall we embark stores?' suggested the admiral.

The hampers and baskets were handed across, and the flag lieutenant helped Sylvia aboard. Maggie was next, and just as she was being helped aboard, Mike arrived. Anita recognized him immediately. 'Mrs. Walmshurst,' he said without any apparent surprise. 'Mike Purdy. We've met, have we not? At the Marsa Club, wasn't it?'

He must surely have known she would be on the picnic, and she had little doubt that he had pulled strings with the Gosthwaites to get himself invited. She might have felt inclined to forgive and forget had there been any small trace of apology or regret or even embarrassment in his manner, but that was not the case. Quite the reverse: he gave her the impression of being inordinately pleased with himself.

She felt tricked and angry. She didn't want to embarrass the Gosthwaites in front of the admiral, but she had a strong feeling that if she went on this picnic a much greater embarrassment might ensue. If she had learnt one thing over the past year it was that it was always better to take a hard decision early than an even harder one later.

'Yes,' she said. 'We have met, and I'm sorry, but I would prefer not to renew the acquaintance.'

She tried to attract Sylvia's attention, but Sylvia was being careful to look the other way. 'Mrs. Gosthwaite! I'm sorry, but I'm going to have to drop out.'

No one appeared to hear. Sylvia and her husband were sitting on the cushioned bench in the bows of the barge, looking out across the creek at the destroyers.

The flag lieutenant offered his hand to Anita. 'May I help you aboard, Mrs. Walmshurst?'

'No,' she said, loudly and clearly. 'I am very sorry; I have decided not to come on the picnic.'

The chatter ceased. Gosthwaite muttered something to his wife. Sylvia hopped out of the barge with remarkable agility, took Anita by the arm, and drew her a few paces away. She spoke in an urgent whisper.

'Now what is all this nonsense about?'

'It is not nonsense, Mrs. Gosthwaite. I've decided not to come on the picnic, that's all.'

'Why, in heaven's name?'

'Because I'm not prepared to share the same boat with Lieutenant Purdy.'

'What do you mean by that?'

'I mean that I do not wish to renew his acquaintance, Mrs. Gosthwaite.'

'But Michael is a delightful chap! He asked particularly to be introduced to you.'

'I'm afraid that only makes matters worse.'

Sylvia Gosthwaite closed her eyes and took a deep breath. 'This is outrageous! How dare you embarrass the commodore in this way? How dare you?'

'I am the one who is embarrassed, Mrs. Gosthwaite. If you had told me that you were inviting Lieutenant Purdy, I would not have accepted your invitation.'

Sylvia tried another approach. 'Is it because you're shy of him?'

'No, I just don't want to be in the same boat with him. If you want me on this picnic, ask him to drop out.'

Sylvia glanced back at the barge. The admiral and his guests were studiously looking the other way, but the petty officer coxswain was standing up in the stern sheets staring across at them.

'That's out of the question.'

'In that case I'm sorry, but my decision stands.'

'This is your last chance, you know. If you don't come today, you won't get another invitation from us.'

'I accept that.'

Sylvia shrugged and shook her head. They went back to the barge. Anita said, 'May I have my basket, please? I'm not coming, after all.'

The flag lieutenant said quietly, 'You can't do this, you know. It's just not done.'

'I've just done it,' said Anita. 'May I have the basket?'

'Come along, Mrs. Walmshurst!' roared the admiral. 'All aboard!'

She looked up at him. 'I apologize, Admiral. But I have no alternative but to drop out. I'm so sorry.'

'Right, well!' roared Admiral Bartelot, as if shouting could disperse embarrassment. 'No one is forcing anyone to do anything. If Mrs. Walmshurst doesn't want to accompany us that is entirely up to her.' He looked aft, over his shoulder. 'Coxswain!'

'Sir!' answered the coxswain.

'Carry on, Petty Officer Jannaway.'

For only a brief instant, as the barge moved away from the landing and Frank looked back to make sure the stern was clear, their eyes met; and then his back was turned again and the barge was heading off down the creek, and boatswain's calls aboard the destroyers were piping the 'still' as the admiral and his picnic guests passed by.

Well, said her Alice voice as she walked back into Sliema, you've certainly burnt your bridges now, haven't you?

She sat down at a table outside Azzopardi's, one of the smarter bar-restaurants which overlooked the creek, and treated herself to a coffee and a custard tart.

Life, it seemed to her, was like going down a canyon in a canoe. She had no control over the force of the blind, relentless maelstrom in which she found herself, only a minuscule power over her personal canoe. All she could do, it seemed, was try to keep it pointing in the right direction and enjoy the ride.

What would happen next? It would certainly be interesting to see. There were times, and this was one of them, when she had the feeling that she was playing a minor part in a Greek comedy. She half expected that at any moment a chorus would pop up from behind the bar among the bottles of Bols and Green Chartreuse, and explain to her what the devil was going on. But then she reflected that the fascination of Greek drama lies in the fact that, while the audience is kept fully informed about what will happen, the characters play out their parts in ignorance of the ironic inevitability of the fate that awaits them. When looked at in this way, the choice of whether or not to contact Frank and try to renew the acquaintance—which, let's face it, was what she was trying to decide—was no longer one between right or wrong or even between acting wisely and acting foolishly. It was nothing more than a toss of a coin.

What was more, whether the coin came down heads or tails would make not the slightest 'difference' to the 'future,' because the way the coin came down was itself a part of that future. So whether she wrote a note inviting Frank to meet her or not made no 'difference' to anything. If she did contact him, she had always been going to, and if she didn't, she had never been going to. If they were destined to meet, they would meet, and if they weren't, they wouldn't. It was as simple as that.

'And anyway,' her Alice-in-Wonderland voice told her as she left Azzopardi's and turned off the waterfront to walk up the hill to Don Rua Street, 'you'd like to drop him a line, wouldn't you?'

'Yes I certainly would,' she replied. So she did.

19

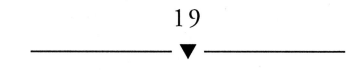

Frank sat on a rock in his best tropical whites cleaning his nails with a matchstick and thinking about Anita.

It was the hottest time of a very hot day. A gentle swell was slapping half-heartedly on the shingle of Tigne beach, and the sun's light was glinting and shimmering on a dark green sea. On the horizon, the mirage of a ship hull-down seemed to float in mid air, and a little way from where he was sitting, in the shade of a brightly painted yellow and blue fishing boat, a mongrel bitch in whelp lay flat out, panting in the heat, snapping at the flies.

He gave up on his nails, took a battered green canvas wallet from his breast pocket, extracted a letter, and read it over to himself. It came from an address in Sliema and the date was given simply as 'Saturday':

Dear Frank,

I've just arrived back after abandoning ship. Did you recognize me? I think you did. Isn't it extraordinary? I had no idea you were in Malta, and would have contacted you before had I known. Anyway, better late than never. I would really love to meet you and find out what tricks Fate has been playing you. Do you know Tanti's bar overlooking Tigne beach? I go there sometimes to read when I need to escape from Sliema. We could meet there if you like. What about next Sunday afternoon at two o'clock? In any case, I shall be there from two to four, so if you're free do please let's rendezvous. It would be so good to meet you again and hear what you've been up to all these years. And I don't suppose we'll be lost for things to talk about, do you? See you at Tanti's on Sunday? I do hope so!

All the best,
Annie.

PS: In case you're wondering, although I'm Mrs. Walmshurst these days, I'm in the middle of a divorce. Oh dear. I hope this doesn't put you off. I'm still the same infuriating me!

He didn't know how many times he had read that letter, but it must have been into double figures. When it arrived, his first thought had been to ignore it, but there was something appealing and sincere about it, and he postponed a decision until the last moment.

It made him smile and stirred up all sorts of memories: of Miss Anita playing tennis with her cousins; Miss Anita on horseback coming along the lane on frosty mornings as he set out for school on his bike; Miss Anita staring at him at the village party after the coronation; Miss Anita swinging her legs when they went over to the Isle of Wight on the ferry; Miss Anita in her sailor suit on Bembridge beach....

He stood up and walked a hundred yards before strolling back, glancing up at the hotels and villas and guesthouses on the sea front to see if there was any sign of her. But no: the only person in sight was a girl in a yellow dress and a straw sunhat swinging her handbag in a rather abandoned way as she walked along. I wouldn't mind a bit of that, he thought to himself—and at the same moment realized with a shock that it was Anita.

He started up the beach towards her. She didn't see him at first, but when she did, she waved vigorously and ran to meet him.

'I'm late, aren't I?' she said as she came up. 'I'm so sorry. I locked myself out, and had to climb back in through the kitchen window to get my key.'

They walked back towards Tanti's bar. His heart was doing somersaults. He felt shy, frightened, and happy. Why me? He wondered. Why should she want to have anything to do with me?

He followed her into the bar and she chose a table under a fan. She took off her hat, shook her hair loose, and sat down. 'I don't know about you,' she said, 'but I'm absolutely terrified.'

'There's no need, Miss Anita. I'm just the same as ever I was.'

'Are you? I'm not sure if I am.' She laughed nervously. 'I don't know what to say. I don't even know where to begin.'

He saw her looking at his hands and was conscious of his broken nails. What does she think of me? he wondered. Not much, I shouldn't think.

Tanti came to take their order, bringing with him a waft of garlic and sweat. 'Sorry about this place,' Anita whispered. 'It was the only one I could think of where we could be private. What are you doing in Malta?'

'I'm the admiral's coxswain.'

'That sounds very grand.' She winced visibly. 'Sorry. That was condescending of me, wasn't it?'

'What about you, Miss Anita?'

She sighed. 'Well. I'm not Miss any more, and sometimes I wonder if I'm Anita.'

Their coffees arrived. She went suddenly quiet and stared down at the table; and when she eventually looked up at him her eyes were full of tears. She opened her bag and rummaged in it. 'Sorry. I'll pull myself together in a moment. Damn! No handkerchief!'

He produced a large, clean white one.

'What an idiot you must think I am!'

'Perhaps this wasn't such a good idea,' he said.

'Yes it was. It certainly was.' She swallowed and smiled. 'You know why I'm like this, don't you? It's because—well, it's just so wonderful to see you again.'

She had golden skin, fair hair, high cheekbones, astonishing dark blue eyes, and a figure to die for. She was as near perfection as he had ever seen.

'Can we sort one thing out straight away?' she said. 'No more "Miss Anita," agreed?'

He said that might be difficult.

'Well please try. Will you? It really makes me *very* uncomfortable. Anyway, never mind about all that. I'm just dying to hear what you've been doing all this time. Do you still play the piano?'

'A bit. Ship's concerts. That sort of thing.'

'What about reading? You used to read an awful lot, didn't you?'

'It's the seamanship manual mostly, these days.'

'And you haven't found yourself a wife?'

'I can't afford one.'

She sipped her coffee. She wore no rings or jewelry. Her fingernails were unvarnished and perfectly shaped, like blanched almonds.

'One of the reasons I wanted to meet,' she said, apparently unaware of the effect she was having on him, 'was that there's something I wanted to say to you. It's long overdue, I'm afraid. I want to apologize for what happened. It was quite unjust of my father to send you off into the Navy like that.'

He shrugged and said nothing.

'Did you feel very bitter?'

He said there was no point in raking all that up.

'The place was never the same after you left, you know. It wasn't just at Meonford Hall, either. It was the whole village. They were all on your side. And then the Roughsedge boy—Alan, wasn't it?—was killed in that awful motor accident. You and he were quite close, weren't you?'

'Yes,' he said. 'We were good pals.'

A priest in a grubby soutane sat down at the next table and ordered a cognac. He looked hard at Anita and licked a blob of saliva from his lip. She glanced back at him with some contempt, and lowered her voice. 'Did you know that poor old Tom Roughsedge lost *all* his sons? Walter was killed only a week before the armistice.' She sighed and shook her head. 'All sorts of rumors went round after Alan died. It was perfectly obvious that whoever did it must have turned straight round and gone back to wherever he'd come from, because there were tire marks in the entrance to a field quite near where it happened. There was a police investigation, but nothing ever came of it. I think they were warned not to look too hard.'

He shook his head, shifting uncomfortably. 'It's got nothing to do with me, Miss Anita.'

She reached across the table and touched his hand. 'I think it has everything to do with you. Don't you see? The upper class always closes ranks to protect itself. For the working class, there's no redress. You have to take what you're given, like it or lump it.' She glanced at the priest, who was studiously looking the other way. 'You know who they say was at the wheel of that car?'

'No?'

'Roddy.'

He didn't know what to say, so said nothing.

'And I think he may well have been responsible for your being sent into the Navy, as well. They found that letter of mine in your room, didn't they? If anyone should have been sent away, it should have been me.'

He remained silent. This was stuff he had put away and forgotten about years before.

'It's so unjust,' she was saying. 'Don't you feel an urge to *do* something about it?'

'I couldn't even if I wanted to. I'd join the Labor Movement if we were allowed. But they've banned the lower deck from forming societies, and we're not allowed to write to our MPs, or the papers, or belong to any sort of political party. It's all forbidden by King's Regulations. In any case, I'm not that political. Not any more.'

'Were you?'

'Oh yes.'

'Why did you change?'

'There's no point, is there? Politics…it's a futile waste of time. You talk about the upper classes oppressing the working class. Well, look at Lloyd George. The way I see it, as soon as people of working class get political power, they cease to be working class, don't they?'

'But don't you agree that the only way to achieve fair shares for all is through a socialist system?'

'Perhaps it is, but it's also pie in the sky.'

The priest was obviously listening in to their conversation. Anita glanced at him. 'It needn't be,' she said. 'Not if the working classes unite. Not if there's a single, unified campaign. Have you read the Communist manifesto? It's positively exhilarating.'

'I'm not that political, Miss Anita.'

'Please don't call me that! Can't you call me Annie?' She leant forward and whispered, 'Shall we go?'

'What a revolting specimen!' she remarked as they walked out into the sunshine. 'He made my skin crawl! Now, then. What do you say? A walk along the beach?'

'Can I make a condition?'

'Go on.'

'No more politics?'

'Done!' she said, and caught his hand, and held it.

They crossed the road and picked their way over the rocks, past brightly colored fishing boats with high prows. The barriers between them came down. He felt increasingly at ease in her company, and he sensed that she felt the same about him. He managed not to call her Miss Anita, and she managed to stay off her political soap box.

She told him about her impending divorce, and being sent out to Malta, and why she was living in digs. She was inclined to chatter on, and he loved it. He felt immensely proud that this beautiful woman was walking at his side, and touched by her warmth and infectious gaiety. He had never experienced anything like it.

They stood looking out over the shimmering sea. Annie—he was calling her that now—picked a small flat stone and sent it skipping out to the horizon.

'Isn't it a funny world?' she said. 'When I saw you last week, in an odd sort of way, I wasn't surprised. It was as if I already *knew* that we would meet. How much longer will you be in Malta?'

'Well,' he said, 'Up until yesterday I expected to be here for another two years. But now I'm not so sure.'

'Don't say you're about to leave just when we've met!'

'I don't know. It's not certain.'

'If you do have to leave, will that be good news or bad?'

'Good, I suppose. Depends how you look at it.'

'You don't sound very sure.'

'I'm not.'

She gave him a push. 'Stop being so cagey! What's all this about?'

'I may be promoted.'

'To chief petty officer?'

'No, this is different. It's something called the Mate Scheme.'

She went into peals of laughter. 'What on earth's that when it's at home?'

He picked up a stone and threw it out over the sea as far as he could. 'They want to see if they can turn me into an officer.'

'Why didn't you tell me before?'

'Well, it's early days.'

'You really are terribly self-effacing. Did you know that?'

'Only with you, Annie. I'm quite different when I'm in charge of a sea boat.'

She said she thought he would make an excellent officer. He said that he had a long way to go before it came about—if it came about.

'It will,' she said. 'I'm sure it will.'

They walked on in silence. He was just wishing that he hadn't told her about the Mate Scheme when she turned to him and said, 'Come back and have a sticky bun at my place. Will you?'

She gave him an iced bun with butter and a cup of tea, and asked him to play the piano. 'I had it tuned,' she told him, 'but it's a bit jangly. When did you last play?'

'In public? Last Christmas. Remember this one?'

'More please,' she said when he finished.

'Something more modern?'

'Can you?'

'How about this?

She leant over his shoulder as he played. Her hair touched his cheek. For a moment her breast brushed against his shoulder.

'What is this?'

'Ragtime.'

'Where did you learn it?'

'I picked it up off a gramophone record.'

'Can you play the Charleston?'

He obliged. If there was any ice left to be broken, that broke it. 'Budge up,' she said. 'Let's play Chopsticks.'

He became a regular visitor. He was allowed all-night leave, so as soon as he was no longer required for duty he walked out through the main gate of the shore establishment known as HMS *Egmont*, down the causeway from Manoel Island and into Sliema, where he stopped at Grech's to buy two iced buns or a bag of Garibaldi biscuits before walking up through the back streets to Number 33.

He was in love. There was no doubt of that. Perhaps Anita was as well, but she never admitted it. Frank wasn't sure where it would lead, and didn't want to question it. All that mattered was that in Annie's company he was really happy for the first time in his life.

He loved it when she caught his hand and they walked along together like a couple of children. That was what was so wonderful about her. She made him feel as if he were ten years old again. Through her, he recaptured some of that sense of innocence he had known in his first years at Meonford Hall, before Roddy pulled him down off the boundary wall and assaulted him.

There was a day when they took a bus and explored along the coast towards St. Paul's Bay. The summer was ending, but the sea was still warm. They took a picnic down a tortuous cliff path to a tiny, rocky beach, where they swam together and lay in the sun together and later walked hand in hand back to the road to wait for the bus.

Bumping back to Sliema, she told him about Basil. He asked why she had married him in the first place. 'Because I was stupid,' she said. 'Stupid and ambitious.'

'Ambitious?'

'Baz said he'd put me on the stage in the West End within the year if I married him. So I sold my birthright for a mess of pottage. Unfortunately it turned out to be all mess and no pottage.' She interlocked her fingers with his and drew his hand up to her lips. He saw her in profile. She had a defiant way of holding her head back and her chin up.

'Annie,' he said quietly. 'I think I ought to tell you something.'

'What?'

'I've fallen in love with you.'

'Oh good,' she said. 'I was so hoping that you would.'

At the end of November he heard that he was to attend the Commander-in-Chief's selection board for the Mate Scheme. When he told Annie, she immediately offered to help him prepare for it.

'They'll want to see if you have the right attitude,' she told him. 'I mean "right" from their point of view.'

He said that he couldn't put on any sort of act.

'I know,' she said. 'All the same, you have to put yourself in the best light, don't you? If I know anything about naval officers, they'll be more interested in whether you'll adapt to wardroom life than whether you can lower a sea boat in a hurricane without drowning the ship's cat. After all, they already know you can handle a sea boat, don't they? But will you fit into a wardroom? That's what they want to know. It doesn't matter so much what answers you give to their questions. What matters is the way you answer them, the sort of person you appear to be. They'll want to find out things like what soap you use, whether you keep your fingernails clean and whether you drop the right aitches. Don't laugh! I'm serious!'

'I can't pretend to be something I'm not.'

'I'm not suggesting you should try. But if you want to be an officer, you'll have to learn how an officer thinks and behaves.'

'You want to turn me into a gentleman?'

'No, because in a sense—the best sense—you are one already. What I'm saying is that you've got to add a bit of—I don't know. Spit and polish.'

He said there was no harm in that.

'For a start, there's your speech.'

'What speech?'

'I mean your way of speaking.'

'My accent?'

'Yes, but the way you say things as well.'

'For example?'

'Well, just now you said, "No harm in that." That isn't officer language.'

'So what should I say?'

'Well you mustn't drop any aitches that shouldn't be dropped, for a start. And try to clip your vowels a bit.'

He put on an officer's accent. 'One can see no objection in that course of action?'

'Well, don't overdo it. And don't show your teeth when you smile. Officers never relax. You've got to look, I don't know—'

'Taut?'

'Exactly. Pretend you're an admiral.'

'Kiss me, Hardy. Every man must do his duty.'

'I couldn't agree more,' she said, and kissed him.

'Frank?' she said a little while later when they paused for breath.

'What?'

'Come to bed with me.'

She was still working in the Fleet Intelligence Office, but as soon as work was over for the day she raced back to Number 33; and as soon as he arrived they used to shut out the world, fall into each other's arms, and make love.

When they weren't making love they talked, played the piano, went for midnight walks, played silly games, and fell asleep cuddled up together, with the gregale rattling the shutters and moaning under the eaves outside.

They enjoyed the same music, the same books, and the same humor. They talked endlessly: about their childhood at Meonford Hall, her father, his mother, class, sex, religion, life, death, the theatre, philosophy, psychology, mysticism, art, war, and—very occasionally—the Navy.

One evening a week before Christmas, he arrived at her place to find her in tears. She had received a letter from her father to say that Basil had committed suicide.

'He's written a letter to me,' she said. 'I haven't been able to bring myself to open it. I've been sitting here staring at it for the past hour.'

He broke the seal, took out the letter, and read it aloud.

Poppy darling,

This is just to say goodbye and good luck. Sorry it had to end in tears, but that's the way of the world. Now, I have an Appointment in Samarra, as Willie Maugham might put it, but before I set off I would like you to know why I've decided to go. The reason, my dear, is that I can't bear the thought of being a divorcee. So infra-dig, don't you think? Also, I've had enough of bronchitis every winter, not to mention my unending battle with General Disapproval and the awareness of the omni-present copper on the corner. There is, however, one plum left in this sorry old pudding, and I've kept it for you. As you know, I managed to fight off your divorce suit, so I shall depart this world with the appearance, if not the reality, of respectability. You will also know that I have no dependants. The chancellor and his forty thieves will take much of the loot I fear, but the house in Cadogan Square will be yours and there should be a tidy sum left over for you as well. Make the most of it, Poppy. It's a quick little life, when all is said and done, which in my case, it is.

By the way, I still believe you have the makings of a great actress, so don't hide your what's-it under a thing-a-me-jig will you? You can always use this letter as an introduction, if push comes to shove.

Yours to the end of time. I really did love you, and love you still.

Basil.

'I don't know why I'm crying,' Annie said. 'I didn't love him one little bit. He was just a dirty old man.' She sighed and thought for a moment, then added rather wistfully, 'But a very funny and generous one.'

She cabled her father for a loan pending the release of the probate and on the strength of it took Frank into Valletta to do some shopping. They went to Mr. Mamo, a cutter for Gieves who did a bit of moonlighting on his own account. She had him fitted out with a new serge uniform in which to attend the selection interview, together with new shoes, shirts, neckties, and stiff white collars with slightly cut-away edges to replace his old fashioned ones. She ordered a white sharkskin dinner jacket for him and for Christmas gave him a set of jet shirt studs and matching cuff links.

They booked a table for dinner at the Hotel Phoenicia on New Year's Eve, and dined on duck. When they took to the floor for the first time he was able to surprise her, as he had had plenty of practice on dance floors since the war ended.

'It's a good thing the selection board won't see you dancing,' she told him.

'Don't I come up to scratch?'

'Quite the reverse. You're too good. Most naval officers tread on one's toes and knock over the furniture.'

Just before midnight, they walked out to the Baracca gardens and stood on the parapet looking out over Grand Harbor. The fleet was in and the ships were dressed with strings of lights. 'Do you remember the fleet review after the coronation?' Annie said. 'Father got into a terrible stew because they got in a muddle over the royal salute. And then we got stuck on the mud. That was when poor Gert was sacked, wasn't it? Do you remember?'

'Of course.'

'You two were close, weren't you?'

'Yes.'

'My governess called her a *femme fatale*. I think she went on the streets. Poor Gert. Poor, lovely Gert.'

Bells rang and fireworks zipped into the night sky, their explosions echoing back and forth across the harbor. As they hugged and kissed and wished each other a Happy New Year, he wondered how long this extraordinary affair of theirs would last.

The Mate Scheme selection board was convened on board the C-in-C's flagship, HMS *Iron Duke*, on the second Monday of January. At seven-thirty that morning, Frank and three other candidates assembled at Customs House Steps, where they were collected by a motor cutter and taken out to the flagship. The interview was held in the Court Martial room. The board consisted of the fleet gunnery officer, the fleet signals officer, the fleet paymaster, and the fleet surgeon. The president of the board was Commodore Gosthwaite.

He was the first to be called in. He stood to attention, looked Gosthwaite in the eye, and said, 'Petty Officer Jannaway reporting for interview, sir.'

Gosthwaite pointed to the upright chair. 'Sit down, Jannaway. What qualities do you suppose you will need as an officer?'

'Leadership qualities, sir. The ability to set an example to the men. And also, the ability to fit into wardroom life.'

'Do you think you have those qualities?'

He paused deliberately, again looked Gosthwaite directly in the eye and said, 'Yes I do, sir.'

'What sports do you play?'

'Football and cricket, sir.'

'Any other interests?'

He had discussed this with Annie. She had said that he was sure to be asked about his interests, and if he said he liked reading, he was bound to be asked what books he had read, which might take him onto easier ground. 'Give them an author they'll recognize,' Annie said, so they went through a list: James, Forster, Stevenson, Hardy, Dickens, Maugham, and HG Wells. But they were all socialist, liberal, or homosexual. Eventually he suggested Kipling. Just the man,' Annie said. 'You can't go wrong with Kipling. All that bit about walking with kings and not losing the common touch. They'll love it.'

Gosthwaite was waiting for an answer.

'I play the piano,' he told him. 'And I enjoy reading.'

The fleet paymaster rose immediately to the bait. 'What do you read?'

'I like Kipling, sir.'

'Which is your favorite?'

'*Captains Courageous*, sir.'

'Good choice, good choice,' murmured the fleet surgeon, and he knew that he had at least one ally on the board.

The fleet gunnery officer asked: 'I see you were twice mentioned in dispatches. When was that?'

'When I was serving in HMS *Campion* in 1915 and in HMS *Essex* in 1916, sir.'

'The latter at Jutland, I take it?'

'Yes, sir.'

'What was your opinion of the outcome of Jutland?'

'I think one has to regard it as more of a win on points than a knock-out, sir.'

The commodore was whispering to the fleet paymaster. They studied his service documents.

'I see your next-of-kin address is given as Meonford Hall,' said Gosthwaite.

'Yes, sir.'

'Isn't that Sir Jervis Yarrow's country seat?'

'Yes, sir. My mother is in service there, sir.'

'How long has she been there?'

'About twenty years, sir.'

'So you spent your childhood there.'

'Yes, sir. From the age of five.'

'Did you ever sail aboard Sir Jervis Yarrow's yacht?' asked the fleet signals officer.

'Yes, sir.'

'What was her name?'

'*Clover* sir. I crewed aboard her at Cowes in 1910.'

'Did you win?' asked the fleet paymaster.

'No, sir. We gybed and lost the topmast.'

The fleet surgeon beamed. 'I remember that very well. I was sailing with Lord Wandsworth, and we lost our mainsail. The Kaiser was racing that day, wasn't he?'

'Yes, sir. We nearly collided with him, but he gave way at the last moment.'

'Were you close-hauled?' asked the fleet gunnery officer.

'Yes, sir. We were on the starboard tack and the Kaiser was on the port. Pun not intended, sir.'

There was a mild show of levity among the members of the board, which Gosthwaite put a stop to by asking, 'You're not married are you?'

'No, sir.'

'Likely to?'

'No, sir.'

'Glad to hear it,' said Gosthwaite. 'What is the name of the Commander-in-Chief of the Mediterranean Fleet?'

He was completely flummoxed.

'Well?'

The fleet surgeon tipped his chair back and mouthed the name to him.

'Admiral de Robeck, sir.'

'Thank you, Jannaway,' said Gosthwaite. 'That will be all.'

A week later, his divisional officer informed him that he had passed the interview and was to be drafted back to England in April to start the Mate's Course at the beginning of May.

He managed to get three days' local leave at the end of March and they went to Gozo. The fields and hedgerows were ablaze with wild flowers. For two days they walked and talked and picked flowers and dreamt of the future. Annie had booked a passage back to England, and was to leave the following week; and three days after that Frank was to take passage home in a cruiser that was paying off in Portsmouth. After that he was due three weeks' leave before starting his course.

They picnicked in a field of poppies and daisies. Annie was in her yellow dress, the one he loved. She lay back, a flower among flowers, lifting one hand to shade her eyes from the sun. 'Let's go on a holiday during your leave,' she said. 'Let's go and build sandcastles on a beach somewhere.'

'Where?'

'Somewhere neither of us have been. What about Bude?'

'We could be very rude in Bude.'

'Or without a care in Weston-super-Mare.'

He rolled over to face her. 'Would you give me a short time in Newcastle-under-Lyme?'

'Really Jannaway! How shockingly vulgar!'

'Beg pardon, m'lady.'

'Now stop being silly and tell me: where shall we go on our last day together? Could you bear to come to the Marsa Club with me?'

He wasn't keen.

'Do let's! They do a curry lunch on Sundays. We don't have to talk to anyone.'

'Just see and be seen?'

'Why not? We can have gin slings and watch the chinless wonders playing polo.'

'No 'arm in that, oi reckon, m'lady.'

She shivered. 'Now you've made me go all slippy-sloppy in the larder.'

'Shall we do something about it?'

'Here?'

'Why not?'

'I never made love in a field before,' she remarked later. 'What about you?'

'Only once.'

'Oh, trust you! Where was this field?'

'Near Lowestoft.'

'Was she nice?'

'Not bad.'

'What was her name?'

'Wilma. She was a nurse. I asked her to marry me, but she said no.'

'During the war?'

'Yes.'

'After your ship was sunk?'

'That's right.'

'What was the war *like* Frank? You never *ever* talk about it, did you know that?'

He lay on his back, and looked at the sky, and the memories flooded back.

'I wish you *would* talk about it,' Annie said.

'There's nothing to say,' he replied. 'It's all been said.'

They abandoned the idea of lunch at the Marsa Club and took a picnic to Birzebuggia instead. That evening, he helped her pack. They talked through the night; and at five o'clock in the morning he slipped out of the house for the last time and walked down through Sliema and over the causeway to Manoel Island.

Three days later he stood on the gun-deck of an elderly cruiser, looking astern as the islands of Malta and Gozo slipped away beneath the eastern horizon.

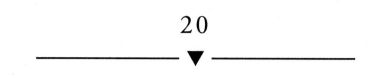

20

On his arrival at Portsmouth, Frank was told that all leave had been cancelled on account of the miners' strike, and that he was to report forthwith to the Royal Naval Barracks for duty with Number Two Naval Reserve Battalion. When he arrived he found scenes reminiscent of those at the outbreak of war. Lorries were loading and unloading bedding and stores, warrant officers were strutting about in khaki gaiters shouting orders, and queues of doleful looking reservists were queuing up to be issued with hammocks and appointed to their duties.

Under the command of Captain Kennedy, Number Two Naval Reserve Battalion was organized on army lines. Frank was appointed as senior rating in Number Four platoon of 'B' company. His platoon commander was an absurdly young looking lieutenant called Crockett, who told him, with a big smile, that he had been required to cancel his honeymoon on the day of his wedding. 'I shall rely heavily on you, Petty Officer Jannaway,' he said. 'I understand you've been selected for the Mate Scheme? Well, this is your chance to show your leadership qualities. I intend to make Four Platoon the best in the battalion, and I can't do that without your assistance.' It quickly became apparent that the whole concept of that ill-fated battalion was fatally flawed. Everyone hated being treated as soldiers, many were in sympathy with the strikers, and no one liked being taken out of their civilian jobs and put back into uniform.

Most of the reservist petty officers were lacking in confidence. One of them, an elderly, quietly spoken man who worked on the production line at the Morris motor car factory in Oxford, pointed out one of the reservist able seamen to Frank and said, 'I'm his superior here, but when I get back to the factory, he's my foreman.'

They had three days to organize themselves before being dispatched by the night train to Newport in Wales. They arrived at their quarters in the Stow Municipal School in the early morning, to discover that no meals had been arranged, no sleeping billets were ready, and all the bedding had been left behind in Portsmouth. No breakfast or midday meal was available, so all ratings were sent into the town with vouchers to buy themselves something to eat. At the end of a fourteen-hour working day, the men had no option but to sleep without bedding on the hard floors of the school class rooms.

An atmosphere of resentment and anger at such incompetence quickly developed, and was shown by acts of passive resistance. No one bothered to salute the officers and everyone seemed hard of hearing when orders were given.

As the cooking equipment hadn't arrived, field kitchens were obtained from the army; but no one liked army victuals and the kitchens and eating arrangements were inadequate to feed upwards of a thousand men.

There was worse to come. Washing and sanitary arrangements were also inadequate, and within days of the battalion's arrival a quarter of the people were suffering from diarrhea. The stink in the heads was abominable.

On top of all this leave was severely restricted. Because of the tense situation in the town no night leave was granted.

The battalion was just beginning to settle into a routine when it was ordered to move to a disused box factory in the dockland outside the town, so that getting into Newport on day leave would be rendered virtually impossible. One company was left to clear up the school. The remaining four companies marched to the new quarters behind a borrowed army band. As they approached the main gates of the box factory, they saw that the whole place was surrounded by high barbed wire fences, and the word went round that the battalion had been sent there as a punishment for slack discipline.

The plan was that the men should be given a packed lunch, which they carried with them and which they would eat as soon as they had stowed their kit in their new quarters. They would then be fallen in on the parade ground, issued with clean hammocks, and provided with a hot meal as soon as it was ready.

This plan was wrecked by another administrative muddle, because the chefs, misunderstanding the order of the day, had gone out of their way to get the meal ready as early as possible, so when the bugle sounded off for the men to fall in for the issue of clean hammocks, it was ignored, because the hot meal was already being served and the mess hall was full of hungry people who were looking forward to steak and kidney pie and who had no intention whatsoever of obeying the order to fall in. It was collective disobedience on a large scale.

Jannaway was summoned by Lieutenant Crockett.

'Right, Petty Officer Jannaway,' he said. 'We shall go into the mess hall, you and I, and you are to call out the members of Four Platoon by name. Is that understood?'

'Understood, sir.'

'Good. Fall in beside me. Are you ready? Bags of bull. By the left, quick, march!'

Off they went, side by side, across the parade ground; and as they entered the mess hall they were greeted by a massive cheer that sent a shiver up Frank's spine. They marched to the head of the hall and halted. Crockett gave Frank a brief nod. He looked down the tables and picked out where Number Four Platoon was sitting. He knew them all by name, and the first man he chose to call out was an able seaman who he knew needed to keep out of trouble.

'Able Seaman Shields! Fall in on the parade ground!'

There were shouts of 'No! No! Why can't we finish our dinners?'

'Fall in, Able Seaman Shields!'

Shields began to get to his feet. There were shouts of 'Sit down!' and 'Scab!'

Frank waited for the noise to die down, and then repeated the order quietly: 'Able Seaman Shields, I am giving you a direct order. Fall in on the parade ground.'

Shields stood up and walked quickly down between the tables, and out of the mess hall.

'Able Seaman Cartwright! Fall in!'

Cartwright followed him. With his heart thundering in his chest, Frank called out more names, until the whole of the remainder of the platoon stood up and obeyed the order.

But that wasn't the end of it. Eight hundred men were still in the mess hall and refusing to move. The commander said he would go in and talk to the men, but Captain Kennedy said he would speak to them himself. All the officers and petty officers accompanied him into the mess hall. As he entered, the whole place fell absolutely silent. He spoke quietly, but with immense authority, pointing out to them the seriousness of their action.

'You are now to go out and fall in with your hammocks,' he said. 'You will be inspected and issued with clean hammocks, after which the parade will be dismissed. I will then see two men from each platoon, who may represent to me personally any grievance in the battalion.'

It did the trick. Quietly, the men made their way out of the mess hall and onto the parade ground.

It was decided by Their Lordships that the battalion was not in a fit state of discipline to do the job assigned to it, so it was ordered back to Portsmouth in disgrace.

At the subsequent inquiry, Captain Kennedy was made the scapegoat. His career came to an abrupt end. He left the Royal Navy soon afterwards, but joined up again at the outbreak of war in 1939. He was placed in command of a lightly armed merchant ship on convoy escort duties, and went down with his ship in the North Sea in the first months of the war when he engaged two German battleships.

21

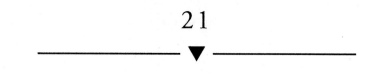

On a grey day in September, Frank traveled by train to Weymouth to join a coal-burning minesweeper in the Fishery Protection Squadron based at Portland. Looking out over the bleak harbor as the taxi sped along the Chesil causeway he thought to himself, well, this is it. My first ship as an officer.

He hadn't seen much of Annie during his Mate's Course. On her return to England she joined a repertory company and started traveling up and down the country, while he was stuck down in Devonport aboard a leaky old wooden ship that served as the Torpedo and Electrical School. They had a few snatched meetings, usually in railway hotels, and when her company came to Plymouth they managed a brief week-end together. But that was all.

It was raining. He paid off the taxi, turned up the collar of his raincoat, jammed his trilby hat more firmly on his head, picked up his suitcase, and walked down the jetty to where the four minesweepers were berthed side by side.

He knew what to expect, but the sight of the four converted trawlers with their tall funnels and tubby sterns caused a drop in the pit of his stomach all the same.

The rain beat down. He went over the brow to the inboard mine-sweeper and surprised a rating who was sitting dejectedly in a black oil-skin, rolling a cigarette. He crossed from boat to boat and boarded his new ship, HMS *Liffey*.

Nobody was about. He put his luggage down, walked aft, and had a look at the sweep deck; then plucked up courage and went in through a screen door and entered the wardroom, over whose door hung a mock pub sign: THE LIFFEY ARMS. Inside, a lieutenant and a sub lieutenant, their uniform jackets unbuttoned and cigarettes hanging out of their mouths, were playing crib with two women, one small and busty with frizzy hair, the other tall and angular with bitten fingernails.

The mess table, which was not much bigger than a large tea tray, was cluttered with bottles, glasses and ashtrays supplied by Watney's Brewery; and the tiny wardroom was filled with the smoke from their four cigarettes.

'Who are you?' asked the lieutenant.

'Acting Mate Jannaway, come aboard to join, sir.'

'My my!' said the busty lady with frizzy hair. 'We are posh.'

Both the captain and first lieutenant of *Liffey* were up from the lower deck. Lieutenant Finch, the captain, had been on the Zeebrugge raid and had been awarded the Distinguished Service Medal. He was a man who said little and drank much. From the start, he seemed to regard Frank with disdain. Barnett, the first lieutenant, was a commissioned boatswain with four rows of campaign medals. He was a chain smoker whose primary interests in life were women and alcohol. He had served in minesweepers throughout the war and had been blown up twice. He had curly black hair, a sulky face, and hooded eyelids.

Frank was put in charge of the cable deck, and he took over as explosives accounting officer, wine and tobacco caterer, and correspondence officer. He supervised the issue of rum every day, stood watches in the wheelhouse at sea, and acted as divisional officer to the stokers, and the torpedo electrician.

The ship was run on lines that bore no resemblance to what Frank had been taught on the Mate's Training Course. Barnett was on familiar terms with the chief boatswain's mate, a gnarled leading seaman called Inches, who in turn was on nick-name terms with the men.

One night when the ship was anchored in Torbay, the anchor dragged, and Frank took charge on the cable deck, assisted by Inches. They were veering more cable and he shouted an order that was not heard; so to get the rating's attention he called him by the nickname he readily responded to: 'Taff.'

The next morning, Barnett buttonholed him at stand-easy. 'I've just had Leading Seaman Inches come to see me with a complaint about you,

Mr. Jannaway,' he said. 'He says that you've been undermining his authority. He told me that last night you gave an order to a rating over his head, and that you called him by his nickname. True or false?'

'It was blowing hard, sir. I gave the order—'

'Don't give me a sob story, Mr. Jannaway. Is it true or isn't it?'

'It's true, sir.'

'In that case you're a fucking idiot.'

It was a cold, wet Christmas. He spent it on board at Portland, acting as the sole duty officer for the four minesweepers. He ate his Christmas dinner, such as it was, alone in the wardroom. On Boxing Day the signalman failed to appear in time for morning colors, so he had to hoist the ensign himself. Five minutes later, when the hands were supposed to turn to, no one appeared, so he went down to the mess deck, found Inches still in his hammock, and told him to turn out and report on deck immediately.

Inches appeared ten minutes later, unshaven.

'What's going on, Leading Seaman Inches? Why haven't the hands fallen in?'

'It's Boxing Day,' he said. 'In case you'd forgotten.'

'I know that. But the hands should have fallen in twenty minutes ago. Get them up here right away.'

Inches stared at him with unconcealed dislike before abruptly asking: 'Can I speak to you man-to-man, sir?'

He said 'yes' before he remembered the advice given on the Mate's course that he should never allow a rating to do such a thing.

Inches came closer and lowered his voice. 'Then just you listen here. You may have a ring on your arm, but I've served longer than you, and I'll not be made a fool of in front of junior rates by a jumped-up ex-PO who thinks he's God all bloody mighty. You're pushing your luck, you are. You're not liked in this ship. Not by the lads, nor by the skipper, nor by the Jimmy neither. If I was you I'd watch my step, see? Because if you go on the way you are, one of these days you might have a bad accident.'

He turned to go, but Frank shouted, 'Wait!' and he turned back. 'Now you listen to me,' Frank said. 'I didn't come down to the mess deck to make a fool of you. I came down to prevent you getting yourself into trouble. You told me what you would do in my shoes. Well, let me tell you what I'd do in yours. I'd go back down to the mess and get the hands turned to. I'd support the officer, because I'd know that one of these days I might need the officer to support me. Do you hear what I'm saying?'

Inches nodded, and mumbled, 'Yes.'

'That's the first and last time we speak man-to-man, Leading Seaman Inches. I'm now going to give you a direct order, and if you don't obey it straight away I shall take disciplinary action.' He stepped away a pace and raised his voice. 'Leading Seaman Inches! Go below and get the hands fallen in.'

Inches saluted, said 'Ay ay, sir,' and obeyed.

Frank walked aft to the stern and put his hands on the gunwale. He looked down at the thin gold rings he wore, one on each sleeve. He was gripping the gunwale so tightly that his knuckles were white. Gradually, he relaxed. He was shaking with relief.

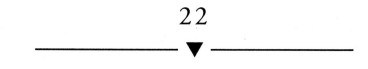

22

After two years at Dartmouth, Roddy moved back to the house in Hyde Park Square in order to attend the naval staff course at Greenwich.

Within days of his return, he and Geraldine were scrapping. Having wielded authority over naval cadets, Roddy did not take well to being treated as one, and Geraldine's cutting remarks about his performance in bed had stung him so often that he was losing interest in her. As for the family Geraldine had wanted, the idea seemed to have been abandoned. 'Do I want a nursery full of screaming kids?' she would say. 'No sir, I do not!'

When he started at Greenwich, he quickly realized that he was going to find the work heavy going. Writing clear English had never been his greatest strength, and the hectic social life that Geraldine expected him to share with her was not conducive to the writing of staff appreciations.

Geraldine had returned to an actively social life, and often when he arrived home after a day of lectures he found the house in Hyde Park Square packed with her society friends drinking his gin, smoking his cigarettes, and talking at the tops of their voices.

After three weeks, he had had enough. He went to live in the Greenwich officers' mess during the working week, coming home to Geraldine at the week-ends. He settled happily into a new routine. He was waited on hand and foot, took his meals in the Painted Hall and had his evenings free to seek whatever entertainment he chose in town.

As one of the few married officers on the course who were living in the mess, and also one of the most senior, he didn't feel it was proper to go on 'runs ashore' with the younger officers, so instead he took to solitary evenings in the West End. It was on one such evening, after attending a show at the Windmill, that he met a young woman called Jacqueline who charged him five pounds for as long as he liked.

Jacqueline appeared to enjoy his company. She praised his physique and his prowess in bed and made him feel like a man. The memory of their times together during the working week helped him to endure Geraldine's sarcasm at the week-ends.

He managed to convince himself that he was not being unfaithful, and that the relief he achieved with Jacqueline was acting as a positive influence on his marriage. There was another important aspect. While the isolated experience with a prostitute he had had some years before had been somewhat perverted, the sex he had with Jacqueline was entirely normal. She even made him laugh. He felt grateful to her for that, and was amazed (and a little confused) to discover that he was becoming fond of her.

But he knew in his heart that what he was doing was a symptom that all was not well in his life, and that his arrangement with this rather charming young prostitute must sooner or later come to an end.

And it did.

He was walking back to his car one bitterly cold evening in March when a man in a fawn Burberry raincoat and bowler hat ran to catch up with him and tapped him on the shoulder.

'Excuse me, Commander,' he said. 'I wonder if I could have a word with you, sir?' He wore a thick muffler and had a waxed moustache. His lips looked blue in the gas-light.

'Certainly not,' said Yarrow, and continued on his way.

The man caught up with him as he reached his car. 'Commander Yarrow, sir! I think we ought to talk. It's in your interests as well as mine.'

'Who are you? How do you know my name?'

'The name's Bootherstone, sir. Ex-army sergeant, military police.'

Roddy felt a pulse of fear. 'All right. Say what you have to say. I'm in a hurry.'

The man glanced down the street and lowered his voice. 'My services have been retained by your lady wife, sir. I am a private detective. I know what you've been up to.'

Roddy thought quickly. 'You can't prove a thing.'

'I'm afraid I can, sir. I've been recording your movements for the past three weeks.'

'I don't believe a word of it.'

'In that case perhaps I can convince you. Here's my card sir, and here's your wife's signed confirmation that she has engaged the services of my agency. Now, if I might make a suggestion, suppose we were to meet for a drink in the public house round the corner? May I impress upon you that it would be greatly to your advantage? You see, I have a proposal to make to you, and I think you would be well advised to consider it.'

The east wind hit him as he came out of the mews and rounded the corner. He entered the pub, went into the saloon bar, and found a small table by the window. The man followed him in and sat down with him.

'I know you're in a hurry, sir,' Bootherstone said when Yarrow had provided him with the whisky of his choice. 'So I shall come straight to the point. As I intimated to you just now, I have, over the past three weeks, on the instructions of your lady wife, kept your good self under observation.' He pulled out a black book and held it up rather in the manner of a witness taking the evidential oath. 'I have written down here in this notebook, sir, eye-witness notes, with dates and times, which prove beyond any doubt that you have been making frequent and regular use of the services of a prostitute.'

Roddy felt sweat trickling down under his arms.

'Right, sir,' Bootherstone continued. 'Perhaps I can square with you. As I told you, I'm a military man, sir. I was at Gallipoli, sir, and if it hadn't been for the Royal Navy I wouldn't be sitting talking to you now, sir. I can't say that I like my job, but it's the one to which I'm best suited, and a man has to earn a living. I've a wife and three fine boys, sir, and I hope they will grow up in a better world than what I did. So you see, sir, I'm what you might call a man with a heart—'

'Get on with it,' said Roddy. 'I haven't got all night.'

Bootherstone smiled. 'No, not tonight you haven't, have you sir? Because tonight's Friday, and your wife will be expecting you home. Very well, I'll come to the point. If the evidence of your nocturnal activities I have collected was to be put into a sworn affidavit, there is no doubt that your wife would be in a position to start divorce proceedings with every confidence of winning her petition before any judge in the land.'

'I don't accept that at all.'

'What is more, sir, your appearance in the divorce court would reduce not only your personal reputation to a state of ruin, but your career in the Senior Service as well. Admit it, sir. You would be left a broken man. I've seen it happen, sir. Oh yes.' Bootherstone leaned forward across the table. 'And that, sir, is why I wish to put a proposal to you.'

'What sort of proposal?'

'I like to think of myself as a man of compassion, sir. I don't like to see a good man ruined. We've both served our King and country, you and me—'

'For God's sake come to the point, man!'

'Right you are, sir. I shall do as you say, sir. What I'm prepared to do, being as you are an officer and a gentleman sir, and me owing a debt of gratitude to the Royal Navy, as I say, what I'm prepared to do, is to omit any reference to your activities with prostitutes in my report to your good lady wife, sir. There, sir. That's my proposal.'

And how much will that cost me?'

'Oh, please, please, sir! I would not stoop to ask for payment. I'm no blackmailer, sir. Oh no. Amazing though it may seem, my motives are philanthropic, sir. We fought to make this country a land fit for heroes, and it's my belief that we who remain have a duty to live up to the sacrifice others have made. While it hurts me to see a gentleman like your good self degrade himself with a common whore, I can understand the stresses and strains that wives can put upon their husbands. Wishing no disrespect, sir, I have met your lady wife, and I would only say that in my experience, blame is seldom to be found on the doorstep of only one party in these matters. Oh no. Might I therefore be permitted to make a suggestion, sir? May I propose to you that you should now return to your good lady and, as husband to wife, confess your misdeeds and ask her forgiveness? And having done so, might I suggest that you put your immoral ways behind you once and for all?'

Roddy frowned. 'Are you some sort of evangelical tub thumper?'

'Suffice it to say that I believe in the Great Architect of the Universe,' said Bootherstone solemnly.

Roddy stared down at the heavy glass ashtray. 'I see. And, if I do as you suggest?'

'If you do as I suggest, sir, I shall be quickly aware of the fact when I see your wife a week today.'

'Why's that?'

'Because if there has been any sort of reconciliation between you, as I sincerely hope there will be, not only shall I discover the fact, but in all probability your wife will dispense with my services. If, on the other hand, it becomes clear to me that you have not had the good sense to resolve this delicate matter with her, I shall have no alternative but to lay the facts before her and advise her accordingly.'

'Are you saying that you would let the whole thing drop?'

'That is precisely what I am saying, sir. You see, sir, I was dragged wounded off the beach at Gallipoli under fire by a brave young midshipman, who couldn't have been more than eighteen years old, sir, and on that day I made a promise that if I could ever do a naval officer a favor, I would. So when your good lady wife showed me your photograph for identification purposes and I saw that you had the Gallipoli medal I said to myself, "Percy Bootherstone," I said, "Here is the opportunity you have been awaiting." So the answer to your question is yes, sir, I will indeed gladly let the matter drop if you will only make it possible for me so to do.'

Roddy pondered this for a few moments. 'I'm most grateful to you, Sergeant. I really don't know what to say.'

'Don't say a thing, sir. Just go back to your lady wife and ask her forgiveness. That way you will be doing all three of us a favor. Wouldn't you say?'

Geraldine was reclining on the sofa when he arrived home. 'What's eating you?' she asked when he appeared at the door of the drawing room. 'You look like you lost a dollar and found a dime.'

He sat down beside her and put his head in his hands.

'Oh Lord!' she said quietly. 'Have you got something to tell me, Piggy Poo?'

Tears were streaming down his face.

'Is it...another woman?'

He went down on his knees and asked her to forgive him. There followed an ominous silence. He looked up at her. She was staring into the fireplace, where the dying embers were turning from red to grey.

Now that he had made a clean breast of things, he felt a great deal better. It had not been nearly as difficult as he had anticipated, and Geraldine seemed to be taking the whole thing extremely well.

'Is it still going on?' she asked.

'No. It's over.'

'Who is this woman?'

He blinked fast. 'What?'

'Who is the lady in question? Anyone I know?'

'No.'

'What's her name?'

'Does it matter?'

'Of course it matters! Come on. Tell me. What's her name?'

'Jacqueline.'

Geraldine shuddered. 'Is she French?'

'Good Lord, no!'

'How old is she?'

'I don't know. About…twenty, I suppose.'

'What is she? A hooker?'

'Of course not!'

'Then what?'

'I don't know. I think she's a typist.'

'A typist?'

'I'm not exactly sure.'

'What did you do with her?'

'I beg your pardon?'

'I said: what did you do with her? Did you take her out?'

'Well…we went out to dinner, yes.'

'Oh you did? Where did you go?'

'Nowhere that you would know.'

'Then tell me. I want to know all about it.'

'I can't remember. Various places.'

'Surely you can remember one of them?'

'It was…pubs, mainly.'

'Which pubs? Where?'

He shook his head. 'What does it matter? We didn't go out all that often.'

'So what did you do? Stay in?'

'Sometimes, yes.'

'Where does she live?'

'What?'

'Stop saying "what" like that. Where does she live?'

'She's in lodgings—'

'Where?'

'Paddington.'

'The red light district?'

'No, of course not! She's perfectly respectable. She lives near Sussex Gardens.'

Geraldine stood up, went to the drinks trolley, and picked up the whisky decanter. 'So what's her address?'

'I can't remember.'

'You can't remember? How the heck did you manage to visit her?'

'Geraldine—surely you don't want to know—'

'Did you sleep with her?'

His heart was racing.

'Well? Did you?'

'Geraldine, I—'

'So you did. You did, didn't you?'

He nodded and bowed his head before her.

'How many times? Come on, you great booby! How many times did you sleep with her?'

He broke down, sobbing. He begged her to forgive him. He said he was sorry. He said that he had learnt his lesson, and swore repeatedly that it would never happen again.

She swung the whisky decanter and hurled it across the room.

'Get out of my house,' she said. 'And don't come back. Ever.'

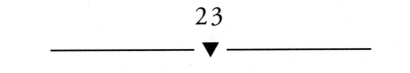

23

Anita was woken at one o'clock on Saturday morning by the telephone ringing. It was Roddy, asking if he could come round to see her.

'What on earth's happened?'

'Geraldine and I have had the most awful bust-up.'

'Where are you?'

'At my club.'

'Couldn't it wait until tomorrow, Roddy? I've got an audition first thing in the morning.'

'I don't know if I can hold out that long. I'm at the end of my tether.'

She said he had better come straight round. She made a pot of tea while she was waiting and opened the front door to him when she heard the taxi draw up. He came in and sat on the sofa in his overcoat and wept. He smelled of whisky and had a dressing on his ear that was seeping blood. He said he was finished, all washed up, done for. 'Just when I was getting somewhere,' he said. 'Just when I thought things were going right for me.' He wiped his eyes with his gloves, leaving a streak of blood on his face.

Annie said it probably wasn't nearly as bad as he imagined.

He shook his head. 'If anything, it's worse. You don't know Geraldine. She'll take revenge. She'll blacken my name. She'll finish me.'

'No she won't! I'm sure she won't. She has a very soft heart.'

'Not with me, she hasn't. I can't do a thing right as far as she's concerned.'

Anita looked at his ear. 'I think I ought to do something about that, Roddy. It's bleeding quite badly.'

He put his hand up, got blood on his fingers, and wiped them on the cushion cover. She took him into the bathroom and removed the plaster the night porter at the Naval Club had given him. The ear was quite badly torn and he had a bruise coming up on the side of his head.

'How on earth did this happen, Roddy?'

'She threw a decanter at me. It was one of a pair. A wedding present from the Collards. Edinburgh crystal.'

She rummaged in a drawer and found a field dressing she had kept after her time as an auxiliary. She applied it, and they went back into the drawing room.

'I wondered if you could give her a call,' he said. 'You know, act as a mediator.' He smiled weakly. 'Isn't that what sisters are for?'

'Hardly!' she said. 'In any case, I'd have to know what the row was about if I was going to be of any help.'

He sighed. 'It's another woman, if you must know. I went to Geraldine and told her about it. I put myself at her mercy. I begged her forgiveness. I told her that the whole thing was over. Which it is. What more can I do?'

'Hope she'll change her mind, I suppose.'

'She won't. I know she won't. You realize she could have killed me with that decanter? I don't know why you're smiling. It's not the slightest bit funny.' He sighed heavily and stood up. 'I might have known that you wouldn't be at all interested. I think I'd better go.'

'Oh, for goodness sake, Roddy! Why don't you stay the night? We can talk for as long as you like tomorrow when I get back. But at the moment I really would like to get some sleep.'

'No. I don't want to be a burden. I shall be living in the mess if she wants to know where I am. You can tell her that she only has to ask, and I'll come back to her. Will you tell her that? It'll come better from you. She'll believe you.' He laughed bitterly. 'She'd believe anyone before she believed me.'

Anita followed him into the hall. He wished her good luck for her audition and added, 'But I don't suppose you need it. I'm sure you'll do quite brilliantly, as ever.' Then suddenly he broke down again and started hiccupping and sniffing and gulping embarrassingly.

'I—I—I've never felt loved—really loved—in my whole life.'

Roddy, do stay the night. Please.'

But he wouldn't, and when he had gone she was suddenly frightened that he might do something awful. She went back to bed and lay awake for three hours before falling asleep, and woke with a start at eight thirty. She threw on her clothes, did without breakfast, and arrived for her audition with a blinding headache and only a minute to spare.

When she arrived back at Cadogan Square in the afternoon, the telephone was ringing. It was Geraldine. She wanted to come round and tell her all about her row with Roddy.

The impasse lasted most of the week. Roddy rang up Geraldine at every hour of the day and night. He tried to get into the house, and hung about outside her front door in the evenings. He sent her a long incoherent letter imploring her to take him back.

On Friday, Geraldine had a meeting with her private detective, who reported that apart from sighting her husband in Soho and following him into a night club, he did not have any concrete evidence of his misbehavior. Geraldine decided to dispense with Mr. Bootherstone's services for the time being, and Mr. Bootherstone said he understood perfectly.

She went home feeling a little better disposed towards Roddy. But on arriving at the house the maid brought her a telegram from her brother that had arrived while she was out. Her father had died of a heart attack the previous evening. The funeral was to take place on Tuesday in New York.

She took a taxi and went to call on Anita. She flopped down on the sofa and said that nothing in her life had ever gone right. Anita rang for the maid and ordered afternoon tea. The telephone rang. Anita answered it, and then put her hand over the mouthpiece. 'It's Roddy. Do you want to speak to him?'

Geraldine shook her head emphatically. 'Tell him I'm not here.'

Anita's patience was wearing thin. There had been telephone calls from Geraldine and Roddy all week. 'I'm not going to lie for you, Geraldine. Do you want to take the call or don't you?'

'Tell him to go to hell.'

'I'm not prepared to do that, either.'

And then Geraldine broke down. 'Oh Daddy!' she wailed. 'Oh Daddy, Daddy, Daddy!'

'Roddy?' said Anita into the phone. 'Your father-in-law died yesterday. Geraldine is very upset. She can't speak to you now. I suggest you try again later.'

The maid brought in the tea trolley. Geraldine perked up. She dried her eyes on a small handkerchief which ended up looking like a burst balloon. 'I loved my Daddy so much,' she said, and bit thoughtfully into a chocolate cake.

The phone rang again. 'I'll answer it,' Geraldine said, and heaved herself to her feet.

'Now listen here you son of a—' She stopped. 'Yes, this is Mrs. Walmshurst's number.' She held the phone out to Annie and said: 'It's for you.'

'Guess what?' said Frank when Annie came on the line. 'I've been confirmed in the rank of sub lieutenant.'

'Wonderful! Many congratulations! Where are you?'

'Chatham. Was that Geraldine who answered the phone?'

'Yes. Are you free this weekend?'

'No, but I am next Friday. How are you? How was the audition?'

'I got the part.'

'Congratulations! Is there some sort of crisis with Geraldine?'

She laughed. 'How did you guess?'

'You can't talk?'

'No.'

'Listen. I'd like to take you out. For a celebration. Are you free next Friday?'

'Yes.'

'This is my treat. Let's go to the Savoy.'

'The Savoy!'

'Well, let's push the boat out, shall we? They do a cabaret and dinner dance on Fridays. Shall I book it?'

'Yes. Come here first.'

'Until Friday. I'll be with you about six.'

'Next Friday,' said Annie, and rang off.

'Well!' said Geraldine. 'You're a dark horse!'

'Not really.'

'How long have you known him?'

'A while.'

Geraldine gave her a searching look. 'You're in love, aren't you?'

'Do you mind if we don't talk about it?'

'Are you ashamed of him?'

'No, but I don't want to talk about him, that's all.'

'Oh, right. It's kind of delicate, yes? But you're in love, that's obvious. I mean look at you. You're all lit up.' Geraldine sighed. 'You're so lucky! I mean, it was obvious listening to you that the two of you are really close. But then you were never short of male company, were you?'

'You haven't done so badly yourself, Geraldine.'

Geraldine shook her head. 'Uh-uh. My friends come to see me because of the booze and the company, not because they like me. You know something? I never felt I could open my heart to a man. I mean, really talk. I never could talk to anyone the way you and that guy of yours were talking just now.'

She sat with her arms out at her sides, occupying the entire sofa. A tear dribbled down her cheek.

'Why don't you try again with Roddy?' Anita said. 'He needs love every bit as much as you do. I think the two of you are far better suited than either of you realize.'

'I don't know,' sobbed Geraldine. 'I don't know.'

24

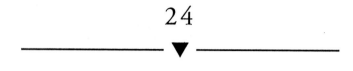

'Sorry I'm late,' Frank said when Annie opened the door to him. 'I had to hang around for the captain.'

'What did he want?'

'Nothing in particular. But the commander can't go ashore until the captain's gone, and the first lieutenant can't go ashore until the commander's gone, and I can't go ashore until the first lieutenant's gone; and every so often the captain takes it into his head to sharpen us all up by staying on until half past five on a Friday afternoon.'

'How very childish.'

'Yes, well, that's life in a blue suit. So—what have you been up to?'

'Playing the agony aunt and attending the wounded.'

She told him about Geraldine and Roddy. They had settled their differences and were back together again. 'It was perfectly obvious from the beginning that they would,' she said. 'Actually, I think Geraldine's quite good for Roddy. He needs to have his ego deflated from time to time.'

She sat on the bathroom stool and they caught up on each other's news while he bathed.

'What's the new appointment?' she asked.

'A cruiser. HMS *Daphne*. On the West Indies station.'

'When do you join?'

'The beginning of April.'

'Are you pleased?'

'I have mixed feelings.'

'Why?'

'Well, what about us?'

'I'll still be here when you come back.'

'I'll be away at least a year and probably two.'

'That won't make any difference. We aren't joined at the hip, are we? We both have our careers.'

He changed into a dinner jacket and they departed by taxi. It sped along Buckingham Gate, round Buckingham Palace and down The Mall towards the Admiralty Arch.

They were both in a party mood, Annie because she had landed a part in *Follies* at the London Hippodrome; Frank because he had bought her a ring and intended to propose.

'Now stop canoodling,' she said as they turned into Savoy Place. 'We've arrived.'

The commissionaire who opened the taxi door as they drew up was Stan Litton, Frank's training petty officer from Shotley. Their eyes met in instant recognition. Frank told Annie about it as they went up the carpeted steps into the vestibule.

'Why didn't you say hello?' she asked.

'I didn't want to embarrass him. Or you, for that matter.'

'Why on earth should I have been embarrassed?'

He didn't have an answer to that.

They were shown to their table. Appropriately enough, the Savoy Quartet was playing 'She's going to marry Yum-Yum' from the *Mikado*. Frank ordered Champagne, and they inspected the *à la carte* menu. Annie couldn't decide whether to have potted shrimps followed by stuffed quails, or *paté foie* followed by *sole meunière*.

The Champagne arrived. The cork popped and they raised their glasses. 'We've come a long way since that coffee we had in Tanti's bar, haven't we?' Annie said. 'Here's to us.'

'Here's to us,' Frank echoed; and when he had set his glass back on the table, put his hand into the side pocket of his dinner jacket and took out a ring. It was only a small sapphire set between two smaller diamonds, but it had made a large hole in his savings. 'Annie,' he said. 'I want to ask you something.'

'Oh—no!' she said, looking past him over his shoulder. 'Don't turn round. Roddy and Geraldine are here.'

He dropped the ring back into his pocket.

'Damn!' said Annie. 'I knew Geraldine's ears were flapping when you phoned last week. I expect she dragged Roddy here with the sole intention of having a look at you.'

'How much does she know?'

'Nothing. Oh God. Here we go. Roddy's coming over.'

'Should we leave?'

'Certainly not! I can handle this. Leave the talking to me.'

Roddy walked briskly across the dance floor and pulled up short, breathing through his mouth like a bull at a fence. Frank hadn't seen him in over ten years but even now, after so long a time, he experienced the same old feelings of fear and hatred.

Anita sat back in her chair, very cool and calm.

'Roddy!' she said. 'How nice to see you and Geraldine on good terms again! Why don't you both join us?'

Roddy ignored her. He turned to Frank. 'Now you,' he said thickly. 'Jannaway. You listen to me. Leave my sister alone, do you hear? Leave her alone or it'll be the worse for you. I'll speak with your commanding officer. I'll finish you. You and your mother. I'll have you stripped of your rank and your mother out on the street where she belongs. Do you hear what I'm saying?'

'Well,' said Anita. 'That's the last time you get any tea and sympathy out of me, big brother.'

Roddy was breathless with anger. 'I'm giving you fair warning. Both of you. I'm not playing games. I'll tell Father. He'll disown you, Annie. You and your lower deck Lothario.'

Anita tipped her chair back, twirling her glass by the stem. 'You're making an ass of yourself, Roddy. As usual.'

His mouth quivered. He went pale at the temples. He could hardly get his words out. He stood over them, shaking his finger. 'You'll regret this. I'll see to that. Within a very short time, you will both regret this.'

As he spoke, the quartet reached a finale, and in the few moments of silence that followed, Annie's retort rang out across the restaurant.

'What an *extremely* unpleasant man you are!'

Frank stood up and took her arm. 'Let's go,' he said quietly.

He gave the waiter five pounds, and moments later they were outside in the noise and bright lights of London's West End.

Annie said she needed fresh air, so instead of taking a cab they walked down to the Thames and crossed the road to the Victoria Embankment.

'It's jealousy,' she said. 'He cannot bear to see us happy. He always has to destroy whatever he can't have for himself.'

Somewhere down in the East India docks, a tug tooted its siren. They leant over the wall, looking down at the river beneath them.

'It doesn't really matter what his motives are,' Frank said. 'The question is, will he do what he said he would do?'

'Knowing Roddy, I'm sure he will.'

'In that case I've as good as had it as far as the Navy's concerned. Unless we give in to him.'

'That's out of the question.'

'I don't mind what he tries to do to me,' he said. 'It's what he might do to my mother that worries me.'

'Yes. Of all the despicable things to say. You can't get much lower than that.'

'But what are we going to *do*?'

'Well one thing's certain in my mind. I am not caving in to Roddy. Or my father. Or anyone. I'm never going to let anyone tell me what to do, or control me in any way whatsoever.' She shivered. 'I'm cold.'

He undid the buttons of his coat and she came into his arms and he hugged her. Big Ben chimed the half-hour. Taxis and buses and cars surged along the Embankment.

'Whatever we decide, we must act quickly,' Annie said. 'He won't wait long. The chances are he'll ring Father tomorrow.' She looked up at him. 'You know what I think?'

'What?'

'Wasn't there something you were just about to ask me? Before Roddy and Geraldine arrived?'

'Yes. I was going to ask you to marry me.'

'There you are, then. That's the solution. We'll get married.'

'How would that help? Roddy can still have my mother sacked. And he can finish me, too.'

'Wait a minute! If we got married and you left the Navy, wouldn't that work?'

'Annie—I've signed an undertaking to serve for another nine years. I can't break that.'

- 199 -

'But you can buy yourself out, can't you?'

'Yes, but it's very expensive.'

'I don't suppose it would stretch my finances unduly.'

'But—what would I do? All I'm trained for is taking mines and torpedoes to pieces and driving an admiral's barge. I doubt if I'd even qualify for a commissionaire's job like old Stan Litton.'

'For goodness sake! You play the piano superbly. You could earn a packet playing at night clubs. We might even work up a double act together. And anyway, you'll have to leave the Navy one day, won't you?'

'What if Roddy has a go at my mother?'

'She could come and live with us.'

'You're a good woman, Annie.'

'I'm damned if I'm going to let that brother of mine wreck everything.'

Frank stared down at the fast flowing river and likened it to his own life, steadily running on with every passing second. Was it so very important to win promotion to lieutenant? What would it prove? Did two gold rings on your sleeve mean any more than one? For that matter, did three, or four, or even five? Would he, as an officer up from the lower deck, ever be able to make any difference at all to the way the Navy was run?

He broke a long silence. 'I think you're right. Let's get married. Let's get married straight away.'

'You'll leave the Navy?'

'Yes. If you can buy me out.'

'We'll have to act quickly.'

'I know. And…I'd like to tell my mother as soon as possible. She's not as strong as she was. If Roddy has her sacked it might be the end of her.'

'Then why not go to Meonford tonight? Yes! Let's do it. Let's just go ahead and do it!'

He took the ring from his pocket. 'I think you'd better have this,' he said, and put it on her finger.

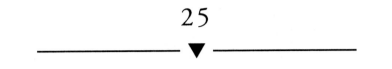

25

Hetty Jannaway sat alone at the long deal table in the kitchen at Meonford Hall and sipped a cup of strong, sweet tea. It was six o'clock in the morning. She liked this peaceful time of day before anyone else was up, when she could think her own thoughts. It was the only time she could really call her own: a brief half hour or so before the sun had risen when she could stop worrying about her housekeeping duties and just *sit*.

She thought about Jack. She often thought about him in the mornings. Her memories of him were like a handful of little snapshots. Meeting him for the first time on the promenade at Plymouth. Sitting with him in the teashop where they shared a penny bun with clotted cream and strawberry preserve. His smile. His slow, Cornish voice. 'Hetty, my dear, you're the loveliest girl I ever laid eyes on, and I want you for my wife.'

Walking with him that evening, his arm round her waist. The wedding in the dockyard church. Jack at her side, looking so smart in his bell bottoms and gold badges. The little room they rented. The sticks of furniture they bought on the never-never.

And then, when he had to sail away to join a battleship in the Mediterranean…the feeling of dread. The sense of foreboding. The inner certainty that she would be made to pay for their brief days of happiness together.

The warrant officer at the door. Stiff, formal. 'Mrs. Jannaway? I have to tell you that your husband….'

The visit from the landlord. Evicted from her rooms. Alone. Wandering in the drizzle. Destitute. Staring out to sea. The grief. The loneliness. The despair.

A touch on her shoulder. A naval officer who smelled of port wine and cigar smoke and expensive soap.

Half a crown for twenty minutes, that was his offer.

When she refused, he told her not to be a silly girl. He said it was obvious what she was up to, and that if she didn't give him what he wanted he would put her in charge for soliciting. She felt powerless to resist him. She knew who he was, that was the trouble. She'd seen him at the Navy Days parade the previous year. He was the Queen's Harbor Master, Sir Jervis Yarrow. How could she disobey a great man like that?

He rescued her from the abyss of destitution. He set her up in rooms on Ebrington Street and made her his kept woman. He made her promise never to lie with another man and to remain utterly discreet, even in the confessional.

He came to see her every Wednesday afternoon at three o'clock on the dot. 'I'll keep your secret if you'll keep mine,' he used to say when he was pulling up his pants or knotting his tie; and then he would wink at her, and smack her on the bottom, and put a florin on the mantelpiece before going out by the back door.

It only lasted a few months, because that summer, on a hot afternoon in July, Lady Laura committed suicide, and a week or two later he came to tell her that he was leaving Devon for good. It was quite a sad parting. He had become fond of her, and said so; and she could not deny that she had become fond of him. He had always treated her decently and with consideration, and she was proud that a poor girl like her could give a great man like him so much pleasure.

He gave her five golden sovereigns by way of a gratuity. She was grateful for that, but didn't dare tell him that she was carrying his child.

The prospect of motherhood engendered in her a steely determination to make provision for her unborn baby. She decided to set herself up as a washerwoman. With the money Sir Jervis gave her, she bought a five gallon water boiler, scrubbing brush, wash board, two tin baths, smoothing irons, ironing board, cake soap, starch, drying lines, and a large quantity of best Welsh coal. She knew she was taking a risk, but she prided herself on her resourcefulness and she had nothing to lose. The alternatives were the street, the workhouse, or suicide.

When the baby was born she entered Jack's name as the father on the birth certificate and ante-dated Frank's birthday by six months. She decided that if the discrepancy were ever noticed, she would tell the truth and shame the devil. But it never was.

For nearly five years she slaved to keep her head above water and provide for Frank. And then, out of the blue, she received through the post a cutting from the *Hampshire Chronicle* that announced that Lady Yarrow of Meonford Hall was seeking applications from suitably qualified women for the position of housekeeper. Enclosed with the cutting was a note that read: 'If you will apply for this post I shall ensure that you are successful. J.Y.'

She finished her tea and set the cup down and heaved a sigh. It would be time to get going soon. She stared down at the tea leaves in the cup. A long time ago, she had believed that you could tell the future from tea leaves. What childish superstition!

She'd never confessed anything of what had happened. She could hardly admit it to herself, let alone tell a priest. She had put it off and put it off and put it off, and now it was too late. How many times had she been to confession? Once a week for twenty years. Twenty times fifty-two. More than a thousand times. A thousand absolutions, tens of thousands of Hail Mary's. Twenty Novenas, at least forty Stations of the Cross.

It was like trying to scrub an oil stain out of stone flags. The mark never came out. Never.

She came back to herself with a jolt. The telephone was ringing upstairs in the library. She pushed herself to her feet and went upstairs to take the call.

'Meonford six-seven, Mrs. Jannaway speaking.'

She heard a whispered, 'It's your mother,' and then Frank's voice: 'Hello Ma! It's me.'

She was short of breath after coming up the stairs. 'Frank?' she said. 'What is it? Are you all right?'

'I'm fine!'

'What's happened?'

'I'm coming to see you.'

'When?'

'This morning.'

She patted her bosom. 'This morning?'

'Yes.'

'Where are you?'

'At Wickham station.'

'Wickham? Why?'

'I'm getting married.'

'Married?'

'Yes. And I'm bringing my bride-to-be with me.'

She broke out in a hot sweat. 'Who is she? Is she a Catholic?'

'You'll find out all about that very soon.'

'When?'

'This morning. In half an hour.'

'Half an hour? Where are you?'

'I told you! Wickham. We're coming to see you. Any chance of a bit of breakfast?'

'But you don't have permission. You're not supposed to come without permission.'

'Don't worry about that. We'll be with you in twenty minutes, all right?'

'But who is it? Who are you going to marry?'

She overheard laughter at the other end of the line, then a voice she recognized.

'Hello Mrs. Jannaway! It's me! Anita!'

'I don't understand—'

'You will!' Frank said. 'The cab's arrived. See you soon!'

The sun was just up, and glinting through the trees. The woods were ringing with birdsong. Outside Meonford, they were held up by Stapleton's dairy herd, which was ambling back to pasture after being milked. They paid off the taxi and walked the last hundred yards into the village before going down the path beside the church yard to the swollen river. Stapleton's cattle plodded up the muddy field on the other side; and beyond the spinney a local train chuffed up the Alton line. They crossed the river by the wooden bridge and pushed the oak door open into the orchard.

Walking up through the walled garden, Annie said, 'You're quite sure about this, aren't you?'

'Yes,' Frank said. 'Quite sure.'

'And we're agreed: nothing and nobody will change our minds.'

'Nothing and nobody,' he said, and they went on up past the rose beds, round the side of the house and into the stable yard, and knocked on the kitchen door.

Eggs and bacon were sizzling on the range. At the head of the table Wilson, the butler, was sitting in his shirt sleeves eating sausages and fried bread. Hetty Jannaway wiped her hands on her apron and looked at them in dismay.

'Hullo Ma!' Frank said. 'Can we have some breakfast? We're both ravenous.'

She raised her hands and shook them, and said: 'I don't understand.'

Frank put his arm round her waist. 'Yes you do. I've asked Annie to marry me. She's going to be my wife.'

She put her hands to her face. Annie said, 'Perhaps you had better sit down, Mrs. Jannaway. I expect it's a bit of a shock, isn't it?'

She slumped down and looked to one side and put her hand to her mouth.

'Come on, Ma!' Frank said. 'It's not as bad as all that!'

'But it is.' Her voice sank to a whisper. 'You don't realize what you've done.' She looked up at Annie. 'Your father won't allow it, Miss Anita. I know he won't.'

'He can't prevent it. We're both over twenty-one and free to marry.'

She put her head in her hands and wept.

'Mrs. Jannaway—please, *please* don't be upset!'

Wilson pushed his chair back, stood up, and took his breakfast plate with him into his pantry.

'What is it?' Annie asked. 'Are you afraid of what my father will say?'

'Well—yes. I'll lose my position, like as not.'

Annie looked at Frank and said, 'We've thought of that. Whatever happens, we'll make sure you're all right. We'd like you to come and live with us in London when you stop work here. So even if you do lose your position, we'll look after you and make sure you're well cared for.'

Hetty was overcome by another fit of sobbing.

'For goodness sake, Ma!' Frank said. 'It's not the end of the world. You should be happy for us!'

She looked up at them, her eyes red. 'You don't know what you've done, the pair of you. You just don't know what you've done.'

'Are the eggs and bacon for us?' Frank asked.

She sniffed and nodded her head, but when she saw Annie about to serve them, pushed herself to her feet and insisted on doing it herself, saying she would set a tray and take it into the billiard room for them.

'We'd rather have it here with you,' Annie said.

'I don't know, I'm sure, Miss Anita. You'd better do as you please.'

They sat down to eat at the deal table, whose feet had rotted and whose legs had been shortened so often that Frank couldn't get his knees under it.

There was an awkward silence. Anita said: 'We'd like to tell you our plans, Mrs. Jannaway.'

She said there was no point in making plans because whatever plans they made they would never be married; at which point Frank lost his patience, put down his knife and fork, and said, 'Ma. Listen: we've made up our minds. We're going to get married. No one's going to stop us. Not even you.'

Anita was gentler. 'I don't understand why you're so against it, Mrs. Jannaway. I mean—is it a lot of reasons or just one? Is it because of what my father will say? Or is it because you're afraid of losing your position? Or because I'm not a Catholic?'

'It's because you're not a Catholic,' Frank said. 'That and the class difference. I really do not know why the hell we bothered to come down here in the first place.'

Anita looked quickly at Frank. There was something about the way he had spoken—something about his manner or tone or the words he used—that reminded her of someone else. And then, in one of those rare flashes of intuition, she knew very well who that someone was.

'I think it might be a good idea,' she said, glancing meaningfully at Frank, 'if your mother and I had a bit of a chat on our own.'

As soon as the door was shut behind him, Anita turned back to face Hetty across the table. 'It isn't either of those things, is it?' she said quietly; and in reply, Hetty stared downward at the scrubbed deal table and shook her head.

Frank paced up and down in the stable yard, smoking a cigarette. He should have known that his mother would react in this way. She couldn't cope with change, that was her trouble. Everything had to be cut and dried. The routine had to run like clockwork, the flags scrubbed spotless, the laundry delivered on time, the meals cooked to a turn. A place for everything and everything in its place. Once a Catholic, always a Catholic. Have you said your prayers? Have you been to Mass? When were you last at Confession? Perfection, perfection, perfection, twenty-four hours a day, three hundred and sixty-five days a year.

But he had Annie on his side now. If anyone could win Ma over, she could. She was marvelous with people. He was sure she'd have Ma eating out of her hand in no time at all.

He strolled to the end of the stable yard, smoking his cigarette. On the train journey down to Wickham, when Annie was asleep with her head on his shoulder, he had undergone a momentary sense of panic at the thought of leaving the Navy. He had put the thought away almost as soon as it entered his head, but it now returned and, in the cold light of early morning it seemed to carry more force.

What will I *do*? he wondered. Could he really metamorphose into a night club pianist? It was all very well to tell his mother that she could come and stay with them in London, but in the light of her present attitude the chances of such an arrangement working satisfactorily seemed remote. If she came to live with them she would inevitably turn herself into their servant, which would be an intolerable situation.

His misgivings were like an incoming tide that creeps up over a flat beach, making little creeks and inroads in the sand. He foresaw that he would lose his sense of direction and purpose. He would become Annie's accessory. She would pay for everything: the taxi fares, the dinners out, his shoes, ties, stiff white collars, shaving soap and toothpaste. She would always take centre stage. He would walk through life three paces behind her with his hands joined behind his back in the way he had been taught on the mate's course. He would pleasure her in bed when she wanted to be pleasured in bed, and he would not pleasure her in bed when she did not wish to be pleasured in bed. He would be her husband in name, but in reality would be little more than her kept man.

But what of it? Didn't he love Annie? And didn't she love him? Although they were of a different class, they had much in common. To a degree, they were both outsiders: her father had cut her out of his will and washed his hands of her, and he was virtually estranged from his mother. And now, on top of all that, Roddy was intent upon destroying their lives.

He took out another cigarette and was preparing to light it when he heard Annie call his name. She was standing at the kitchen door, beckoning urgently.

He hurried back across the stable yard and entered the kitchen. His mother was lying flat out on the stone flags. He knelt beside her and took her hand. She stared up into his eyes and tried to say something. For a fleeting moment, he felt her hand tighten on his. Then she was gone.

In the confusion that followed, Annie drew him to one side and told him that it would be best if they kept apart for the time being, so after phoning his ship and obtaining four days' compassionate leave, he went to stay with Mr. Roughsedge at Stocks Cottage.

On Sunday, he went to Mass for the first time in many years. Hearing the old familiar Latin took him back to his earliest days at Meonford when his innocence was intact and the world was a beautiful, happy place. He came out of the church feeling guilty and distraught. He knew very well what his mother would have said to him, had she been able, in those last moments before she died. She would have begged him once more to come back to the Catholic Faith. That was undoubtedly her dying wish, and the fact that she had been unable to express it aloud did not lessen the force of it one whit.

On Monday, he went to her room and sorted out her things. She left pitifully little behind: her missal, her rosary, her wedding certificate, a few letters rolled up and tied with a boot lace; her caps, collars and aprons, her every day clothes, her Sunday best.

Under her mattress he found an envelope with 'To pay for my funeral' on it. There were two five-pound notes inside. On the little boxwood chest of drawers stood a framed photograph of himself aged seven after his confirmation, and the faded snap of his father, Jack Jannaway, with his cap flat aback, standing on the promenade at Plymouth.

'At the bottom of the deep blue sea, my darling,' he whispered, and his eyes filled with tears.

Hetty Jannaway was buried at Fareham on the Tuesday, Frank's last day of leave. He hired a motor coach so that the kitchen staff and a dozen people from the village could attend the funeral. Lady Yarrow came, but Sir Jervis stayed behind.

After the funeral Mass, they sang 'Lord, for tomorrow and its needs,' which was Hetty's favorite. Then they went out into the blustery day, and when the priest had said the burial rite, Hetty's remains were lowered into the ground.

Frank had agreed with Annie that they should meet on Wickham station to catch the six-thirty train to London, and he left his baggage at the station so that he would not have to return to Meonford after the funeral. He arrived in good time and sat down on a bench on the platform to wait. For the time being, he set aside the question of marriage and leaving the Navy. He had been unable to speak at any length to Annie since his mother had died, but outside the church before the service she had said simply, 'We have to talk.' He agreed with that.

Anita had lain awake all night, struggling with the problem of what to say. Now, sitting on the green leather seat in the back of the taxi as it sped along the Alton Road towards Wickham Station, her mind was made up. After going round and round in circles, she had come to the conclusion that the only way—the *only* way—was to cut clean. She must end their liaison; and in doing so she must not drop even the most obscure hint about her reasons for doing so. She must close off every possible avenue of hope that they could ever meet again.

It would mean putting on an act, she knew that. Two years before, she had failed to resist Sylvia Gosthwaite's interrogation. This time, she must not fail. She knew what she was going to say, and had rehearsed her lines until she had them to perfection. But for all that, as she walked through the booking hall and onto the platform, she was shaking with nerves.

She arrived on the platform with only a minute to spare before the train was due.

'Annie!' Frank said the moment he saw her. 'What on earth's happened? Where's your baggage?'

'I'm not coming with you,' she said, and her voice sounded unnaturally high-pitched and strained. 'I'm sorry, Frank. I've been thinking very hard about everything, and I've come to the conclusion I've got to call a halt to the whole thing. It's over between us. I think I've been deceiving myself about you for a long time. I've been putting on an act. We're not the same class, are we? It simply wouldn't work, would it? Our...affair—it was a wonderful fragile sort of bubble, wasn't it? But that's all it was: a bubble. And now it's burst. Please don't look at me like that, Frank. You've had a good run for your money. Heaven knows how much I've spent on you. It's finally dawned on me what you're up to. I've seen through you. I realized last night for the first time what a nerve you've got. Roddy was quite right to say what he did. You're a fortune hunter, aren't you? You expect me to buy you out of the Navy and then what? Sponge off me for the rest of your life? Don't you think that's a bit much? I mean—what's in it for me? Nothing as far as I can see.'

He felt a great ache in his chest. 'I don't believe you mean what you're saying,' he said.

'I can assure you that I do. I've given a great deal of thought to it all—indeed, I've thought about little else for the last three days. I could have written all this in a letter, but I thought I'd do the decent thing and tell you to your face. I hope you appreciate that, and I hope you appreciate everything else I've done for you, the way I coached you for your interview and built up your confidence and taught you how to behave like an officer.'

She pressed the engagement ring into his hand. 'Take this back,' she said. 'Find someone else. Someone of your own class.'

The rails rumbled as the London train approached the platform. He had to shout to make himself heard as it came into the station. 'I don't believe you mean any of this,' he shouted. 'You still love me! I know you do. Why can't you look at me, Annie? You *do* love me, don't you?'

She was shaking her head. 'No. And I don't think I ever did, either. It was just the sex, that was all. Not love. Not real, deep love. That was all an act.'

He heard his own voice as if it were someone else's. 'How can you say that? It wasn't an act! I know it wasn't! This is the act. *This!*'

The train came to a halt. Doors slammed.

'You have to believe me,' Anita said. 'It's over. Finished.'

His eyes held a wild look. He was like an animal in a trap.

'I'm not going,' he said. 'I don't believe you. There's something behind this. I intend to find out what it is.'

'There is nothing behind it! I'm finished with you! Do you hear me? Finished!'

'Listen,' he said. 'I'm quite sure we can sort this out—'

'No! No! You listen! I don't want to see you again Frank. I don't want to have anything to do with you. If you don't get on the train—now—I'm going to call the stationmaster.'

'Then let me write to you. I can't believe—'

'No. Please *don't* write. Please don't try to contact me in any way. It's over. You'll never change my mind. Please—please get on the train.'

The train began to move. He put his hands on her shoulders and looked down into her eyes, and said, 'I shall love you to the end of my life.'

He stepped aboard at the last moment, slammed the door shut, and lowered the window by the strap. When he put his head out and looked back, Anita was already running away down the platform. But although he could not see her face he knew with complete certainty that she was in tears, and that she did still love him, and that either great pressure had been brought to bear on her by her parents, or she had been told something that had convinced her to bring their wonderful love affair to this bitter, bitter end.

PART III

▼

1929–1931

26

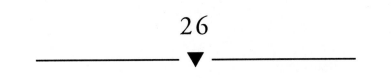

'That is cracking news!' announced Roddy at breakfast one morning a week before Christmas. He held up a letter he had been reading. 'Listen to this. It's from old Fortnightly.'

'Who?'

'Come on, Gerry! You remember Ernle Fairfax-Notley. We were at Osborne together. He's Director of Naval Appointments at the Mad House.'

'The what?'

'The Admiralty. He's the chap who pulls names out of the hat for officer appointments. Roddy waved the letter in triumph. 'Listen, listen! "Dear Yarrow, I am delighted to be able to inform you, in advance of the official notice in the Gazette, that you have been selected for promotion to Captain on the Post List and that you are to be appointed to HMS *Winchester* in command from 15th March 1930. If you would care to give my office a call, I should be delighted to arrange a mutually convenient day for you to come in so that I can brief you on your ship and her officers."' He looked up. 'Well? Are you going to congratulate me?'

'What for?'

'For God's sake! I've got a sea command! Of a cruiser in the Second Cruiser Squadron! I'll be right under the eye of the C-in-C Atlantic Fleet. You can't ask for much better than that. I tell you what: I'll take you out to lunch at Brown's. We'll have a celebration.'

But Geraldine had a previous engagement and declined, so Roddy took himself out to lunch and had a long, hard think about the style of command that he would adopt. He was still quite dazed by the news. Thoughts and ideas jostled in his head. At last, at long, long last, his career had taken an upturn. He thought about all his past commanding officers, and how they had imposed their personality on their ships. That was what you had to do when in command at sea. Every aspect of the ship, from the smartness of her boats to the behavior of her men ashore or even the cleanliness of her heads and bathrooms, was seen as a direct reflection of the leadership and authority of her captain.

I shall start out as I mean to continue, he told himself, echoing the words of at least two of his previous captains. I shall crack down hard on the officers. Accept only the highest possible standards. Uphold the finest traditions of the Service. Work hard and play hard. Demand one hundred and one percent and a little bit more besides.

He joined HMS *Winchester* in Portsmouth, where she was in the last week of an extended refit. He wasted no time in establishing his own peculiar style of authority. He spoke to his officers collectively and individually. He conducted a written test of one hundred questions for all bridge watch-keeping officers, for which the pass-mark was set at ninety per cent, and when this was not achieved he summoned the first lieutenant and demanded to know the reason why.

The first lieutenant, a small, harassed Scot called Finlay, defended the results, saying that they were remarkably good, all things considered.

Roddy exploded. He had taken an instant dislike to Finlay. He told him to re-run the test and go on re-running it until the required result was achieved, stopping the leave of those officers who failed.

The result was a noticeable tautening of the atmosphere throughout the ship, and Roddy was pleased to note that Finlay appeared to be frightened of him. He took to wandering round the upper deck and sending for Finlay whenever he found anything amiss.

'Will you kindly do me a great favor?' he said quietly to Finlay one day when he had found a rope's end dangling over the side.

'Yes sir?'

'Will you very kindly—' Roddy's face contorted and he suddenly yelled, 'SHARPEN UP!'

It was such an effective little trick that he extended it and perfected it, preparing the ground with sweet gentleness and then, when an officer's guard was down, lashing him with the verbal equivalent of a cat o' nine tails.

He also clashed with the senior engineer, a humorous and well-liked lieutenant commander known universally as 'Spike' who had stood by the ship throughout her refit and who, for his pains, had been passed over for promotion. As a result of the bad odor with the new captain he asked to be relieved early. Roddy was pleased to see him go. It was proof positive that the pips were beginning to squeak.

The next to go was the commissioned gunner, who collapsed with a perforated ulcer during the gun functioning trials and was landed that evening and carried off the ship on a stretcher.

The ship completed her sea acceptance trials and was ordered to Portland for shake-down and work-up. This involved practicing emergency drills, proving the Watch and Quarter Bills, and exercising every seamanship evolution and weapon firing that HMS *Winchester* might be called upon to perform.

Boats were lowered and hoisted; landing parties and boarding parties were mustered, briefed, armed, and sent away in the boats; darken-ship screens were rigged and night firings exercised. There were fire drills, damage control drills, man overboard drills, and sea boat drills. All the ceremonial gear had to be taken out and made to work. Awnings were rigged, accommodation ladders lowered and hoisted, and the ship dressed overall.

'Would you very kindly SHARPEN UP!' Roddy would shout when a drill or evolution was performed less than perfectly. It became a saying in the wardroom.

With the exception of the captain's favorite, Lieutenant Oram, the officers became united in their dislike of Captain Yarrow; while on the lower deck, he became known as Piggy Grunt.

It was Finlay who took the brunt of the terror. Instead of sharpening him up, Roddy only succeeded in wrecking his first lieutenant's self-confidence, and Finlay developed a nervous twitch.

One evening when the ship was at anchor in Weymouth Bay, Roddy sent for Commander Lethbridge, his second-in-command, and ordered that the following morning the anchor was to be weighed by hand, and that the first lieutenant was to take charge of the operation on the forecastle.

Weighing anchor by hand was a laborious business that involved clearing lower deck of all hands to heave in the cable by stages using two heavy three-fold purchases that were rigged 'luff upon luff.' It was an exercise that was rarely carried out in earnest, but an old favorite of flag officers when the fleet was at general drill.

The gear was lugged up from the boatswain's store and, during the morning watch, laid out on the forecastle in accordance with the seamanship manual. But when Captain Yarrow appeared on the bridge a little after seven, Lieutenant Commander Finlay was not present to report that all was ready.

'What's going on?' said Yarrow as he hoisted himself up into his high chair. Where's the first lieutenant? Snotty!'

Midshipman Norsworthy stopped picking his nose and sprang to attention. 'Sir!'

'Find the first lieutenant and inform him that his presence is required on the bridge.'

The midshipman doubled away. Finlay appeared a few minutes later.

'What the hell are you up to, first lieutenant?'

'I apologize, sir. I was—'

'Are you ready to weigh anchor by deck tackle?'

'Yes, sir.'

'Then why, pray, have you not reported the fact?'

'Sir—I—'

Yarrow leaned forward in his chair and said softly, 'Will you very kindly do me a favor, first lieutenant?'

And then, poor Finlay cracked. He broke down completely, and wept in front of everyone on the bridge: the captain, the commander, the officer of the watch, the midshipman of the watch, the yeoman of signals, the navigating officer and the padre, the last having come to the bridge to watch the fun. The padre took him down to his cabin. Weighing by deck tackle was abandoned, and that evening when HMS *Winchester* arrived back inside the breakwaters of the Portland naval base, Lieutenant Commander Finlay was landed and sent, as Yarrow put it when he spoke to the commander that evening, 'to have his head shrunk by the trick cyclist in the funny farm at Netley.'

The problem of a replacement arose. The next executive lieutenant in seniority after Finlay was Lieutenant Oram, the captain's favorite. David Oram was a tall, fair haired, blue-eyed, smooth-mannered Etonian. Yarrow sent for him and told him to take over the first lieutenant's duties immediately. Oram was delighted to do so, but pointed out that he was already heavily burdened with duties: he was the commander's assistant and ran the commander's office; he was in charge of ratings' training classes, and he was also the ship's signals officer.

Yarrow therefore signaled Admiralty requesting an immediate relief for Finlay, recommending that as Oram already knew the ship, he should take over as the first lieutenant and that his duties should be taken over by whoever was sent as Finlay's relief.

Forty-eight hours later, a signal was received in the ship to the effect that Lieutenant F.J. Jannaway had been appointed to fill the vacancy.

Within five minutes of reading the signal, Yarrow was in his picket boat on his way to the naval base ashore, where he rang Jannaway's appointing officer and told him that the lieutenant in question was not acceptable.

The appointing officer said there was nothing he could do, so Roddy demanded to speak personally to Rear Admiral Fairfax-Notley. 'Can't you open another box of lieutenants, old man?' he said when Fairfax-Notley came on the line. 'This one just won't do.'

'Why not?' asked Fairfax-Notley.

'He's an ex-mate. He won't fit in. Not in my wardroom, at any rate.'

'Oh, I think you'll find that he will,' said Fairfax-Notley. He has an excellent record.'

'I don't care what he's got. I don't want him in my ship.'

'Well, I suppose it might be possible to find an alternative, but I wouldn't recommend it. You've gone through three officers in six weeks as it is. If you turn this one down, I think there is a very considerable risk that it might reflect adversely on yourself. Had you thought of that?'

Roddy returned to his ship in a foul mood. A dark cloud descended. When his personal servant brought him his customary glass of Sackville amontillado sherry before dinner, he found the captain stamping up and down in his stateroom muttering, 'Bloody hell, bloody hell, bloody hell!'

Lieutenant Jannaway was interviewed by Commander Lethbridge on the morning following his arrival. Lethbridge informed him that he would be taking over the duties that Lieutenant Oram had performed, namely those of Commander's Assistant, Officer in Charge of Training Classes, and Signals Officer. Jannaway pointed out that, while he had extensive experience as a boats and regatta training officer, he had no experience at all as a signals officer. Lethbridge made a note of the fact and said that he would mention it to the captain, who was keen for the ship to do well in the Atlantic Fleet regatta to be held the following autumn.

'Do I understand that you and Captain Yarrow have served together before?' Lethbridge asked as Jannaway was about to leave.

'No, sir,' said Jannaway, and left it at that.

'I shall make no secret of the fact,' Yarrow began when he saw Jannaway the following day, 'that I did not ask to have you in my ship, that I did not wish to have you in my ship and that I did everything possible to have your appointment cancelled so that you might never set foot aboard my ship. However you are here now; and I am obliged to make the best of a bad job.' He paused to fix a malevolent stare at Jannaway, who remained quite impassive, standing to attention and keeping his eyes fixed on the bulkhead, upon which hung the framed photographs and crests of previous ships in which Roddy had served. 'I will therefore say to you what I have said to every other officer under my command. It is my intention to make HMS *Winchester* the best ship not only in the Second Cruiser Squadron, but in the Atlantic Fleet. I intend that she will be the best at gunnery, the fastest at evolutions, the smartest in harbor, and the most efficient and prompt in acknowledging signals and making her returns to the Commander-in-Chief. Any officer—*any* officer—who fails to come up to the highest possible standards, will get short shrift from me.' Yarrow lowered his voice. 'But in your case, Jannaway, in your case, if I detect any tendency on your part to inefficiency, or slackness, or disloyalty, I will have you *crucified*.'

Jannaway returned to the wardroom soon after stand-easy had been piped and found the officers gathering for a mid-morning cup of tea. They sat in armchairs and on the bar fender, chatting and sipping their tea and scanning the newspapers. As Jannaway entered, a hush fell and they all looked his way. Then, with one accord, they chanted the *Winchester* wardroom motto: 'So…will…you…very…kindly…SHARPEN UP!'

As the laughter died down, Commander Lethbridge entered the wardroom. 'Change of program, chaps,' he said.

There was a groan.

'What a bore,' said Oram. 'Am I going to miss Derby Day?'

'I'm afraid you are,' said Lethbridge. '*Cardiff* has problems with her main bearings. She was due to visit the city of Cardiff next week. We're standing in for her.'

'I say, that's a bit of luck!' said Lanyon, the baby-faced navigating officer. 'I've only just completed the chart corrections for the Severn Estuary.'

'Are we likely to spread awnings?' Oram asked.

'Almost certainly, yes. We shall also be giving a children's party on Saturday, the day after our arrival. Any volunteers to organize it?'

'Give it to the sub,' said Busby, the gunnery officer.

Sub Lieutenant Entwistle pretended to hide behind a cushion.

'I'll take that on, sir,' Jannaway said.

'Good man!' said Lethbridge. 'And, by the way, I put your request to the captain about not taking on the signals department, but the answer was "not granted," so you *will* be taking over signals from the first lieutenant.'

'Ay ay, sir.'

'So…will…you…very…kindly…SHARPEN UP!' chanted the wardroom officers, and once again they roared with laughter.

27

▼

Dora Williams clapped her hands for silence. 'David Evans! Stop talking this minute! Susan Roberts! Stop slouching and sit up straight.'

A hand went up at the back of the class.

'Yes?'

'Please Miss, it's stopped raining!'

'Thank you, William, I am aware of that. Now listen to me, all of you. We are going to visit a ship of the Royal Navy today. The name of the ship is HMS *Winchester*.'

'Please Miss!'

'What is it, Gwyneth?'

'Well, Miss, last week Miss Jones said it was HMS *Cardiff*, like. So why's it changed?'

'There is no need to say "like" at the end of a sentence, Gwyneth, I have told you that before. I believe that HMS *Winchester* is visiting the city because HMS *Cardiff* has had mechanical difficulties.'

'Did her boiler burst, Miss?'

'I have no idea, Owen. Now pay attention. We shall walk in crocodile and there is to be no talking on the way. Once we get on board the ship, you are all to listen to what the officers say to you and do what you are told. Blodwyn Parker, you may walk with me at the head of the crocodile. Mary Evans, you are to walk at the back and keep order. And remember: you are all to be sensible and on you best behavior. Come along!'

They were met by a lieutenant in uniform. He was very suntanned and smart, and he had two rows of medal ribbons on his chest, with oak leaves on two of them, which she knew meant that he had been twice mentioned in dispatches. The children stared at him as if he were from another planet. He saluted, and Dora realized, a little too late, that he was saluting her.

'How do you do?' he said. He was every inch a naval officer: very debonair and full of vigor. 'I'm in charge of the children's party. The name's Jannaway. Frank Jannaway.'

'I'm very pleased to meet you, sir,' said Dora. She was feeling quite funny inside.

'It's Miss Jones, I believe?'

'No, sir. I'm Miss Williams. Miss Jones is poorly, sir.'

'I see.' He hesitated a moment, then said. 'There really is no need to call me "sir," Miss Williams. I'm a very ordinary mortal. The uniform doesn't mean a thing.'

'Oh,' she said. 'Oh.'

He looked at the children. 'They're very quiet.'

'They're not allowed to talk, sir.'

He had sad eyes, but a nice, homely smile. 'May I take over?'

She smiled back. 'With the greatest of pleasure,' she said.

He walked down the crocodile, and fifty pairs of eyes followed him. He stopped half-way down and talked to the smallest boy in the school, who wore short trousers that were too long for him and a flat cap that was too big.

'What's your name?'

'Evan Thomas.'

He sat down on his haunches and beckoned to the children to gather round. 'There may be pirates on board,' he whispered. So if anyone sees a pirate, you must tell me, see?'

Fifty heads nodded solemnly.

He led the way up the gang plank, or whatever they called it in the Navy, onto the forecastle. He stood in front of the gun turret and sat them down on benches facing him.

Then he started talking about the ship. Dora was just thinking that this was far above the children's heads when a sailor dressed up as a pirate, with a cardboard cutlass between his teeth, came stealthily round the side of the turret.

Blodwyn Evans giggled suddenly.

'What is it?' said the officer.

'Please sir, there's a pirate behind you, like.'

'What did you say?'

'There's a pirate, sir! Behind you.'

And of course when he looked round the pirate was gone. He started again, but only a few moments later, two pirates appeared. Again he turned round just too late. The third time there were four pirates and the fourth there were eight, and when it happened a fifth time and sixteen pirates put their heads round the gun turret, the children were giggling and shouting and Dora was laughing so much she was crying.

After that, the pirates took over. The children were given their own pirate hats and false beards and eye patches to wear. They were split up into ten groups of five, and went running about all over the ship. There was a slide and a swing rigged on the upper deck. They went up to the bridge and sat in the captain's chair; they went into the wheelhouse and took it in turns to turn the wheel and shout up the voice-pipe things like, 'Hard a starboard, ay-ay, sir!' and 'Full astern on the engines!'

At four o'clock, all pirates were piped to muster on the seamen's mess deck, where they were served with sausage rolls and biscuits and cakes and jellies and custard pies.

'I expect you'd like a cup of tea yourself?' said the officer, and led her through a maze of corridors to the pile carpets and chintz furnishings of the wardroom anteroom.

He introduced her to the second in command, Commander Lethbridge, who put down his book, took a pipe out of his mouth, and sprang to his feet.

'Has he been looking after you properly, Miss Williams?'

'Oh—wonderfully, sir. The children have had a marvelous time. I have myself, indeed.'

A steward in a white jacket served hot buttered toast and they drank tea from cups which bore the Admiralty crest. 'This is such a treat,' Dora said. 'You've no idea.'

'It's a pleasure,' said Frank.

'Have you children of your own?'

'No. I'm not married.'

'I'm so sorry. I shouldn't have asked a personal question like that.'

'Not at all.'

She felt terribly embarrassed.

'It's a Catholic school, isn't it?' he asked.

'Yes,' she said, grateful to change the subject.

'I'm a Catholic myself.'

'Oh,' she said. 'Well then. That explains a lot, doesn't it?' Their eyes met and they both smiled at the same moment. He asked which church she went to and what time Mass was. He said that he was free tomorrow, which was Sunday, and would she mind if he came to the same Mass as she went to?

'Not one bit,' she said.

He came to Mass in a very nice suit. They knelt side by side to receive communion from the priest, and afterwards, when he was kneeling beside her, she glanced at him and thought to herself what a good, strong face he had.

After the dismissal, they sang 'Faith of our Fathers,' which she always loved. He had a beautiful voice. A lovely strong bass, it was. Walking out into the June sunshine and seeing him say good-morning to Monsignor Morgan, Dora thought wistfully to herself that this handsome lieutenant was just the sort man she would really like to have as a husband.

Don't be so silly, girl, she told herself. He wouldn't look twice at you, he's an officer.

But he did look twice. His ship stayed at Cardiff for the whole week. He took her out to tea in the city and they walked in the city park. She couldn't believe it really. She told herself that he probably did this in every port, but she was sure in her heart of hearts that it could not be so. He asked her about herself; and she told him about her father, who died in a pit disaster, and her four brothers, two of whom were killed in the same trench at the second battle of the Somme.

He didn't say anything about himself and she didn't think it proper to ask questions. He seemed a rather lonely man. He never knew his father, and his mother had died some years before. He had no relations. 'Or at least,' he said, 'none that I know of.'

On the Wednesday, he took her on board for the official cocktail party. She felt out of place among the city dignitaries and their ladies, but Frank was very nice to her and never left her on her own; and afterwards, when he took her out to a restaurant for dinner, he told her that he didn't like cocktail parties much, either.

He was on duty on the Thursday, but free on Friday, and he asked if she would like to go to the pictures with him. But she hardly took in any of what happened on the silver screen because he held her hand almost all the way through; and when they came out into the bright evening sunshine her feelings were in a turmoil.

'I've got the day off tomorrow,' he said. 'I thought we might take a picnic along the coast.'

'That'll be nice,' she said. 'I expect you'll enjoy that.'

'I'd like you to come too, Dora. Would you?'

'Will there be other officers going?'

'No. It would be just you and me.'

'I'm not sure,' she said.

'Why aren't you sure?'

'I'm not sure if it would be proper.'

His eyes twinkled in that way he had. 'In that case let's be improper, shall we?'

They had a lovely day out. They caught the bus to St. Athan, where she used to go for summer holidays before the war when she was small. His steward had packed a picnic, complete with real damask serviettes, and they sat on the dunes by the sea and ate veal and ham pie and lettuce and tomato sandwiches and drank lemonade from the bottle, because the wardroom attendant had forgotten to put in the pony glasses.

In the bus on the way back, Frank said he had enjoyed the past week more than any week he could remember for a very long time. 'I have too,' she said, and the words came out in a funny sort of way that didn't sound like her own voice at all.

He took her out to dinner that evening, and the following day they went to Mass. Afterwards, when they were sitting in the park watching the sparrows hop about for crumbs, he said, 'It's no good, Dora, I have to tell you something.'

Her heart sank. It was his last day, wasn't it? He had to end it somehow.

'I'm in love,' he said.

'Oh,' she said. 'Oh. That's nice.'

She watched the sparrows. Well really, she thought. What did you expect, girl?

He was sitting beside her, staring ahead as if he were driving a car. 'I would like to marry her,' he said. 'But I'm not sure if she would have me.'

She smiled. 'Haven't you asked her, then?'

He turned to her and looked right into her eyes, and took both her hands in his. 'No,' he said. 'But I'm asking her now.'

Well yes, it was all very sudden, but she knew in her heart that he was right for her because he was a Catholic and he was so good with children. Perhaps she should have played hard to get, but she was nearly thirty and there weren't many nice men left over to marry. She didn't want to be left on the shelf, did she?

He didn't exactly rush her into it, but he didn't give her much time, either. Perhaps that was a good thing, because she might have said no and lost him. All the same, there was just a little corner of her mind which wondered why he hadn't married before and why he looked so sad and thoughtful sometimes. But he was a good man, she was sure of that. Hadn't she liked him from the first instant of their meeting on the quay side? No, he wasn't the sort to deceive her. He wasn't the sort that would change overnight as soon as they were married—at least, she didn't think so.

All the same it was very sudden, because when she said 'yes' that afternoon in the city park, he said that they could get married when he was on leave in August.

'That's very quick, Frank,' she said. 'We've only known each other a week.'

'But if you're sure you want to marry me, there's no point in waiting, is there?'

She was trying to think of an answer to that when he said, 'Come here,' and he reached out and took her in his arms and kissed her; and all her doubts fled away.

She gave up her teaching at the end of the summer term and they were married in Portsmouth at the beginning of August. They went on a four day honeymoon in the New Forest. He was a lovely husband to her and with every day that passed she felt herself falling more deeply in love with him. They took a flat in Southsea and she made her nest. She had an early miscarriage in October, which was upsetting, but she got over it, and Frank was very loving to her. They had a quiet Christmas at home, just the two of them, walking along the wintry front at Southsea and making toast in front of the gas fire, and really beginning to get to know each other for the first time; and in the new year when she wrote and told him that she thought she might be pregnant again, he wrote back and asked her to promise that she would take great care of herself this time; and that was what she did.

28

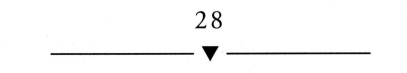

Early in the New Year there was a mutiny on board the submarine depot ship *Lucia*, which lay alongside in Devonport most of the year, but which had been ordered to join the Atlantic Fleet for the spring cruise. HMS *Lucia* was a coal-burning ship, and suffered from the usual conflict between spit-and-polish and coal dust, which the advent of furnace fuel oil had largely turned into a thing of the past. The other ingredients for discontent were old chestnuts: a first lieutenant with an unfortunate manner, a misunderstanding over hours that would be worked, and a last-minute curtailment of ship's company leave, coupled with extra work in foul weather.

The upshot was that when both watches of seamen were piped to fall in one morning after stand-easy, they stayed in their mess deck, pulled the hatch down over their heads and started singing hymns, with the result that HMS *Lucia* was paid off, her captain, first lieutenant, and boatswain were placed on half pay, several ratings were court-martialed and dismissed or given sentences of detention, and the remainder were distributed among other ships, sewing the seeds of discontent far and wide across the Atlantic Fleet.

One such seed was Able Seaman Steven Lewtas who, having just completed a sixty-day stint at the Royal Naval Detention Quarters, was waiting on the jetty with his kitbag when HMS *Winchester* returned to Portsmouth to give Easter leave. He came aboard over the forward brow and was ordered to report to the regulating office, where he went through the usual joining routine.

'Last ship?' asked the regulating petty officer.

'*Lucia*.'

'Oh yes? Well just watch your step, see? We'll be keeping a close eye on you.'

He was told which watch he belonged to, allocated a hammock billet in the forward seamen's mess deck, asked for his next of kin details, checked in for victuals, rum and tobacco, given his kit locker number, and told the name of his divisional officer.

'Jannaway?' he said. 'Did you say Jannaway?'

'Lieutenant Jannaway to you.'

'Is he up from the lower deck?'

'That's no concern of yours.'

'I wonder,' said Steve Lewtas as he ambled up the main passage to his mess deck. 'I wonder.'

He didn't have to wonder long, because Lieutenant Jannaway sent for him that afternoon after secure had been piped. The cabin door was open, so Lewtas knocked on the door post and received a brisk, 'Come in!'

He stepped over the cabin coaming and entered. In a glance, he took in a shelf with a row of books, a desk with a half-written letter on it, and a leather-framed photograph of a smiling young lady on the bunk-side shelf.

Jannaway got to his feet and shook him by the hand. 'Well Steve?' he said. 'How's tricks?' And straight away, Lewtas knew that his divisional officer was still the same old Jan he'd known as a nozzer at Shotley naval training establishment.

But of course he was not the same, otherwise he would still have been an able seaman. Not that he was at all stuck up or posh, no, there was nothing of that about him. But he was an officer wasn't he? He was an officer all the way through like the pink writing in a stick of Blackpool rock.

Jannaway took Lewtas's records out of their cardboard envelope. 'You're in your last year of service,' he said, referring to the service certificate. 'Are you going to sign on for another five?'

'Like as not, sir,' said Lewtas. 'There's no work outside, is there?'

'And you're married. What about family? Do you have any children?'

'Do I ever, sir! I've got five sprogs.'

'And your wife?'

'Maureen, sir. She's all right. But she talks a lot.'

'You're in lodgings?'

'In Portsmouth, ay, sir.'

'Any questions you want to ask?'

Lewtas shook his head. 'I'll find out, soon enough, sir.'

'You lost your good conduct badges after the *Lucia* business, did you?'

'Ay, sir.'

Jannaway nodded. 'Well as far as I'm concerned, that's over, past and forgotten.'

'Sir,' said Lewtas, and nodded stiffly.

'Outside this cabin, we can't be on the same old terms we once were, Steve. I'm sure you realize that. But if ever you want to come and see me on a private matter, you only have to ask.'

'Thank you sir,' said Lewtas, leaving the cabin backwards. 'Thank you very much, sir.'

After Easter leave, the ship returned to Portland to carry out trials with the Fairey floatplane. The pilot, a tall, gangly, humorous sub lieutenant by the name of Horsey, fitted himself into the cockpit and, when his diminutive observer had strapped in behind him, started up the engine with a spluttering roar, deafening everyone on the bridge and sending a fine spray of oil over them for good measure.

There was a delay while the requirement to turn into wind, not down-wind, was explained to the captain. When this had been achieved, and when the captain had been persuaded, against his better judgment, to give permission for the floatplane to be launched, the catapult fired.

After a few nail-biting moments when the floatplane seemed certain to plunge into the sea, it managed to climb away, returning a few minutes later to fly past the ship at full throttle and below masthead height.

After establishing radio communication with the ship, the plane flew around exercising spotting tactics for twenty minutes or so before returning to alight on the water and be hoisted in on the derrick.

Lieutenant Jannaway was in charge of the hoisting operation. The derrick was swung out on the starboard side, ratings were detailed to pass steadying lines, and the lifting hook was lowered on its wire pendant. But just as the plane was taxiing up to be hooked on and hoisted, it was drenched by a wave, and the engine cut and would not restart. This meant that the ship would now have to come alongside the plane to pick it up instead of vice-versa.

Yarrow was not renowned for his ship handling ability, and did not relish the prospect of maneuvering his twenty thousand ton cruiser alongside a flimsy and expensive aircraft. On the first attempt the ship missed by twenty feet or so. The second attempt was closer, but still not close enough. The third time went much better. The floatplane passed gently down the starboard side right under the hook pendant. The pilot and observer were standing on the main plane above the cockpit, ready to accept the steadying lines and hook on. As the ship came slowly by, Horsey reached up to grab the pendant, but at the same moment the ship rolled, and the hook pass inches beyond his grasp.

'Round again!' he shouted tiredly up to the bridge, 'Too high!'

There was a shout of laughter from the hands working on the upper deck.

'What's all that laughing?' Yarrow demanded from his high chair on the bridge. 'What the hell's going on?'

'I think it was some sort of air service joke, sir,' Lethbridge said.

'Lieutenant Jannaway report to the bridge,' Roddy said very quietly.

Lethbridge leaned forward. 'I beg your pardon, sir?'

Roddy looked round at him. 'Have you got cloth ears, Commander? I said, LIEUTENANT JANNAWAY REPORT TO THE BRIDGE!'

Jannaway came onto the bridge within the minute. He glanced at the commander, who indicated that he was to report directly to the captain. He approached the captain's chair. Yarrow was gazing forward.

'You sent for me, sir,' Jannaway said, and saluted.

'Yes I did. What's going on? What went wrong?'

'The lifting hook was lowered sir, but the ship rolled to port as the plane came alongside and the hook was just out of the pilot's reach. If I may make a suggestion, it may be easier to hook on if we make our approach head to sea with the floatplane just to leeward.'

Roddy kept his eyes fixed on the horizon. 'Are you trying to teach me my job, by any chance?' he asked.

'No, sir,' said Jannaway.

'In that case, would you do me a favor?'

'Sir?'

'Would you very kindly take your thumb out of your bum and SHARPEN UP!'

Jannaway went back down to the starboard derrick. 'Right, Petty Officer Banyard!' he said briskly and in the hearing of the junior ratings, 'The captain's going to make another approach. Let's get it right this time, shall we?'

That summer of 1931 was not a happy one. The dole queues were lengthening, the weather was foul, and the country was edging ever closer to the precipice of national bankruptcy. Worst of all, it seemed likely that Sir George May's Economy Committee would recommend cuts in pay in the public services, and that the Navy's 1919 pay scale, regarded as sacrosanct on the lower deck, was going to be cut.

The world of admirals was not a happy one either. Because of his handling of the *Royal Oak* episode, in which Rear Admiral Collard called Bandmaster Barnacle a 'bugger,' Admiral Keyes had displeased the King, so forfeiting a life-long ambition to become First Sea Lord. The result was a game of musical chairs. Keyes was sent to serve his time out as C-in-C Portsmouth; Chatfield was moved from the Atlantic Fleet to the Mediterranean Fleet and Admiral Hodges was appointed to the post of Commander-in-Chief, Atlantic Fleet.

One foggy evening in June, when HMS *Winchester* was swinging round a buoy in Portland harbor, Yarrow sent for his commander.

'Fleet regatta,' he said. 'What are you doing about it?'

'The first lieutenant has it in hand, sir.'

'I'd like to put up a better showing than we did last year.'

Lethbridge smiled. 'I think we're all agreed on that, sir.'

Yarrow pulled at his nose and grunted. He glanced up at Lethbridge. 'Do you think Oram's the best man for the job?'

Although Oram was the captain's favorite, he had been involved in two unfortunate experiences on the forecastle in recent weeks. He had parted the picking up rope while coming to a buoy in Portland harbor the week before, and had strained the starboard anchor cable by running it out to a clench while anchoring in a high wind.

Lethbridge trod carefully. 'He's very competent, sir.'

'That wasn't my question.'

'No, sir.'

'Well?'

'Oram is certainly a very able and energetic officer.'

'Go on.'

'But…I think the men might respond better to someone with what one might call the common touch, sir.'

'Meaning Jannaway, I suppose?'

'Yes sir.'

'Hmm,' went Yarrow.

'Jannaway is a fine seaman,' Lethbridge said, 'and the men respect him for it. He's also doing very well in charge of the boys' training classes.'

'So you're telling me to make him regatta officer, is that it?'

'No sir, I'm saying that if you wish to make a change, Jannaway would be the officer I would recommend.'

Yarrow stroked his chin for some time. 'Very well,' he said eventually. 'If he's as able as you suggest, let's make use of his ability. As of today, he takes over as regatta officer—and as forecastle officer. You can tell him from me that if we aren't cock of the fleet this time next month I'll have his guts for garters.'

The fleet assembled in the Channel at the end of June, and after twenty-four hours of maneuvers, the C-in-C ordered that the fleet would anchor in formation in Weymouth Bay for the night, using flag hoists only for communication.

As with every other evolution performed under the eye of the C-in-C, Yarrow was aware that he would be judged on the performance of his ship. In the case of a fleet anchorage, this meant maintaining strict station within the formation and anchoring precisely when and where the admiral intended.

Special sea duty men were closed up well in advance. The chief quarter-master took the wheel. The navigating officer was at the bridge chart table with the plan of the anchorage drawn out on the chart. Sub Lieutenant Entwistle was using the distance meter and singing out ranges on the line guide, HMS *Norfolk*, four cables on the beam. The yeoman of signals was keeping his telescope focused on HMS *Nelson*'s flag deck in order to be able to spot the C-in-C's signal hoists as they were hoisted. Lieutenant Busby was the officer-of-the-watch, ready to pass the captain's wheel and engine orders down the polished copper voice-pipe to the wheelhouse.

On the forecastle, Jannaway had prepared the anchors for letting go, and the chief shipwright was standing by with a sledge hammer to knock the Blake slip off when the captain gave the order to anchor.

It was a dreary, drizzly afternoon with poor visibility. All went well until, at about eight cables to go to the anchorage, there appeared out of the drizzle a small coaster moored close to the position in which the flagship intended to anchor.

Immediately, a signal was hoisted in HMS *Nelson*. 'Answer at the dip!' yelled the yeoman to the flag deck; and a moment later when he had read the signal, he reported to the captain 'Ships turn together twenty degrees to starboard, sir!'

'Very good!' replied Yarrow.

'Stand by sir! Stand by! Executive signal, sir!'

'Starboard ten,' ordered Yarrow; and Lieutenant Busby repeated the order down the voice-pipe to the quartermaster.

'Signal from the flagship!' sang out the yeoman as another hoist of flags fluttered up HMS *Nelson's* signal halyards. 'Amended anchorage position, sir,' he reported. 'Ships will anchor four cables eastward of planned positions.'

'Very good,' said the captain.

Lanyon rushed to his chart table to place the new anchorage position on the chart. A minute or so later he looked up. 'Captain, sir!'

'Yes?'

'There is a wreck marked close to our anchorage position, sir.'

'How close?'

'Under half a cable, sir.'

'Very good.'

Lanyon took a couple of bearings and reported, 'Six cables to go, sir.'

'Very good,' said Yarrow. 'Are we in station, sub lieutenant?'

'In station!' reported Entwistle.

'Five cables to go, sir!' reported Lanyon, and then, after taking rapid bearings of points on the shore line, 'This course will take us very close to the wreck, sir.'

Yarrow raised his binoculars and studied the coast. He planned to spend the weekend with friends at Osmington Mills, and wondered if he could spot the village.

'Four cables to go, sir.' reported Lanyon. 'And I estimate four and a quarter cables to the wreck.'

'Very good,' said Yarrow, who was still studying the coastline.

'Still in station sir!' reported Entwistle.

Lanyon took another bearing from the compass repeat on the bridge wing. 'Three cables to go, sir! May I recommend we anchor half a cable short in order to give safe clearance from the wreck?'

Roddy lowered his binoculars and turned to look back at Lanyon. 'Anchor out of station? Certainly not!'

Lanyon sighed and shook his head.

The yeoman was reading a flag hoist in HMS *Norfolk*. 'From the line guide sir,' he reported, "Stop engines."'

'Stop both engines!' ordered Busby.

'Two cables to go!' reported Lanyon.

'In station!' reported Entwistle.

'Very good,' said Yarrow.

'One cable to go, sir.'

'From the guide,' reported the Yeoman, "Stand by to anchor," sir!'

Yarrow raised a green hand-flag, which was the signal to the cable party to stand by. On the cable deck, the chief shipwright picked up the sledge hammer and held it ready to knock off the Blake slip and let the anchor go.

'Half a cable to go, sir.'

'Very good.'

'Quarter of a cable to go, sir,' reported Lanyon. 'Captain Sir, may I recommend that we anchor *now*? Otherwise we shall be dangerously close to the wreck.'

Yarrow ignored him.

'Still in station, sir!' reported Entwistle.

The ship moved slowly on through the water.

'Stand by sir!' shouted the yeoman. Stand by…stand by…Let go, sir!'

Yarrow brought his green flag smartly down. On the forecastle, Lieutenant Jannaway bellowed, 'Let go!' and the shipwright swung the sledge hammer, knocked off the slip, and sent the chain cable thundering out through the hawse pipe.

'Exactly in station on anchoring, sir!' reported Entwistle, smiling broadly.

Lanyon used parallel rulers to put the anchor bearings on the chart and fix the exact position of the anchor on the sea bed. Yarrow got down from his high chair and came to have a look.

'All well, pilot?'

Lanyon straightened and moved aside so that Yarrow could see the chart.

'According to the fix I took on letting go, we appear to have dropped the hook fifty yards north-west of the wreck, sir.'

'Well then. A miss is as good as a mile.'

'From C-in-C to all ships, sir!' reported the yeoman. 'Maneuver well executed.'

Yarrow punched the air. 'Excellent! Excellent!' He clapped Lanyon on the shoulder. 'Cheer up, Pilot, it may never happen!'

That evening, Yarrow paced his quarterdeck with his commander. There were ten days to go before the regatta, and the seamen's cutter had been lowered for practice. Jannaway was in the boat with the coxswain. They were practicing starts, giving ten quick strokes to get the boat moving, twenty longer ones to establish a lead and then a transition to the steady rhythm that had to be maintained over the three mile course.

'How do they look to you?' Yarrow asked.

'Pretty good, sir,' said Lethbridge. 'Jannaway's doing a good job.'

'That doesn't mean to say we'll beat *Norfolk*.'

'No sir, but we're in with a chance. Morale is high. I think we'll give them a good run for their money.'

Yarrow scowled. Jannaway was becoming a lot too influential in the ship for his liking.

On reaching the stern, the two officers, their telescopes under their arms, their hands behind their backs, turned at the same moment and paced back along the quarterdeck towards 'Y' turret.

'Would you care to dine with us in the wardroom tonight?' asked Lethbridge.

'That's very civil of you,' said Yarrow. 'What's the occasion?'

'It's the first lieutenant's birthday, sir.'

'In that case, I'd be delighted. WMP.'

Oram asked Jannaway to stand in for Lieutenant Busby as officer-of-the-watch from eight to midnight that evening so that Busby could attend the birthday dinner. Late in the evening, a signal came up to the bridge in the bucket which was hoisted up on a string through a pipe from the WT office. The signal was from the C-in-C, and informed all ships in company that general drill would be conducted the following morning, and that ships were to be prepared to weigh anchor by hand. Jannaway sent the signal straight down to the captain in the wardroom. He also passed the message to the chief boatswain's mate and the petty officer of the watch on deck and gave instructions for all necessary gear to be brought up and ranged on the forecastle by the morning watchmen.

Shortly before midnight, Oram came onto the bridge somewhat the worse for drink. 'I've got news for you, my old mate,' he said. 'Father wants you to be in charge on the forecastle tomorrow when we weigh anchor by deck tackle.'

The day dawned sunny. The marine bugler sounded Charlie at five a.m., and forty-five minutes later, both watches of seamen were mustered and detailed off to clean guns, scrub decks, and polish bright work. At six-forty-five, the pipe 'Clear lower deck, all hands muster by parts of ship, stand by for general drill,' was made, and when Yarrow arrived on the bridge ten minutes later the commander reported to him that all hands were closed up and ready.

Yarrow hoisted himself into his chair and squeezed his hands between his thighs. He was in a good mood that morning. At the birthday dinner the previous night his officers had seemed unusually well disposed towards him.

Jannaway came onto the bridge and reported, 'Ready to weigh by deck-tackle, sir.'

'Very good,' said Yarrow.

Jannaway saluted and was about to go when Yarrow called him back. 'Let's see if we can beat the *Norfolk*'s shall we?'

'Ay ay, sir,' said Jannaway. 'We'll do our best.'

He disappeared down the ladder. A minute or two later the signal for general drill was hoisted in the flagship. Yarrow slapped the arm of his high chair. 'Off we go!' he said. 'Sound general drill!'

The bugle call sounded off through the loudspeakers on the upper deck, and within seconds the first drills were being read out by the yeoman of signals. 'All ships sound six short blasts, sir! Galley to provide one unbroken fried egg on the bridge! Stokers lower the cutter and pull once round the ship!'

While the orders were passed and reports made, Roddy sat slapping the arm of his chair, muttering, 'Come on, come on, come on!' when an evolution seemed to be taking too long.

A gun's crew was required to rig sheer legs. The ship's flight was ordered to make a kite and fly it. The first lieutenant was ordered to rig the whaler for sailing and sail round the ship using an officer-only crew. Oram took charge of this last evolution, but soon after getting under way the boat's mainsail fell into the sea.

'Foolish fellow!' Yarrow roared good-naturedly down at him from the bridge. 'Do better!'

'Captain, sir!' yelled the yeoman. 'From C-in-C, all ships to weigh anchor by deck tackle!'

It was the moment everyone had been waiting for. 'Come on, come on, come on!' said Yarrow, slapping the arm rest of his high chair with the flat of his hand. 'Let's get on with it!' But the words were hardly out of his mouth when the midshipman manning the bridge telephone reported, 'Forecastle ready to start heaving in, sir!'

As the bugler sounded the 'commence,' a spontaneous cheer went up on the forecastle. The hands manning the deck tackle heaved away, and the heavy chain cable came thumping in through the hawse pipe until the two blocks of the purchase came together and the 'halt' was sounded. Then, when the weight of the cable had been taken on the parting strop, the two blocks were pulled apart by ten seamen manning the overhauling pendant, the deck tackle was re-connected to the cable, and the operation repeated.

As more cable came in, the strain increased, and it was no longer possible for the men to run away as they heaved. First they plodded, later it became more like a tug of war.

'From the bridge, sir,' reported Midshipman Ainslie, who was manning the telephone on the cable deck, 'What is the delay?'

Jannaway went to the bows and looked down at the cable. 'Report to the bridge that the cable is up and down, bar taut,' he told the midshipman. 'I suspect we have a foul anchor.'

The sound of cheering came to them across the water. HMS *Norfolk* had successfully completed the evolution.

On the bridge of HMS *Winchester*, Yarrow was winding himself up into a fury. Jannaway was sent for. He came up to the bridge and reported that the strain on the cable was such that weighing by hand was no longer possible. Yarrow turned to Lanyon. 'I suppose this is your wreck, is it?'

'I fear it might be,' said Lanyon.

'I thought you said we'd anchored clear of it?'

'The charted position may not be entirely accurate, sir. The Fleet Hydrographer doesn't guarantee one hundred percent accuracy.'

Yarrow scowled. 'Yeoman! Make a signal to C-in-C. "Foul anchor. Am attempting to weigh by steam capstan."'

Down on the cable deck, Jannaway ordered the deck tackle to be unshackled and the gear cleared away. The cable was brought to the capstan, the capstan was connected up, and the order 'heave in' was given.

Slowly, with each link of the cable grinding and complaining as it came inboard, the capstan began bringing the cable home. But not for long. There was a spurt of steam, a scream of metal, and the capstan came to an abrupt halt.

'Tell the bridge that we definitely have a foul anchor,' Jannaway ordered.

'From the Captain,' reported Midshipman Ainslie a few moments later. 'What do you intend to do about it?'

'Tell the captain I'm coming up to report to him personally,' Jannaway said, and then, before leaving the forecastle, gave the order to the chief shipwright to put the brake on the capstan and to disconnect it from the steam winch.

'What the bloody hell are you buggers playing at on the forecastle?' Yarrow asked when Jannaway arrived on the bridge. 'Do you realize that the fleet's sailing without us?'

'We have a foul anchor, sir. I recommend we veer a shackle of cable and then send the diver down.'

'And how long will that take?'

'I could have a diver in the water within fifteen minutes, sir.'

Yarrow grunted and shook his head. 'Balls to that. We'll break the anchor out with main engines.'

'Ay ay, sir,' said Jannaway, and left the bridge.

As soon as his head disappeared down the ladder, Yarrow ordered, 'Slow astern both engines.'

Lanyon turned back quickly from the chart table. 'Sir!'

'What do you want?' snapped Yarrow.

'Are they ready on the forecastle, sir?'

'Ready? What do you mean, ready?'

'For breaking the anchor out, sir.'

'Are you trying to teach me my job, pilot?'

'No sir.'

'Then will you do me a favor? Will you very kindly SHUT UP?'

When Jannaway arrived back on the forecastle, the petty officer stoker, the shipwright and Able Seaman Lewtas were struggling with the hand wheel to disconnect the capstan from the cable. 'Can't shift it, sir!' shouted the shipwright. 'Too much strain on it!'

At the same moment, they felt the shudder of the deck as the ship started coming astern.

'What the fuck's he doing?' said Lewtas. 'We're still connected up and he's put the fucking engines astern!'

Jannaway ran to the capstan and added his weight to the hand wheel to disconnect the capstan. At the same time, out of the corner of his eye, he saw the anchor cable beginning to rise up out of the water as the ship came astern. 'Clear the forecastle!' he ordered, and the men didn't have to be told twice. They ran aft and took cover behind the gun turret. As they did so, Jannaway turned aft, looked up at the bridge and shouted, 'Stop coming astern! We're still connected up!'

What happened next seemed to take place in slow motion. The cable rose out of the water, and began to vibrate, making a deep, throbbing hum. Flakes of rust peeled off the steel links of the anchor cable leaving bare, blue metal.

Jannaway heard a shout: 'Jan! Get back!' He turned, and saw Steve Lewtas run out from behind the gun turret. At the same moment, there was a sound like a rifle shot as the cable parted. It rose up into the sky, flailing like a monstrous anaconda, and came hurtling down on the cable deck and up against the gun turret.

Jannaway stepped over the piled heaps of cable to where Lewtas lay. He knelt down, and gently rolled him over onto his back. Steve had taken the full force of the cable. His head was smashed to pulp.

Captain Yarrow peered down over the dodger at Lieutenant Jannaway.

'No one hurt, I trust?' he shouted.

Frank got to his feet and looked back at Roddy. In rage and in sorrow, he raised his fists above his head and shook them; and he shook them again, and again, and again, and again.

29

Yarrow sat in his high chair and issued his orders.

'Commander!'

'Sir!'

'The first lieutenant is to take over on the forecastle. Lieutenant Jannaway is to be confined to his cabin.'

'Ay ay, sir.'

'Yeoman!'

'Sir!'

'Make a signal to the Senior Officer, Second Cruiser Squadron.' He paused, blinking and grunting while he concentrated on the wording. 'Regret to report that I have parted my main cable while attempting to break the anchor out with main engines.' Then he shook his head. 'No. Belay that.' He pulled at his nose. He didn't like having to regret anything, especially to his senior officer. Nor did he like the implication that the parting of the cable was in any way his fault. After a lot of crossing out and re-writing on the yeoman's part, the final signal read:

> MAIN CABLE PARTED WHILE ATTEMPTING TO BREAK OUT ANCHOR WITH MAIN ENGINES. ONE MAN FATALLY INJURED. CONDUCTING IMMEDIATE INVESTIGATION.

The reply came back ten minutes later:

> PROCEED PORTSMOUTH FORTHWITH TO DISEMBARK CORPSE AND EMBARK REPLACEMENT ANCHOR AND CABLE REJOINING FLEET AS SOON AS POSSIBLE THEREAFTER. BOARD OF INQUIRY WILL CONVENE ON ARRIVAL SCAPA FLOW.

As soon as the ship was on course for Portsmouth, Yarrow went down to his cabin and sent for the commander. His servant brought coffee in. The ship was thundering along at twenty-six knots. The vibration sent the cups and saucers rattling.

'Did you see what Jannaway did?' Yarrow asked. 'After the cable parted?'

'No, sir,' said Lethbridge.

'He shook his fists at me.'

'Are you sure it was at you personally, sir?'

'No doubt about it. He stood up and looked directly at me and shook his fists.'

'That's a very serious charge, sir.'

'I know damn well it is. But I can't overlook it, can I? I'm going to have to do something about it. If I don't, Jannaway will be seen by the ship's company to have got away with an act of gross insubordination. It's the thin end of the wedge, commander. That's what it is. The thin end of the wedge.'

Lethbridge nodded but said nothing.

Yarrow helped himself to sugar and milk and stirred his coffee for a lot longer than was necessary. Suddenly, he looked up. 'I think Jannaway's cooked his goose. Don't you?'

'Was the cable in date for survey?' asked Lanyon at Stand Easy in the wardroom.

Oram sat on the bar fender and sipped his tea. 'Not quite, damn it. It's booked in to be done when we dock in August.'

'I shouldn't think that'll affect the issue one way or another,' Busby remarked. 'Any cable would have parted with that strain on it.'

Lanyon was pacing up and down looking gloomy. 'If we'd anchored short as I recommended, we wouldn't have had a foul anchor in the first place.'

'For God's sake, Pilot!' Oram said. 'It isn't the end of the world.'

'It might be the end of my career.'

'If it's the end of anyone's career, it'll be Jannaway's.' Oram put his hands between his knees and rubbed them together in a self-satisfied sort of way. 'After all, he was the one who left the cable connected up, wasn't he?'

'I think we were bloody lucky to lose only one man,' said the padre, an oily individual called Dunstan who made a point of swearing occasionally in order to be one of the chaps.

Oram drained his cup. 'Yes. And what's more he was one of the *Lucia* mutineers. So I don't suppose Father will eat a slice of plum pudding the less at *his* demise.'

An unmarked van was waiting on the quay when HMS *Winchester* berthed alongside at Portsmouth. The hands were fallen out and sent to dinner as soon as the berthing wires had been secured. Five minutes later, when the decks were clear of onlookers, the body of Able Seaman Lewtas was brought up from the sick bay in a canvas bag and taken down the brow and into the van, which drove quickly off through the dockyard.

After dinner, both watches of seamen were mustered and the boatswain took charge of off-loading what remained of the starboard anchor cable in preparation for embarking its replacement; and when the captain had finished his lunch, he sent for his commander and began his preliminary investigation.

Roddy was aware that the whole affair could explode in his face unless handled very carefully. He had experience of investigations of this nature and knew of the danger of fogging the issue with irrelevant factors or hypothetical suppositions.

What was necessary was to get at the single root cause of the anchor cable parting. He was aware that he should have waited for Jannaway to report that they were ready on the forecastle before he used main engines, and was worried that if the fact that he did not wait for that report became known to higher authority, he might have to share part of the blame. That was quite unacceptable. It was essential for him to 'clear his yard-arm'—to emerge from the incident free of any blame.

Before seeing any witnesses, he decided to do his homework. He took the manual of seamanship down from the bookshelf over his desk and turned to the chapter on anchor work; and under the heading 'Weighing Anchor' found the paragraph which laid down that whenever it was necessary to maneuver a ship with an anchor on the bottom, or to break an anchor out using main engines, the cable holders should be disconnected from the spindles and the brake should be on, so that in the event of undue strain coming on the cable, it could be readily paid out by easing the brake.

He saw Oram first and established that the cable was only just out of date for its survey; but also got from him a useful statement to the effect that the ship's program had rendered it impossible to carry out that survey within the period laid down in King's Regulations. Then he saw Lanyon and obtained a navigational narrative of events, including confirmation that Lanyon had assured him on anchoring that the anchor was clear of the wreck. He then questioned the commander as to why Jannaway and not Oram was in charge on the forecastle that morning, so giving himself an opportunity to make the point that Jannaway had been given the job as part of his further training, a line Yarrow liked particularly, as it made him out to be a captain who was concerned about the furtherance of his officers' careers.

The next witness was the chief petty officer shipwright, a powerfully built Glaswegian with a thick black beard called Silletto. A few months before, Silletto had made a formal complaint about being required to attend evening quarters at a time when he had a heavy work load. Yarrow had dismissed the complaint as frivolous, and since then Silletto had been marked down in the ship as a trouble-maker.

'Chief Shipwright, were you on the forecastle this morning for weighing anchor?'

'Ay, sir.'

'To your knowledge, was the cable holder connected or disconnected when the cable parted?'

'It was connected, sir.'

'Who ordered it to be connected?'

'Well, sir, what happened was—'

'I asked you a simple question, Chief Shipwright Silletto. Kindly answer it. Who gave the order for the cable holder to be connected?'

'Lieutenant Jannaway, sir.'

'Thank you very much. That will be all.'

Silletto's mouth opened and shut. Yarrow glared at him and shouted, 'I said, that will be all, thank you, Chief Shipwright.'

After Silletto had gone, Yarrow looked down at the papers on his desk and said very quietly, 'I'll see Jannaway next.'

The secretary, a pale, bespectacled Paymaster Lieutenant called Burleigh, leant forward and said, 'I beg your pardon, sir?'

Jannaway had gone over the sequence of events in his mind several times, and by the time the secretary called him into the captain's cabin he was confident that he would be able to justify all his actions on the forecastle that morning. But he was not ready for the ambush Yarrow had prepared for him.

'Stand there!' the captain barked as he entered; and immediately launched his attack. 'I've heard the evidence of several witnesses, and it is clear beyond any possible doubt that the anchor cable parted for one reason and one reason alone, namely that the cable holder was connected up when main engines were being used to break out the anchor. It has furthermore been ascertained from evidence that the officer who ordered the cable holder to be connected was you. Do you dispute that?'

Jannaway was caught off balance. It was true, the cable holder had been connected, and he had been the officer who had ordered it so; but at the same time it was not true, because he had ordered the cable holder to be disconnected.

'I said, do you dispute that?' Yarrow repeated. 'Do you dispute that the cable holder was connected up on your orders?'

'No, sir.'

'Thank you. Thank you very much.'

'May I have permission to make an observation, sir?'

'Well?'

'Although I ordered the cable to be connected up, before I came up to the bridge to report to you, I ordered it to be disconnected.'

'And was that order carried out?'

'Three ratings attempted to carry it out, sir, but on returning to the forecastle I discovered that they had been unable to do so because of the strain on the cable.'

Yarrow started blinking and grunting. This was a fresh piece of evidence that he had not taken into account.

Then he saw a way round it. 'If, as you say, you gave the order to disconnect, why did you not see to it that your order was obeyed? Is it not your normal practice to ensure that when you give an order it is carried out?'

'Yes it is sir, but I was aware that it was necessary to weigh anchor and rejoin the fleet as quickly as possible.'

'So you gave an order but did not wait to see it carried out because you were in a hurry to report to the bridge, is that correct?'

'Yes sir.'

'I see,' said Yarrow. 'In that case, why did you not report to me the fact that you had not seen your order carried out when you came to the bridge?'

'Sir, I didn't consider that—'

'Did I not clearly inform you that it was my intention to use main engines to break the anchor out?'

'Yes, sir. But—'

'Surely you of all people, a one time seaman petty officer and ex-mate, must be aware of the instructions in the seamanship manual on the subject of disconnecting the cable holder when main engines are to be used?'

'Yes, sir. I am.'

'Then I repeat, why did you not inform me straight away, when you heard that I intended to use main engines, that you had not confirmed that a vital order you had given had been carried out?'

'I admit that in that respect, I was at fault, sir.'

Yarrow nodded for some seconds.

'And after the cable parted? What did you do?'

'I went to attend the injured man, sir.'

'And then?'

Jannaway clamped his jaws tight shut and shook his head.

'And then what did you do, Lieutenant Jannaway? You stood up, did you not?'

'Yes sir.'

'And which way were you facing when you stood up?'

'I was facing aft, sir.'

'And you were looking up, were you not?'

'Yes sir.'

'You were looking up at the bridge, yes?'

'Yes, sir.'

'And then? When you had stood up and were looking up at the bridge, what did you do?'

'I shook my fists, sir.'

'And who could you see on the bridge?' Yarrow asked very quietly.

'I beg your pardon, sir?'

'I said, WHO COULD YOU SEE ON THE BRIDGE?'

'You, sir.'

'And what was I doing?'

'You were looking down at the cable deck over the dodger, sir.'

'Did you see anyone else?'

'No sir.'

'So when you shook your fists, it was not at the bridge you were shaking them, but at me, your captain.'

'Sir,' said Jannaway, 'I wish to apologize unreservedly for an action that was done in the heat of the moment and without the intention of any sort of insubordination.'

'But you do admit that, in the presence of a large number of junior ratings, you shook your fists at me, your captain?'

'Yes sir. And I deeply regret doing so.'

There was a long silence.

'Very well. This preliminary investigation is concluded. I shall report my findings direct to the Senior Officer forthwith by signal. In the meantime I direct that you are to be relieved by the first lieutenant of your duties as regatta and boats officer. You are also to be required on board for duty until further notice. Furthermore, as I see no reason for imposing an extra burden of duties on your brother officers, you are to be released to fulfill your normal duties in the ship. However, as you have admitted to me that (a) you failed to ensure that a most vital order had been carried out, (b) failed to inform me that it had not been carried out, and (c) made an open and highly insubordinate gesture to me your commanding officer in the presence of junior ratings, you give me no alternative but to apply to the Commander-in-Chief for your trial by court-martial.'

There was an auction of the dead man's kit that evening. It was held on the seamen's mess deck, and Lieutenant Jannaway was the only officer present. When he came down the ladder and asked the leading hand's permission to enter, he was received with quiet respect.

Lewtas's gear had been laid out on the mess table: his cap, his blue and white suits, his boots, his lanyards, silks, money belt, and boatswain's call. The articles went for shillings and pennies only. No one could afford more, and although Lewtas had been well liked, he had not been in the ship very long. Jannaway bid for Steve's boatswain's call, which had been issued to him twenty years before at Shotley; and having bought it for three shillings put it back on the pile and bid for it a second and a third time, paying two pounds for it in the end.

After the auction, he returned to the wardroom for dinner.

'By the way,' Lethbridge said to him over the soup, 'You have been nominated to inform the widow. Transport will be on the jetty at nine o'clock tomorrow morning.'

There were road works in the street where the Lewtas family lived, so the naval staff car parked at the end, and Jannaway walked the rest of the way.

It was a Saturday. Dozens of children were playing in the street. Filthy-faced toddlers sat in the gutters and stared as he went by. Little girls playing hop-scotch whispered and giggled behind their hands. A gang of boys stopped kicking an old tennis ball about and came marching along behind him.

The front door of number sixty-six was open. A little girl of five sat on the step playing with a doll that was missing an arm.

'Is Mrs. Lewtas at home?' Frank asked her.

'What for?' said the child.

'I want to talk to her.'

The girl jerked her head. 'She's out the back.'

He went into the house and was met by a steamy smell of washed clothes that took him right back to his days in Devonport when his mother took in washing for warrant officers.

He found Steve's wife hanging out washing in the yard, which backed onto the railway line.

'Mrs. Lewtas?'

She turned. 'Yes?'

'My name's Frank Jannaway. I'm in the same ship as your husband.'

'Oh yes? What do you want?'

'I'm afraid I've got bad news.'

Her look changed from surprise to suspicion and from suspicion to anger. 'Is he in trouble?'

'Shall we go into the house?'

She shook her head. 'You can say what you must out here.'

'There was an accident yesterday on board HMS *Winchester*. The anchor cable parted. Your husband was hit by the cable. He was killed.'

She stopped hanging the washing, and shook her head, unable to take it in.

'Did you see it happen?' she asked.

'Yes.'

'Why? Why did it happen?'

'It was an accident.'

'Whose fault was it?'

He shook his head. 'It was an accident, Mrs. Lewtas. That's all I can tell you.'

A solitary shunting engine came panting along the railway sidings behind the house. She finished pegging up a white shirt and turned away. Her shoulders began to shake. He went to comfort her, but she recoiled from him, her head bowed, her face in her hands.

He said, 'I have to ask you this. Will you be all right financially?'

She whipped round to face him, her eyes red with tears. 'All right? That's a joke, that is! We're up to our eyes! And we'll be kicked out of this place, like as not.'

'You will qualify for a widow's pension. And there's this.' He handed her an envelope. 'It's from the sale of his kit.'

She looked at the envelope and then back at him. 'I suppose that makes everything all right, does it?'

He gave her some details about the pension she would be entitled to and said he would arrange for one of the naval charities to get in touch. She dissolved into quiet tears and said she was sorry she had been rude to him.

'It's all right,' he said gently. 'I understand.'

At that, her temper ignited. 'Understand? Understand? You don't understand *nothing*!' She ordered him out of the house and followed him to the front door; and as he was walking away, she screamed, weeping, after him, 'Bloody officers! Bloody Navy! Bloody Navy! Fuck the lot of you! Fuck the bloody lot of you!'

The ship sailed early on Monday morning, having embarked a new anchor and a replacement cable over the weekend. The rest of the fleet had spent the week-end at Portland, and HMS *Winchester* rejoined the squadron off the Isle of Wight for the passage north to Scapa Flow.

The buzz was already round the ship that Jannaway was in trouble, and he was left in no doubt by the ship's company that they sympathized with him. This was made obvious one evening when he did night rounds of the ship accompanied by the master-at-arms. As usual, they started right forward in the paint shop and worked their way aft, visiting every compartment, passage way and mess deck. When they arrived in the seamen's mess deck where Lewtas had slung his hammock, Jannaway was received with punctilious respect by the leading hand; and as he departed up the ladder an anonymous voice shouted, 'We're with you, Jan!'

'I didn't hear that, sir,' said the master-at-arms as they strode on along the main passageway to the stokers' mess deck.

When the fleet arrived at Scapa Flow, the Flag Officer Commanding the Second Cruiser Squadron, Rear Admiral Astley Rushton, sent for Yarrow, who was piped over the side in full dress uniform with sword and medals. HMS *Winchester*'s petty officer writer had by this time typed out Yarrow's report of his investigation into the accident, and the buzz was round the ship that Jannaway was going to take the rap.

The official board of inquiry was convened on board HMS *Exeter* that afternoon. The president of the board was the captain of HMS *Norfolk*, a punctilious ex-gunnery officer called Prickett. He was assisted by two commanders and a lieutenant commander with a law degree. The whole thing took three hours from start to finish, so that the officers of the Board were able to return to their ships in time for the cocktail party to be held in HMS *Dorsetshire*'s wardroom that evening.

The following morning, Jannaway was brought before Yarrow by Commander Lethbridge to be formally informed of the decision of the Board. Lieutenant Burleigh was in attendance, standing at the captain's elbow clasping to his chest a copy of B.R. 11, the bible of court martial procedure, and a bulky and much-amended copy of King's Regulations and Admiralty Instructions.

Jannaway stood stiffly to attention before the captain's desk, his hat under his arm, cap badge to the front.

'Lieutenant Jannaway, sir,' said Lethbridge.

Yarrow held his hand out to Burleigh. 'His file, if you please, Secretary.'

Burleigh handed over a buff file marked PERSONAL. Yarrow opened it and took out Admiralty Form S.206, the confidential report, which he had completed in red ink.

'Right,' said Yarrow, grunting and pulling at his nose. 'Right. The Flag Officer, Second Cruiser Squadron, has received my application for your court-martial, and it will be forwarded to the Commander-in-Chief for his consideration. In the meantime, I have been directed to submit a special confidential report on you; and, because that report is adverse, I am required by King's Regulations and Admiralty Instructions to read it to you, and you are similarly required to sign it and acknowledge that you understand its contents. Is that clear?'

'Yes, sir,' said Jannaway.

'Very well. This is what I have written. "Since joining HMS *Winchester*, Lieutenant Jannaway has made little effort to integrate himself with his fellow officers. His manner towards the ratings has been over-friendly and his attitude towards his superiors, particularly to myself, has been cold and, on one occasion, grossly insubordinate. He lacks the social qualities of an officer, and has proved to be a misfit both in the wardroom and the ship. Although his professional knowledge is, on the whole, sound, his lack of judgment, his lack of leadership, and his slackness in ensuring that his orders are properly carried out have resulted in a fatal accident to a member of my ship's company. On these grounds, and in view of his low average score of two point nine for officer qualities, it is my recommendation that this officer be placed on Admiralty Quarterly Report and that, if he does not demonstrate an immediate and visible improvement, Their Lordships should give consideration to his removal from the Service."'

Yarrow spun the form round on his desk, and pushed it towards Jannaway, who accepted a pen from Lieutenant Burleigh and signed his name at the bottom of the report.

'Now get out,' said Yarrow.

He went out onto the forecastle and looked out over the bleak Orkney islands. He thought of the weeks and months he had spent in that place during the war, and of the shipmates he had known who had lost their lives.

So many lives, so much service, such dedicated loyalty....

His thoughts drifted. Why had he become an officer in the first place? So that he could improve conditions on the lower deck, wasn't that it?

He looked down at the new chain cable. The old cable had been over-strained and condemned. There was a lesson in that, too. They were all links in a chain: Steve Lewtas, himself, Roddy, the admiral. And wasn't that chain of loyalty already dangerously overstrained? The conundrum was that if you wanted to get on in order to change things, you had to give the outward and visible signs of being obedient to the system. You had to keep your mouth shut and your nose clean. But the question that remained was that if you went along with the system temporarily, at what stage did you return to your true loyalty? When was the right time? Was it ever possible? And even if it was, could there ever *be* a right time?

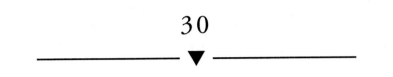

30

Dora felt quite shy of Frank when his ship came back into Portsmouth at the end of July. She was eight months pregnant and worried that he might not like her, now that she had lost her shape. But she needn't have worried because he was so kind and nice to her.

'I love 'ee true,' he said, and nibbled her ear; and she tickled him, which sent him into paroxysms, and she said, 'Come on, boy, where's your self control?' and went on tickling him until he ended up begging her to stop, crying with laughter and saying 'I can't stand it, I can't stand it!' and she said, very Welsh, because he liked it when she talked that way, 'Got no self control, boy, that's your trouble.'

He advertised in the Portsmouth Evening News for 'a piano in first rate condition for next to nothing,' and do you believe it he got one for a pound providing he could remove it. He got some of his sailors to help him; and they put it on a barrow and wheeled it through the city and out to Southsea, and it went in the front room. She gave the sailors tea and jam sandwiches, and Frank played the piano. Brilliant, he was. He could pick up any tune you liked to name and play it by ear.

The sailors were so polite and nice to her. They called her 'Mrs. Jannaway,' which gave her a sort of warm glow inside, because she hadn't been called that before; and when she thanked them all for helping with the piano they thanked her back, and she watched them walk off across the common with their bell bottomed trousers pressed against their legs by the wind, walking with that funny rolling gait sailors have. She turned back to Frank and wept in his arms, because she was so happy and proud to be married to him and to be carrying his baby.

Frank was allowed home for the night whenever he wasn't the duty officer. On the Sunday when he was on duty he sent a taxi for her and she went to have lunch on board with him. It was very quiet because nearly all the other officers were on leave. After lunch they sat in the anteroom and had coffee, and Frank picked up the local Portsmouth paper.

'Ye gods!' he said, all of a sudden. 'They can't do that!'

'What can't they do?' Dora asked.

He shook his head and put the paper down. 'It looks as though the government's going to cut naval pay.'

'Well, fair's fair,' she said. 'The teachers and police are going to get theirs cut too, aren't they?'

He picked up the newspaper and read it again and shook his head again. 'This isn't a fair cut,' he said.

'Well, is any cut fair?' she said. 'At least everyone's being treated the same, aren't they?'

'No they're not.' said Frank. 'Not if they do what they say they'll do.'

He explained about the Navy's different pay scales. He said that it looked as if they were going to put all the men on the 1919 scale onto the 1925 scale. 'Well that seems to make sense,' she said.

'No it doesn't. The 1925 pay scale is twenty-five percent *lower* than the 1919 scale; and it was Admiral Beatty himself who promised the 1919 men that that their pay would never be cut.'

'Oh,' she said. 'I suppose that does make a bit of a difference, doesn't it?'

She stayed on board all afternoon, and in the evening they watched the Royal Marines beating the retreat, which was lovely because at the end they put a spotlight on the white ensign flying from Nelson's old ship the *Victory*, and bugles played the sunset call while the band played *The day thou gavest, Lord, is ended*. It gave her quite a lump in the throat, that.

August was an awful month for weather, but it didn't seem to matter because they were both excited about the baby's arrival.

Every morning of his leave, Frank brought her breakfast in bed. One morning he cupped his hands on her stomach and spoke to the baby. 'Can you hear me in there?' he said. 'You're to hurry up and come out before I go off to sea again, do you hear?'

'He's kicking, Frank!' Dora said. 'Just feel! See? I think he heard you!'

When he came home on leave in the middle of August he said he didn't want to think about ships or look at his uniform for the whole fourteen days. He seemed quite tired and sad about something, so she asked him what the matter was; and he told her about the man who died when the cable broke, and how he visited his widow and had seen the poverty she lived in.

'I'd forgotten what it was like,' he said, and she was shocked to see tears in his eyes. He came to her and she held him in her arms; and he told her about his friends who had died in the war, how it made him feel guilty to be alive, how he had struggled to be an officer to help improve conditions on the lower deck, but how it hadn't worked, and how he had less influence now than he had when he was a petty officer in charge of an admiral's barge. And now there was this rumor going round of a big pay cut and he felt powerless to do anything about it, even if he knew what he should do, which he didn't.

They went for a walk on Southsea Common. A seaplane was flying overhead. Frank said it was practicing for the Schneider Trophy. They went to the seashore and looked across the Solent at the big yachts racing, and he said, 'I was a deckhand aboard a yacht like that when I was a boy.'

There was such a lot that she didn't know about him. It was as if there were a big crater in his life that he didn't like to look into. She didn't like to ask him about it because she was still in awe of him.

One evening when he was reading the paper after supper he said, 'Well, well, well.'

'What is it?' she asked.

He looked up as if he had forgotten she was there. 'The captain's sister's just got married.'

'I didn't know he had a sister,' she said.

'Didn't you?' he said. 'She's an actress. Anita Yarrow.'

She looked blank. 'Who has she married?'

He looked back at the paper. 'A South African tennis player called Lasbury.'

'Oh well,' she said, 'He's famous. Even I've heard of Stewart Lasbury.'

He tuned the piano himself and played it every day that summer leave. He said that now that he was married he wanted to be more of a family man and less of a naval officer. He said that as soon as he had qualified for the minimum pension, which would be in five or six years' time, he would leave the Navy and do something else with the rest of his life. She was a bit worried by that because she thought the security of a good pension was important. But she didn't like to say anything. Most of the time he was very cheerful and funny and relaxed, but every now and then she saw a different side to him, one that seemed torn by some problem he wrestled with.

One night he walked in his sleep. He jumped out of bed and threw the sash window up and put out his head and shouted something unintelligible, and she had to go to him and bring him back to bed; and when he woke up he was shaking and sweating and he said he'd had a nightmare about a tidal wave. She held his head against her breast and soothed him. He was tight all over, like a piece of wire. 'It's all right, Frank love,' she whispered. 'I'm here. It was only a dream.'

On his last day of leave, which was a Sunday, they went to early Mass; and afterwards he took her over to the Isle of Wight for an outing to Bembridge, and they had an expensive lunch in a hotel restaurant overlooking the sea. They watched the sailing boats. He said that one day he would like to have a boat of his own. 'I'll teach you to sail, Dora,' he said. 'Would you like that?'

'I don't know,' she said. 'I've never tried.'

He suggested going for a walk after lunch, but she was feeling large and heavy, so she sat in the window and watched him walk along the beach on his own. She looked at him and she thought: that man is my husband. Then she had a pain and when he arrived back she said, 'I think I've started.'

He paid the bill and they caught the first ferry and went straight back to Southsea. By the time they arrived at Portsmouth harbor her pains were coming quite close together and she was terrified that her waters would break before she got home. But they didn't, and Frank did all the right things in the right order; and the midwife came straight away and the baby was born at five o'clock the following morning.

It was a boy. 'I can hardly believe it!' Frank said.

Dora blew her cheeks out. 'I can,' she said.

He sat on the bed and held the baby for the first time. 'Isn't he perfect?' he whispered. 'What shall we call him?'

'You choose,' she said.

'Alan,' he said. 'His name is Alan.'

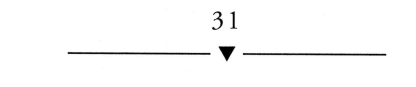

31

There was a cocktail party on board HMS *Warspite* on Friday evening, to which the first lieutenant and two officers from HMS *Winchester* were invited. Because it was the last week-end before the ship sailed for the autumn exercises, no one wanted to take up the invitation; but naval etiquette dictated that each ship should be represented, so Oram detailed off Lieutenant Jannaway and Sub Lieutenant Entwistle to go.

Frank had never enjoyed wardroom cocktail parties. More often than not an atmosphere of false bonhomie prevailed. There was always much back slapping and hearty laughter. First lieutenants talked to first lieutenants about watch routines, darken ship screens and the problems of keeping the flats and passages clean. Engineers talked to engineers about generators and evaporators. Sub lieutenants talked to sub lieutenants about beer, cars, and runs ashore, and lieutenant commanders talked to lieutenant commanders about their promotion chances.

That evening, Frank was button-holed by an elderly lieutenant commander with graying hair and a well-used face. 'You're the ex-mate from *Winchester*, I believe?' he said as they shook hands. 'Harry Pursey. I'm an ex-mate myself.'

Within minutes they were discussing the expected pay cuts. A few days before, an anonymous letter signed 'Neutralis' had appeared in the September issue of *The Fleet* magazine, in which the writer had made a veiled warning about what might happen if the Board of Admiralty allowed the cuts to go ahead.

'I'm not wondering "what will happen—IF,"' Pursey said, quoting the last line of the letter. 'It's quite obvious what will happen. The lower deck will go on strike, that's what'll happen. What a shambles they've made of things! This must be the worst Board of Admiralty in living memory. Look at them—we're in the middle of a national crisis, and they're all on leave! Field's a nice enough bloke, but quite ineffectual. As for Dreyer, he's all gong and no dinner.'

Frank found it a great relief to find someone he could talk to openly. They agreed that it would be disastrous if the 1919 pay scale was cut, as the lower deck would see it as an act of treachery on the part of the Admiralty.

'And that's exactly what it would be,' Pursey said.

'I think the long and short of it is that the top brass are completely out of touch with the lower deck,' Frank remarked.

'Oh yes?' said Oram, who appeared from nowhere. 'This sounds like a very interesting conversation. Can anyone join in?'

Frank was the duty officer on Sunday. As all was quiet in the afternoon, he went down to the commander's office to put in some time on the back-log of paperwork. When he lifted the files out of his in-tray he found a sealed envelope marked for his personal attention. It contained a request from Petty Officer Telegraphist Devereux, and read: 'To see officer of division on a private matter.'

Devereux was a quiet, rather nervous individual who kept very much to himself and carried out his duties in the WT office with meticulous attention to detail. He was the sort of person who faded into the background, and it seemed odd that he should have put in this request.

Frank went along to the WT office and found Devereux mustering the code books. 'I've received your request,' he said. 'If you'd like to come to my cabin this evening after nine, I'll see you then.'

Devereux stepped into the cramped little cabin and drew the curtain across the door. 'So what can I do for you?' Frank asked when he had taken the spare chair.

He hesitated before speaking. 'It's a tricky subject, sir. Have you seen the latest issue of *The Fleet?*'

'Yes.'

'In that case you know about the Neutralis letter.'

'Doesn't everyone?'

Again, Devereux hesitated. 'Before I say anything more, sir, may I have an assurance that nothing of what I'm about to tell you will be repeated by you, and that you will never report that this interview took place?'

'That's a tall order,' Frank said.

'I know that, sir but I wouldn't like to commit myself further until you can give me that assurance.'

'Why is it so important?'

Devereux wiped his upper lip with his knuckle. 'Sir—information has come into my possession in a way contrary to regulations. I believe it's my duty to pass on that information, but if I do, I shall lay myself open to a charge.'

'What sort of charge? A breach of security?'

'Yes, sir. And perhaps a much more serious one than that. But I feel it's my duty to tell an officer what I know and—well, the only person in the ship I can approach is you.'

'I see.'

Devereux swallowed nervously. 'What I have to say is for the good of the Service, sir, but I—I need to be able to speak freely, and without fear of being penalized later.'

Frank knew exactly what Devereux was getting at. The Royal Navy had no compunction about crushing those who dared to criticize it in any way. 'All right,' he said. 'You have my word that I'll preserve the strictest confidence. Nothing you say will go beyond the four walls of this cabin. So what's this all about?'

'The pay cut, sir.'

'We don't know for certain that we're getting one.'

'Yes we do, sir. At least, the C-in-C does.'

He pulled a sheet of paper from his pocket and put it on the desk. It was a carbon copy of a signal from Admiralty, and was addressed to all nine commanders-in-chief, including C-in-C Portsmouth and C-in-C Atlantic Fleet.

'I'm not sure if I want to read this,' Frank said after reading the first line.

Devereux tilted his head. 'I think you've gone too far to back out, now, sir.'

So he read it, and became immediately aware that it was dynamite:

FOR YOUR CONFIDENTIAL GUIDANCE. THE FINANCIAL CRISIS OBLIGES HM GOVERNMENT TO TAKE IMMEDIATE AND STRINGENT MEASURES TO BALANCE THE BUDGET. THESE MEASURES WILL INVOLVE SACRIFICES FOR ALL CLASSES OF THE COMMUNITY AND REDUCTIONS IN PAY IN PUBLIC SERVICES. H.M. GOVERNMENT HAVE DECIDED THAT THEY ARE OBLIGED TO CALL UPON THE FIGHTING SERVICES TO MAKE THIS CONTRIBUTION TO THE COMMON END. FOR THE NAVY THE SACRIFICE INVOLVES THE ACCEPTANCE OF THE RECOMMENDATIONS OF THE REPORT OF THE COMMITTEE ON NATIONAL EXPENDITURE AND THESE INCLUDE PLACING ALL OFFICERS AND MEN AT PRESENT IN RECEIPT OF PAY ON 1919 SCALES ON THE REVISED SCALE INTRODUCED IN 1925 AND REDUCING ALL STANDARD RATES OF PAY OF OFFICERS BY 11 INSTEAD OF 8 PER CENT AS PREVIOUSLY DECIDED TO COME INTO FORCE IN JULY LAST. THE NEW REGULATIONS ARE TO COME INTO FORCE FROM 1ST OCTOBER NEXT.

Frank could hardly believe what he had read. The Government, with the Admiralty's full support and approval, were going to cut the 1919 pay scale back to the 1925 pay scale, and then cut the 1925 pay scale as well.

'Where did you get this?'

'I'm not at liberty to tell you that, sir.'

'Why did you bring it to me?'

'Isn't it obvious, sir? I had to do something, didn't I? I mean—we're being kept in the dark, aren't we? The C-in-C's pulling a fast one.'

'Admiral Hodges is sick.'

'With respect, sir, what's his chief staff officer for? Besides, it's gone to Admiral Keyes as well, hasn't it? And what's he done about it? Nothing.'

Frank looked at the signal again. It had been released three days before.

'If you ask me, sir, they're so frightened of the row it'll cause they're deliberately withholding it from the fleet until the ships have sailed from the home ports. They don't want trouble in their own back yards.'

He understood now why Devereux had been so insistent about confidentiality. Here was a signal addressed for the personal attention of commanders-in-chief, which would have been encrypted and transmitted by a highly secure means designed to ensure that none but the addressees or their chief staff officers or signal officers should see it. That a petty officer from the most junior ship in the cruiser squadron should have got hold of it was proof in itself of a most serious breach of security regulations somewhere along the line, and unless he reported the matter to higher authority straight away, he would be equally culpable of the same offence.

'Did you decrypt this signal yourself?'

'No, sir. It was given me.'

'Why you?'

'Because I'm a PO Tel, sir. And—'

'And what?'

'Because I'm in the same ship as you.' Devereux gave a nervous little cough. 'I think you're better known in the fleet than you realize, sir.'

'So…are you expecting me to take some sort of action?'

'Sir—I've been in the Service just on eighteen years. It's my life. I came to you because I knew you'd understand. I thought—well, I thought you might be able to do something about it.'

Frank looked at him. 'It's not as easy as that.'

'Nothing's easy in the situation we're in now, sir. And if something isn't done soon, things are likely to get a lot harder before we're through.'

'What do you mean by that?'

'You know what I'm talking about, sir. You've read the newspapers. You've seen the Neutralis letter. And now you've seen that signal. It's obvious, isn't it? The Admiralty's going to sell us down the river and the C-in-C's aren't going to lift a finger to stop them. They may think they're making economies, but it'll cost them dear in the long run. It'll cost them the good will of the lower deck, what's left of it. They may think they can get away with it, but they won't, will they? I mean, if you were a three-badge AB on the 1919 scale with a wife and kids, and your furniture on the never-never, what would you do? You'd have to be deaf and blind not to know what's going on, sir. I don't want to see the fleet go on strike, but that's the way we're heading.'

'Are there people in this ship who would take an active part? If it came to a strike?'

'There are people in *every* ship. Every ship in the fleet—every ship in the Navy.'

'What do you expect from me?'

Devereux's eyes moved from side to side. 'You're the officer, sir. You're supposed to know what to do.'

'Does anyone else in the ship know about this signal?'

'The only person—no sir. No one in this ship.'

'Do you know if any other officers have been approached in the same way you have approached me?'

'I think it's extremely unlikely, sir.'

Frank thought for a few moments. 'Let's be quite open about this, Devereux. What exactly have you come here to tell me?'

Devereux paused for a long time before giving his answer, and when he did, Frank felt the hairs stand on the back of his neck.

'I think there's going to be a fleet mutiny,' he said. 'That's what I've come to tell you.'

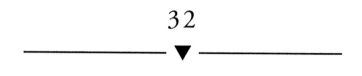

32

Dora put on her mackintosh and dressed Alan up in the smock and boo-tees and the knitted cap his Granny had made for him. She put him in his pram with the waterproof cover on and the hood up. Very carefully, she lowered the pram down the steps from the house, and pushed it along the path across Southsea Common.

She joined the wives and families who had gathered on the foreshore to wave goodbye to the men who were sailing with the Atlantic Fleet for the autumn exercises. They stood on the pebble beach, close to the memorial that marked the spot where, in 1805, Nelson had embarked to sail in the *Victory* before the battle of Trafalgar.

Frank had managed to get his last night off duty, and they had talked about Alan's future. Frank said that one day he would introduce Alan to the arts—to music and literature. He said he wanted him to grow up to have a much larger view of life than he had himself. 'Whatever else he does,' he said, 'he must not join the Royal Navy.'

'You haven't done so badly,' she said.

'Perhaps not. But the Navy puts blinkers on a man. I wouldn't wish that on Alan.' And then he added: 'I think the duty of a father is to make it possible for his son to become a better person, and lead a fuller life than he did himself, don't you?'

He was a lovely man, Frank. Funny, and kind, and gentle, and loving. And every so often he would come out with these quiet thoughts of his that made her ever more determined to be the sort of wife he needed.

With the blue-jackets ranged in neat lines on their forecastles, gun decks and quarterdecks, the ships of the Atlantic Fleet came slowly and majestically out through the narrow entrance of Portsmouth harbor. First came the battle cruisers *Hood, Warspite* and *Valiant*; and now the cruisers *Norfolk, York, Dorsetshire, Exeter,* and, at the end of the line, *Winchester,* Frank's ship.

On the shore, mothers bent over their children and pointed. Some waved handkerchiefs. Others stared in awe at the might of Great Britain's naval power. 'Look Alan,' Dora said. 'Here comes Daddy's ship.'

But Alan had just found his thumb, and was more interested in it than HMS *Winchester*, or any other ship in the Atlantic Fleet.

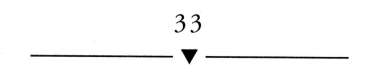

33

Roddy was glad to be back on board and away from Geraldine. With Geraldine, he was in a permanent state of tension. Life in her company was like an unending competition that he was never allowed to win. On board his ship, all that changed. He was the focus of attention for five hundred officers and men. He was piped on board, waited upon, reported to, and deferred to. But it was not only the personal attention he received that he found so pleasant about shipboard life. It was the regular routine, the bugle calls, the meals at exactly the same time, and the steady progression of identical events through the day, from the ceremony of Colors each morning to the evening report of the commander at pipe-down every night at sea.

'All well Commander?'

'All well, sir.'

'Have the new midshipmen been put into watches?'

'They have, sir.'

'Keep an eye on young Courtenay, will you? He's a distant cousin of mine. Who's his Sea Daddy?'

'Jannaway, sir.'

'Swap him. Give him to Number One.'

'Ay ay, sir.' Lethbridge hesitated a moment. 'As a matter of fact, I wanted to speak to you about Jannaway, sir.'

'Oh?'

'He's asked to see you on a private matter. He stressed that it was important and urgent.'

Yarrow breathed out through his teeth. 'That man will try my patience too far one of these days. What's it about, do you know?'

'He didn't tell me, but my guess is that it'll be to do with this pay cut.'

'That's hardly a private matter.'

'I tried to discourage him, but he was insistent.'

'That bloody man!'

'To give him his due, he does have his finger on the pulse as far as the lower deck is concerned. And it is his right. You say in your standing orders—'

'I know very well what I say in my orders, thank you very much, Commander.' Yarrow heaved a sigh. 'Very well. Let's get it over and done with. I'll see him right away.'

'Now, sir? He has the middle watch. He'll be turned in.'

'Turn him out. If I don't see him now, I won't see him at all.'

'Well get on with it,' Yarrow said as soon as Jannaway entered. 'I haven't got all night.'

The ship was rolling in a quartering sea and the wooden furniture was creaking as it worked against the bulkhead.

'Sir,' Jannaway said, 'I believe that if the government implements these pay cuts in the way that's been reported in the papers, there is a serious danger of a major breakdown of discipline.'

Yarrow sat back in his chair and said, 'Drivel.'

'With all due respect,' Jannaway said, 'Do you think I would request to see you if I had any doubts at all about the seriousness of the situation?'

'Well go on,' said Yarrow. 'Say what you have to.'

'If the recommendations of the May Committee are implemented, and it looks as if they will be, some able rates on the 1919 pay scale will lose a quarter of their pay.'

'They'll have to tighten their belts then, won't they?'

'They won't be able to make ends meet, sir. They won't be able to support their wives and families. They can't afford to buy houses. They have to pay rent for lodgings. They can't even afford to buy furniture—they get it all on hire purchase. If their pay is cut, they'll face repossession of their furniture or eviction from their lodgings, and in some cases, both. Some are afraid that their wives will be driven into prostitution.'

'Balls,' said Yarrow. 'Complete and utter balls.'

'No, sir,' Jannaway said. 'It is *not* balls.' He met Yarrow's eye and held it. 'These men have no savings to fall back on. They *can't* tighten their belts. Their only weapon—'

'Go on,' said Yarrow. 'What is their only weapon?'

'To go on strike, sir.'

Yarrow tipped back his chair, gave a snort and then a shout of laughter. 'So you think there's going to be a mutiny, is that it?'

'I think it's quite possible sir. Probable, if the situation isn't nipped in the bud. The whole fleet is in a state of tense apprehension.'

'I think you would rather like a mutiny, wouldn't you, Jannaway? I think you would relish it.'

'That is the reverse of the truth, sir,' Jannaway said quietly.

Yarrow grunted a few times. 'And…this mutiny of yours. Have you any suggestions as to how we might avert it?'

'I think the most important thing to do, first, is for the Admiralty to stop keeping us in the dark.

'"Us," did you say? "Us?" Are you acting as some sort of trade union leader for the fleet by any chance?'

'I'm speaking out of a sense of duty, sir. I became aware of the concern felt by the men in my division, and I believe it my duty to make you aware of it.'

Yarrow backed off a little. For a moment, Jannaway felt that that there might be the beginnings of a rapport between them.

'So what do you expect me to do about it?'

'For a start, I think that if the cuts are to be made, the fact should be made known to the fleet immediately. Secondly, it would prudent *not* to assemble the fleet at Invergordon, because as soon as the fleet is assembled, the men will be able to plan concerted action.'

'So you're saying we should disperse the fleet?'

'I think it's the only way to avert a strike, sir.'

'So let's see, have I got this right? You want to cancel the entire fleet program at Invergordon, do you? Cancel the sports program. Cancel the advancement boards for petty officer. Cancel the officers' Inverness Ball. Cancel all the children's parties. Cancel the senior officer's call on the King at Balmoral. Cancel the Highland Games. And what about the people of Invergordon and Alness and Cromarty? What about the butchers and bakers and candlestick makers? What about the pubs and dance halls and hotels? What about all the newspapers and fresh milk? What about the lorry loads of tinned beans and cabbages and new-laid eggs? I suppose they can all be left in the garbage bins on the jetty can they? I'm sure the locals will really jump for joy to hear that their biggest single source of income of the whole year has just gone down the drain. Had you thought of that?'

'Sir—the consequences of a fleet mutiny would be far more damaging. It would damage the Navy in a way that might take generations to repair.'

But Yarrow wasn't listening, he was laughing. 'So what you're suggesting is that I make a signal to Admiral Tomkinson, the Senior Officer of the Atlantic Fleet, saying, "Please sir, I don't think we ought to go to Invergordon this year, because Lieutenant Jannaway says the men may call a strike." Is that it?'

Jannaway looked down at the patterned carpet. 'I don't have anything more to add, sir.'

'Well I do,' said Yarrow. 'I most certainly do. Let us make no bones about this, Jannaway. If you think that you can take some sort of revenge on me for what was a boyhood prank…if you think you can stir up any sort of communist trouble on this ship out of some warped sense of sticking up for your class, then I recommend to you that you think again. It's my opinion that you should never have been made up to officer in the first place. You are a trouble maker, that's what you are. A trouble maker and a jumped-up lower-deck lawyer. Now get out of my sight, and don't waste any more of my time.'

34

▼

MUTINY

Soon after seven o'clock on the morning of Saturday, September 12th 1931, the ships of the Atlantic Fleet slipped in through the narrow entrance to the Cromarty Firth and came to their moorings in the fleet anchorage off the town of Invergordon, which stands at the foot of the Easter Ross mountains, twenty miles north of Inverness, in Scotland.

As soon as HMS *Winchester's* anchors were down, booms and ladders were lowered. Within minutes, the ship's motor cutter was on its way inshore to collect fresh milk, mail, and newspapers.

One of the men in the motor cutter was Able Seaman Bennett, who worked as Lieutenant Jannaway's typist in the commander's office, and who was landing to collect the ship's official mail.

The diesel engine thumped away as the motor cutter punched through the choppy water of the Firth, and as the boat approached the jetty, the coxswain sounded four short blasts on his whistle to order 'Slow,' and then a single blast for 'Stop.'

Once alongside, Bennett waited for the petty officers and leading hands to disembark before going up the steps to the jetty, where he was met by his opposite number from HMS *Norfolk*, Able Seaman Hill.

Hill ran the ship's company radio on board *Norfolk*, and during the passage north had been listening in to the BBC news reports of the debate on pay cuts in the House of Commons. There was now no doubt at all that the cuts were to be implemented.

'We're going to hold a private strike meeting this afternoon,' Hill said as they walked up to the mail office. 'In the canteen at two o'clock. We want a representative from each ship. Will you represent *Winchester*?'

Lieutenant Jannaway was using the typewriter in the commander's office when Bennett returned on board with the official mail. As soon as he entered, Jannaway removed the sheet of paper in the typewriter and placed it face down on the desk.

'The AFOs have arrived, sir,' Bennett said, and handed over an envelope marked ON HIS MAJESTY'S SERVICE. Jannaway opened it and took out the Admiralty Fleet Order that had been issued the previous week. It officially confirmed the contents of the C-in-C's signal that Devereux had brought to him. Whether through incompetence or design, the Admiralty had chosen to send it through the post to the fleet rather than by signal.

'They're going ahead with the cuts, aren't they, sir?' Bennett said.

'How do you know?'

'My opposite number in *Norfolk* heard it on the BBC news last night. And it's in all the newspapers.'

Jannaway shook his head, but said nothing.

'Can I ask you a question, sir? Off the record?'

'Yes?'

'I think there's going to be trouble. Big trouble.'

'Go on.'

'Well...what would you do, sir? If you were in our shoes? I mean...they're pushing us into a corner, aren't they? That AFO's an insult. Why were we the last to hear? Everyone in the country heard about this pay cut before we did. People are getting angry, sir. Things are getting out of control. The question is—'

'What?'

'Nobody wants it to get out of hand, sir. That's the last thing anyone wants. But something's got to be done. There's no question of us accepting it. The question is, what do we do, and how do we do it?'

Jannaway picked up the sheet of paper from the desk, studied it for a few moments, and then folded it in half and half again.

'This may be of some help,' he said. 'I wish I could do more, but I've already done all I can.'

Bennett landed with the ship's soccer team that afternoon, but instead of going to the sports ground, he went up the path to the junior rates' canteen, a long, narrow building painted green, with a tin roof supported by iron rafters.

Inside, he joined a group of about a dozen sailors who were sitting away from the window at one of the long tables at the far end of the building, smoking and drinking squash. Apart from them, the canteen was empty. They looked like an innocent bunch of sailors enjoying a quiet afternoon ashore.

But they were not enjoying a quiet afternoon, nor were they innocent. They were plotting a mutiny.

Later, after it was all over, no one remembered exactly who said what, but just about everyone remembered what was said.

'It's got to be properly organized.

'And it's got to be solid.'

'We've got to have a lead ship.'

'That should be the flagship. *Nelson*.'

'She doesn't arrive till Monday.'

'What about *Hood*?'

'No. Let's make it *Rodney*.'

'*Rodney* till *Nelson* arrives?'

'Better stick to one ship all the way through.'

'*Rodney* then. *Rodney* to the end.'

'When?'

'Eight o'clock Tuesday morning, when we're due to sail. We go up on the forecastles and sit on the cables. We stop the fleet from sailing.'

'And if that doesn't work?'

'We'll commandeer the boats. We'll raid ships' stores. We'll get the stokers to take over trains and buses. We'll go down to London. We'll march on the Houses of Parliament and rub their fucking noses in it.'

'Bloody hell!'

'How else are we going to make the bastards listen to us?'

Bennett took out a fold of paper that was tucked inside his hat and threw it down on the table. 'This may be of interest, gentlemen.'

Hill picked it up and looked at it. It was a sheet of foolscap with the Admiralty crest at its head. There were just ten lines, typed in capitals. Hill read them out to the meeting.

CONCERTED ACTION

NO VIOLENCE

NO RINGLEADERS

MINIMUM DISOBEDIENCE

CHEERS BETWEEN SHIPS

MAINTAIN ESSENTIAL SERVICES

NO INSOLENCE

NO BAD LANGUAGE

COURTESY AND RESPECT TO OFFICERS

GOOD LUCK

'Fucking hell!' someone muttered. 'Where did that come from?'

'My boss,' Bennett said. 'Lieutenant Jannaway.'

'Is he all right?'

'Yes. He's all right.'

Hill picked up the sheet of paper and looked at it again. 'I reckon it makes a lot of sense.'

'What's that about cheers between ships?'

'It's like a tradition—what we always do. It's to show solidarity. Keep spirits up.'

'So are we going to do it?'

'We've got to, haven't we? We've got no choice.'

'It'll take some organizing.'

'We need a manifesto.'

'And a committee.'

'That's us, isn't it?'

'No. It's got to be done democratically. We can't elect ourselves.'

'So we elect a committee, right? And a chairman. We'll have a strike meeting. If we're going to do it, we've got to do it properly.'

'So when we do we have this meeting? Tomorrow?'

'*Nelson* won't be in.'

'Bugger *Nelson*!'

'It's *got* to be tomorrow. There's no other time we can do it. We've got to have the whole thing sorted by Tuesday.'

'We could leave it till next week-end.'

'No way! They'd split the fleet up and stop us.'

'So it's Tuesday, agreed? Tuesday when the fleet sails.'

'Tuesday when fleet *doesn't* sail!'

'So what about this meeting? Are we agreed for tomorrow afternoon?'

'There won't be much time to spread the buzz.'

'We can start doing that this evening.'

'We want as many as possible. The whole watch ashore. They need to be convinced. We've got to make sure it's solid. I vote for tomorrow evening.'

'Why not both? Afternoon and evening? We can pass the buzz today, now. On the sports ground. Everyone ashore tomorrow afternoon.'

'What about the RC's?'

'What about them?'

'Well, there's only one RC Mass, isn't there? And Catholics go from every ship in the fleet to it. Which ship's holding Catholic Mass on board tomorrow?'

'*Malaya*, isn't it?'

'There you are then. You're an RC, aren't you Wiggy? You can go to Mass in *Malaya* and spread the buzz. That way the message will go back to every ship in the fleet.'

On Sunday, the fleet canteen started to fill up as soon as the first liberty men came ashore. Normally only a handful of men from each ship would have taken leave on a Sunday afternoon at Invergordon, but that day there was an unprecedented rush to go ashore.

Shortly after two o'clock, Len Wincott, a smiling, moonfaced able seaman from HMS *Norfolk*, who had removed the name tally from his cap, entered the already crowded fleet canteen. He found the last remaining empty table and jumped onto it. The buzz of conversation stopped. All eyes turned in his direction.

'I'm not a politician,' he said. 'And I don't know how to conduct a meeting. But what I do know is this, my friends. We must strike. Like the miners. They went on strike five years ago and they got what they wanted. If they can do it so can we. If we don't strike, what's left to us? Poverty and degradation. Our families being evicted from lodgings because we can't pay the rent. Hire purchase firms taking back our furniture. Our wives going on the street. That's why we've got to strike. Look at the money it's cost to bring the fleet up here. Thousands and thousands of pounds. And what for? So the admirals can play war games and the officers can have their cocktail parties and their ball in Inverness, that's what for. So what's the answer? I've told you already, comrades. They've given us no choice. We've got to strike. They've pushed us up against the wall and if we do nothing they'll push us further till we're crushed. So we must strike, comrades. Like the miners. We must withhold our labor. Tuesday morning, first thing, we down tools. We go up to the forecastles and sit on the anchor cables and strike!'

There was no clapping or cheering, but heads were nodding in agreement.

'But if we're going to strike, we've got to strike together and we've got to hold out until they give in—all of us solid, no wavering. We've got to stop our ships going to sea. But to do that, we've got to be organized. So I'm asking now for one representative from each ship to come forward and volunteer to spread the proposal for strike action in his ship.'

For a moment, it looked as if no one would come forward and the whole idea would collapse; but then there was a sudden rush to volunteer. Men were crowding round Wincott's table, and he was scribbling each representative's name and ship down on the back of a packet of Ardath cigarettes.

S.O.A.F. to Admiralty, 1025, 14th September

IMPORTANT. THERE WAS A SLIGHT DISTURBANCE IN THE ROYAL NAVAL CANTEEN, INVERGORDON, YESTERDAY, SUNDAY EVENING, CAUSED BY ONE OR TWO RATINGS ENDEAVOURING TO ADDRESS THOSE PRESENT ON THE SUBJECT OF REDUCTION IN PAY. I ATTACH NO IMPORTANCE TO THE INCIDENT FROM A GENERAL DISCIPLINARY POINT OF VIEW; BUT IT IS POSSIBLE IT MAY BE REPORTED IN AN EXAGGERATED FORM BY THE PRESS. MATTER IS BEING INVESTIGATED.

The rush to go ashore on Monday was even greater than on Sunday. As leave was given to the watch that had remained on board the previous day, the effect was that there was a port watch strike meeting on Sunday and a starboard watch strike meeting on Monday.

Len Wincott was duty watch that day and would not have been able to get ashore without the co-operation of his friend George Hill, who agreed to stand substitute for him. He landed at four o'clock and went up to the canteen, where he found another meeting under way. As he entered, a hollow-cheeked stoker was making a speech in which he was urging a march on London.

'What do we do for food?' shouted someone.

'We take what we need from the fields. Turnips—mangel worzels. We can—'

He was drowned out by laughter, which was stopped by a banging and rattling on the door and shouts of 'Open this door immediately!'

The door was opened, and in walked Lieutenant Elkins, the officer of the patrol from HMS *Norfolk*, accompanied by three ratings of his patrol that had remained with him, the rest having put discretion before valor and made themselves scarce.

'Stop this meeting!' bellowed Elkins. 'If any man speaks I shall arrest him!' He forced his way into the crowd and lost contact with the remnants of his patrol in the process. He was half way between the bar and the door, and surrounded by a press of men, who were making it impossible for him to go forward or back.

'I shall remain here until I am satisfied that what is being discussed is not to the prejudice of discipline!' he bellowed over the din.

'That stops the meeting!' shouted someone. Then a hand went up and a beer glass flew, and smashed against one of the iron roof supports. Elkins crouched down, hunching his shoulders up and protecting his head. The way to the door opened and pressure was applied. He was pushed outside, and the door locked against him.

As the time of expiry of shore leave approached, men began streaming down to the jetty in their hundreds. A few were drunk, but most were simply excited. A crowd from the *Rodney* came along the road singing the 'Red Flag.' No one bothered to salute the officer of the patrol. Everyone was shouting to everyone else.

'Don't forget, *Winchester*!'

'OK, *Norfolk*?'

'Don't forget—six o'clock tomorrow morning!'

'Six o'clock!'

'OK, *York*?'

'Six o'clock tomorrow!'

When Frank came on deck at five forty-five on Tuesday morning, everything looked normal. The stokers had flashed up the boilers in preparation
for sailing at eight o'clock, power was on the main derrick for hoisting the
picket boat, and steam was on the capstan for unmooring. The only sign
that anything might be about to happen was that someone had put a line
through the copy of daily orders on the ship's company notice board and
had scrawled CANCELLED across it. But at six o'clock, when the marine
bugler sounded 'hands fall in,' only the petty officers and a few of the leading seamen appeared on deck.

Midshipman Courtenay reported to him. He saluted and said, 'First
Lieutenant's compliments, sir, would you see him in the wardroom right
away.'

Oram was walking about in the wardroom with a cup of coffee in one
hand, using the back of his other hand to catch the drips. 'I want you to

take charge on the forecastle and unmoor,' he said. Use the petty officers and midshipmen as necessary. Understood?'

Frank returned to the forecastle and took charge of re-connecting the mooring shackle, weighing the port anchor, and shortening in the starboard anchor cable in preparation for weighing at eight o'clock. That done, he went aft to report to the captain. On his way, he met Oram, who told him that he had been unable to find enough hands to work the main derrick to hoist the boats. 'I managed to get a party of marines to man the guys,' he said, 'but as soon as they did, someone shouted "Drop that or you'll get killed," and they all disappeared. How have you got on?'

'We've unmoored,' Frank told him. 'And we're ready for weighing anchor. I'm on my way to report to Father now.'

'Leave that to me,' said Oram. 'I'll do that.'

He left Oram to score his points with the captain, and went up to the signal bridge to make sure that the signals ratings were carrying out their duties, which they were, as were the electric light party, the engine room watch keepers, and the cooks and wardroom attendants; so it seemed that essential services were being maintained. However, when he returned to the forecastle, a much larger crowd of men had assembled, and there were similar crowds on the bows of the battleships *Valiant*, *Hood* and *Rodney* and the cruisers *Norfolk*, *Dorsetshire*, *Exeter*, and *York*.

Moments after his arrival on the forecastle, the men aboard *Valiant* gave three hearty and well-disciplined cheers that were immediately answered by cheers aboard the minelayer *Adventure* and the battleship *Rodney*. It was then that Frank realized that what he was witnessing was a full scale, mass mutiny.

The guard and band paraded for the ceremony of Colors at eight o'clock, and everyone faced aft and stood to attention with noticeably more than usual smartness. But the stokers had not turned to, so there was no hope of sailing on time. Soon after the 'carry on' had been sounded, they heard *Norfolk* sound the bugle call to clear lower deck. Minutes later, *Winchester* followed suit.

Frank went aft and fell in with the officers on the quarterdeck, facing forward at the crowd of men who had obeyed the order to muster. The captain came briskly aft, his telescope under his left arm, a white silk handkerchief in his breast pocket. Commander Lethbridge called the ship's company to attention and reported, 'Lower deck cleared for your address, sir.' Yarrow returned his salute, stepped up on to a bollard grating, and made what was obviously a carefully prepared speech.

'I have called you here today,' he said, in that pompous naval accent of his that made Frank wince inwardly, 'because I understand from the commander that a proportion of you have got some wild idea into your heads about making a protest over the reductions in pay. That is extremely foolish. The consequences of individual disobedience, laid down and authorized by the Articles of War, are harsh; but the consequences of a combined refusal of duty are harsher yet. If any of you have grievances, there is a proper way, authorized by the Naval Discipline Act, for you to state them.'

He paused for a moment, and in that pause someone in the crowd grunted like a pig. His face darkened. 'Do you realize that reports of your behavior ashore have already reached the national press? Do you realize that, as a result of your action, millions of pounds have already been knocked off the value of British shares in the Argentine alone?'

Men began drifting away from the back of the crowd. The pig grunted again. There was laughter.

Yarrow's lips quivered. Two pale spots appeared on his forehead. His hands were shaking visibly. 'For God's sake, don't you realize that if the Navy goes wrong, the whole nation's credit will collapse?'

But it was no good. The drift away from the quarterdeck turned into a rush, and the petty officers made no attempt to stop it. The captain ordered Divisions to be sounded off, but the men went back up to the forecastle and refused to obey.

Frank went back to the forecastle. A few minutes later he was joined by Commander Lethbridge, who told him that he had orders from the captain to identify the ringleaders, arrest them, and put them in cells. Frank said that it would be an impossible task. Undeterred, Lethbridge tried to take the names of the men who appeared to be at the forefront, but each time he did so they scattered and dived back into the crowd. He stood up on a bollard and called for silence. 'If you will file past me one by one,' he told them, 'I will make a note of all grievances and take them straight to the captain.'

'And get ourselves put over the bleedin' wall?' shouted someone from the center of the crowd. 'Not bloody likely!'

Minutes later, a picket boat went by with an admiral on board. Immediately, the whole body of men stood to attention as a mark of respect. But as soon as the picket boat was clear, someone shouted, 'Hip hip!' and there was a huge cheer that was immediately answered by similar cheers from *Valiant, Norfolk* and *Adventure.*

It was now well after eight o'clock, but the captain was not on the bridge and the ship was not ready for sea. The *Valiant,* which had been due to sail at the same time, was still at anchor; and on the forecastle of the minelayer *Adventure* men were cheering and catcalling.

S.O.A.F. to Admiralty, 0916, 15th September

IMMEDIATE. SITUATION 0900 TODAY. HMS *REPULSE* HAS PROCEEDED TO SEA FOR EXERCISES; OTHER SHIPS HAVE NOT PROCEEDED; AND CONSIDERABLE PORTIONS OF SHIPS' COMPANIES HAVE ABSENTED THEMSELVES FROM DUTY. ATTITUDE OF ALL RATINGS TOWARDS THEIR OFFICERS IS AT PRESENT CORRECT. I HAVE RECALLED SHIPS NOW EXERCISING AND STOPPED LEAVE OF OFFICERS AND MEN. CHIEF OF STAFF LEAVES HERE TODAY, ARRIVING ADMIRALTY EARLY TOMORROW MORNING.

After being relieved on the forecastle by Lieutenant Busby, Frank went below, washed and shaved, and went to the wardroom for breakfast, where he found his fellow officers sitting about in gloomy silence.

Oram looked at him and said, 'You knew this was going to happen, didn't you?'

He said, 'I think we all did, didn't we?'

A signalman knocked on the door and brought in a clip-board with a signal from the Senior Officer, Atlantic Fleet, which he showed to Oram and Lanyon. It cancelled the order for ships to sail and ordered the *Repulse, Warspite, Malaya,* and *Exeter,* which had already sailed, to return to harbor.

'This is madness!' Lanyon remarked. 'The last thing we should do is bring the others back into harbor. After all, they're clear out of the trouble, aren't they? This'll only make things a hundred times worse.'

'Oh, I don't know about that,' Oram said. 'With the fleet in one place, at least we'll be able to keep the press from sticking their noses in.' He turned to Frank. 'Take charge of re-mooring, will you?'

Sporadic cheering went on between the ships throughout the forenoon. After Stand Easy, Yarrow sent for the commander, the master-at-arms, and the first lieutenant for a council of war in his cabin.

Master-at-Arms Holden was a home-loving man who, until six months before, had believed he would never go to sea again and would be able to spend the rest of his life tending the roses in his cottage garden at Bosham.

'It's a bad business, sir,' he said, when Yarrow asked him for an assessment of the situation. 'The men are perfectly respectful, but those who aren't on the forecastle are down on their mess decks, and whenever an officer tries to give them an order they just melt away.'

Yarrow turned to Lethbridge. 'Have you any comments Commander?'

Lethbridge shook his head. 'I regret not, sir. I fear that this will have to be resolved at a much higher level.'

Yarrow turned to Oram. 'What about you, David?'

Oram pushed back a lock of flaxen hair, glanced at Lethbridge, and sniffed. 'I think we should play it by the book, sir. I think we should parade the marine detachment with rifles and fixed bayonets, and clear the forecastle. I suggest you read the Articles of War to the whole ship's company and make it clear that this is not a strike but a mutiny, and that you will take whatever steps and use whatever force necessary to restore discipline.'

Yarrow stuck his tongue into his cheek and said, 'Hmm,' and after some thought added, 'No. No, I don't think so.'

'If authority is not asserted,' Oram said quietly, 'it is lost altogether.'

'Very well,' said Yarrow. 'We shall assert it. We shall go down to the seamen's mess deck now—the three of us together—and I shall order the men to turn to.' He stood up. 'Lead the way, Master-at-Arms.'

They followed Holden down from the cabin flat, along a passageway and down through the hatch to the seamen's mess deck, where they found a couple of dozen ratings sitting at mess tables.

'I am giving you men a direct order,' Yarrow said. 'Go on deck and report for duty immediately.'

They sat and stared at him in silence. His mouth opened and shut. He blinked rapidly, went red in the face—and then turned round and went back up the ladder.

Admiralty to S.O.A.F., 1205, 15ᵗʰ September

IMMEDIATE. YOUR 0916, THEIR LORDSHIPS ENTIRELY APPROVE OF THE ACTION WHICH YOU HAVE TAKEN. ANY REPRESENTATIONS WHICH YOU THINK IT IS RIGHT TO MAKE AS THE RESULT OF YOUR INVESTIGATIONS WILL BE CAREFULLY CONSIDERED BY THE BOARD. MEANWHILE, OFFICERS SHOULD TAKE EVERY OPPORTUNITY OF LAYING STRESS ON THE FACT THAT GREAT SACRIFICES ARE BEING REQUIRED FROM ALL CLASSES OF THE COMMUNITY, AND THAT, UNLESS THESE ARE CHEERFULLY ACCEPTED BY ALL CONCERNED, THE FINANCIAL RECOVERY OF THE COUNTRY WILL BE IMPOSSIBLE. SIMILAR CHANGES OF PAY HAVE BEEN MADE IN THE ARMY AND THE ROYAL AIR FORCE.

In the dog watches, the padre went up to the forecastle and tried to lead the men in community hymn-singing. This was not a success: he received a concerted raspberry for his pains. But it gave the men the idea to hold their own concert, so the ship's company piano was brought up from the junior rates' recreation space and manhandled onto the forecastle.

A little after six, Roddy ventured out onto the quarterdeck. Hearing the sound of singing, he sent for Oram and told him to put a stop to the concert because he thought it might put the ship in a bad light with the senior officer. But Oram was apprehensive of dealing with the men, so he sent for Jannaway and told him to do it on his behalf.

Frank was greeted with a cheer when he arrived on the forecastle, and someone shouted, 'Give us a tune, Jan!'

He sat down and played his own ragtime version of Yankee Doodle Dandy, which had gone down well a few months before at a ship's company concert. There was embarrassing applause for his effort, and he was bombarded with requests for dance tunes, songs, and jazz.

'What next?' he asked after a while.

'Play your favorite, sir,' someone said, so he played Chopin's Prelude No. 7 in A Major, the piece he had played for Miss Pinkham all those years before. The playing of it left him feeling emotional.

When he had finished, he sat at the piano, filled with a sense of futility. The men were quiet. 'We're not mutineers,' somebody said. 'Wouldn't you have done exactly the same, sir?' asked another.

He sat at the piano and nodded his head.

'Sir?'

'Yes?'

'When this is over, will you put in a good word for us?'

'We don't want any ringleaders named,' a voice called out from the back.

'I don't know of any,' Frank said. 'And if I did, I wouldn't name them.' He stood up. 'Get this piano down below now. Otherwise the dew will spoil it.'

It was the custom in HMS *Winchester*'s wardroom to have potato crisps with evening drinks. That evening the wardroom chef had made the crisps particularly well, and they were served in silver dishes by the wardroom attendant.

Admiralty to S.O.A.F., 2101, 15th September

IMMEDIATE. PENDING INVESTIGATION AND SUBSEQUENT CONSIDERATION BY THE ADMIRALTY OF REPRESENTATIONS AS TO HARDSHIP CAUSED BY NEW RATES OF PAY, THE BOARD HAVE APPROVED THE TEMPORARY SUSPENSION OF THE ATLANTIC FLEET PRACTICE PROGRAMME.

The next morning when 'hands fall in' was sounded, no one bothered to appear except the petty officers. The mutiny had taken firm hold now. There was sporadic cheering and counter-cheering between ships for most of the forenoon. In HMS *Winchester*, the loyalty of the Royal Marines had collapsed. They took up position in the eyes of the ship, with the stokers and seamen forming a solid wall round them so that they could not be identified or called out by officers or petty officers.

S.O.A.F. to Admiralty, 1148, 16th September

MOST IMMEDIATE. I AM OF THE OPINION THE SITUATION WILL GET ENTIRELY OUT OF HAND UNLESS AN IMMEDIATE CONCESSION IS MADE. SUGGEST (A) THAT PERCENTAGE CUT IN PAY, WITHOUT ALLOWANCES, FOR RATINGS BELOW PETTY OFFICER BE PROPOR-

TIONATELY THAT OF HIGHER RATINGS; (B) THAT MARRIAGE ALLOW-
ANCE BE APPLIED TO THOSE RATINGS UNDER TWENTY-FIVE WHO
HAVE MARRIED ON OLD SCALE OF PAY. FURTHER, I RECOMMEND A
REPRESENTATIVE OF BOARD SHOULD VISIT ME TO DISCUSS MATTERS
ON SPOT.

S.O.A.F. to Atlantic Fleet, 1320, 16th September

I AM INFORMED BY THE ADMIRALTY THAT THE CABINET WERE SIT-
TING AT NOON TODAY TO CONSIDER THE POINTS REPRESENTED BY
ME CONCERNING REDUCTIONS IN PAY.

S.O.A.F. to Admiralty, 1406, 16th September

MOST IMMEDIATE. SITUATION AT 1400. FLEET HAVE BEEN
INFORMED CABINET WERE SITTING AT NOON. MORE SHIPS HAVE
CEASED ORDINARY HARBOUR WORK; AND MEN ARE MASSING ON
FORECASTLES AT INTERVALS, ADJACENT SHIPS CHEERING EACH
OTHER. INTERFERENCE WITH RUNNING MACHINERY AND FORCED
INTER-SHIP COMMUNICATION MAY BE NEXT STEP.

Behind the scenes, other forces were at work. Enraged by the way the Sea
Lords had bungled the announcement of the pay cuts, and fearing that the
mutiny might spark a copy of the Bolshevik revolution of 1917, the King
summoned Admiral Kelly from retirement.

Kelly had had fought at Jutland and was the admiral who was the best
liked and most respected on the lower deck. If there was one man the men
would listen to and trust, it was Kelly.

He traveled north to Balmoral overnight, where he spent the day in dis-
cussion with the King George. On Wednesday morning Mr. Corbett, the
barman at the Royal Hotel in Invergordon, saw him talking informally
with a group of sailors near the Invergordon landing stage.

Later that morning, the men on the forecastle of HMS *York* were
amazed to see Kelly come aboard by climbing the Jacob's ladder onto the
lower boom. The buzz went quickly round the ship that Kelly was on
board, and when 'clear lower deck' was sounded, all but thirty or forty
men mustered to listen to the old admiral's address.

When the captain sent the marine lieutenant to order the people still on the forecastle to lay aft, Kelly said, 'No! Leave them where they are! If they don't want to hear me, that's okay by me, they'll hear it from the people who do.'

The moment Kelly started to speak it was obvious that he had lost none of his charisma. He stood up on a bollard, invited the men to gather round him, and talked to them like a father to his children.

'As you know,' he began, 'I've been retired for a number of years, but the King has asked me to come up and see what I can do about this so-called mutiny of yours. I know that some of you older men have been treated pretty rough. But you 1925 men don't have a thing to worry about. It doesn't affect you one bit. So what I'm going to do is this. Tomorrow, I'll go back down to London and straight to the Admiralty, and as soon as I'm inside the door I'll take my boots off so they can't sling me out again. I'll bang on the First Sea Lord's door and argue your case with him. But I won't be able to do any of that unless I can report to him that the fleet is under proper discipline, and is on its way back to the home ports. So we're going to have to cut out all this rot about mutiny right away. That's my plan then. I'm sending you all back to your home ports and giving you a spot of leave so that you can go home and work out with your wives how you can fix things up.'

When he had addressed the ship's companies of *York* and *Repulse*, Admiral Kelly went on board *Hood*, from where he made a personal telephone call to Admiral Field, the First Sea Lord. An hour later Rear Admiral Tomkinson received a signal whose tone was in stark contrast to every other signal he had received from Admiralty in the previous three days:

Admiralty to S.O.A.F., 1445, 16th September

MOST IMMEDIATE. THE BOARD OF ADMIRALTY IS FULLY ALIVE TO THE FACT THAT, AMONGST CERTAIN CLASSES OF RATINGS, SPECIAL HARDSHIP WILL RESULT FROM THE REDUCTION OF PAY ORDERED BY HM GOVERNMENT. IT IS THEIR DIRECTION THAT SHIPS OF THE ATLANTIC FLEET ARE TO PROCEED TO THEIR HOME PORTS FORTH-WITH TO ENABLE PERSONAL INVESTIGATION TO BE MADE BY THE COMMANDERS IN CHIEF AND REPRESENTATIVES OF THE ADMIRALTY, WITH A VIEW TO NECESSARY ALLEVIATION BEING MADE. ANY FUR-

THER REFUSALS OF INDIVIDUALS TO CARRY OUT ORDERS WILL BE
DEALT WITH UNDER THE NAVAL DISCIPLINE ACT. THIS ORDER IS TO
BE PROMULGATED TO THE FLEET FORTHWITH.

Soon after Tomkinson's signal was received in HMS *Winchester*, Lethbridge came into the wardroom and announced that all divisional officers
were to explain the implications of the signal to the men in their divisions,
and that 'clear lower deck' would then be ordered and the captain would
address the ship's company personally. This was done; but when the bugle
sounded off, only thirty or forty men, most of them petty officers and
leading hands, mustered on the quarterdeck.

Yarrow ordered Lethbridge, Oram, and Jannaway to go up to the forecastle and repeat the order, but when they arrived on the forecastle, they
were greeted by cheering and booing.

Lethbridge took the Admiralty signal out of his pocket and read it to
them. 'Now listen!' he shouted. 'Listen! You've got what you wanted! The
Senior Officer is—'

'All right commander, I'll take over now,' said Yarrow, who had
appeared unannounced.

Lethbridge stepped aside. As Yarrow stood up on the centre-line bollards and looked down at the crowd, Frank's heart sank.

'I wonder if you realize,' Yarrow began, 'the extent of the damage which
you are doing and indeed have already done to the Service and the country. I wonder if you realize that your unforgivable behavior has caused a
massive slide on the London stock exchange. I wonder if you realize that
Britain is, thanks to your action, now in dire danger of being forced off the
Gold Standard. And why? Because you've acted like a lot of sheep. You've
been led by the nose by the Devonport ships into this. Oh yes. Make no
mistake. I tell you this—'

Someone blew a raspberry. There was laughter. Someone else shouted
'Fuck the Gold Standard! What about our fucking living standard?'

Yarrow shook his finger at them. 'You've had the signal read to you.
This is your last warning—'

'Fuck off, Piggy Grunt!'

At that, Yarrow got down off his bollard, his face white with fury.
'Commander! My cabin, if you please! All officers are to muster in the
wardroom immediately.' He turned to Oram. 'Find the gunnery officer.

Have the machine guns brought aft, and pistols issued to all officers. At the rush!'

Roddy turned on his heel and left the forecastle. Lethbridge and Oram followed him, but Frank stayed where he was. As soon as the others were out of earshot, he turned back and stood up on the centre-line bollards.

'Will you listen to me?' he asked.

The shouting and catcalling stopped. Faces turned up towards him. They were waiting for him to speak. The words, unrehearsed, seemed to say themselves, as if another person were speaking through him.

'Last July, after Steve Lewtas was killed, one of you shouted as I was going up the ladder on rounds, "We're with you, Jan." Well, I want to thank whoever it was who said that, because he lifted my spirits when I most needed it. Now I want to do something for you in return. I'm not going to plead with you. All I want to say is this. You've won your case, gentlemen. This pay cut's not going to go through. Why? Because the Admiralty's climbed down, that's why. I've seen every signal that's been received in this ship in the last five days and it's obvious to me that the Admiralty has caved in. They would never have made a signal like this otherwise. Why am I saying this? Because I don't want this to end with the lower deck getting the worst of it, that's why. You said you were with me—well, I'm with you. I may mess in the wardroom, but my heart's on the lower deck—it always was, and it always will be, because that's where the real people are.'

He looked round at their faces. Some of the older men were in tears. 'Well, I don't know about anyone else,' he said. 'But I'm going to obey the order now, and lay aft.'

He stepped down off the bollards and walked alone off the forecastle; but by the time he was half way to the quarterdeck he became aware that the men were following along behind him in a single body, and that their mutiny was over.

'Ye gods!' Lanyon muttered as Frank fell in beside him. 'How in hell's name did you manage that?'

It was dark by the time HMS *Winchester* left the Firth of Cromarty and started the passage back to Portsmouth. Frank had stood in for Oram on the cable deck again, and now that the cables had been lashed for sea and the cable party had gone below for their supper, he remained on deck alone for a few minutes longer.

The shore lights slipped by as the ship headed east along the coast of Nairn. He looked aft at the beam of the Cromarty lighthouse as it swept round and round. Suddenly he knew that within the space of a week the Royal Navy's priceless tradition of pride and self-confidence had died and that, though it might one day be replaced by a lesser substitute, it could never be resurrected.

PART IV

▼

1943

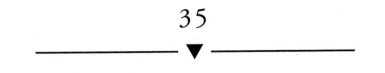

35

The Exeter train had been delayed, but whether by the blizzard or air raids Anita had no idea. It had come to a halt soon after leaving Reading and had remained stationary for nearly three hours before going slowly back, by a succession of stops and starts, into the station.

A porter went down the carriages opening all the doors and shouting, 'All change!'

The soldiers and sailors and airmen poured out onto the platform, and made a rush to join the tea queue. Anita took her overnight bag down from the rack and made her way to the ladies' waiting room, which she found already packed. She was about to go out again when a plump blonde in WAAF uniform came smiling up to her.

'Excuse me, Miss? Could you settle an argument for us? Are you Anita Yarrow?'

'Yes, I am.'

'I knew it,' said the girl.

'I was looking for somewhere to sit,' Anita said.

'Oh! Oh—well, I'm sure we could make room for you. If you don't mind a bit of a crush, that is.'

She went and sat with them. They introduced each other with lots of laughter and excitement: Brenda, Mavis, Irene, Kitty, and Joyce. She signed her autograph for them on the back of their cigarette packets.

'It's ever such a thrill meeting you,' said Brenda. 'You've no idea.'

The train moved out empty.

'I saw you in *Goodbye Piccadilly*,' said Irene. 'I cried all the way through.'

'What are you all doing?' she asked.

They looked at each other. 'We're not supposed to say,' said Brenda. 'But we're plotters.'

They settled down to wait. After twenty minutes or so, another train came in. The voice of the station announcer boomed out, 'Reading! Reading! This train will call at Didcot, Oxford, Banbury, and Coventry only. Change here for Paddington. Change here for Paddington, platform three.'

It remained in the station for some time, and while it was there Anita left her place and went along to join the queue for the ladies' lavatory.

When she came out, the train had left, leaving the opposite platform almost empty. Walking back to the waiting room she saw, sitting by himself on one of the benches, a naval lieutenant in a greatcoat with the collar turned up.

It was Frank.

She mingled with the crowd and made her way back to the waiting room. The WAAFs welcomed her back and took the coat from the place they were saving for her.

'Are you all right, Miss Yarrow?' Kitty asked. 'Joyce's gone for some teas. I said to get you one. I expect you could do with a hot drink? Are you sure you're all right?'

'Well,' said Mavis, 'At least Gerry won't be busy tonight, what with this weather.'

'That doesn't make any difference,' said Irene. 'They're dropping them blind, these days.'

Joyce came through the crush holding three mugs in each hand. 'There's four with and two without,' she said. 'Do you take sugar, Miss Yarrow?'

'I won't have one, thank you,' Annie said. She stood up. 'Thank you all so much for being so kind. I think I'll go out onto the platform now.'

He was still there. She crossed over to the other platform and walked along towards him. The collar of his greatcoat was turned even higher now. He was dozing. Yes, it was definitely Frank. She walked past him to the other end of the platform, wondering whether to speak to him. Part of her wanted to, but another part said she should leave well alone. But she couldn't do that. She simply couldn't.

She went back and stood in front of him.

'Frank?'

His eyes opened slowly, then his whole body jerked awake and he straightened up, staring at her.

'Can I sit down?' she asked.

He nodded. She sat.

'I always knew we'd bump into each other one day.'

He said nothing, staring straight ahead.

'And it would *have* to be on a railway station, wouldn't it?'

She looked at him more closely. He had aged. He had gone grey. He looked dead tired.

'Don't you want to speak to me?'

'Is there anything to say?'

'I think there is.'

She wondered if it would be better to take it no further, but couldn't bring herself to walk away.

'How are you?'

'Surviving,' he said. 'Like everyone else.'

'Do you mind if I stay and talk?'

He stared across at the other platform. 'I'm not sure,' he said, then he turned to look at her, and her heart did a somersault, just as it always used to.

'Why aren't you sure?'

'Why? Because...' He seemed to be struggling to find words. 'Because...because I never stopped loving you, that's why.'

'Perhaps I'd better go.'

'No!' he said quickly. 'Stay and talk to me. Tell me what you're doing.' He turned to her, smiling. 'I haven't seen any of your films. I keep away from them.'

'You haven't missed much.'

'I knew you'd do well. You're married, aren't you?'

'Yes. You?'

'Yes.'

'That's good. I'm glad. You must have been in the Navy over thirty years.'

He shook his head. 'I left in thirty-two, and joined up again in thirty-nine with everyone else.'

It seemed that they had run out of things to say to each other.

'How is your family?' he asked, rather formally. 'Are your parents still alive?'

'My mother is. But not my father. He committed suicide.'

He shook his head in disbelief. 'Why?'

She looked away, remembering.

'Why?' he asked again.

'It…happened on Christmas Day. After the Invergordon mutiny. We'd had a lot of rain, and the Meon had flooded. Part of the boundary wall had come down. We had a new gardener. Bloodworth. You remember the Bloodworth family?'

He nodded. 'I shared a school bench with Doris Bloodworth.'

'Well, Bloodworth brought my father a little model steam engine, very rusty, that he'd found in the wall. Apparently Roddy hid it there years before, when he was a cadet at Osborne. Father summoned him to the library and they had the most dreadful shouting match that went on and on and on. Eventually my mother sent me in to calm them down, but Roddy stormed out, and I was subjected to a similar onslaught. I took Roddy's side—Father had always had a down on Roddy—and I said something…something unforgivable. The result was that we had the most ghastly Christmas dinner party imaginable, and when we'd passed the port and drunk the loyal toast, Father retired to the library and he—shot himself.' Anita smiled quickly. 'I'm sorry. Perhaps I shouldn't have told you all that.'

'What about your mother?'

'She married a cellist and went to live in San Francisco.'

'And Roddy?'

'He's a rear admiral commanding a desk in Whitehall at the moment. What about you, Frank? Do you have children?'

'Two boys. Alan and Steven. Eleven and four, nearly five.'

'Are they like you?'

'Alan is. I think Steve's going to be more like his mother.'

'Are you happy?'

'Is that of importance?'

She looked away so that he could not see her face. 'Of course it is.'

'Of course?'

'Yes.'

'Do you have children?'

'One. Peter. He's eight.'

There was a long silence.

'What was the reason?' he asked.

'What reason?'

'The one you didn't dare give me on Wickham station. You said that your bubble had burst. You said it was an illusion. But it wasn't, was it? There was more to it than that.' He looked across at the opposite platform where some air force girls were flirting with a group of soldiers. 'It was a good act, but I never believed it.'

'Is it any use saying I'm sorry?'

'Are you?'

Their eyes met.

'Yes,' he said softly. 'Yes, I believe you are.'

She pushed her hand towards him and he took it and held it.

'Can we go somewhere else?' she asked. 'There are some people over there. I don't want—'

'Your public?'

'It sounds awful, but it's a fact of life.'

They went off the platform and stood outside the station under partial cover from the blizzard.

'What are you doing, Frank? Have you just come back from sea?'

'No. I'm too old for that. I'm pushing fifty.'

'Well, I'm over forty.'

'You don't look it.'

'So what *are* you doing?'

'Nothing very exciting.'

'Aren't you going to tell me?'

'I'm a cog in the war machine, Annie. Like everyone else.'

The snowflakes whirled round them. She said she was cold and needed a hug. He undid the brass buttons of his greatcoat and held her in his arms. His tears were wet on her cheek.

'It wasn't an illusion, was it?' he said.

'No,' she whispered. 'It was real.'

'I still think about you,' he said. 'Almost every day. Especially recently. I don't know why.'

'Telepathy,' said Anita. 'We were always telepathic, weren't we?'

'Why did you do it, Annie?'

She looked into his eyes and for a moment was back in the kitchen below stairs, sitting opposite Hetty Jannaway at the deal table; and Hetty was clutching at her chest in pain and saying, 'You must never tell him, Miss Annie. For God's sake, please, please, never tell him.'

She shook her head. 'I can't tell you, Frank. Not now, at any rate. When the war's over, perhaps. But not now. Even then—'

'What?'

'I couldn't be sure that what I was telling you was the truth. If it's any consolation, I didn't do it willingly. It broke my heart. But I had no alternative. Can you understand that?'

He shook his head. 'Not really.'

The wind whistled round the station building, bringing with it a flurry of snowflakes.

'We could go to a hotel,' she said. 'I don't mean for—I just thought it would be nice to be together for a little while.'

'I'm on my way home, Annie. I haven't seen my boys in eight months.'

He frowned in a way that frightened her. At the same moment the station loudspeakers boomed out over their heads that the train approaching platform three was for Paddington only.

He released her, buttoned up his coat, picked up his grip, and led the way through the booking hall. The train drew to a screeching halt. She said, 'I can't bear the thought that I might never see you again.'

He shrugged. 'It's the way it is, isn't it?' And then, as if on a sudden impulse, he opened up his grip, felt deep inside it and brought out two stiff-backed notebooks.

'I want you to have these,' he said. 'They're not for publication. At least, not yet. But perhaps one day...one day they may be of interest to someone, somewhere. And—maybe they'll help you to understand.'

Anita felt a sense of panic. 'Will I ever see you again? Can't we keep in contact?'

He shook his head. 'Better not,' he said. 'No, better not.'

She caught his hand, trying to pull him back, but he made her let go, and stepped up onto the running board. He entered the train, slammed the door, lowered the window, and looked out. A whistle blew. She reached out to him. Their fingers touched.

'Keep safe,' she said. And then: 'God bless you, Frank. God bless you.'

The train jerked forward and gathered speed, the carriages banging out of the station. She stood back on the platform and raised her hand high above her head—and then the guard's van went clattering past, and its dimmed red tail lights were quickly swallowed up in the driving snow.

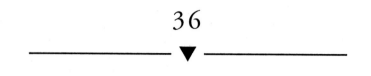

36

Frank had a special way of knocking on the door in Morse code, so that Dora always knew who it was when he arrived home. Di-di-daa-di, di-daa-daa-daa it went early that January morning. She dried her hands on a tea towel and rushed to the front door. He came in and stamped on the doormat. There was snow on his greatcoat and cap. His train had been delayed. He had been up all night.

Alan and Steven came into the hall. Steven put his fingers in his mouth and stared up at his father. 'How's Alan?' Frank asked. 'And how's Captain Oates?' He hoisted Steven up and gave him a hug. 'What have you been up to, young man?'

'Having breakfast,' said Steven.

'Would you like some?' Dora asked. 'It's only porridge and toast.'

'I don't mind if I do,' he said, mimicking Colonel Chinstrap.

She dashed into the kitchen to make more toast and tea. She stirred up the last of the porridge and put it on a plate.

'You're looking thinner,' she told him. 'You aren't eating enough.'

'You're looking more beautiful than ever,' he said. 'I'm not seeing you enough.'

He took her in his arms. She burnt the toast and scraped the charcoal off into the sink.

Alan said, 'Mummy's always doing that.'

They sat in the dining room and watched him have his breakfast.

'When is Daddy going to shave?' Steven asked his mother.

'He's very anxious to see you shave,' she explained.

'I've already had a shave, Captain Oates. You'll have to wait until tomorrow morning.'

She put her hand on his arm. 'I want to take a snap of you before you change out of your uniform.'

He finished his tea and sat back. 'What do you want a snap of me for? You don't want a picture of my ugly mug!'

Steven pushed his forefinger into the curl of gold braid on his father's sleeve and said very sternly, 'Yes we *do*!'

They went outside to the narrow little garden, which backed onto the allotments and the stream. A thick covering of snow had fallen in the night and the branches of the apple tree which grew by the coal shed were heavy with it. Steven ran about making new footprints and pretending he was a railway engine by blowing out steam.

'Put your cap on, Frank,' Dora said. 'I want you with your cap on.' She opened up her Kodak Brownie and he tipped the peak of his cap over his eyes and grinned obligingly. The shutter clicked. 'Now me!' said Steven.

'I've only one left. I'll take one of all three of you.'

'All your men, Mummy,' Alan said.

Dora took the snap and they went inside.

Upstairs, they closed the bedroom door and greeted each other again. He changed out of uniform into grey flannels and a tweed jacket.

Dora hung his uniform in the wardrobe. 'I'll be glad when you never have to wear this again,' she said.

Downstairs, he rubbed his hands together and said, 'Now then, what's for mending?'

He adjusted the brakes on her bike and put a new washer in the kitchen tap. He put a book shelf up in Alan's bedroom and he climbed into the loft to make sure the cistern wasn't leaking. The house filled with the smell of his tobacco and the sound of his voice; and after lunch Steven said, '*Now* will you shave?'

Frank took him on his knee and sang 'This is the way the gentlemen ride,' bumping him up and down until he was helpless with laughter.

'Daddy,' Steven said.

'Yes?'

'Can we go boganning?'

'Boganning?'

'He means tobogganing,' Alan said. 'We haven't got a toboggan,' he told Steven. 'So we can't.'

'Then we'll use tea trays,' said Frank. 'Nothing like a tea tray for a good bit of bogganing.'

Frank helped Steven put on his leggings and mittens, and they set out along the cinder track to the gap in the railings. Dora took Alan's arm, and Frank carried Steven on his shoulders. They went down the path past the tennis club pavilion to the stream, which was frozen at the edges, and on the way across the bridge Frank dangled Steven over the water. They went over the deserted golf course and up the steep bank by the railway line. The sun broke through the mist and glinted on the snow.

Frank went first to show the boys how. He lay chest down on a Silver Jubilee tray, and descended at high speed. Dora sat on the other tray, which refused to budge. Alan took over the tray from his father, but fell off after only a few yards.

Then it was Steven's turn. He had already climbed to the top of the bank. 'Not from up there, Steven!' Dora called. 'Start further down!'

But he was already on his way down, and there was no stopping him. He came skittering head-first past them at great speed, becoming airborne as he went over a bunker, and disappearing from view as he went on down to the stream at the bottom of the slope.

They chased after him. Frank slithered down a steep clay bank and found him in two inches of nearly frozen water, still clinging to the tray, his nose a few inches from a discarded cistern. He picked him up and put him under his arm like a pig for market. 'We'll have to have another go at that, won't we?' he said, putting Steven down. Then he took his hand and ran with him all the way to the top of the hill.

Dora stayed at the bottom. 'Don't be silly, Frank!' she called. 'It's dangerous!'

But he called back, 'We're not being silly!' He turned to Steven and said, 'You're not afraid, are you?

Steven shook his head emphatically, though in fact he didn't know what being afraid was like. His father pointed him in a safer direction and told him how to dig his toes in if he wanted to slow down or change direction. Then he let go of the tray and Steven went hurtling off again, coming to a stop a few yards from the third hole.

Dora leant against Frank. 'I suppose it's like going up the mast again after you've fallen off, isn't it?' she said.

On the way home she walked between Alan and Frank, her arms linked in theirs. Steven held his father's hand and tried to keep step with him by jumping along in big strides. When they got home, Dora hung the wet clothes in the kitchen and gave Steven a hot bath while Frank lit the fire in the sitting room.

That evening, they gathered round the piano and Frank played some of the songs they used to sing before the war. When he played 'You are my sunshine,' Dora got out her handkerchief and blew her nose.

'That one always makes Mummy cry,' Alan said.

Steven insisted that his father carry him upstairs to bed. Frank hoisted him over his shoulder like a sack of potatoes, and pretended he was going to let him slip when they were halfway up.

Steven hung head down, held by the heels, and watched the carpet rods recede beneath him. His father didn't know that Panda was supposed to clean his teeth or that Monk the monkey with a half peeled banana was supposed to join in the prayers.

Dora came in with Alan and they sat on the bed while Frank read *The Tale of Pigling Bland*, which Steven had chosen because it was the longest of all the Beatrix Potter stories, and he liked the picture of Pigling Bland dancing with Susie at the end.

His father kissed him goodnight and told him to be a good boy and go to sleep. Steven lay in the bed looking very small. 'Tell me when you're going to shave, Daddy,' he said.

They switched out the light and went onto the landing. 'I think he'll remember today, won't he?' Frank whispered.

'I think we all shall,' she said.

There was an air raid in the night, but they didn't bother to move downstairs and Steven slept through it without waking. When the lorry arrived outside the front door, Frank was awake immediately. It was just after six, and still dark. He rubbed his fist on the window pane to get rid of the hoar frost.

'It's Jock,' he said, and hurried downstairs to open the front door. Dora got out of bed and put on her dressing gown. She went down to the hall. The able seaman had left the door open and a chill draught had followed him in.

'I'm being called out,' Frank said. 'Sorry.'

She made them a cup of tea. Frank came downstairs five minutes later, his uniform buttoned over a white polo-necked sweater. He gulped down the tea and prepared to leave.

'When will we see you again?' she asked.

'Can't promise anything. I'll try to get tomorrow off.'

He kissed her goodbye and she stood in the bay window to watch him go. As the lorry drove off, its roof scraped against the branches of a birch tree, brushing the frosty snow off, and leaving behind it a pale silver cloud that hung for a moment outside the window.

The naval staff car arrived at the door at seven o'clock that same Sunday evening when she had just put Steven to bed. She went to the front door and opened it to a naval commander in uniform.

'Mrs. Jannaway?'

'Yes.'

'May I come in?'

'Yes.'

Alan was listening to the wireless in the sitting room, so she took the commander into the front room. She knew immediately why he had come, but it was somehow better to let him tell her in his own way.

It was cold. The gas fire was unlit. The commander looked very young, she thought. He held his hat like a steering wheel in his hands, turning it round and round as if driving a lorry round a corner. He glanced nervously about him at the shelves of books and the photographs on the mantle piece.

'It's bad news, isn't it?'

'I'm afraid so.'

'Is…he dead?'

'Yes.'

How unbelievable it seemed later, when she thought about the way he told her and the calm manner in which she accepted the news. They stood in silence, he looking down at his cap, Dora steadying herself with her hands behind her against the piano lid.

'I expected it,' she heard herself say. 'Sooner or later.'

The commander said: 'He died in the most courageous circumstances. He was defusing a land mine. He insisted on tackling it single handed, so there were no other casualties.'

She was not really surprised at that. It was typical of Frank.

The commander began telling her things that she was unable to take in. He gave her useless pieces of information about pensions and benevolent trusts, none of which would bring Frank back. He said that some naval charity would be getting in touch with her.

And then he seemed to be in a rush to go, to be out of the house, to leave this little tragedy behind him, and get on with the war.

When the front door was closed and the naval staff car had driven off, she went up to Steven's bedroom and helped him put on his dressing gown and slippers, and brought him downstairs to sit with her and Alan by the fire in the sitting room. She took Steven on her lap, and Alan sat on the arm of her chair with his arm round her shoulders. She was grimly determined that she would not break down in front of them. She felt she owed that to Frank. She knew he would want her to be brave, as he had been brave.

'Now then,' she said. 'I'm going to tell you something about Daddy.'

The investiture took place four months later. Dora decided not to buy a new suit for herself, but bought a new grey shirt and a pair of grey trousers for Alan. She bought a tie for Steven—it was his first tie—and put water on his hair to make it stay down when she brushed it.

The Admiralty sent a car to take them to Buckingham Palace. They were met by a naval captain, who was some sort of equerry or aide-de-camp. He conducted them along a wide, carpeted corridor and up a short flight of gilded stairs. While they waited, he tried to put Dora at her ease, but he wasn't nearly as good at it as Frank had been in Cardiff when she went aboard his ship for the children's party.

They were beckoned through into a high-ceilinged room and were presented to the King, who was wearing the uniform of Admiral of the Fleet. Dora was impressed by how small he was, and by the size of the Queen's hat. The King said that Frank had given his life to save others, and had displayed courage that was in the finest traditions of the Service. He referred to him as 'your very courageous husband.'

'Mummy,' said Steven as they moved back to resume their seats, 'Was *that* the King?'

Outside the Palace railings, they were met by several press reporters and photographers.

'Can we have the little boy on his own, Mrs. Jannaway?' one of the photographers asked. 'On his own, with the medal, please.'

She showed Steven how to hold the box with the George Cross medal in it.

'Look up here, sonny!' the photographer said. 'Look up at my hand here!' And the next morning, on the front page of the *Daily Herald*, under the banner headline SON OF A HERO, there was a picture of a little boy in short trousers, with his necktie not quite straight, holding his father's medal in its box, and looking perplexedly up at the sky.

EPILOGUE

▼

In the fall of 1995 I went to La Jolla to attend the marriage of my step daughter and, thanks to the good offices of the bridegroom's mother, I was introduced to Rowena Rambler, a retired Hollywood gossip columnist.

We met at the Rancho Santa Fé Country Club. Rowena was in her early eighties, a diminutive, craggy figure in a frothy white blouse and a pink mini-skirt. I had been told that she was interested in meeting me because she was planning to write a piece about Anglo-American marriages for a local paper. But things didn't quite turn out that way, because I quickly discovered that her real mission was to talk me into ghosting her autobiography.

We sat on the deck by the tennis courts and sipped iced coffee through rainbow straws, while two sun-kissed hunks belted a tennis ball monotonously back and forth from the baselines.

Rowena told me about herself. As a cub reporter on the *Ranch and Coast* she had been sometimes mistaken for Ginger Rogers. She'd lived all over Los Angeles: on Venice Beach, in Santa Monica, Westwood, Hollywood, and Beverley Hills. From what I gathered there wasn't a star she hadn't dined with, been mistaken for, interviewed, or danced with.

She dropped names by the score. She had interviewed Rogers and Astaire, Crosby, Sinatra, Day, Hope, Mitchum and the Rat Pack. She'd danced to Glenn Miller's band with Stewart Granger, she'd lunched with Cary Grant; and with her late husband, who was an undertaker to the rich and famous, had bought a house from Marilyn Monroe.

She was into astrology and insisted on knowing my birth date. When I told her she got excited because I was on the cusp between Leo and Virgo. 'That's spooky!' she said. 'I'm on the cusp between Aquarius and Pisces.'

It was forty minutes since we sat down, and I was beginning to feel rest-less. I said that I ought to be getting back to La Jolla, as I was expected for lunch. We strolled out to the car park agreeing, repeatedly, how fascinat-ing it had been to meet each other.

Then, as I fitted the key into the door of my hired car, I asked her a question. I shall never know why I asked it. Perhaps it was because, after such an orgy of name dropping, I gave in to an impulse to drop the only name I knew. Or perhaps telepathy was at work. Or maybe it was in the stars, or Apollo sent from his shining silver quiver one of his golden arrows plucked from the bosom of the wine-dark Californian sky.

'Did you,' I asked, 'ever hear of a British film actress by the name of Anita Yarrow?'

Rowena did a double-take, as if struck on the shoulder by a bullet. She took two steps back and, with a sharp intake of breath, put her hands up as if to ward off evil spirits. 'Did I hear you correctly? Did you say Anita Yar-row?'

'Yes, I did.'

'How in heaven's name do you know Annie?'

'I don't know her. But I did know her son.'

'Which son was that?'

'Her only son, Peter. A friend of mine was his first lieutenant in the Royal Navy back in the seventies.'

'You were in the British Royal Navy?'

'For twenty-five years.'

'Never!'

'Do you know Anita well?'

She clutched my arm. 'My dear young man,' she said, 'Annie and I go back a very long way indeed. She was the first movie actress I ever inter-viewed.'

I said how interesting that was, and was about to get into the car when she stopped me. 'Would you consider changing your schedule?' she asked. 'I think you have a story to tell, and I would like to hear it. What do you say? Will you take lunch with me?'

I used her mobile to cancel my lunch appointment and we drove up the hill and parked under the pines outside the Rancho Santa Fé Restaurant. We strolled into the bar for an aperitif. Over a gin-martini (shaken not stirred: Sean Connery was an old friend) she confided that the waiter—a massively built, baby-faced, bull-necked individual with golden curls and a pearly white smile—was an ex-champion surfer whose clothing company had recently gone under thanks to some shenanigans in Tokyo.

After our aperitif, we sat down to a Mexican salad. On Rowena's prompting I told her about my connection with Anita Yarrow.

I explained that I'd joined the Royal Navy as a cadet back in 1955, at the same time as Steven Jannaway. He was a chunkily built, dark-haired cheerful rogue, with an obstreperous manner and a knack of saying the wrong thing to the wrong person at the wrong time. He got an admiral's daughter pregnant out in Malta in the sixties (under water, so he told me) and had to give up his childhood sweetheart in order to marry her. Then he joined the Fleet Air Arm, banged out of a Vampire jet at low level while under training, damaged his back, and went on to fly cumbersome aircraft called Gannets from the abominably small decks of British aircraft carriers.

Rowena fingered her Aquarian pendant and gazed at me. 'So you actually knew this Steven Jannaway?'

'Yes. He was a close friend.'

'And his father? Did you know him too?'

'No. He was killed defusing a land mine in the Second World War. He was awarded a posthumous George Cross.'

'That's an award for gallantry?'

'Yes.'

'He was a hero?'

'I suppose he was.'

Rowena made an impatient noise. 'Don't be so English! Of course he was a hero!'

She took out a silver propelling pencil and made a short note on a small pad. Then she looked up and became business-like. 'I'm going to ask a favor of you. I am just so excited to meet you, and I know that Annie will want to meet you too.'

'Do you know her well?'

'My dear, Annie and I go back a *very* long way. Annie was the first actress I ever interviewed for the *Ranch and Coast*. She's my closest friend. A real sweetie, if ever there was one.'

'She must be quite an age now.'

'Her age goes with the year. She was ninety-five in January last. She is quite, quite amazing.'

'Well,' I said, 'I suppose I could look her up when I get back to England, if you have her address.'

She laughed, shaking her head. 'My dear young man! She doesn't live in England. She lives right here in Rancho Santa Fé!'

And that was how I got to meet Anita Yarrow, the thirties heartthrob, star of forties blockbusters like *Some Sunny Day*, *Dakota Farewell*, and *Cry Me a River*.

Anita's house was tucked away in a pine wood in an area that was encircled by a high security fence. Admittance to this area was via high wrought-iron gates manned, behind bullet-proof glass, by a uniformed guard. Following the security guard's directions, I drove uphill through the trees. The gates to her house swung open at my approach.

Feeling oddly nervous, I rang the bell.

The door was opened immediately by the butler, a man in his early seventies, partly bald, with a neatly trimmed goatee beard and intelligent eyes.

'Hi,' he boomed. 'I'm Oliver.'

'Hi,' I returned, my eyes drawn to the original Hockney on the wall behind him.

'Miss Yarrow is having her rest. Will you come this way?'

I followed him along a wide, tiled corridor into an open plan living space which shouted two messages that came over loud and clear: this lady has money, and this lady has class. There were fine Persian rugs on the floor, an abundance of creamy leather sofas, a corner cabinet of Sevres porcelain, and wide shelves of books. On the Bechstein grand piano under the high windows stood a dozen or more silver framed photographs—the captured family memories of more than a hundred years.

But it was the original oil paintings on the walls that were the most striking feature of all. This was the collection of someone who knew about art and knew what she liked. There were originals by Cassat, Sergeant, Whistler, Sickert, Matisse, and Hopper; and, tucked away in a corner over the writing desk, there was a charming little Degas of racing at Deauville.

I was admiring it when Anita came into the room. I would not have believed that a woman of her age could get away with designer jeans and a classic cream shirt, but that's what Anita Yarrow was wearing, and, with her white hair and startling blue eyes, she and her surroundings were like a fabulous piece of jewelry sparkling in the Californian desert. She was tall, she was elegant, and she was every inch a lady.

We shook hands and sat down, she in a high-backed armchair, I on a sofa.

I said that it was very kind of her to invite me.

'I didn't,' she said.

'Well all the same it's very kind—'

She stopped me with a wave of her hand. 'Rowena said you are a writer. What have you written?'

'A few novels. Some television. A screenplay.'

'What are you writing at the moment?'

'I'm researching a novel.'

'About?'

'The Royal Navy.'

Her penciled eyebrows went up. 'Is that why you were so insistent upon coming to see me?'

'I was under the impression that you were insisting on seeing me, Miss Yarrow.'

'Rowena's been up to her old tricks,' she remarked. Then we were interrupted by the arrival of Oliver with the tea trolley.

It was all very English. While Oliver poured the Earl Grey, I glanced round at the room. Tucked away in the corner under the bookshelves beside Anita's high-backed chair, there was a side table with a lamp, a bowl of silk roses the color of burnt meringues, and a silver-framed photograph of a cheerful-looking British naval officer, World War II vintage, with the peak of his dark cap tipped slightly over one eye.

When I saw that photograph, I felt goose bumps. You see, I had seen the same photograph in Steven Jannaway's cabin forty years before when I was under training at Dartmouth Naval College.

'Do you recognize him?' Anita asked.

'Yes,' I said. 'It's Frank Jannaway, isn't it?'

She had used a subtle hint of blusher, but there now came to her cheeks more color than had been there before. 'Yes,' she said. 'That's Frank. He was a very dear friend of mine.' She looked away for a few moments. 'So now,' she said rather distantly, 'I suppose you want to know how I came to know him, don't you?'

'Oh—no,' I fluffed. 'Not at all—I really wouldn't like—'

'Don't be so silly, of course you would. Besides, hasn't it occurred to you that I might like to tell you? Do you realize that you are the first person I've met in over fifty years who knew the Jannaway family?'

There were tears in the old lady's eyes now, and I was feeling emotional myself. I didn't know what to say, and told her as much. She told me to help myself to a cucumber sandwich and tell me more about Steven. I said that I had put much of what I knew, with some fictional elaboration, into a novel called *The Raging of the Sea*.

'So that's who you are,' she said when I told her the title. 'I read it from cover to cover. I think your Julietta character has a great deal to answer for. Or was that one of the fictional bits?'

'Not entirely. It was a mixture.'

'You novelists,' she sighed. 'You're all challenged by the truth, aren't you? Tell me about this book you're planning. What is it about?'

'A mutiny.'

'Which one?'

'The Invergordon mutiny of 1931. Does that mean anything to you?'

She smiled. 'Roddy—that's my brother—was at Invergordon. He was the captain of HMS *Winchester*, a cruiser in the same squadron as Captain Prickett. Now that's a name you really should know.'

I did. I had lunched with Prickett's grandson only a year or so before, when he was working for Elton John.

'Prickett was the captain of HMS *Norfolk*, wasn't he? That was Len Wincott's ship.'

'Wincott. Yes. I've heard that name. How did he fit in?'

'He was one of the ringleaders. He was thrown out of the Navy and defected to Russia. They gave him the Order of Lenin.' I saw her nodding. 'But—wasn't Frank Jannaway at Invergordon as well? And how did you come to know him? Was it through your son?'

She shook her head. 'No. I knew Frank long before that. He was our housekeeper's boy at Meonford Hall. He used to polish boots and clean grates.'

'Is that the Meonford Hall in Hampshire? Where the Braddle family lived?'

'Yes. They bought it after my father died. Did you know the Braddle family?'

'Not personally, but Henry Braddle was the Flag Officer Flotillas in Malta when I was serving in a minesweeper there. I went to a party once at Meonford Hall. It was soon after Steve and Julietta were married, before they moved into Stocks Cottage.'

She smiled, and shook her head, remembering. 'Stocks Cottage! That was where our gamekeeper lived. Tom Roughsedge. He had four sons. All killed. Three in the Great War, one in a motor accident.' She went into a reverie for a few moments, and then turned back to me. 'Do you play the piano?'

'No.'

'Frank was superb. He's played that piano. What about his sons? Were they musical?'

'Well, I don't know if you know, but the elder son, Alan, is a paraplegic. But Steve plays. I think he could have been quite good if he hadn't joined the Navy.'

'What happened to him?'

'He took early retirement as a lieutenant commander. He fell out with one or two senior officers—said things they didn't want to hear.'

'What a silly thing to do.'

She picked up a brass bell from the table by her chair and rang it. 'Ollie,' she said when the butler appeared. 'Bring in Roddy's tuck box, would you?'

Oliver withdrew, and a minute later returned bearing an English school tuck box made of varnished pine and bound with lamp-blacked metal bands and corner pieces. He placed it on the glass-topped coffee table. For a few moments, Anita looked at it. Then she turned to me. 'You open it. I can't manage the catches.'

I raised the lid. It was stuffed full of notebooks, diaries, and Admiralty files marked ON HIS MAJESTY'S SERVICE.

'Most of these are my brother's papers,' Annie said. 'I had a trunk full, but threw a lot out about forty years ago.'

As I began looking at the contents of those faded files, it dawned on me that they were of priceless historical value. Had they been in the Public Records Office, I doubt if they would have been available to public view. There were hand-written memoirs dating back to before 1914. There were drafts of confidential reports on officers. There were duplicates of reports of proceedings, reports of accidents, copies of letters marked PERSONAL about officers, and comments on Fleet exercises and gunnery trials. There were letters and notes drafted in Captain Yarrow's own hand. In another file I found Captain Yarrow's standing orders. Then I found two thick files marked INVERGORDON: REFUSALS OF DUTY. When I saw them, I knew I had struck gold.

I looked up. 'These are priceless.'

'Take the whole lot out, darling. You'll find a couple of notebooks at the bottom.'

I found them. They were not Admiralty issue, but bought from a stationer: two one-hundred page hard-back foolscap notebooks, with every line of every page covered in the same neat handwriting. As I glanced through them, it began to dawn on me what was being described.

'Who?' I asked, but Anita waited for me to find out for myself. I turned to the first page of the first notebook. It was set out like the title page of a book:

REASONS IN WRITING
1905–1931
F.J.J.

'Francis John Jannaway?'

'Yes.'

I asked why she was letting me see it. She said she thought that it was a story that needed to be told. 'The Admiralty has virtually erased the name Invergordon from the history books,' she said. 'But this is one event that should never be forgotten. After all, it marked the end of the British Empire, didn't it?' She fixed me with her lovely sapphire eyes. 'You have a good track record as a writer. I'm sure you could do it. As fiction, perhaps. You could make it accessible. What do you say? Could you take it on?'

'I fly back to England tomorrow.'

She made an impatient sound. 'I thought you were a professional! If you're serious about this book you say you want to write, you'll cancel your flight. I won't allow those papers out of this house. You would have to read them here. You can stay as my guest.'

I said I needed time to think about it. She said there was no time. 'If you can't make up your mind here and now, you're not the person I want to write this book.'

'But my wife—'

'Let her fly back on her own. She'll be glad to be shot of you. Come along now. You have to take a decision.'

I thought fast. I knew that this was a once-in-a-lifetime opportunity. Research doesn't often fall into one's lap like that.

'May I make a condition?' I asked. 'If I'm going to do this book, I'll have to tape some conversations with you. I want to ask you about your brother, about Frank, your father, what it was like. I want to know the *whole* story. I want to know it so well that I can tell it as if I had been there, as if it had happened to me. I want to get right inside Frank's mind. And your brother's, and yours. I want to look out through your eyes. I want to experience what you experienced, see what you saw, and remember what each one of you remembered.'

She gave me a radiant smile. 'Attaboy,' she said. 'Let's do it.'

So we did.

© Charles Gidley Wheeler
Tetbury, 2005

0-595-33956-5

Printed in the United Kingdom
by Lightning Source UK Ltd.
103923UKS00001B/94-105